ROADS TO VAROSHA

Roads to Varosha

To Angela
I hope you enjoy the book

Best Wishes

Krystof Carel *Krystof*

29/11/16

Roads to Varosha
Krystof Carel

Published by Aspect Design 2016
Malvern, Worcestershire, United Kingdom.

Designed, printed and bound by Aspect Design
89 Newtown Road, Malvern, Worcs. WR14 1PD
United Kingdom
Tel: 01684 561567
E-mail: allan@aspect-design.net
Website: www.aspect-design.net

ISBN 978-1-908832-96-2

For Liz and for Rob.
With Love.

Cast of Main Characters

Michael Blidworth, reporter; son of Barbara and Tom.

Georghios Ioannis Panayiotis, (Ioannis), cousin once removed to Costas, Takis and Tassos.

Mavro, leader of a right-wing group in Athens.

Tassos P. Panayiotis, cousin of Costas and Takis, ex police officer.

George Holdsworth, civil servant in the British Administration in Cyprus.

Stavros Christos Charalambou, civil servant in the British Administration in Cyprus, grew up in Myrsina.

Private Alf Holdsworth, George's son, stationed on the British Army base in Cyprus.

Captain Peter Jarvis, officer in charge of the quartermaster service on the British Army base in Cyprus.

Mehmet, member of Turkish Cypriot terrorist group, grew up in Myrsina.

Takis P. Charalambou, Stavros's son and childhood friend of Mehmet, member of Greek Cypriot terrorist group.

Costas X. Charalambou, Stavros's younger son, Takis's brother, member of Greek Cypriot terrorist group.

Simon Holdsworth, son of Alf, grandson of George, charity worker.

Mphatso, Mozambican emigre, British citizen, business owner in Athens, charity worker.

Zoe, flatmate of Simon Holdsworth.

Glossary

BFBS: British Forces Broadcasting Service provided radio services for HM Forces.

CB: confinement to barracks.

Chewa: People of Bantu origin who are the largest ethnic group in Malawi, with other communities across central and southern Africa, also called Nyanja; their language is Chichewa/Chinyanja/Cinianja.

CM: Court martial.

CO: commanding officer.

EOKA: National Organisation of Cypriot Fighters (a Greek Cypriot nationalist guerrilla organisation that fought a campaign for the end of British rule in Cyprus and for the island's self-determination and union with Greece).

NAAFI: Navy, Army and Air Force Institutes (an organisation which runs the recreational establishments needed by the British Armed Forces, and which sells goods to servicemen and their families).

NCO: non-commissioned officer.

OIC RMP: officer-in-charge of the Royal Military Police.

QMS: quartermaster service or store.

RSM: regimental sergeant major.

TMT: Türk Mukavemet Teşkilatı, the Turkish Resistance Organisation, a paramilitary group opposing EOKA with the objective of forcing partition, or Taksim, of Cyprus.

UNFICYP: United Nations Peacekeeping Force in Cyprus, formed in 1964 to prevent inter-communal violence.

WO2: warrant officer class two.

PART ONE

Chapter One
Michael, Athens, November 2013

Mike barked in mock frustration at his friend and editor in London. He frenetically tapped the laptop keyboard, making last second amendments to his piece, attaching it to the e-mail and pressing the send button.

The mobile broadband icon traced a laboured vortex for a few seconds before a confirmation message was displayed. 'Bloody wi-fi.' then a pause in his conversation. 'Right, it's gone! I'll be out and about now to dig for more information, so text me or call if you have to.'

'OK. Bye.'

THE ESCALATOR TO NOWHERE.

Michael Blidworth, Middle East Editor, reports from Athens on the catastrophe engulfing the country and its inhabitants in 2013, witnessing the ultimate price an innocent individual has paid.

In the tourist honey pot of Monastirakis in the weak autumn sunshine, the visitor would be forgiven for believing the migrant crisis that has engulfed this EU outpost is a fallacy. Shops peddle familiar goods, shoppers carry bags from niche and high-end retailers, cafés and restaurants are bustling and their tables spill into plazas and side streets alike. Tourists are the providers of metaphorical gold and silver. Only the persistent hawkers give away the slightest hint of tarnish. Apologists for the deep economic and social calamity into which Greece has stumbled have invented countless bogey men upon which to heap blame, attempting to deflect the population's ire from failures of State and a fractured economy. Failures, some would argue at least in part, forced upon Greece's leaders by an unconcerned European bureaucracy.

Tourists might be forgiven for believing the multi-national retail outlets bundled into new-era shopping malls in fashionable suburbs portray the economic situation as little different to any other European capital. Stray beyond Athens-in-a-day in search of 'A' list sights and your impression of Athens is challenged.

Two Metro stops from the tourist hub, still in sight of the majestic Acropolis, tourists alight in search of the iconic Archaeological Museum where, for several hours, one can immerse oneself in the history of a once-great empire. Clasping their mobile phones, street maps and bottles of water, the inquisitive tourist walks a few hundred metres between Victoria station and the museum entrance. About them the cityscape has changed. The built environment is markedly shabbier, the atmosphere less relaxed. More than half the shop fronts are abandoned to poster hangers, slogans and taggers. Street furniture is defaced, uprooted, mangled. Beggars line the route, young men hang around the station exits.

Local resident Alexis takes me to the local department store where he used to work, reduced in its death throes to displaying a few items of remaindered stock on the ground floor. Tourist maps and brochures proudly advertise this store. Unwitting customers ascend pointless escalators and lifts which spew their passengers onto darkened, empty floors, barricaded at their first step by stacked shop fittings. From one hundred and fifty personnel, the store now has a staff of one, a security guard doubling as a cashier for the unexpected instance a purchase is proffered. A forlorn-looking supermarket, not connected to the department store, half-heartedly peddles its wares to a few dejected customers in the basement of the otherwise empty carcass. This is one reality, among myriad thousands, of the economic collapse in Greece.

'It's all gone horribly wrong in Athens,' he volunteers, as we walk back onto the main thoroughfare. 'This used to be a fashionable neighbourhood, but look how it has been pulled to its knees by the economic crisis.'

A pristine, white-painted building across the road is virtually the only functioning business along this wide thoroughfare. A member of staff cleans the remainder of last night's graffiti from the building's walls, beneath its shining neon sign: Marks and Spencer. The juxtaposition of Western retail icons and the decrepitude of the neighbourhood is a striking image of how badly things have gone wrong.

At his apartment in a side street, Alexis proudly shows me family photographs of the area in the 1960s.

'When my parents lived here, this was such a good area. The apartment blocks, many built in the inter-war years, were palatial. Celebrities and stars lived here. The fortunate have now deserted the area for the affluent suburbs. Those that remain are the forgotten many.' His balcony displays a Greek flag on its pole, his claim to sovereign territory a message to the heterogeneous population, now more immigrant than indigenous.

Alexis vents spleen about how migrants have taken the area down several notches further.

'They just hang around in groups, there's nothing for them to do. They can't move on because without money there's nowhere to go, no means of getting anywhere. Nobody cares about them anymore than they care for how this neighbourhood has dived into catastrophe.'

It isn't as if migrants pose a threat to others. Their safety is more precarious than any resident, but the sheer numbers now forced into their marginal existence, sleeping in the squares, the parks, in doorways, squatting in abandoned office blocks, makes it feel more like a zone of conflict, a netherworld where one takes care where one goes.

Alexis takes me to the huge municipal park. *En route* we pass a derelict building, crumbling render belying its turn of the century splendour, its wooden shutters rotting and dangling by rusty hinges. A few young migrants peel back a sheet of corrugated iron fence around the property and spill out onto the street. Peering within, I catch sight of rubble and refuse waste. The stench of human excreta wafts from the darkened entrance of a once-desirable address.

At the park, unmaintained for months since the bankrupt municipality forced gardeners into redundancy, grasses and unkempt bushes mask dozens of makeshift polythene-clad tents. There's a menacing atmosphere. Scruffy individuals, mostly men, group and regroup with some kind of unfathomable purpose. Women and children shout from beyond the pathways in foreign tongues. Amongst all the migrants, the more established occupants, alcoholics, drug addicts and prostitutes vie for territory. Alexis wears a look of shame as he guides me along the once-maintained pathways beside weed-filled borders. This is a snapshot of the crisis in Greece.

He, not wishing either of us to loiter unnecessarily,

guided me out of the park gates, onto a busy arterial road where Athenians go about their daily business oblivious to, or in denial of, the dystopia inside the park railings.

In the evening, I strayed again towards Victoria Square. A fine drizzle has set in, but young migrants still congregate around the exits. Imran, a twenty-year-old Afghan, engages me in conversation, using his broken English.

'We are here because where else can we go? We have no homes, we have no possessions. Nobody wants us to be anywhere.'

I ask him where he wants to be.

'England, London—my city! I will get there even if I must walk.'

He has most recently come from Turkey, accompanied by others of like mind, each seeking their own Eden. I ask him if he wants to remain in Greece.

'No; why I stay here? No job, no money. Why? No Greek people like us or want us to stay.'

I suggest that he conveniently forgets the numerous acts of charity he and his colleagues receive each day, as ordinary people bring food and clothing. He hastily acknowledges the kindness of others, but his tone is dismissive, as if there is a harder, pressing truth. As I remain with him for the evening, I am appraised of that truth.

Late in the evening the police clear the square and send the migrants scurrying down side streets. We take flight toward the towering dome of St Pantaleimon church. But there is trouble ahead. Imran, familiar with escape routes, guides me around the trouble until we reach the abandoned block that is his temporary home. We scurry up the dilapidated stair well, seeking a place of shelter. We look out over the narrow street, watching the riot police pass by. I become aware of a rearguard of dark-clad men, not police. Theirs is a more brutal passage, as they lash out at any unfortunate passer-by who doesn't fit their image of a Greek patriot. There are plenty. Charity workers, anarchists, communists, students. Few migrants remain in the street long enough to be the focus of the black-clad shock force.

We look on incredulously and with concern, as a couple of men become ensnared by one baseball-bat-carrying paramilitary. He attacks the pair and relentlessly beats, kicks and punches one, then he abandons his prey and moves away. Other colleagues pass by unconcerned. The police, having passed earlier, are unaware of the incident. The second of the cornered men is now comforting the victim, but there appear to be no signs of life from the victim.

Imran turns to me, without words, conveying with his expression the significance of the event, and his reason for wanting to move on, move to England.

'This is what happens to us,' he finally says.

Bystanders gather to assist. An ambulance eventually arrives, half an hour later. Battle-weary paramedics scoop the victim into the vehicle and drive off, seeming fearful of the return of the perpetrators, as if the crew will be targeted too.

Meanwhile, in Monastirakis, tourists continue their culinary and cultural autumn visits in high spirits and with laughter. Another night in Athens.

Mike left his hotel room with his tools of trade and cagoule, descended the stairs to rejoin Imran who was self-consciously, uncomfortably, perched in a corner seat, holding a glass of water, wary of onlooking guests and staff. They could tell he wasn't a guest, but Mike had bribed the concierge to ensure he could wait there unchallenged. Mike's next stop would be the emergency room at the hospital, seeking the identity of the victim whose beating he had so recently witnessed.

Chapter Two
Ioannis Georghios Panayiotis, 2011

Mavro, the man to whom Ioannis had been introduced by Uncle Tassos, to be known forthwith only as Mavro, sat in a flourescent-lit room above a food store in the commercial section of Zeyfiri. Ioannis regarded him with suspicion because this was not the kind of person, by appearances, that he had imagined would be able to shape and provide purpose to his life. Mavro was a broad, muscular man, of about forty, perhaps 1.65 metres tall, dark, with sleaked back black hair, with at least a day's beard growth, both showing signs of greying. He was dressed, appropriately for his moniker, in black combat trousers, t-shirt and shoes. He did not reveal any emotion; it was like the interview from hell. His face seemed chiselled into a hard, unforgiving stare, his dark eyes fixed on Ioannis, seeking what lay deep in his thoughts. Mavro's rough accent and voice at once evoked a hard peasant life and a liking for cigarettes.

Ioannis was uncharacteristically quiet, meek.

'Your uncle has spoken to me. Your uncle thinks you would be a good member of our cause. Has he talked about what it is?'

Ioannis let him talk about his 'uncle', even though Tassos wasn't his uncle. He was his father's cousin, but had always been called 'uncle' and his wife, Adonia, 'auntie'.

'No,' uncertain as to whether he should have said 'No, sir,' but nevertheless not that bothered.

'No? No? Is that all you have to say for yourself? Your uncle tells me you usually are only too eager to mouth off exactly what you think to any unfortunate soul who happens to cross your path. He tells me you are pretty keen to mouth off at the custody officers. And all you can say to me is "no"?'

'He hasn't told me much about what I am going to be doing. I don't really know what your cause is.'

'Listen kid,'—Ioannis hated that everyone thought he was still a kid. He was in his twenties. OK, he didn't look that old, but he was surely a man because of his age—'how do you feel about how we live in Greece today? What do you think about the humiliating situation Europe has brought Greece to today? Who do you think is making sure all the shops are going out of business, the jobs are drying up, money is scarce, immigrants are invading our islands and city centres? Why is all that happening?'

Ioannis once again regretted that he didn't really think much about this stuff these days, didn't read the papers, didn't own a TV, hadn't listened to the talking radio since the time Nico had called him a dick. He knew what he knew because his friends had told him things, or he had read news headlines on his mobile. The Romany community, if that's what Mavro meant by immigrants, had always been the resented element in the Zeyfiri neighbourhood. They were accused of thievery, lawlessness, drug dealing, and taking the jobs of Greeks. Ever since Ioannis had been at school it had been the same banter. He thought most people, except those with money, lived like he did, maybe a bit more comfortably, a bit more family-like, but everyone he knew was on the breadline these days. In Zeyfiri, he knew there weren't many people with money. It wasn't the sort of place to show off your wealth. Maybe, he thought, Mavro was also talking about beyond Zeyfiri when he talked about immigrants. Maybe he meant the refugees. Ioannis thought that he knew what the difference was between migrants and refugees, but Mavro talked as if there was no difference.

'I dunno, perhaps it's politics, but I don't know much politics. That's for rich and powerful people. It doesn't make a difference to us, to me. I just live my life, see what each day brings.'

Mavro seemed unimpressed, but it was difficult to tell. He had a scowl, but he had had it from the beginning. He cast a fleeting glance at Tassos, as if to query the wisdom of him nominating this prick.

'Let me ask you then, are you Greek?'

'Of course!'

'And is your father Greek?'

'He was. He was a great supporter of the Greek nation. And my grandfather's sister's son, Costas, was a very big man in history.'

Mavro was vaguely aware of the family history from his discussions with Tassos.

'And what did this relative of yours do?'

'Costas was in the Greek army. He was a fighter in Cyprus for EOKA. My father only did national service.'

'What do you know about Costas's time in Greece?'

'He belonged to a paramilitary group called "X". I don't know much more, but my father was proud of his record.'

'Do you know what EOKA stood for?'

'For enosis, the union of Greece and Cyprus, the removal of the British from Cyprus, to finish any ideas that Turkey had about partition of the island.'

'And how does that make you feel today?'

'I dunno, that's another place. I was born here. I'm not Cypriot. I know about Cyprus's history, but it doesn't interest me.'

'What does interest you?'

'Nothing really.'

Ioannis thought Mavro was going to explode at that response. His face went red and his veins stood out at his temple. He must have reckoned that he was getting somewhere by calling up the patriotism inside Ioannis, but had been disappointed at his last answer.

'Who did you vote for, what party do you support in elections, in municipal elections?'

'I don't vote. It doesn't make any difference. The same people get in and say the same things.'

'But what one thing would make things better?'

'I dunno. Get rid of the immigrants; put money in everyone's pockets. Give us back our Drachma.'

Still Mavro got nothing he wanted to hear. He terminated the interview.

'Come here again tomorrow night. You will meet Steven who is going to be your mentor. Welcome to the cause. Close the door on the way out. Your uncle and I have some talking to do.'

'Listen Tassos, you've brought me a dud one in that lad. Are you trying to test me or something?'

'I know he's a difficult one to manage, but he's a good lad under it all; at least he was before he started to build a list of charges as long as your arm. I have a responsibility to discharge. Neither his mother nor my wife will give me a moment's rest until I have put him on a path to some kind of respectability. He's angry, hot-headed, lost. You can surely mould him. I don't want to burden you. But your guys can work on him.'

'He's a liability, first and foremost. In his current condition I can't do anything with him. I can't be seen to be involved myself; that's why I have allocated him to a mentor. Steven will knock him into form. But if he turns out to be a savage, I can't vouch for his future.

'Why didn't you drop him in it and send him off for conscription?'

'He's not going to cope well with discipline. What would the military do? Put him on charges each time he crossed a line. He would be discharged within weeks, or even if he lasted to the end, I'd still be stuck with him afterwards. Adonia wouldn't like that and what you might call her "favours" would be withdrawn; as they still are in danger of being if I don't convince you to take him on. He can't even look after himself, let alone follow orders. I just thought you might offer a flexible approach with the same tough discipline, but no discharge. I think he'll pull himself up by his boot straps, learn to obey, follow instructions and, maybe, control his temper. If he doesn't do that after a few months, you can drive him to the door of the Hellenic Army and make sure he signs his draft papers.'

Tassos was conscious he was not holding a very strong bargaining hand. Tassos still thought there was a cell waiting for Ioannis in Korydallos Prison.

Mavro was still unconvinced, and Tassos played his last card, and final sanction, 'I realise you are reluctant, but be aware, Mavro, that the impunity with which you are allowed to operate in Zeyfiri can change at any moment, at the flick of a switch.'

Mavro, realising this was Tassos's most high stake chip, had little option but to acquiesce.

PART TWO

Chapter Three
George and Stavros, 1931

George sat silently in the hide next to Hassan, observing birds in their natural habitat. In the lull between sightings, he reflected on how he had reached this spot.

George had been posted to Cyprus six months previously, in 1929. Stavros was a Cypriot working for the colonial administration, just like himself, he was a single, twenty-three-year-old civil servant. Generations of Stavros's family and friends were residents of Myrsina. The village had several hundred inhabitants and was situated on the windy plain against the backdrop of the Kyrenia mountains. Surrounding the village was abundant wildlife in a timeless, dust-infused, rural, agricultural setting under harsh, interrogative sunlight.

George's visit to the village was at the invitation of Stavros, and had arisen out of their growing friendship. Their office routine was regimented, colonial, administrative. 'Native workers' were treated differently because of where they were born, a fact of colonial life that George couldn't stomach. He made amends by breaching separatism one person at a time.

The first time he spoke to the Stavros, whose demeanour was restrained, careful not to raise attention to himself, they were sitting adjacent to each other on the wall outside their workplace. George with a cigarette, Stavros with his lunch of bread, cheese and olives.

'You want some bread?' He proffered the snack, his arms

extending from the too-short arms of his suit jacket, revealing tanned, downy arms. His face, similarly dark and handsome, hair cut short, brilliantined and combed to one side.

'No, y'er alright, mate,' His Yorkshire accent was not always tamed, sometimes escaping unexpectedly like now when he was caught off-guard socially.

'How you can work all day on just cigarettes?' A lightly accented phrase that nonetheless revealed hard work on a second language. 'Here,' insistently passing some of the coarse, off-white loaf, opened up and filled with white cheese. Greek hospitality, never take no for an answer, thought George, gratefully.

'You sure, mate? I don't want to take yer meal away from you.'

'I am sure! Here, take.'

George discarded his stub and took the crusty offering, biting into it thankfully. He had no lunch because his money had run out until pay day. 'Ta! Very good of you.'

'You are working in the governor's office, yes?'

'That's right mate, and you?' chewing, his palate serrated by the hard crust, tantalised by the tastes of freshly baked bread and acidic tangy cheese.

'Accounts, second floor. I am a clerk. My name is Stavros.'

'George,' speaking through a mouthful of bread. Four incompatible tasks at once: hold bread, chew, shake hands, talk. 'How long have you worked here?'

'Two months. I graduated from gymnasium in Lefkosia—in English you say Nicosia. I have been very lucky to get this job.'

'Everyone's lucky to have a job at the moment. I've been here six months, give or take.'

'Give or take?' querying the meaning, intonation raised at the end.

'More or less?' Another question, as if checking he had understood, which the nod confirmed. 'You speak English well.'

'It was a major subject for me at gymnasium. I am not so sure of many things, so I still need practice.'

'Where are you from?'

'My home is a village called Myrsina, but in Lefkosia I stay with some friends of my cousin. They have,' pausing for thought, correcting his tense, '*had*, space for me and they need money.'

'You look like you're about my age, twenty-three?'

'Twenty-three, me also.'

Stavros's fresh young face lit up as the conversation continued, the mask of anonymity slowly dismantled, the budding shoots of a friendship nurtured over shared lunch.

They probed each other for commonality: football, Cyprus, the governor, family, relationships, food, until their allotted break had ended.

'Listen, Stavros, we could meet up again. How about tomorrow?'

'I would like that. We can talk some more.'

They walked back past the governor's house, its wooden oriental-styled frontage masking the administrative hub of this colonial outpost. George had found out the house was built in sections in the UK and was destined for India, Ceylon or somewhere, but a former governor had taken a liking to it and had it intercepted *en route* before its passage through the Suez canal. They parted at the entrance stairwell to their office building to go to their respective sections.

George and Stavros had thus become friends as much out of curiosity—on both of their parts—as to how the other lived their lives, as out of getting on well and genuinely liking each other. George had mentioned bird watching shortly after meeting Stavros, another snippet of information revealing something about himself. Finding new friends was a process of familiarisation, like catching a glimpse of actors through a chink in a theatre curtain before an eagerly anticipated production. Whilst his tendency was to fall in with people from the UK of similar age, of which there were a few at work, George also allowed his curiosity about Stavros to develop. Being honest, he preferred being with Stavros because he found most of the British he worked with to be stuck up, decadent, living or carving a dream life in colonial service. He was a Sheffield lad and had no truck with that.

They met again, it became a comfortable routine at lunchtime on those February weekdays, the caution of earlier conversation cast away, matey banter taking its place, probing further each other's preferences.

A cold grey sky of fast moving clouds dredged the plains toward the mountains, dropping their burden like a veil across the foothills before shrouding the mountain peaks. There was a chill wind and they were both clad in heavy wool coats with the collars turned up. Stavros also wore a scarf, although George thought he was fine without.

'You remember I wrote to my mother and told her you were my new friend?' George listened to the intonation of English spoken by a Cypriot. Stavros pronounced 'mA-therr', his *r*'s rolled and extended. It helped George when listening to other Greek Cypriots. He was privately amused at the prospect of Cypriots listening to him and taking on his Rotherham accent. He nodded in response.

'Then my mother, who cannot write, had a letter written in return. She has invited you and I to visit Myrsina. She says that a villager friend of my father'—*fA-therr*—'is interested in birds and he says that a good range of birds could be sighted, best time is during late March or April, so we can go meet my family and you can go watching the birds.'

George knew it was frowned on and potentially unsafe for British civil servants to travel around the island in this unfettered way, even more so associating with locals. Colonial stalwarts—of which there were plenty where George and Stavros worked—disapproved of those breaching the boundary between ruler and ruled. George didn't much care for their views. He was both apprehensive and thrilled to have been invited, his friendship with Stavros had built mutual trust and no scenario he could imagine for such a trip involved other than benign intentions. He wasn't worried about what people would think, nor what privations he would be obliged to endure. His apprehension originated from his belief that he lacked the etiquette and language to carry it off.

'That's a very kind offer, but, Stavros, I can't speak Greek, as you know, and I don't know all the customs. I might cause your family offence without even intending it.'

'Don't worry, they know something about you already because I wrote how you are new in Cyprus and your life is different before you are coming here. They will be happy to see you.'

'Well, it seems like a good opportunity, if you think it will be safe to travel, I am honoured to be invited and accept, but you must be my guide. If I am doing something wrong or something that causes offence, you must tell me.'

'Of course,' said as if there was no likelihood of disaster. 'You will just need to smile your friendly smile and my mother will forgive anything. She will say you have the face of an angel. Trust me!'

'Then I accept!'

The trip was agreed upon, Stavros made arrangements in the ensuing weeks. The brother of the family he was boarding with was a driver. He regularly travelled out of Nicosia towards Famagusta port and a lift was organised for the pair, but the exact weekend would be dependent on the driver's schedule.

The economic and political situation was not ideal. 1926 was five painful years ago. George knew he had been lucky to escape the consequences and his South Yorkshire upbringing. No part of the world was unaffected by the circumstances that had reduced millions to abject poverty. Cyprus was no exception. He knew the local population was prone to poverty because the bulk of the economy was based upon agriculture and labouring. Stavros had described the set up. Almost every villager was involved in some way or other with the production of food from a family plot, fields or farm. Stavros's extended family worked isolated plots of land spread across a large area surrounding the village. They grew wheat, fruits and vegetables. Herds of goats and sheep were shepherded by either the youngest, the eldest, or males least capable of doing anything else.

George knew from his involvement with an agricultural reform programme at work that the position of each plot was neither random accident nor design. They were a consequence of inheritance and gender, the paths between them trodden by their kin folk as if choreographed by their genes, the footsteps gently mutating from generation to generation, plots becoming increasingly divided.

Stavros and George set out together on a Friday afternoon. The journey was about an hour. They'd sat on the open back of the lorry amongst the cargo packages, discussing their work, the passing countryside, joking and laughing.

The driver dropped them off at a crossroads two miles from the village. They had walked the remaining distance along an unmetalled side-road across the open, flat fieldscape, toward the tightly clustered village of white buildings topped with red tiles.

Chapter Four
A Trip to Myrsina

When they arrived they were welcomed warmly, Stavros was the returning son—not a frequent returnee to the village now that he lived in Lefkosia—and was respected by most people for having such a prestigious job. The first adult male that they encountered coming into the village had diverted them into the first tavern and ordered glasses of ouzo to celebrate their visit. George met several other men of a certain age, all wearing similar coarse black baggy vra'ka trousers, cotton striped shirts, black sleeveless yilekkos or long sleeved zibouni jackets, long leather boots meeting their vra'ka at the knee, some with headgear, and all with a thick moustache, virtually identical in dress and style. He was introduced one by one to them, Dimitri, Spiros, Yannis, Giorgiou; they spoke in broken English, with translations through Stavros. Younger men were not present in the tavern, but he had noted that they were more likely to be dressed in the contemporary western clothes that he and Stavros wore.

As news of their arrival permeated through the village, Stavros's father, Christos, ran down to the tavern to join in the celebrations. There was much hugging, chatter and humour in the small rustic tavern and a great deal of high spirited talk as the ouzo flowed. George, who had been imprinted with the hygiene standards of a colonial existence—boil all water, be careful what you eat—viewed the jug of water he was given with the ouzo with some suspicion until Stavros told him that the water in the village came from a clean, reliable spring. Reassured, he poured the water into the ouzo and watched clear spirit and water transform into a cloudy white liquid, the unmistakable smell of aniseed assailing his nostrils. As he swallowed, the inevitable burning sensation filled his chest as the rough spirit made its way down his throat. Stavros's father, it turned out, spoke English well enough to communicate directly with George. He introduced George to every individual that came into, or walked past, the tavern. He spoke with enthusiasm about the planned birding sortie. An hour passed in this pleasant way before a small girl ran into the tavern, received by Stavros who swept her into his arms and kissed her on the cheek, making a fuss of her. She, distracted by this intervention by Stavros, but giggling with joy, wrestled away from Stavros to address Christos like a child reciting a new poem from memory, careful not to forget what she had been told to say, before looking uncertainly at George and running back out without awaiting a reply. Stavros explained that the child was his niece and had been sent with a message from The Matriarch—Stavros's mother, Eleni—to ensure that the party made its way to the family home because food was about to be served. Stavros explained this to George and conveyed his amusement that rather than referring to her by name, his father always called his wife 'The Matriarch'. The tradition had maintained itself throughout Stavros's childhood. Eleni, apparently, took it in her stride 'as long as you know, old man, who is wearing the vra'ka'—the implied social order within the household held well and did not impact on their deep affection for each other.

The group had made its way from the tavern and along the dirt road that ran through the centre of the village, attracting the attention of the other villagers. Stavros explained that there was a plan to link the village to the main road with a tarmacadam road. The church and the colonial authorities had been reluctant to release the finances because not enough tax had been collected from the neighbourhood. It was thought that other communities were more deserving of the resources. This irked many in the village because they argued that the taxes were unfair and unaffordable and that the main reason that the tax revenue was so low was because there were less inhabitants in their village than elsewhere. As a community of subsistence farmers, they had no cash crop grown to sell on through the markets, so there was little money in the local economy, therefore little opportunity to tax. George was aware that this prioritisation of resources was always going to be an issue, especially in times of economic torpor. The austerity of the villagers' lives had been there in the ruggedness of their locally woven clothing, the lack of creature comforts and the fact that all transportation was by wooden cart drawn by cattle or donkeys. It was a world apart from his life in Nicosia, but George genuinely felt the warmth of the community. He put to the back of his mind the questions he wanted to ask about the villagers' lives; there would be a better time for a private conversation with Stavros.

They approached the family home—an unprepossessing single-storey building with a roof of clay tiles and rendered clay walls broken by two shuttered windows and the main doorway—to be met by the entire extended family who ran out to greet Stavros and his guest.

George was treated to warm hospitality. The family treated him as one of their own, offering him a bedroom in their home for the weekend.

There had been a great deal of high-spirited chatter culminating in George's introduction to The Matriarch, Eleni. She was a woman of a certain age, with timeless attractiveness, nonetheless looking as if she had had a difficult life. The spirit of her soul was conveyed in bright, sparkling eyes, the crow's feet around their edges highlighted in the open, friendly smile she reserved for George and her son. George had found himself at home in this grouping, accepted by all, even the niece who had previously regarded him with suspicion. The assembly outside the house attracted the attention of others in the street. Each neighbouring household poured forth its inquisitive, friendly human content in the direction of Stavros's family home. A party had been ignited like a bush fire after a lightning strike in this quiet village far from the busy city of Nicosia. It was not long before a number of the men in the village had gathered their instruments and started playing traditional Greek music. Everybody became unwitting guests in a huge street party. Tables were set up in the street on rustic trestles. Food began to appear from the family home and was placed on the tables: bread, cheeses, olives, salads, hummus, aubergines, yoghurt, figs, fruits, more cheese, eggs, potatoes, chicken, seasonal vegetables and so on. At a spoken command, small children had rushed around neighbouring houses gathering chairs and placing them round the trestle tables. Eleni encouraged her neighbours to bring food and join the party. Even as dusk took over and the clear night sky presented itself, the party continued amid strategically placed oil lamps. The party atmosphere continued past midnight; children began to curl up and sleep on chairs, parents' laps or indoors; adults began to slump on their chairs from overindulgence. The band played on and people danced their traditional folk dances. It became clear that some of the band were similarly inebriated. Their music became more inaccurate as time wore on, but it didn't matter to those assembled. They were having a good time and it was all because of George.

After midnight, George was shown to a small rustic room within the house, his bed a mattress stuffed with straw on a clay base built up from the floor. The room was sparsely furnished with a hand-built, reed-seated chair, a handmade table and several wooden pegs on the wall for clothing. There was no door, only a heavy curtain across the doorway. There was a shuttered window, closed to keep out the chill of a spring night. George was inebriated and paid less attention than he might have done to his surroundings, but he was grateful for whatever hospitality he had been offered. In his tiredness, after relieving himself in the latrine outside the building, he slumped fully-clothed onto the mattress and fell asleep. He was awoken at dawn by the crowing of cocks and the braying of donkeys. The dawn chorus was fully under way and he recognised, even in his hungover state, the calls and song of many different birds. As he hauled himself off the mattress, which had afforded him a surprisingly good night's sleep, the household was already fully awake and dealing with the chores of early morning. It was 6 am on Saturday and the smaller children were being prepared for school, which was some two miles away in a neighbouring village. He was informed that they would be at school from 8 am until one in the afternoon and would make the journey on foot. On Sunday there was no school, but they would be expected to dress in their best clothes to attend the small Greek Orthodox church in the village, unless they were Muslim. Muslims attended the mosque on Fridays.

He drew back the doorway curtain and entered the main room of the house, which doubled as a dining area and a kitchen. Everybody was engrossed in some domestic activity or other. Everyone, nonetheless, found time to greet him. Another meal was under preparation, but his offers to help were politely declined. He was handed a mug of hot sweet tea. It was made of honey, water and dried heads of chamomile, stuffed into the mug so the stalks protruded from the mug. Stavros joked with him that it was good for hangovers. George reflected in a gentle voice that it might be a useful drink. He washed using a bowl outside the house, then attempted to shave but abandoned the effort.

During breakfast the talk returned to the topic of birding. Christos outlined the plan they had for George over the weekend. He was to join Hassan in walking several miles into the foothills where they would construct a hide and watch from within. George had been warned that whilst he was here to observe the wildlife, there were others equally likely to hunt his birds. George had already heard about a local dish made with birds. Preparations continued for his excursion. Shortly after they had eaten a frugal repast of bread, cheese and meats, he was handed a lunch pack tied up in a cloth on a stick and marched out to meet his guide. Hassan had a friendly, welcoming, warm personality, whilst speaking virtually no English, he was able to convey limited information to George in broken English-Turkish, doing the actions to help interpretation of phrases, like a game of charades. Hassan announced their departure and, as one, the extended family had accompanied the pair to the boundaries of the village and watched as they trekked away. At this stage the temperature was around 60 °F. The sun had appeared and was following its trajectory across a pale blue sky. George, resplendent in his khaki kit and pith helmet, was well prepared for a day in searing heat. Whilst nobody in the village had made comment, it was clear that some humour was being extracted at his expense on account of his bizarre outfit as the two shrank further into the landscape.

Their destination was reached quickly, a secluded hillside spot adjacent to a small and rapidly drying out dew pond. This was adjoined by a grove of olive trees edged by a line of cypress, affording shelter to the birds who would come to the pond to take the water. Overhead, birds of prey were circling on thermals. Hassan had made preparations: a hide made from a tarpaulin draped over some hazel twigs had been constructed with a viewing slot. Two large boulders had been utilised to act as seating. On arrival at the spot, George surveyed the surroundings, keeping an eye out for birds and different wildlife. He looked at the hide and quickly settled into it, although he wasn't sure how long he would be able to endure the midday heat under the tarpaulin.

For now, it was pleasantly cool. With his field glasses to hand he continued to survey the land and with whispers and gesticulations communicated near silently with Hassan. For several hours they continued their watch. George was making copious notes of his observations, drawing the marking features of species he was unable to identify on the spot. Hassan contributed by spotting birds that George hadn't yet seen and gave each their Turkish name, which George interpreted to the best of his ability. His list and enthusiasm grew exponentially for the first couple of hours: rock thrush, Cyprus warblers (*Sylvia melanothorax*) and Sardinian warbler, falcon, buzzard, roller, wheatear, bunting, swift, nightingale, jay, tree creeper, and so on.

He had not managed to see such a broad selection of bird life in one spot since arriving in Cyprus, although he had been fortunate enough to travel to the salt lakes outside Larnaca and observe huge flocks of greater flamingo, *Phoenicopterus ruber roseus*, hovering on their stilt-like legs above the surface, constantly moving in flocks of dozens up to several thousand. That had been a stupendous sighting. He had previously seen ospreys in northern England, but this was something better, not only the birds themselves, but the setting, the Larnaca salt lakes, which at that time of the year were filled with water. Salt was a tax-earning commodity, harvested at this lake and others throughout the history of Cyprus and its respective occupations. The waters were shimmering in front of the ancient Islamic mosque with its calling tower, a slender finger reaching for the blue infinity, called the Tekke. The site was surrounded by tall palm trees, the distant Kyrenia range of mountains acting as a hazy backdrop, their peaks shrouded in heavy grey cloud. George had thought it was one of the most exotic sights he could expect to see in a near Eastern posting—it was so different to anything he could have imagined. The architecture of the mosque, the palm trees waving in the autumn breeze, the expanses of water rimmed by harvested salt mounds, the colourful display of the pink birds. Amazing!

George knew he was privileged to be able to roam this land with its hospitable and friendly inhabitants and captivating wildlife. The villagers seemed to bear no grudge against their British occupiers. As the heat of the spring day began to build and the birds became less in evidence, the two men prepared to return to the village, firstly sharing the lunchpack that Eleni had provided and drinking a gourd full of spring water that Hassan carried. As they walked in silence George began to think again about the family and the villagers. His thoughts were interrupted occasionally by a bird sighting, something Hassan pointed out and named, or by needing to concentrate whilst negotiating difficult terrain.

He had been led to understand that there was little in common between Turkish Cypriot and Greek Cypriot, coming as they did from such different religious and cultural backgrounds. But it did not appear to be the case; Hassan, a Turkish Cypriot—as were many of the villagers—seemed to be an integral member of the village, accepted as he was by Greek Cypriots, and they likewise by him. He had his land; they socialised together, were present at each others' family's vital events, their children went to school alongside each other, shared much in terms of kinship, sense of place, burden. He was unable to discuss it with Hassan; neither of them had enough of a common vocabulary. It was not something he had yet felt able to discuss with Stavros. He undertook to have that discussion and try to understand the subtleties involved in the relationships between villagers. It didn't seem to make sense to George, imbued as he was with the colonial view that the two sides were different, wanted different things politically and were frequently at loggerheads in history. All his acquired wisdom was being challenged during his visit to the village.

Chapter Five
Under the Mimosa Tree

George, returning from their expedition, was introduced to Hassan's heavily pregnant wife, three children, grandmother, and those members of the extended family still living in the village. It was difficult to communicate across the language barrier other than with smiles, laughter and the demonstrable gratitude that George showed towards his hosts. The family was afflicted by the poverty he had recognised in Stavros's household. The quality and quantity of furnishings was minimal, functional rather than beautiful, the building itself was rustic. The only noticeable differences between this and Stavros's family home were the denomination of religious artefacts, this being a Mohammedan household. He parted after his hospitable hosts had plied him with tea and sweetmeats, returning to Stavros's household shortly after 2 pm.

Stavros was reading at the kitchen table when he returned. He suggested they sit in the square in front of the church, under the mimosa trees. The second of two taverns in the village was nearby, so they could have a coffee and wait for the rest of the household to return before the afternoon meal. Stavros feigned an interest in the bird spotting expedition, although George thought it small talk. They sat in the spring warmth under fresh lime-green foliage and yellow blossom whilst the village slept through the siesta. A hospitable tavern keeper brought coffee and glasses of water on a round metallic tray. George steered the conversation towards the issues he had been unable to discuss with Hassan.

'Stavros, everybody appears to be very poor in this village.'

'Of course. It is an agricultural community. People have no money, little education.'

'Has it always been the same?'

'As long as I can remember, as long as my father can remember these villagers have had very little.' He leaned forward to take a slurp of the grainy coffee. 'There is no cash economy; *almost* no cash,' he corrected himself, having realised that the taverns ran on cash, evidently. 'Everybody needs some money. For that families rely upon people like myself who have been blessed with an education and have moved to work in the towns and cities. We send money back to the family and this is what sustains them, allows them to buy seed and fertiliser and equipment. Otherwise, the only money circulating in the community is from what we sell amongst ourselves and at market. Once a week the women go to the markets in Varosha to sell what produce they have, whatever the season. That is why the village is quiet today.'

'But if there's not much money, how do people manage to buy essentials, clothes, equipment, foodstuffs?'

'Apart from the way that I was telling you, there are, of course, moneylenders. There are two moneylenders in our sister village and almost every villager here is in debt to them. Even my father.'

'Are moneylenders controlled? Does the government have any control over them?'

'No!' His intonation implied the naivety of the question. He cleared his throat with a noisy hawk. Perhaps, thought George, a signal of impatience. Stavros's chatter continued, assuming a tone of restrained perseverance.

'The government goes about its business and doesn't legislate, doesn't help villagers. We pay taxes, carry our debts. We repay them when we can, but all the time there are new demands. Recently there has been talk of introduction of new import taxes and increases in the salt tariff. These things are a burden on villagers. The only solutions available are to borrow more money or sell more produce.'

George, newly enlightened and oblivious to Stavros's agitation and thinning veil of congeniality, said 'So moneylenders control villagers' lives and the debt collectors pursue families for the repayment of debts. Are there other things that stop villagers participating in the economy?'

'Of course, the merchants. We have none in this village except for tavern and shop owners. Merchants do as they always do and take opportunities for financial gain. The villagers are at the mercy of the merchants and their prices. When we cannot afford the goods we have to go back to the moneylenders. It is a vicious circle.'

'Does the church not assist? Is the church not speaking out on behalf of the poor?'

George noticed Stavros shift on his seat. He turned to face George more squarely. George immediately regretted the religious intrusion and thought he wouldn't get an answer. When Stavros began again his voice was louder, his pitch more strained.

'Look! The church is very powerful, maybe not our priest, but the bishops have big power over peasants, especially those who have limited literacy or education. Those people with no education, like my parents and the elders, believe what the church is telling them. As a good Orthodox son, I would find it difficult to challenge the church or what the priest is telling me because that would be to disrespect my elders. You must understand that the church is part of the problem of the rural poor. In the past, the church was the tax collector for the Turkish Ottomans. Even after the British took control, they continued to allow the church to play this role. Nobody forgets such things, but they do not challenge. I think older people do not challenge enough.'

Non-Yorkshire folk would have thought George's persistence was insensitive to Stavros's evident discomfort and agitation. George continued saying what he was thinking.

'I've often wondered what role the church plays in each village to whip up any sentiments towards or against unionisation of workforce an, of course, union with Greece.' He was drawing on intelligence he had gained at work.

Stavros, increasingly resentful and suspicious of George's motives, turned away from George momentarily. He kicked at a trail of ants moving toward the trunk of the mimosa tree. He avoided looking directly at George when answering. The smile on his face was now a barricade, no longer welcoming. This time he spoke more rapidly and with higher pitch.

'Ah, you are discussing a tricky area for me, my friend. I talk with you as a friend, but you are also a work colleague employed by the colonial government. So I wear two hats, one as a Greek Cypriot Orthodox and one as an employee of the colonial administration. I don't have myself any voice about how the colonial administration manages its population. I am not different, then, to my less fortunate peasant villager. Also, my friend, in common with all of my fellow citizens, I have a British passport. In answer to your question, you are right to think that the church would have a position and that from the pulpit it would promote its position. It depends on where you are and which church and which priest is doing the preaching. There is, of course, also a political viewpoint that the church puts forward, especially in respect of union with Greece, which the archbishops support. They have the support of the Orthodox Church in Greece. But in this village, the priest can see that there is little to be gained for the villagers in promoting a strong pro-union view. These are peasant farmers living at subsistence.' In his discomfort he abandoned correctness of diction and resumed his oration. His voice was now louder. 'My compatriots have little interest beyond the village, their kin folk, their religion, and the dowry of their daughters. So, the priest does not spend much energy trying to generate debate or influence opinion in favour of union with Greece, enosis. There are some in the village who are strong supporters of enosis. They are ones you will see raising the Greek flag on holidays. There are many young people for whom union with Greece is logical, given their cultural and religious background. They may also have been influenced by their education to think of the idea of a Greek nation encompassing all the Greek speakers of the world.'

Stavros mentally rehearsed oaths directed at George, seething with internalised anger at this relentless interrogation.

George was by now conscious that his questions and the manner of his questioning were unfair, indelicate. The faster pace of Stavros' speech, his more strident and higher pitched voice made it clear that he was getting worked up. George wanted to understand, but he couldn't push the point, and didn't want to further offend his host. He had so many questions, so much to piece together. Stavros himself had belied the notion of a peaceful coexistence of Greek and Turk by focusing only on a Greek view of things when he was flustered. Why, thought George, did he not consider whether Turks would countenance a partisan future sculpted only by Greeks?

He thanked Stavros for his candidness and patience. The two of them lapsed into an awkward silence, broken only by the barking of a dog, the birdsong in the square, the squeaking of rusty shutters opening, the awakening villagers about to continue their afternoon, and some distance away, the noise of a vehicle. As if to signal a timely curtailment, the previously suspicious niece ran into the square to call the pair for lunch. Whilst summoning the tavern keeper to be paid, George reiterated his gratitude to Stavros, saying that he had learnt a lot during that tranquil time under the mimosa trees and had gained new and boundless respect for his local colleague. With true feeling, he said that Stavros was both his superior in being able to speak two languages fluently, for being articulate in his second language and for being so knowledgeable on local political and cultural issues in a way that George would find difficult to match with British culture and history. They returned home, eventually to be treated to another feast, this time of boiled lamb and potatoes, wine and bread. He was taught to pronounce the name of the dish by Eleni—*kleftiko*. The wonderful aromas had seduced them like a temptress as they walked along the street. George was salivating even before sitting at the table in the courtyard covered by grape vines behind the house. Stavros, recovering from his grilling, once again warmed to George as the food smoothed his vexation. When they had first returned, Stavros, away from George in another part of the house, had launched into an explosive and agitated monologue in Greek, with his parents the unwitting recipients of his irritation with George. His warmth towards George only returned after his parents' patient and soothing counsel had taken effect. The rest of the day, however, was as pleasant as George could have imagined. If there were agitators here for enosis, around the table they were being very subdued. If he had offended Stavros, it was no longer apparent.

That night, George lay in his bed robbed of sleep by many distractions: dogs barking their dialogue across the plains, cicada beetles, sheep bells as flocks moved in search of good grass, but mostly by his own jumbled thoughts. The experiences of the weekend challenged his view of the country and its people. In the six months since his arrival in Cyprus, he had had little opportunity to form views other than of his comfortable colonial civil servant lifestyle with its living accommodation, formal dinners and patriotic pomp and circumstance. This was the first time he had been the privileged guest of a local family. He had taken the opportunity to discuss those things that were on his mind, but he had more questions. His view of Cyprus would not be the same again. On reflection he had decided his handling of the conversation with Stavros was reckless.

He committed to treading more sensitively. He would apologise when the opportunity arose.

The next day was warm and sunny, the dust blowing in vortices across the landscape like a diva dismissively contemptuous of her audience. Stavros and George prepared to travel back to Nicosia. George thanked his hosts and Hassan and his family profusely and with genuine humility. On departure, he handed them small gifts he had hidden away in his luggage. Stavros and George were similarly treated to packaged food, fruit and dried goods, like sons whose mother thought they needed feeding up, her love travelling with them. Hassan, speaking through Stavros, requested that they return in several weeks for the christening of his soon-to-be-born fourth child. The grateful pair left on foot, shouting further thanks and goodbyes as they passed through the village. They walked to the main road where they planned to wait for a British vehicle to pass, failing that, one of the few local omnibuses travelling to Nicosia. As it was a Sunday there were few vehicles travelling towards the city from Famagusta or Lefkoniko, so they sat on the roadside and fell into conversation again.

'When we were talking yesterday, I think I caused you offence. I really want to apologise. It was not my intention. The part of England I come from is known for its straight talking and I'm behaving just like I would at home. I am grateful to you for letting me understand your life.'

'You know, I was very angry when we were talking under the mimosa tree. I went to my parents and spoke to them. I said you were asking questions. They told me to be more understanding. They said I should imagine myself in your country and think what questions I would want to ask. Then I thought your questions were maybe not so bad. But I want to know whether you were asking me because you suspect me of being a supporter of enosis; is the governor asking you to find out about me?'

George, taken aback that his friend should think such a thing, was quick to deny this and place his interest in context, to try to remove any suspicion that Stavros might have that he was anything other than a friend.

'Your life has been—*is*—so different to mine, I just want to understand. Our conversations are private, between ourselves. I wouldn't repeat anything we discussed. Your political views are your own and no, I am not vetting you and your views. I have been unfair to you because we have not spoken of the political views that I myself hold. It was a one way discussion, so I apologise.'

Stavros, placated by the apology and reassurance, a smile of friendship returning to his face after a prolonged absence, grasped his friend's hand, holding it as they talked, as male friends do in his culture, promising George he will be less of a fool. George, eager to be accepted on common ground and equally relieved, also tried to disengage his hand at the earliest opportunity, not sure about the relevance of this gesture.

No vehicles passed in the next fifteen minutes. Their conversation continued, sometimes small talk, sometimes probing. George, still inquisitive, thought he could once again ask his searching questions.

'I wanted to ask about your experience of Turkish- and Greek-speaking families living side by side in peace. In my ignorance, I'd thought that there was little contact between communities, different villages, different lifestyles. In your village, there were Turkish speakers like Hassan and Greek-speaking families living alongside each other. In England, there are very few people outside London who are not English by birth, there are almost no places where there are Christians and Muslims living in the same communities.'

'First and foremost, in Cyprus, one's life is one's family and kinfolk, one's loyalty is, after that, to your community, to your religion, to those of the same class as yourself. There is no need to make the distinction on racial differences. In the village, and in others like it, there are no differences between us apart from going to different places of worship.'

A lorry passed, but showed no signs of stopping for the pair, so Stavros continued.

'Of course, the local priests, mullahs, and what have you, are powerful forces of influence, but peasant farmers are of the same class as each other, so their family and community are more important than other things. We all live together because of these things. In the cities it is different because so many people have migrated from elsewhere and don't have local family, local land. Then other loyalties bind people together, perhaps religion, perhaps patronage of merchants and moneylenders, now unions too. And, of course, political agitation can increasingly influence and divide people. The Orthodox Church is, as you already know, a strong political force.'

A shepherd approached across the open fields with a herd of perhaps two hundred goats seeking good pasture, their bells clanging as they went past the pair, engulfing them in a transient cacophony and dust cloud. The shepherd greeted Stavros by name. A conversation ensued. A dust storm blew up several fields away, highlighting the unseasonable dryness of the land. A car passed by, fully loaded with passengers, the driver swerving to avoid errant sheep grazing on the verge. George shifted his attention from Stavros and the shepherd and drew patterns in the dust with a stick, deep in contemplation. Stavros's partisan political stance didn't seem to fit with the idyll he was now describing.

After the herd had passed and the car disappeared into the shimmer of heat haze, Stavros continued his dialogue with George.

'There are big changes going on. The colonial bureaucracy is blind to these things. It seeks to divide and rule. Through its policies, its patronage, and its political meddling it tries to set Greek and Turk against each other. Why? Because it succeeds! Take the police. Almost all police officers who are not British are Turkish Cypriots. The bureaucratic councils who make local decisions are tipped to favour Turkish interests because Turks are more compliant in their support of the British. But things are changing. There is a new Turkish politician on the National Council who always votes with the Greek minority. Of course, you only have my view of these things so you need to ask others their views, but, I think, my friend, that my views are right!'

Eventually, a local bus came along, a converted covered charabanc exported to the island after the Great War, and still running. They hailed it and attempted to board. It had the atmosphere of a mobile marketplace. The crowded space was filled with bags, large woven baskets, women in scarves, children, chickens tied together by one foot, goats in the aisle. On top of the bus were more woven baskets of produce, potatoes, leaves, gourds, garlic, onions, livestock in woven cages, suitcases and wooden crates of bottles, all tied down to a luggage platform with ropes. Inside, there was animated discussion and much laughter amongst the women. Children were screaming, crying, sleeping, staring at the passing countryside, clinging to their mothers, staring at the new passengers, especially the one with the pith helmet. There was neither spare seating, nor much space to move further into the bus. The two men stood in the foot well adjacent to the driver for the fifteen-mile journey, although more passengers and their baggage were boarded at two further stops. Conversation was curtailed by the whine of the engine and the overwhelming cacophony of their fellow passengers' conversation, and the bleating goats under the seats of row three. The bus was so overcrowded that it crawled along the road at about ten miles an hour.

At the bus station the two men parted company, George once again thanking Stavros for the weekend visit and taking pains to impress upon Stavros how much he had valued the experience, the birdwatching, and the conversations the two of them had. Stavros, was genuinely relieved that George seemed to not have been offended in any way by his experience, and was instead demonstrating empathy with the villagers. They arranged to meet again after work the following Wednesday, although they would meet up at lunchtime each day on the wall outside Government House.

Chapter Six
George and Stavros Gather Information

One hot midweek lunchtime, George told Stavros he'd seen ΕΝΩΣΗΣ slogans on many walls in Nicosia, and asked whether there was a recent surge in support. He also knew that his employer was removing the slogans around Nicosia as fast as they appeared.

'Many young Greek Cypriots think it logical given their cultural and religious backgrounds. If they are Greek they have been influenced through their education to think of the idea of a broader Greek nation encompassing all the Greek speakers of the world. Now, the government is planning changes to the Education Act, to remove any opportunity to influence the syllabus.'

'I thought you might mention that. Many people in positions of power are strongly set against any change to that Act. It appears that their opposition might be a spark that alights disturbances,' said George.

'If there are going to be disturbances that might be one of the contributing factors. There are others, of course. We have discussed trade unions before. These days there is pressure to join unions, to obtain the benefits that as individuals we could not hope to achieve. The KKK union has grown in recent months as it recruits more and more young people.'

'I can't deny my own views. Industrial workers in the UK would be expected to join a union. It's a political obligation. They'd be blacked if they didn't. Everyone hates the bosses who suck the life spirit out of their workers and strip assets to line their own pockets. Do your unions also have a political message?'

'Your first point explains why unions are on the rise in Cyprus. But it is also why enosis is a popular cause. Is it not true that the very colonial administration you and I work for is the evil boss who, as you say, "sucks spirit" from the poor peasants of Cyprus?'

'Okay, I understand that sentiment, but it does not reflect my own view. Why should the government take the blame for all ills? Why has a long-promoted association with Greece suddenly transformed into an even bigger stick with which to beat the administration?'

'Absolutely. A complicated set of factors are at play in Cyprus. The great agitators of the moment are the youths. They are being organised, with the support of the unions and the church, to challenge so many different things. They support enosis, improvement of working conditions and salaries, are concerned about the economic situation, and are in favour of a stronger voice for the Greek and Turkish Cypriot people. It amounts to a minor revolution and the natural target is the colonial administration.'

'Don't you think the colonial administration has as its prime interest the support and prosperity of its subjects? Don't they see that?'

'George, you cannot be so naive as to think that! Look around you, look at the poverty. Where do you see any sign of support, prosperity, progress or development? My village has looked the same for a hundred years. The British have been in charge for the last fifty years. So what have they done for us?'

George found himself boxed into a corner. He hadn't any coherent counter-argument, but he objected to the view that resistance could be explained by the actions of the administration. He continued to probe, 'There has been a lot of unrest recently, anti-British feeling. Do you think this will incite the people of Cyprus to rise up against the administration?'

'It could have happened already. Just when the poor of Cyprus think that things have got as bad as they can, that is usually the time when the British make some arbitrary decision to increase tariffs, taxes, or change something else and things become even worse. Of course, some of us know that it isn't just the British who are creating the depression, but facts rarely get in the way of agitation. People either lose the will to continue, or they resist. The same has happened here. Perhaps around the corner there is another decision, another spark that ignites smouldering resistance. It is entirely likely that if the British keep taking from the people there will come a point when the peasants start active resistance.

'Is that your own opinion?' George reflected on the sounds and meanings of Stavros's words, thinking that his friend was either becoming a master wordsmith, weaving a carefully nuanced dialogue to convey his own political views, or conversely his command of English was not sufficiently precise.

'George, you should know me better. As long as I wear the badge of my employer, I do not hold views of my own.' A smile appeared briefly, then disappeared.

George thought it was the former.

In subsequent weeks, George was careful not to overplay his friendship with Stavros. George cultivated stronger links with the lads who were his peers, people who were his age and British: Pete, Lofty, Gerald. They boarded in the same building, they sometimes socialised in a particular café, a favourite bar, they talked about their own popular culture which they had in common. With Stavros he was learning new things all the time. With these lads, he comfortably coasted in neutral, but was not fully engaged. He didn't have to work at the relationships because they were predictably shallow. In neither company was there much chance of meeting women he desired. Colonial employment was a celibate condition for George—a male-dominated world. Sure enough there were opportunities, but these women were not really his cup of tea.

* * *

In October, long after a second trip to Myrsina with Stavros during which he attended the christening of Oran, Hassan and his wife's fourth child, George met Stavros one evening for a drink. Neither had much money, so it was a long evening nursing a single glass of beer. Heavy rain the previous evening had caused storm drains along the roadside to overflow. Flotsam congregated in unexpected pools. The bar's veranda was, as a consequence, flooded and unusable, so they sat indoors even though it was a humid night.

Stavros briefed George on a development at work: 'Several local men who work in the administration, including myself, have been recruited to do a job'

'Oh yeah, what's it doing?'

'We have been asked to observe and report on the public meeting that is scheduled to take place tomorrow, when political speakers will address the audience. We received a briefing from the police commander's deputy, asking us to report back whatever happened, who was present, any familiar agitators, that sort of thing.'

George had heard about the meeting.

'Hell, Stavros, that's like spying on your own people. Are you sure this is a good idea? Listen, I haven't spoken to anybody about your beliefs, but it doesn't sound like this task is compatible with them.'

'True, and I have had a battle with myself about it.'

'Do you think you can carry it off? What if you're recognised? What if the police arrest you?'

'It is a worry. I was thinking perhaps I need to be very quiet, not really visible.'

'You need a lot of luck and chutzpah to carry it off. Why did you agree?'

'Chuz-pa? I don't know what that word means.'

'Chutzpah or luck?' said George, smiling. 'It means nerve, audacity. Are you sure you can do it?'

'Maybe yes, maybe no. I didn't get much choice. I get extra pay.'

'OK, is that the best excuse you can come up with? I'm pretty sure every sinew in your body wants to resist.'

'My heart says I shouldn't do it, my mind says I should—it might help with my career—and what would my employer have thought if I had refused? That would have made them suspicious, no?'

'Perhaps, but if you're spotted—if you are identified—they'll either think you're rebelling or you're collaborating. They'd guess rebelling in full sight of law enforcers would not be your style and then they'd conclude you're collaborating. Depends on who sees you. You could come a cropper. Be careful.'

'OK, this conversation is finished now. Let's imagine we haven't had it.'

'Whatever. *Be careful!*'

George returned home perplexed about Stavros's motives. Stavros melted into the darkness as if he was harbouring a deadly secret.

Chapter Seven
Riot!

Stavros was dressed to blend in with his young compatriots. His sentiments were aligned with those of the assembled crowd, but his loyalty to his employer meant he needed to keep his distance, not be recognised, and absolutely not be arrested. He and his three Cypriot colleagues behaved as if they did not know each other. His crisis of allegiance, being of the crowd but not in it, and simultaneously vice versa, was a problem for him. He worked hard to keep his political views close to his chest within the workplace. He had only opened up to George, not even to other Cypriots. Perhaps he was chosen by his manager because he successfully cultivated an apolitical identity. More likely it was because he was about the right age and had Greek Cypriot features. He was confident that his views recently shared with George had not precipitated his selection for the task. The police had posted several officers along the route, but by planting Stavros and his colleagues in the crowd they were expecting qualitative assessment from within.

He kept to the margins of the demonstration. The crowd was increasing in size throughout the cool early autumn evening. Church bells across the city had been rung as a signal to gather; the clergy were the messengers. This was a significant congregation.

Anti-British sentiment had once more been ratcheted up. A blunt anti-democratic instrument called Imperial Order in Council had been used by the administration to override a decision by the democratic body, which had voted against increased import taxes.

This had been the third time in quick succession that an Imperial Order in Council had been used. Democratic process had not aligned with the will of the colonial bureaucracy. Elected members were outraged to have been over-ruled when resisting tax increases, voting down the budget and resisting the imposition of an education bill which sought to limit the role of religious bodies in designing the curriculum in schools.

Stavros was familiar with the twists and turns of government and the manipulation it relied upon. Now, prompted by a shift in political allegiance within the National Council, there was renewed advocacy for union with Greece. Each issue was fanning the flames of anti-British feeling. Amongst Greek Cypriots, who made up the majority of the demonstrators, the main chant was for enosis. In the autumn evening darkness, thousands, mostly young, gathered, dressed to resist the autumn chill. Stavros noted some individuals were organising and managing the gathering. Other people marshalled the crowd. The proponents of enosis mustered their support from youth clubs, student groups and the scout movement, as well as the anti-communist unions. Makeshift banners were carried proudly by their membership. The gathering had structure. The crowd was behaving as if choreographed.

Everyone was aware that several speakers had recently resigned from the National Council in protest at the imposition of anti-democratic interference. Now these men clambered clumsily onto the stage, each in turn testing the microphone with a blow of hot breath and a tap of their fingers, the result akin to a small incendiary explosion emanating from the teetering gantry of loudspeakers. They each spoke passionately, excitedly, in their support of enosis, prompting a noisy, confused chant from the crowd about beating the colonial oppressor, then the recognisable chant 'enosis'. The last speaker on the stage announced that they had a petition to present to the Governor.

It was difficult for Stavros to stand by dispassionately whilst taking in what was going on. He had to react to the messages from time to time. His brief was to report back as soon as possible after the meeting had finished. George had agreed to remain in the office at Government House until Stavros returned and been debriefed. He wanted to offer moral support.

Without drawing attention to himself, Stavros made a mental note of the speakers, the general thrust of their speeches, and the identities of the organisers. He was not surprised when a priest from the main church, a known pro-enosist with a reputation for hot-headed gestures, struggled onto the stage. He looked ungainly in his ecclesiastical dress brandishing a huge Greek flag on a long flagpole whose centre of gravity threatened to topple its bearer. Once in his position of elevation, he spoke animatedly for some minutes, his booming voice concluding with an invitation to those gathered: 'Revolution!'

A huge cheer of support went up from the highly charged and vocal—and exclusively male—crowd. Amongst the chaos, Stavros heard people shouting 'Gia tin Kyvérnisi Voulí!' ('To Government House!').

It was now dark. The crowd was marshalled towards their intended destination, about a mile and a half away. Young people, high on emotion and hormones, moved noisily to the front of the procession, flanking the three keynote speakers who were marching purposefully to petition the Governor. Youthful agitators, some with flags in hand, grabbed sticks and stakes as they proceeded and became increasingly unmanageable. Stavros knew that neither this procession—nor its scale—had been anticipated by the police, nor would the limited police presence be able to control it. He held back, hoping neither to be recognised nor be embroiled in any unrest. He had to adapt to achieve his task, think on his own. His colleagues, presumably also responding to circumstances, were nowhere to be seen. Stavros sidestepped an invitation, the proffering of a wooden stake, to take up arms. The crowd shuffled noisily, chaotically forward. Street lamps were being systematically smashed by hundreds of hot heads in the increasingly aggressive crowd. Parked vehicles were vandalised by some youths, their running boards, engine covers and lamps damaged by sticks and sharp implements. Stavros expected to recognise some of the demonstrators who were his age, but it seemed many of these young men were not from the area, or his peers had the sense to avoid open agitation. The only people he fleetingly recognised in the darkness were his colleagues.

The front of the baying crowd reached Government House. They repeatedly chanted slogans: 'Down with the occupiers!' 'Up with enosis!' spoiling for a fight. Further down the street, those not yet reaching their destination were still shouting 'To Government House!' As he approached the forecourt of Government House, Stavros noted his suspicion had been confirmed: very few soldiers or police were present beyond its open gateway. They had been caught, literally, off guard. He could see two dozen or so officers, half a dozen on horseback and finding it difficult to handle their mounts in the chaos. By no means all of the crowd were angry nor armed, many further back in the procession simply sympathised with the sentiments of the petitioners, as indeed might Stavros have done in other circumstances. The head of the crowd generated its own uproarious, anarchic, violent momentum. The three keynote speakers intent on delivering their petition and talking to the Governor slipped from view, knowing they had lost control of the crowd and would not achieve their objective. The activists in the crowd were by then delivering their own direct message. Parts of the crowd dissipated, sensing that things were getting out of hand. Stavros spotted signs of organised combat at the head of the angry dissenting crowd. Stavros could hear and see instructions passing from one youth to another, further and further backwards down the procession. Clusters of perhaps six to ten youths were operating as teams of agitators, directing other demonstrators to weapons, some initiating new chants, some organising themselves into wrecking parties. It seemed all the remaining young men had armed themselves with stones *en route*, their pockets bulging by the time they reached Government House. Most were carrying slings. At each opportunity to chant, propel something, or vandalise, the crowd became more animated. The police were the initial target of the crowd's venom and were quickly overwhelmed. The forecourt of the building was overrun with demonstrators. Police horses bolted, unseating at least one officer, who fell into the crowd and was set upon. The few foot police mounted repeated baton charges, but were engulfed by the crowd, which meted punishment on individual officers unable to escape. Stavros watched from the periphery, bewildered, as the police withdrew to a position of shelter. He wondered how he could continue with his task now things had gone beyond any chance of control. Windows were shattering as slingshots found their targets. Backup police and guardsmen were drafted in. A group of police reinforcements forced their way through the baying crowd by car and into the forecourt. They clambered out, terror disfiguring their features. Their cars were almost immediately overturned in the forecourt and set on fire as their occupants fled to safety.

Several minutes later, most of the windows in the front of the building had been smashed under sustained onslaught from slingshot. A raging petrol fire took hold in the forecourt enabling rioters to light their sticks. Parts of the predominantly wooden structure caught alight. Soft furnishings were burning inside broken windows. Other flammable materials facilitated the blaze. From a vantage point on the stone steps against a backdrop of flames and choking smoke, the District Commissioner appeared in a vain attempt to order the crowd away. His timid admonishments were lost in the cacophony. The crowd lunged towards him, forcing him to retreat behind the main door. The second time he appeared he instigated a further baton charge by police. That also failed, but caused injuries to those at the front of the gathering.

* * *

George, believing himself to be relatively safe within the building and behind a police guard, was shocked at the turn of events. The District Commissioner then implemented his riot contingency arrangements. He appeared once more, as would an apprehensive amateur actor entering stage left, and read the Riot Act. His attempts were drowned out by the shouts of the now confident and highly energised crowd, but the consequences of the reading were about to come to them. Inside the building, the main door was being hastily reinforced. Frantic efforts were under way to barricade the smashed windows; the deputy DC was organising an orderly evacuation of the Governor, his family and staff to police HQ. Lower grade civil servants remaining in the building were assigned roles—manning barricades, fighting fire, facilitating the evacuation, dealing with injuries caused by broken glass and missiles. Eventually, as fire gained a firm hold, everyone was evacuated.

The Riot Act was implemented. What followed is testament to the power of weaponry and gunpowder. The reinforced police now took up their positions as the fire continued to take hold and fired single shots directly into the crowd to disperse them. Stavros backed away from the area and was carried along a side street amongst a chaotic stream of retreating rioters. Several individuals fell victim to police bullets and lay disabled and bleeding in the forecourt and on the nearby street. The police pursued the crowd, which soon dispersed in all directions, leaving the façade of Government House burning and bedecked with the injured who were isolated amongst the chaotic aftermath of the disturbance. Stavros took stock in a darkened doorway. Traumatised by what had happened, he quickly split from the demonstrators and melted into the night. Making sure he had not been followed by rioters nor police, he zigzagged back to his rendezvous point. He and his colleagues were due to be debriefed immediately, but the trouble had thrown out any plans. Only one of his colleagues joined him, the DC was elsewhere. Nobody assumed responsibility, so he returned to his office, settled at his desk in the middle of the night, falling into and out of sleep.

By daylight, the compound had been surrounded by a cordon of barbed wire, manned by troops. No part of the ornate wooden façade of Government House remained. The detritus of the riot was strewn about the neighbourhood, which was eerily quiet, the residual stinking smoke still filling one's lungs.

Chapter Eight
The Friendship Wanes

For George, the days that followed were frenetic. The Governor called up troop reinforcements, aircraft and battleships in support—'a show of force', as he called it. The riot in Nicosia had dissipated and no further trouble had been reported. George was astonished to learn that several other towns had experienced simultaneous demonstrations, each lead by pro-enosis politicians and religious leaders. The District Commissioner met to discuss strategy, and before the week was over, a draconian regime had been implemented to stifle further dissent. Police and troops acted together to arrest each of the suspected ringleaders. They were quickly taken away, deported from the island. Without its ringleaders, the dissent quickly lost its momentum, and the stifling bans on press freedom, telecommunications and personal freedoms ensured its dissolution. George, though, realised that the freedom he had experienced since he had arrived would not be returning. Soon afterwards, Stavros told him that Myrsina was, as usual, peaceful and took no part in the troubles of that year, but he realised it was probably impossible to visit again.

Stavros did, the following day, go through debriefing, providing important corroborating evidence. He was rewarded for his loyalty and thanked, if only as part of a written message of gratitude from the Governor to all the Cypriot civil servants. His memory of the night of 21 October would remain with him. His political views, still hidden from his employers, strengthened in the wake of the riots.

George and Stavros continued to meet for lunch, although this was the limit of their association. Their subsequent letters plotted the divergent lives of the friends.

Sheffield,

10 December 1934.

Dear Stavros,

Warm greetings from a very cold Yorkshire. I trust you and your family are well.

It is now a whole year since I completed my tour of duty in Cyprus. I have fond memories of your beautiful island, your compatriots, and your family. Please pass on my warm regards to Christos, Eleni, your sisters, nieces and nephews.

This year has been eventful. I returned to the UK in December '33, just before Christmas, and spent the festive holiday with my parents, who are well. I was fortunate to have been placed into a Civil Service job in a nearby city, Sheffield. Now I am settled into my job. The people I work with are good company. My boarding accommodation is not bad.

I wonder how things are in Cyprus? Perhaps you could let me know what is happening on the island. I know Governor Palmer is unpopular for many reasons. The one reason I read about here is the banning of any trade unions and the demonstrations that have followed the ban. It seems to me that the Governor just wants to stamp out any Cypriot political ideas. How does that affect you, as a civil servant? Do you think it will work?

Here in England I can tell you that in the summer the British Empire Games took place in London instead of South Africa. You will, I expect, know all about it, England and Canada taking most of the medals. The White City Stadium and Empire Pool venues in London looked very modern in the photographs. I expect their construction brought many jobs to the battered economy. There are so many new things being built these days.

In terms of other news, two of the great British composers of classical music, Sir Edward Elgar and Gustav Holst both passed away. Their music has had great impact and they will be missed. Also there was a terrible coal mining accident in Wales this year when almost three hundred people lost their lives. The newspapers were full of the event. It was a national tragedy. So sad. On a happier note, I was fortunate to be able to see the launch of RMS *Queen Mary* in Glasgow. What a beautiful ship, full of the latest machinery and very luxurious! I was very lucky that I was on a walking holiday of Scotland and was passing through Glasgow by train at the time of the launch.

In politics, in which I know you are always interested, the main events have been a huge expansion of the Royal Air Force. This, perhaps, has just arrived in time, because there are rumblings of political activity and rearming once again in Germany, which British politicians are becoming very jumpy about. Even in this country, a man called Oswald Mosely has addressed a meeting of British Fascists. It pains me to think that a new threat from Germany is present after all the losses we all suffered in the war. I hope we do not have to suffer them again.

I look forward to hearing from you. Very best wishes to you and your family.

George

P.S. I am courting a young lady. Next time I write I will let you know how things are going.

Lefkosia,

February 1934.

Yasou, George!

I hope you are well. Thank you for your letter of December 10th.

It seems like you and your country are making a fast recovery from the Depression. I wish the same was true of Cyprus, but there is little to be optimistic about. You are correct about the union ban and the unrest that has followed. It has been very destabilising and the military has put further pressure on the people, so our lives are very much suppressed these days. All the Cypriot people feel they live under the unbearable burden of the Colonial power. As for myself, I am finding it increasingly difficult to work as a native civil servant because it sets me apart from my own people. Even the District Commissioner accepts that people like me are in a half-way trap between the British and our own people. We are separated by our loyalty to the Colony and we cannot be truly the Greeks we want to be.

I think by the next time I write to you, I may not be the clerk you once knew!

My new wife, Vassiliki, and I are well and we send you our best wishes. We have a child, Takis, who is nearly one year old. My parents and relatives send you their warmest wishes.

Your friend, always

Stavros

Kalamata, Greece,

February 1936.

Dear George,

I am writing briefly to let you know my new address. I am no longer in Cyprus. I will write to you soon.

Stavros

Sheffield,

December 1936.

Dear Stavros,

I have not heard from you since you moved to Greece so I am writing to you, again at Christmas time, to update you on my life, and to possibly prompt a response from you. I am very interested to hear from you and to understand why you decided to move to Greece.

Here we are living under the increasingly dark shadow of the fascist spectre in Germany, although Mr Baldwin's government seems to be playing it down. In the short time since my last letter, the rise of Mr Hitler and his National Socialist Party has shocked everybody. We have, of course, seen the worst face of Germany throughout the Olympic Games. The newsreels played in the picture houses are very telling. I am not sure what it would be like to live in Germany at the moment, but I fear for people like Jews and Gypsies.

Mr Baldwin seems much more interested in the problems of our monarchy. Just this week, the king, who succeeded his father in January, has abdicated so he can marry Mrs Simpson—hugely significant! Mr Baldwin is running around like a dizzy hare trying to solve the constitutional crisis. There isn't really much else to read in the newspapers.

Since last writing to you I have also married. My lovely wife is also from Sheffield and we met in a dance hall. We were courting for eighteen months before getting engaged. Our wedding was this year. We are very much in love and looking forward to starting a family.

I am still working as a civil servant.

Very best wishes to you.

George

Kalamata, Greece,

July 1937.

Dear George,

I am so sorry I have not responded sooner to your letter in December. If you are aware of the events in Greece at the moment, you will realise that all the people are wrapped up in the political situation led by Metaxas who is supported by the monarch. He was appointed prime minister by the king to counter the Communist threat. This he has done by the most draconian means possible, so that all free speech, association, and political membership is banned and everyone is spying on one another. It seems that Metaxas has learnt much from Mussolini and Herr Hitler. I have to be very careful what I say or write. I will be in contact when I am able, but you should not write to me.

You remain my good friend

Stavros

Athens,

October 1943.

Do you remember me, George? It is Stavros.

You may have forgotten me. I would be sorry if it were so.

I have become involved in the battle for the heart and soul of Greece, unable to write to you for fear that I would give myself away if our letters were intercepted. The Germans and their Italian and Bulgarian allies are suffocating us with their occupation. The British and their allies are struggling against them. I am a fighter also, but I cannot tell you more.

Greece is like a fighting pit full of wild dogs. We even fight our own people. It is a dark time in history my friend. Times are very hard here and many people are dying. I am sure there are hardships also with you.

If I, my wife and two children—Takis, ten; and Costas, eight—survive, I will be in touch. With good fortune the Hellenic State will survive.

Stay safe.

S.

PART THREE

Chapter Nine
Alf Holdsworth, 1958

Alf's company had been on manoeuvres day and night, bivouacking in abandoned houses and shepherds' shelters. They were never further than a few miles from camp. There had been skirmishes between Greek Cypriot and Turkish Cypriot communities, but none had been serious. There were no reports of casualties on either side for several days, but rifle fire resonated sporadically across the wadi to the north, giving the impression someone was letting off firecrackers. When the wind was right it was possible to hear shock waves from gunfire echoing across the plain. The company, prominent and dressed in khaki fatigues, moved in clear daylight. It was a typical hot early summer day, the sun had risen about 0530 and the relative cool of night time had been driven off by 0700. The full intensity of the daytime heat had been limited by a bank of unseasonal cloud to the East.

The contrast between the camp and the surrounding countryside was striking. Inside the camp were tarmacadam roads and parade grounds; regimented eucalyptus and mimosa trees; white-painted kerb stones, and their complimentary white pebbles, defining significant areas; the ordered symmetry of Nissen huts and tents in which men were barracked in neat rows of beds: all very British and disciplined. Beyond the camp the vegetation defined its own boundaries on the undulating land, an alien place, harnessing different symmetries driven by the features of the landscape: wadi edges; rock outcrops; low, tree-topped hills; and dusty plains.

anemones, thyme and chamomile grew wild between the scrubland
bushes and cacti, lending a scent to the land that changed with
the seasons. Stone walls marked boundaries of land ownership,
their convolutions tracing the outcome of acrimonious disputes
over generations. It was whilst passing through these villages on
exercises or manoeuvres that he reminisced about the stories his
father had told him when he was younger. Alf had been in awe of
his father, George, with his colourful descriptions of his several
years here. The thirties had been a time of considerable unrest, not
unlike that in which Alf now found himself an unwilling witness.
George had had a keen interest in ornithology and managed to
indulge his interest at every opportunity. He would take a leave
pass from his civil service job and had escaped to a local village
called Myrsina. His dad, who was so far from Rotherham where his
neighbours were all pigeon fanciers bar none, had found the bird
life of Cyprus to be exotic and varied. For some reason, his dad's
stories had always been narrated in the broadest of Rotherham
accents, even though he could speak the Queen's English as well
as the next man. Of his hosts, his dad would say, 'They had been
hospitable, offering coffee and pastries as soon as you engaged in
conversation. I remember that the coffee were very tasty, hot and
sweet, boiled up in a little pouring pan on t'stove. By, it looked like
sludge and tha were in for a bloody shock if tha drank more than
half way down t'cup.'

Dad, recalled Alf, was very admiring of the locals, whose
forebears had lived through endless occupations. Their faces—
deeply furrowed and tanned to the hue of a walnut by long
summers—reflected the hardships of their rustic lives, their simple
clothing of black for the women and baggy trousers, long socks
and hobnailed leather boots for the men, was an oft-repeated detail
Alf remembered from his dad's expansive stories. George described
his trips as a release from the confines of an expatriate life. Because

he visited more then once, the local villagers had taken him to their bosom, although he hadn't known until later that they had shielded him from the more antagonistic villagers, particularly the younger generation whose politics were anti-British and anti-Government. His host had apparently said, 'There are hotheads too, but they will learn there is no pleasure in having a hot head all the time.' The use of spoken English in small villages in the 1930s could not have been very extensive and Alf had always wondered whether there had been some embellishment of the dialogues his father had claimed to have. George had clearly warmed to the people. He said it was with a heavy heart that he had had to return to his Nicosia garrison at the expiry of his leave pass.

It was these recollections that Alf recalled any time his gaze drifted beyond the fences of the camp boundary or, as now, when he was marching across the stubbly wheat fields, or whilst they were bivvied overnight and he was on sentry duty. His fellow servicemen saw the landscape as barren and unforgiving. Alf perceived a softness in the gentle pace and contents of a life dictated by nature in a landscape that had been sculpted to support the villagers' survival. Outside the villages there were precious few houses because of adversaries like wild dogs, terrorists and robbers. Villagers would leave their village for the fields in the early morning, perhaps walking for an hour to reach a distant field of crops. Alf and the company would sometimes be marching along a wall over the brow of a hill and be met by the gaze of a dozen women, their backs straightening briefly from their hoeing or tending duties to watch the troops' passage. In a largely empty landscape, it was always odd to see these curious, guarded gaggles of women—always women—take a rest from their back-breaking task to watch the company pass. Then they would they return to their work. Alf would hear animated chatter and laughter with, on occasion, a salacious edge to it. He assumed the conversation was similar to that in Catterick where women would share comments about virile squaddies, egging the men on, looking for a bit of fun.

The only other souls found in this landscape were the shepherds, staff in hand, sheepskin coats stained by the red-brown soil, their dog never far away. The sheep seemed instinctively to make their way without help or guidance from the shepherd. Alf and his squad would often chance across a sleeping shepherd in a rock cave on the edge of a wadi, or beneath a solitary tree which offered the only shade from the midday sun, startled into consciousness by the armed soldiers. The sheep were doing what they always did, seeking what limited nourishment they could find on the flat Messaoria plain. Sometimes the shepherds were old men, sometimes children and teenagers yet to be introduced to a more demanding vocation, or too lacking in prospects to do anything else.

Otherwise the landscape was empty. It had a beauty and integrity that Alf felt lent it a familiar and attractive air. He admired this country and its people. Alf was, however, frequently reminded by his fellow squaddies that their view of the island and its inhabitants was at odds with his own. Not that he trumpeted his admiration from the rooftops, he was just more forgiving and less aggressive in conversation about what was happening to the country.

Alf often thought about the fact that he had never actually killed anyone; a show of force was usually sufficient to calm inflamed situations. He didn't know how he would feel if he did have to kill someone, especially as the victims are likely to be Cypriots. Despite his interest, Cyprus had not been Alf's preference for his National Service; he would rather would have gone to Germany where there were lots of opportunities to develop his interest in radio communications; and perhaps meet a girl, marry, and have a family. Unfortunately, as a National Serviceman, all decisions were made for him. Here he was, twenty-three, single and in Cyprus. He was told he was having the time of his life. He wasn't sure he could subscribe to that view, but in National Service the camaraderie and friendships one built could be priceless. There was always some prank, joke or jape being played, and his mates were all high spirited, which made for a good life. However, there were some in his billet who were by no measure having the time of their lives. Ewan, one of a dozen in Alf's tent, had done previous service in Egypt, was contemptuous of Cyprus and everything Cypriot. This had come out during a conversation after tea in their mess room, a Nissen hut with a toilet to the left of the door in the half-moon, bricked, end wall. He and his fellow squaddies had been subjected to a day of pointless square bashing, mess cleaning, bull and kit inspection. A normal day. The conversation had started benignly enough, but was developing an edge that was drawing others in the room to take sides, like a local soccer derby being discussed in a pub. Unfortunately, Alf was on his own. Ewan, forthright in his opinions and liking the sound of his own Scottish accent, had declared, 'These guys have been fighting everyone and each other for centuries. They need controlling, suppressing. That's what we're here to do.'

'In this part of the Med they're right at the centre of all the historical territorial disputes. It's not that they fight *anyone*, they just defend themselves and resist conquerors,' said Alf. 'We're just another conqueror to them. Greek Cypriots think the Ottomans were the only recent conquerors, but the Brits have done it twice.'

'That's bollocks,' said a new contributor called Roy, taking sides with Ewan, as he did in any argument, 'these guys have no reason to fuckin' hate us—we brought them prosperity and order—yet we've been fighting with them and been taking casualties for all this last year that we've been in this shit hole. We lost Chalky White only six months ago outside Varosha, don't forget that poor bastard got shot then stabbed dozens of times before he died. It's only the last few months it's quietened down. They're fuckin' savages.'

'Chalky was a great guy,' began Alf, 'he'd stand up for all of us, but he was off duty and messing with some local married woman. If he'd done that in Yorkshire he'd have got his 'ead kicked in. Who's been ambushed and killed on duty in the last five years in this company? Nobody. Except that Gurkha chap who was shot accidentally on the parade ground by Eric Smith. Eric didn't mean it, his gun went off when he dropped it. The Cypriots, in the main, like us, at least they *did*, until Grivas brought his terrorist ways back from Greece a few years back.'

Their principal adversary was EOKA, the reason so many British troops were on the island. It was headed by George Grivas, also called Dighenis by his followers, a man who universally elicited passionate, conflicting emotions. He was elusive, as were his close-knit senior command. They were at the same time murderers, criminals and liberators of the Cypriots from the yoke of Colonial rule. He had been born in Famagusta district the same year as the British assumed their rule over the island.

'*Like* us?' replied Ewan. 'Don't give me that shit, you know Grivas has tens of thousands of supporters here, ready to rip the head off anyone who'll get in the way of union with Greece. That means us and the Turks, pal. I hate this fucking place, just like I hated Egypt.'

Murmurs of agreement spread through the gathering group, now nine or ten strong. It was no secret that Ewan had been pulled out of Egypt and reallocated to their battalion as a punishment because he was regularly brutal with locals. He was a difficult character to share a billet with because he was always confrontational, a bruiser. With other lads, especially those whose tour of duty was the same as his, the experience of being billeted together strengthened comradeship and friendship. But Ewan wasn't in that game.

'Alf's right,' said Jack Gatbrook, a younger, more recently arrived conscript. Alf thought him well-read and intelligent. 'There's only a tiny proportion of people working against us, the rest get on with their lives in the way they always have, pay the taxes they've always been forced to pay, and keep out of trouble. EOKA torture and execute them as well.'

'I remember my dad talking about being posted to Nicosia,' said Alf, 'he used to visit a village near——'

'We don't give a toss what your dad did and what he didn't,' interrupted Ewan contemptuously. 'Listen, you and us are never going to see eye to eye. We're different, Holdsworth; I'm not the one who's out shagging the local lads.'

This groundless, malicious comment, one of many similarly hurled at him by Ewan, didn't hit its mark because Alf had been immunised through a lifetime of such jibes in childhood, but it did annoy him. 'Fuck off,' he retorted. But the mess canteen signalled time for snap, saving him from an escalation in hostilities. The participants, who were only distracting themselves from their hunger, piled out of the hut to the mess block drawn by the familiar smell of fish and chips. The demarcated lines of engagement were reinforced within their billet after that exchange. Alf and Gatbrook on one side, Ewan and his less cerebral supporters on the other.

Chapter Ten
Captain Peter Jarvis

'What a godforsaken hole,' thought Peter as he left the aircraft cabin and stepped onto the tarmac. 'No luxuriant vegetation like Hong Kong, nor greenery like England, just a landscape of whitish rock, red soil and dried up scrub.' He had previously done service in Aden, which was, in his opinion, 100 per cent godforsaken hole. He had expected better of Cyprus as a holiday destination for the better-off during the post-war years. 'Perhaps I am being harsh—it could be the relentless sun stripping the countryside of detail,' he thought, as he was transferred by Jeep to his base several hours away. Later in the journey he thought, 'Maybe I'm just grouchy because I didn't sleep on the flight.'

Peter's assessment on reaching his destination was that first impressions were usually reliable.

After being allocated a room and settling in at the officers' mess, he reported to his commanding officer. After formalities were over, he was briefed on his specific role. The CO instructed him that to all outward appearances Peter was to be officer in charge of the quartermaster service at the base, nominally overseeing the quartermaster. He was told the ex-RSM was perfectly able to run the stores without oversight, and his only additional burden would be to have a weekly update meeting with Peter, on the premise that Peter was doing an island-wide review.

'Otherwise,' said the CO, 'you are tasked with restoring the locals' trust in us by identifying and rooting out any individuals from amongst our ranks who cannot be trusted. Here's some further details and intelligence.'

The CO handed Peter a buff quarto envelope with treasury tag closures. 'You will need to "go native" to gain some insight. I have selected you because of your previous Special Investigations Branch experience. You're a rare beast in this camp because you're an army officer and have intelligence experience, in addition to which you have been posted without any colleagues—so you are an unknown quantity. Without allegiances. Or any sort of reputation.'

Peter's role had sounded rather vague when he was briefed in the UK. He thought about the implications as the CO continued his monologue which was delivered in a rapid-fire machine gun style.

'You'll need to read up on the island. Its people. Politics. The history of the situation in Cyprus. Look at past triggers for dissent among the ranks.'

'I'm aware, sir, of the history on the island. I prepared before leaving the UK by catching up on some reading. I'll work on the role.'

'Good,' said the CO, although privately he thought that the books weren't going to help. 'I think there's a three-month opportunity to rid the camp of any bad eggs. We need to bring the reputation of the military back to an acceptable level amongst the locals. That's how long you have. It's up to you how you obtain intelligence. I want results! Just don't break cover, man. The only person who will know your business is Redcap Lieutenant Surridge, who's OIC RMP in the camp. Communicate with him, but not face-to-face unless it can't be avoided. Report to me weekly in person. My clerk has your induction pack and house keys. He's booked weekly meetings under the cover of the QMS (quartermaster service) review updates. Good luck, captain.'

The CO stood up and turned his back to a still-seated Peter to face the large window overlooking the parade ground where servicemen were being put through a drill: clearly a signal that the meeting was now over. Peter stood, saluted to the CO's back and withdrew from the office.

Corporal Simes handed Peter another large envelope, a set of keys, and a map of the base. The envelope, he was informed, contained details and inventory of his married quarters. The map had been marked with a route to his house and to QMS. Peter, on leaving the building, took a long detour round the camp to place the various facilities, before rejoining the marked route.

His wife was due to follow in several weeks, the interim period would give him opportunity to develop his cover. He found the NAAFI and purchased some basic supplies, tea, soft drinks, evaporated milk, washing up liquid, bread and biscuits, air mail writing paper and envelopes. He went to the forces post office to buy stamps. He visited his quarters and dumped the provisions. He would stay at the officers' mess for the first few days, he thought. His first task was to sort his house out and check the inventory. His second was to locate his packing cases—which had been sent in advance of him and would be in store somewhere on the camp—in one of which were his books. His third task would be to write to his wife. He made his way back to the officers' mess. He thought about writing a letter to Vicky but, having had no sleep since the UK, thought, 'I'm going to have a nap before writing to Vicky.'

Several days into his tour of duty, Peter had made progress on the domestic and operational front. His house was becoming organised and his books had been largely extracted from their packing cases. He'd set up regular meetings with the quartermaster. He spent most evenings revisiting parts of relevant documents, refreshing his knowledge and placing what he had read, or learnt into the context of his task. The intelligence reports identified opinion leaders amongst the ranks on the camp and an assessment of any subversive activity. A military police summary for the last year identified errant soldiers and details of charges. A separate report listed the men confined to barracks for minor misdemeanours. Cross-referencing these he produced an initial short list of suspects.

The absence of his wife was one of those things he had become used to over the course of their short wedded life; it was the same for most forces families who were rent apart on a regular basis to meet the demands of the military machine. Yet he longed for company. This wasn't a posting he'd particularly welcomed and the nature of his role meant that he needed to be on guard against forming allegiances, let alone friendships. The arrival date for Victoria had been put back a couple of weeks again, so he faced the best part of six weeks without company and, to be blunt, without sex.

Chapter Eleven

The Incident at the Sentry Post

Alf reflected absent-mindedly on his sparring match with Ewan several days previously. He stood on duty at the small white-painted sentry hut at a gated break in the middle of a long stretch of triple-layered, barbed-wired perimeter fencing where the garrison's married quarters abutted onto the camp. Beside the fence was a strip of tinder-dry brushwood, chamomile, thyme, and thistle beaten down under foot in places, neglected and yet taking hold in stands. Parts of it had recently caught fire so extensive black patches emitted the smell of old bonfires. Bisecting the scrub past the hut was a narrow concrete footpath along which married squaddies would walk or cycle from their comfy family homes to take up military duties within the camp. During the day mothers and pre-school children would pass by visiting the health centre, NAAFI, church, officers' mess or social club. This was a lonesome post, one to which Alf had been detailed because the military police were short-staffed on account of an unseasonably late flu outbreak, devastating in its spread. Several perfectly healthy men had been hospitalised with pneumonia because of the virulence of the bug. The company RSM had 'asked'—if that was a word in the RSM's vocabulary—for volunteers to do sentry duty, but when none were forthcoming he had sought out soldiers against whom he held a grudge, including Alf, to report to the military police officer in charge of sentry duties. Sentry duty was not very popular. This was Alf's first stretch on this particular sentry post, and because it wasn't a strategic entry point, there was no particular requirement to be upright and alert, weapon ready for use. By 11 am the sun was almost overhead, beating down on the hut, which at only about four feet by three, and with only one tiny window, was akin to a sweat chamber. He wore summer mufti, light khaki shorts and short-sleeved shirt, cap, blacked boots and itchy, khaki, knee-length socks. The breeze, when there was one, pushed hot, dry air around the scrub and into the hut.

Nobody had passed for more than fifteen minutes. With so few interruptions, Alf was becoming somewhat sleepy. Neither his task, nor any of the natural distractions such as a butterfly, lizard, or gecko on the hut ceiling, were able to keep him alert. He drifted into that delicious hinterland between sleep and wakefulness where he was struggling to keep his eyes open and focused. He needed to open his eyes, but his brain abdicated responsibility. He succumbed to the exquisite sensation of sleepy-wakefulness. Reality was partial, his coordination disabled, his arms dropping to his side, his rifle butt slipped from his hand, falling to the floor, the noise then returning him to a semi-awake state. He experienced a physical sensation of submission and sexual arousal.

* * *

On Thursday, after an early meeting with the RSM, Peter had an opportunity to return to his married quarters and develop his covert role. The morning heat reflected back off the parade ground and the concrete path toward the perimeter sentry hut, burning him from above and below. Lizards scattered into the scrub on his approach, the dried vegetation bristling in response. He was deep in thought as he walked, and arrived at the sentry post quickly.

* * *

Alf became aware of somebody at a distance approaching from the direction of the camp parade ground. Conscious of his duty, he straightened up, propped himself up from his slouch against the hut wall, picked up his rifle and stood in a posture approximating standing to attention. As the individual came into view, Alf could see the stripes on the arm of the man's shirt and realised it was an officer who he had not previously seen. In a belated attempt to display he was fully alert, he saluted. The officer—by now it was clear he was a captain—approached, walking briskly in the formal way all officers walked down the path from Alf's left. He hovered to a halt, turning to face him. The pleasurable feeling associated with Alf's half wakefulness had all but dissipated. He was hauled briskly back into the now-world, adrenaline coursing through his veins in anticipation of the bollocking he was now likely to receive.

* * *

Peter thought the soldier had been dozing and couldn't let the incident go unchallenged. 'At ease,' he said in a clipped manner, his expression hardening before he continued. He took in the soldier's physical appearance, early twenties, good physique, upper body muscle, appealing face, dreamy brown eyes and lovely ears, not unlike a previous acquaintance in the Far East, Joe Matthews. He and Matthews, under similar circumstances of separation from their partners (although Joe was unmarried) had conducted a mutually beneficial relationship for some months a couple of years back. He'd almost forgotten the episode until now, but there was no mistaking the similarity between Joe and this soldier.

'Soldier, I couldn't see well as I walked towards you, but it appeared you were slouched in your hut and not ready to act. Were you asleep on duty, private?'

'No, sir,' replied Alf, bringing his saluting arm to his side.

'I would suggest that you were.'

'No, sir, I can definitely say I wasn't asleep, sir.' Alf, maybe not quite over the sensation, looked directly at the officer as he spoke, his eyes retaining some of the hangover from slumber, his pupils not quite reacting promptly to the sunlight.

'Asleep on duty, soldier, is an offence. Look at your uniform man, it looks like you have been sleeping rough. I could have you on a charge.'

Until then, Alf had not realised his shorts were not straight and his shirt tail was out. He attempted to tidy his appearance up. It could not be hidden from the captain that his slumber had left Alf with a discernible bulge in his shorts. The captain, suddenly easing back on his interrogation, looked Alf eye to eye, and appeared to read Alf's discomfort. A very tight-lipped smirk fleetingly crossed his face.

'I suppose it is a difficult post to man, having so few passers-by,' he said, 'but you should remain alert, private. Don't let me catch you again.'

'Sir.'

The need to protect his covert role got the better of Peter. Having meted out his reprimand and asked for the private's surname and number, he continued along the path, through the fence, and out of view, but not without a last once-over visual of all the lad had to offer. He had to be careful not to raise suspicion, otherwise the camp would be full of gossip. He thought he'd managed to behave as if nothing had just happened.

* * *

Alf watched the officer move ever further way before he turned a corner beyond the perimeter, wondering quite what had just happened. He knew the officer had realised he had been aroused, and though not wishing to entertain the idea that this was what had averted a charge, was nonetheless grateful for the outcome. Nothing else of significance occurred that day. Alf was relieved at 1330 hours by one of his colleagues.

Chapter Twelve

Peter Continues His Covert Activities

It was becoming clear to Peter that two or three different factions of, to be frank, thugs and pranksters were carrying out subversive activities both within the camp and amongst groups of expatriates. EOKA was heavily reliant on a small army of itinerant youth to intimidate its own Greek Cypriot followers, as well as unsophisticated leaflets, pamphlets and graffiti to taunt its oppressor. Possession of, or possession of the means to produce, materials were sufficient ground to arrest and charge locals in house-to-house and roadblock searches. Some servicemen, frustrated at what they thought to be the emasculation of the British in the face of such propaganda, countered with a subversive campaign of their own, peddling messages of hate and intolerance toward the terrorists and the local population, all of whom were, inaccurately, accused by these groups of supporting EOKA. In the early days of 1956, an organisation called Saddleback was a prolific pedlar of anti-Cypriot propaganda. Some evidence existed of campaigns of violence against innocent local populations. Spontaneous meting out of rough justice and violent behaviour by British forces had been reported. Since that time, organised British anti-EOKA campaigns had been spawned, with pamphlets being disseminated, graffiti appearing, and missives from a group calling itself Black Sheep had been written, as well as material from Saddleback itself. Identification of the individuals involved had never been successful, the campaign was unofficial but was widely believed to come from within the forces in response to the continuing anti-British activities of EOKA and the resulting regular confinement to barracks (CBs) suffered by the troops.

Peter had heard about the CBs from the NCOs in the QMS. 'We're bored off our tits in camp when we're CB, sir. You have to expect some sort of response from the lads; somebody letting off steam at EOKA's expense at least raises our spirits.'

Peter surmised that much of the activity was both ill-conceived and uninformed; no great surprise since serving NCOs and national servicemen were provided with little understanding of what they were fighting against, nor why there was a fight in the first place. It was rare to find anyone below officer rank who showed the slightest interest in the politics and causes of the conflict. What was notable was that the two-year posting of national servicemen, and the usual three-year stint of other ranks, was not consistent with the longevity of these campaigns. Somebody, whoever it was, was present for the long term and had overall strategic control, at least of Saddleback. Most of the lower ranks were probably just recruited and indoctrinated on the back of their frustrations.

Peter quickly discounted several more obscure lines of enquiry and concentrated on Black Sheep and Saddleback as being key threats to the perception of British even-handedness. They required neutralising. The focus of their activity might not be in the camp itself, but there were going to be supporters in the camp. He thought he'd identified likely suspects, sympathisers to the cause, men one might label as thugs in civvy street. He had to find a way of ingratiating himself with them and their colleagues.

Peter believed a soldier named Cartwright was responsible for an unprovoked physical attack on a group of young Cypriot students some weeks earlier. The circumstances of that attack were unclear and undocumented: the duty log in the barrack room made no mention of the altercation at all, although hospital reports, complaints and local press coverage made it clear that some catalyst had resulted in three of the group being severely bloodied. The response, under the circumstance, was probably disproportionate rather than criminal, but it adversely affected the inhabitants' perception of the British forces as being fair in their occupation. Greek Cypriot youth were the main recruits for EOKA campaigns of intimidation, but the affected students were not described in the press as activists or known sympathisers.

Cartwright was known to frequent one of several bars in the centre of town when he was off-duty. So, one August afternoon in Famagusta, Peter was to be found was trying to engineer a chat with Lance Corporal Cartwright who had signed out on a leave pass that afternoon. That same afternoon, Alf and Gatbrook, finding themselves simultaneously awarded some free time, took a taxi to the local town. Their intention was to try and obtain a recent 45″ single of a popular music group. They were dropped off outside the only music shop in town that stocked British and American pop records. They were disappointed to hear that it was not in stock. Gatbrook had apparently been to a performance of the band in London and rated them highly. Crestfallen, the pair mooched around the fruit and vegetable market and other shops, buying grapes and air mail writing paper. On a whim, they entered a local bar having scraped together just enough of their meagre pay to each buy a cooling bottle of Keo beer. After downing his beer, Gatbrook took his leave to buy a book in a nearby book store. Alf took his time with the beer, relaxed, and considered whether he could afford a second.

In the first three bars Peter visited, Cartwright was not to be found, nor any British customers, forces or not. In the fourth, he found a sole customer—who he was surprised to recognise, as was the customer to be recognised. It was the dozing sentry guard, Holdsworth, and he appeared to be on his own. Peter acted as nonchalantly as he could. After a couple of beers in the previous bars, he was fairly relaxed.

Alf was sitting in one of the rush-seated, high-backed wooden chairs, nursing his beer, watching life pass by the open doorway, listening to the noises of the town: car horns, diesel engines, shouting voices, builders hammering out a piece of metalwork, a cement mixer somewhere nearby. Greek music was issuing forth from the jukebox in the corner, although there had been several English language records on earlier. Several minutes after Gatbrook's departure, a strange coincidence occurred: the captain who had bollocked him for sleeping on duty came into the bar.

'Private Holdsworth, is it?'

'Y'sir.'

'Mind if I join you for a moment?' He ordered a beer whilst settling into his seat. Holdsworth's bottle was only half empty so he wouldn't offer him another, otherwise he may find himself seated longer than necessary.

'Holdsworth, can I call you by your Christian name?'

'Alfred, shortened to Alf, sir. Could I enquire as to your surname, sir?'

To Alf this was highly unusual, since there were few occasions in the military when officers and other ranks would interact socially beyond rather stuffy mess functions (when the other ranks would be waiting or serving). Even those events could not be referred to as mixing. Vinegar and milk, more like.

'Jarvis, Peter Jarvis. Lets not call each other "sir" and "private" in here, eh?'

'OK, sir,' said Alf, automatically uttering the required response, self-conscious, and a little curious about why an officer would wish to consort with him.

Peter felt a frosty defensiveness from Holdsworth. He thought, 'Is this man suspicious, does anyone know my business here?'

'Are you with anyone at the moment?'

'Just Gatbrook, a fellow from my billet. He's off to buy a book. He likes reading.'

'So what brought you into town?'

'We'd both got a pass and were off-duty today, so thought we'd get down here to buy a record. Only the shop doesn't have the one we wanted. So here we are getting a beer before going back.'

'Do you use this bar a lot?'

'No, its the first time I've been here. Normally, we'd be in the Forces Club, but that was out of our way for getting the taxi later.'

'Do you know, I've only just arrived, but I'm getting a good feel for this place. I did some pre-reading just before being posted, but I didn't know how relaxed and friendly the locals would be.'

'They're really good people, a bit aggressive if you're seen to have money to spend, savvy business people, charm the money out of your pocket, if you know what I mean. Socially, they seem warm.'

'Have you been here long? It sounds like you know the place well.'

'A year so far, always in this camp. The reason I know as much as I do is because my dad was a civil servant out here in the thirties, before I was born, and he used to tell me stories about his trips to the villages.'

'Where was he based?'

'Nicosia. He was there when Government House was burnt down.'

'I haven't managed to get there yet. I hear the shops are good.'

'Yes. What is your role in the camp, sir?' said Alf, briefly forgetting the abandonment of formality.

'I'm OIC Quartermaster's Store. Doing an island-wide review. Nothing too out of the ordinary. So, coming back to the Cypriots, you don't see them as the enemy?'

'No, most of them are peaceful, warm-hearted and gracious. Some of the younger ones are more hot-headed, but that's the same anywhere, isn't it? The EOKA footsoldiers are a bit different though, terrorists, they terrorise us and their own people, you'd think they were modelled on the Hitler youth the way they control neighbourhoods. Violent too. The ordinary Cypriots, whether Greek or Turk, don't deserve that.'

Peter remembered Grivas, the elusive architect of the EOKA struggle, who had fought the war in Greece with a force that at times used the techniques they'd learnt from that country's fascist occupiers. He thought Alf's opinion was astute.

Peter acted very relaxed during this conversation, unlike Alf who looked uneasy. Changing tack, Peter said, 'I'm looking for household equipment today, taking the opportunity before Victoria, my wife, arrives. Do you know where I might find kitchen stuff? The army stock issue is not as comprehensive as Victoria would want and I have been posted a list by her to purchase. She's one of those women who socialises by over-cooking for dinner party guests. That's why I wander around in her absence like a lost soul—she's the bubbly social secretary, I've no skills in that area.'

Alf nodded to signal he was listening, not sure how to respond, except by directing him to hardware shops in the street behind the market. He decided to take the opportunity to find out more about the man.

'How long have you been married?'

'Two years, though we were courting five years before that. It followed my passing out from Sandhurst in fifty-two, now I'm thirty and married, posted via Hong Kong to Cyprus, with only a brief spell back home in between. Hardly got the opportunity to get to the Proms in the short time we had, but I managed to catch a couple of concerts with Vicky.'

'I've not been to London, but I hear that the Albert Hall is a spectacular building, and by all accounts, the Proms were something to try and get to just once.'

'London is my home, specifically West London, Ealing. I think it is by far the most relaxed of the West London suburbs. My parents live in Gloucestershire, but they had a small flat in Ealing that they gave to Vicky and me after the wedding.'

Alf gathered that the family were farmers, moderately well off, and Peter's younger brothers were working the farm. Peter had a yearning for something more interesting. He was introduced to his wife-to-be at a Young Farmers event in Cirencester.

'Victoria was bundled into this event by a school friend, she didn't know a soul, but had the personality to get me talking and coming out on my shell.'

'You don't seem to be very shy to me,' said Alf, thinking there had now been two occasions when Jarvis had engaged him.

'I'm not the same with men, comes with all that time at public school. Interesting what you say about EOKA. So you don't think that everyone's EOKA then in Cyprus?'

'Not at all. Most just want to farm and have families. They're focused on land, olives, goats, education for their sons, and dowries for their daughters.'

'You do seem well informed for a private, if I may say so.'

'I learnt a lot off my dad. Cyprus was something of a teenage obsession. Even after school I was down the public library reading the newspaper stories and getting out books on Cyprus. Then my interest waned.'

'Do you like reading?'

'No, I didn't do well at school. "Factory fodder" they used to call us kids, fit for nowt else.'

'People like you and me can still relate to each other. We have an education, all of us are fortunate to have it provided for us—look at the chaps in Africa, no structure or privilege to their upbringing. Nonetheless, I've met very intelligent people from all backgrounds, even Africans, at Sandhurst. I wouldn't have thought of you as "factory fodder", there's that spark of interest in your surroundings, a spirit of enquiry.'

Alf didn't know much about Africa. He kept that to himself.

'As I said, t'were pit, steelworks or factory'—Alf slid into dialect against his better judgement. He was careful to speak in a more cultured way normally, thinking it might open the right doors— 'but National Service dragged me away from my surroundings, and for that I was grateful. I'd like to work as a radio operator.'

'Well, you've landed in the right place here if you want to develop that interest. This is one of the stations the forces want to expand.'

Alf was somewhat taken aback to hear this. What limited part of the army mission he knew about led him to think he was just posted to a remote camp where holding the peace was the only task.

'I'll have a word and see what opportunities exist for people to learn those skills,' said Peter.

Alf was once again uneasy, he was unused to people facilitating his progress, taking an interest in him, steering him into a vocation. He hadn't trusted the careers advice man at school. He was wary of anybody making life-changing propositions. As a serviceman, you were told what to do and when, no questions; you didn't need to think about anything other than blacking your boots and presenting you and your billet tidily, not getting drunk, and not getting CBs.

'That would be very kind of you, sir,' said Alf politely, conscious that a door might be opening here, but guarded about the captain's motives.

Peter couldn't really spot anything in this relatively articulate man's story, nor in his demeanour and attitude towards the locals. Nothing yet gave him cause to think he was associated with Black Sheep and Saddleback, but he thought it would be useful to try and extract some more from him later.

'Now I must be away. I've got a driver picking me up from the Forces Club front entrance at three. Sorry, I can't give you a lift.'

He downed what remained of the now lukewarm beer and stood to leave, paying the tavern keeper the required shiny new currency whilst addressing Alf from across the bar: 'Tell you what, why don't you come round one evening to my house. The packing cases have just arrived and there's a good range of books about Cyprus from my Sandhurst days to be unpacked. Say after seven on Tuesday?'

Alf was being catapulted into this arrangement, whilst not entirely happy to socialise in this way with the ranks, but the friendship seemed genuine.

'Your offer next Tuesday is kind, but to be honest I have never been to an officer's quarters, I'd feel a bit out of place.'

'Come round, we'll have a beer and look through the books. That's settled then. 14 Edward Road. 1900 hours.'

Alf didn't think it was settled at all, but the man was out the door before he could wriggle out of it.

Peter was convinced that acceptance would indicate either a real interest in the topic or an interest in himself. He decided that Alf's body language suggested that the appeal lay with him.

* * *

In the several remaining minutes before Gatbrook returned—he must have been consumed by the bookshop he'd been so long—Alf considered again what had just happened. Not usually one to be forced into things, he felt somehow that he had been coaxed, at the very least, by a man whose intentions he couldn't fathom. There was a risk that the man could be following desires that had been kindled by Alf's previous embarrassing state, but nothing in the exchange in the bar in any way suggested that. Alf reckoned he could spot a dodgy sort and had clocked several men whose sense of decorum was suspect—especially after a heavy night on the beer. Alf himself, whilst having a liking for female company, was awkward with women and clumsy in conversation with them; but he was clear in his heart that his sexual interest lay with women. Sure, in cramped quarters with men whom you trust and reciprocally trust you, potentially with their lives, there was some banter and solo masturbation at night. Alf considered himself a champion of covert wanking. After all, they were all men with natural sexual appetites. The two other men in the tent they had as a billet were similarly careful not to hold a stick—as it were—to any other in the matter of gratification. If they wanted and could afford female company they'd make their way to the areas of town where that service was available. Alf, though, didn't really relish this emotion-free solution. Only once had he been with pals to shadier parts of Varosha to exercise natural urges. Opportunities for courting a girl were pretty limited in a camp full of men; and outside of camp he reckoned his chances were zero. Like other lads, it didn't take much to excite him. His tumescent member was a feature of his entire teenage life. Now he was flying solo most of the time out of necessity.

Alf, trying to preserve what was left of his beer, decided he could handle any eventuality, decided to commit to the following Tuesday and was frankly more concerned about the ribbing both he and Peter would get if the wider camp got wind of the two associating.

Gatbrook reappeared, flustered by having spent so much time engrossed in one book after another during his bookshop visit. He'd been unaware of the time until the owner indicated that he was about to roll down the shutters for the siesta. Alf and Gatbrook made their way to the taxi rank and returned to camp.

Chapter Thirteen
Skirmishes Near the Old City Walls

Almost immediately on Alf and Gatbrook's leave pass ending, their company was once again called out to patrol an area close to the Old City walls. This was a frequent venue for Greek on Turk violence, the area close to the towering Crusader battlements, the de facto barrier between two communities. There was always an army presence along the wide tree-lined street leading away from the town gate in the city walls because it was also the colonial administrative centre. The main post office, town council, police headquarters and civilian general hospital were all arranged along the street, whilst a municipal park lined one side behind a five-foot high walled and fenced perimeter. Civic pride oozed from the honey stone buildings, the carefully maintained lighting, bus shelters, planters full of tropical colour and freshly painted benches, all in top condition as if they were pin-ups for tourist brochures. The *pièce de résistance* was a moderate-sized steam locomotive stranded like a beached whale on ten metres of isolated railway line that reminded viewers of a long-lost colonial railway heritage.

Preservation of normality was always the task on these occasions. Trouble flared up every few weeks or months depending on the weather; the cooler it was, the more likely it was to happen. The company was tasked with setting up additional stop and search roadblocks at entry points to the long thoroughfare. Guards were placed on key buildings, allowing the civic administration to continue to function, albeit to a soundtrack of sporadic gunfire;

like the intrusive punctuation of a typewritten account of quotidian commerce.

Alf was rostered for three days on this post. It was generally understood that there was little risk to the British troops. Flare-ups were inter-ethnic, limited to relatively small numbers of combatants. The general line of fire was between the safety and vantage afforded by the top of the city walls and the exposed urban landscape of boatyards, industrial units and chandlers' shops below and across the main road to the port. There was virtually no British fire during these events, which tended to burn themselves out over a period of hours to days; angry and frustrated young men taking issue with their most convenient adversaries. One side initiated the fight, the other would retaliate. Ultimately they would tire of the pointless exchanges, or be distracted by some other pressing paramilitary imperative.

Alf worked purposefully in the hot sun, under the regulation steel helmet that baked his brain. Frequent rest breaks were arranged so that the men could cool off, smoke and drink iced water. His daily routine continued until Sunday: reveille at 0500, breakfast at 0645, muster on the parade ground at 0730, transport to the action zone by 0800, relieve the last watch, snap at 1300, back to camp at 1900, kit inspections, dinner and bed.

Sergeant Davis convened the company in their billet on Sunday at 2100 and announced the stand-down rota during the week. Alf and several others were to have Monday and Tuesday off, the remainder would have two other days until the trouble had exhausted itself. That would have been fine, except they were still needed for general duties within the barracks. On Monday there was parade ground practice for a forthcoming visit by the governor. Alf's remaining time was taken up with washing clothes, ironing shirts, blacking boots, darning socks and writing a letter home. He wasn't a great letter writer, but he knew that his mum appreciated a regular envelope through the postbox. His dad, whilst retaining an interest in his son's exploits, had lost interest in things over recent years, and so the letters were always written with his mum in mind as the reader. He could imagine the pair of them sitting in their little Sheffield living room in front of the Bush radio, dad listening to the gardening programme advice about preserving dahlias in wet weather, mum reading out the letter to dad, bringing in the contents of previous letters where relevant.

BFPO Cyprus

May 19th 1958

Dear Mum and Dad,

I hope you are well and dad has got over his recent cold.

Before I forget, I have to tell dad that Bill Morris went birding last week and says he spotted a Demoiselle Crane and a Great Bustard.

Life here goes on as usual, no terrible violence, just the normal flare-ups. The weather is heating up now and the spring flowers are almost all finished. The orange blossom is very fragrant and even in the camp we get a waft from time to time from groves about half a mile away. We have been told that the ablutions block is to be replaced and new hot showers are going to be installed before September.

We are currently on barricade duty in Famagusta, but I have been given leave for two days. I met an interesting chap several weeks ago, a ranking officer who seems friendly enough, no airs or graces. He has an interest and appreciation of Cyprus, just like me and dad (although I know dad has lost interest recently). He's invited me to look though some of his book collection on the history of the island. I think it would be interesting to fill in any gaps in what I know. He also said he would see what opportunities there are for me to get involved in the radio and electronics side of things, so I'm hoping something will come of that. You never know, the family could have the next William Shockley (tell dad he was the chap who won the Nobel Prize last year, 'cos he won't know who he is).

I've got a mess do in a week or so; we've been practising on the parade ground. Sir Hugh Foot, the governor, is coming to the camp. I'm on waiter duty in the officers' mess, well, OK, plate-clearing duty. At least I'll get to eat some of the mess catering, so that'll be a bonus. I just hope it isn't roast beef and all the trimmings because it's too hot for that.

Anyway, I must close now. Give my love to John and sis, tell them I miss them both and I miss a good pint in The Feathers with John. That would be my second stop if I came home, after coming to see you of course, ha ha! Give my love to everyone else and if you run into Julie Marshall tell her I'll try and write to her soon.

All my love

Alf

xxx

P.S. yes, it's OK if you take the Meccano set to the pawnshop.

Alf placed the folded airmail paper into the blue envelope and wrote his home and recipient address, licked a stamp, sealed the envelope and put it on the footlocker at the end of his bed for posting. Then he went to the ablutions block whilst it was quiet. Whilst showering, he began to think about Julie Marshall. This led him to take a longer than usual shower. Refreshed and exhilarated, he returned to his billet and fell asleep.

On Tuesday morning he was given the opportunity to go to the armed forces club at the beach and spent the morning sunbathing and swimming in the warm water of the bay. This was a regular haunt for Alf. Going to the beach was what everyone in the camp did when they got the opportunity. Whether good swimmers or not, the buoyant salinity of the warm water ensured even non-swimmers bobbed along the surface. Alf wasn't a good swimmer, despite his athletic physique he had never really taken to the idea at home, where the public baths were always too crowded. Slow swimmers were always bullied by the swimmers who powered their way up and down the lanes, scattering others in their wake.

For now he was content to float face down among the painted fishing boats in solitude. Shoals of small fish traced their way beneath the shadows cast by the boats. The heat of the sun and sand at midday was such that no matter how desirable a swim, the trudge across the burning hot sand was like walking on coals to the waters' edge. Most people just stayed in the clubhouse where they ate and drank a cool beer when the sun was at its hottest. This was how Alf passed the rest of his time before his return to camp.

That evening, Alf, dressed conservatively in slacks and a short-sleeved blue shirt and sandals, made his way to the married quarters. Along the path a lamp post with a solitary bulb lit the way. Moths clustered. Geckos lay in silent anticipation of their prey. Cicadas chirruped in the scrub. The pathway past his sentry post was unmanned and exit-only at night. On his return, he'd have to walk around the perimeter fence to the main camp entrance. He hoped none of his colleagues would be there to probe about where he had come from.

Despite the warmth of the summer night, the shutters, windows and mosquito screens were closed; Peter didn't like to go through the palaver of locking up every time he left. His default was a stuffy, airless house, the turgid atmosphere moving only in response to the ceiling fan's evening dervish. One day it would, he thought, completely detach itself from the ceiling. Each evening he'd open the verandah doors and shutters and sit outside for a few minutes reading or writing a letter to Vicky or his parents. It was the latter that he was doing when he heard a knock at the door. He returned indoors and purposefully closed up the verandah shutters and doors; he didn't want his domestic life to be on show. Peter quickly prepared mentally for the possible outcomes of the evening.

Alf found Albert Road easily enough amongst the grid of streets. North–south street names were royalty, east–west streets bore Scottish Regiment names. Nineteen Albert Road was a rendered, pink-painted, two-storey semi behind a low, rendered perimeter wall. White-painted wooden shutters and a pitched terracotta roof contrasted with the hue of the walls. The garden extended on three sides and a gated, high-walled yard stood to the left of the house. Neighbouring houses were painted other candy colours, arranged like a tray of brightly coloured confectionery. In the garden were neatly stacked empty packing cases, boxes and tea chests. In the dim light emanating from the lone outside bulb, he saw the black stencilled markings on the crates: 'Southampton, c/o Capt. P. F. Jarvis,' 'Fine Ceylon,' 'Catterick,' 'Crosse and Blackwell,' 'BFPO, Hong Kong'. This, to Alf, was the epitome of a forces life: moving around the pink bits on the world map with one's jetsam trailing behind in recycled wooden packaging. It was a family life to some, but a solitary life to him; all his belongings fitted in the one packing crate with rope handles, which also doubled as the footlocker at the end of his billet. Since he wasn't well travelled, his crate only had his name, rank, number, and below that, 'BFPO, Cyprus' and the regiment address.

Peter answered the door after a short few moments and invited him into a bare hall with magnolia rendered walls and ceramic floors. The living room, into which he was next ushered, had identical décor, but contained a whirring ceiling fan and war-department-stamped standard issue furniture: a three-piece suite in brown leather, a coffee table, a standard lamp with a tasselled shade, a dining table with four chairs, and a sideboard, all in matching wood. There was also an empty bookshelf and, in one corner, a pile of books; and deposited temporarily around the room were a stack of crockery, a pile of towels, and some foodstuffs.

'Sorry about the mess, but I've just been doing a bit of unpacking, then I got looking in my books and nothing else has been done since. Sit down and let me get you a drink.'

Alf sat uneasily on the edge of the sofa.

'What will you have? I can offer Coca Cola, Kean orange or some squash, or perhaps a can of lager.'

Alf opted, as a squaddie would, for a can of Tennants. Peter went into the linked kitchen, pulled two cans from a fridge visible through the doorway, located the can opener, and cut two holes in opposite sides of each can top.

'Hope you don't mind drinking from the can, I haven't unpacked the glasses yet.'

'No problem.' Losing the 'sir' was becoming easier.

'So how have you been? Were you detailed to the trouble in Famagusta?'

'Yes, at the end of last week and over the weekend. It was fine, nothing untoward.'

'I understand one or two visitors to the hospital were injured in the crossfire last Friday.'

'So I believe, but I wasn't at that end of the road, I was closer to the town hall end.'

'Ah,' said Peter, as he sat down on the other end of the sofa.

'Nice beer, very welcome, thanks.'

'Don't mention it, but I warn you that you have now reached the limit of what hospitality I can offer.'

'That's fine, thanks. I wouldn't have room for anything else after the mess dinner.'

'Likewise.'

Peter noted how very similar this lad was to Joe. He had the eyes, which in the toned-down light being cast by the standard lamp in the corner had darkened, his pupils were large black discs surrounded by hazel irises. His hair was dark, but bleached a lighter shade by the sun, and trimmed to the standard short back and sides. Peter sensed brilliantine. His skin was a beautiful even brown, his forearms covered by fine fair hairs, his ears delightfully sculptured and tanned. In his civvies, the lad looked a very pleasant picture. He thought to himself that a first hurdle had been overcome, the lad was here, so he hadn't bottled it. Now it was for Peter to discount his involvement in the trouble and thereafter to discover why he had come.

Alf glanced once more around the room and at Peter, whilst the latter was proffering disparaging remarks about the heaviness of camp mess catering. Peter was wearing khaki shorts and a flannel checked, short-sleeved shirt and sandals on socked feet. He looked quite relaxed and entirely at ease. His slim physique, whilst perhaps not as toned as a squaddie's was, for an officer, well maintained. Alf's glance centred on the pile of books, sipping his beer, he said, 'Are those the books you were talking about?'

'Yes, I thought we could have a look through them to see whether any are familiar to you. I know their texts, so I can give you some gen if you need. Just ask any question.' He rose to cross the room and picked up a pile of books and placed them on the dining table.

'Come over here to the table and we'll work through them.'

Alf crossed the room and sat where the chairs were placed, so the two of them were sat adjacently at the table.

Peter arranged a couple of coasters for the drinks. 'This first book focuses on the transfer of occupation from the Turkish Ottomans to the British in 1878.'

Alf had not been minded to think so far back, his interest in the country prompted only by reminiscences of his father, Alf's knowledge dated back only to the 1920s. Alf took the weighty quarto book and leafed through the dense text uncertain what he was meant to be doing.

Peter began to outline the book's content. 'There are some startling revelations about the transfer in here. For instance, the Ottoman occupation was essentially an exercise in bleeding the resources of the island dry, extracting the maximum amount of tax from the locals and offering little back in terms of infrastructure. I was surprised to find that the Greek Orthodox bishops were happy to continue as tax collectors for the Turks. Also, the British secured occupation by paying a tribute of vast quantities of salt to the sultans of the Ottoman Empire. Even after the British occupation, the tax structure initiated by the Turks didn't get dismantled. Instead, they continued some of the taxes and overlaid more taxes to raise money for the exchequer. Cypriots didn't cease to be Turkish citizens until 1914, and to avoid conscription they had to pay the Turks a poll tax. No wonder there is stinging resentment of the Turks to this day, and that it spread to resentment of the British because of their complicity.'

Whilst not disinterested, Alf struggled because his knowledge was somewhat more superficial. It felt like he was in a history lesson back in Rotherham with an overly enthusiastic teacher. He hadn't been in a classroom for many years and was taken aback at the barrage of facts and figures assailing him here in a house in Cyprus. He chose to silently persevere.

'Of course, the British overcame initial scepticism and their role in Cyprus has been much more like benevolent colonialism, putting the infrastructure in place and investing in the people. Schooling, healthcare and communications have all been down to the British. But that doesn't change the fact that if you are a peasant farmer—Greek or Turk—you are virtually destitute. There is a very difficult route out of that. Even schooling takes away manpower, or rather child power, from rural tasks. Illiteracy hasn't been eliminated yet and the main drain on rural families remains the dowry that goes with a bride. In some households, the dowry accounts for a significant proportion of the value of the family estate. The move from farms to cities in Cyprus is partly a symptom of dwindling dowry pots. In the end, families didn't even have plots of land to pass to the newly-weds, so the younger generation started to move to the towns and cities to try to improve their fortunes.'

Alf was hoping he could move the lesson forward, conscious that he may have taken on something he wasn't at all equipped for. Nevertheless, he silently asserted to himself whilst picking up a second book, 'I wasn't given much opportunity to say "no" to tonight, so it's not my problem if I'm disinterested.'

There followed several minutes more trawling through facts and figures, eventually reaching the 1931 riots. During this time, Alf was hoping his body language reflected engagement and interest. He suppressed a yawn.

Peter, until now comfortable in the role of lecturer, spotted the yawn out of the corner of his eye. He attempted to open up other lines of chit-chat, wondering if there was any point in probing about Black Sheep and Saddleback.

'Sorry, I do rather go on when I'm interested in a topic. I should let you talk. Where does your interest in Cyprus start?'

Alf perked up a bit, describing his father's role and his descriptions of life at the time of his employment in the colonial civil service.

Peter mused to himself that you can often seem to be reaching for the same goal, but for entirely different and misunderstood reasons. Peter wondered whether his insight into Alf could be similarly misguided. He wanted to think Alf was here for precisely the reason he himself believed. The articulate reciting of facts and descriptions by Alf, without even having taken note of Peter's books, signalled to him that this was no subversive activist. His knowledge and empathy for the local population did not fit the profile he was seeking. He thought it was time to test his other theory.

Alf sensed that the interest Peter had in his books had shifted and that Alf himself was now the focus of Peter's attention. Peter had swung round on his dining chair so his legs now faced Alf; whilst Alf was talking, Peter's gaze moved from his eyes to neck, to ears, to chest, back to eyes, then to lower abdomen, and so on. Alf continued to talk, becoming more acutely aware of his companion's interest. At a certain point in the conversation, Peter shifted himself on his chair to face Alf from his left and his bare legs touched Alf's left thigh. Alf felt a burst of adrenaline shoot through his system, which made him suddenly alert. His gaze rapidly diverted to meet Peter's, carrying in it a fleeting look of incomprehension as if to convey unspoken questions: 'What?' 'Why?' Peter seemed oblivious to the unspoken enquiry and acted very much as if his physical contact was neither deliberate nor unreasonable. However, Alf similarly shifted his thigh imperceptibly further from Peter under the pretence of reaching for his can of beer. He was uncertain whether or not this represented the entrée to a subtle pass, but was not unaware of a level of excitement within himself, if not quite describable as arousal.

The topic shifted, as did Peter, standing as he proposed they move back to the sofa.

'I can see that we may have a shared interest in history, but I realise my school teacherliness isn't to everyone's taste. Let's sit on the sofa again and talk about something different.'

Peter caught Alf's elbow and guided him lightly to the sofa. Alf now realised that this second physical contact indicated a level of familiarity that could go one of two ways. He was wrestling with his emotions; not quite sure whether the situation that he thought was developing should be repelled, ignored or embraced.

He wanted to normalise any uneasiness and allow them to be just acquaintances, like his mates in his billet. Weighing up the options, mindful of the opportunity that was in prospect of being positioned for an electronics technician job, he decided to go with a middle line and to ignore what had happened in case his wild interpretations were wrong.

Peter was convincing himself that Alf and he were thinking along similar lines, thinking Alf's disinterest in historical fact was a sure sign that Alf was here for something else. A shot of adrenaline coursed through his body at the thought. 'Fight or flight,' he decided.

He decided to test this hypothesis by suggesting the lad told him about his interests. He began to feel himself shivering, not from cold—for it was stuffy in the enclosed room—but from excitement. Peter was certain, his judgement reinforced by his hormonal rush, that there would be a good outcome. Peter commented on Alf's suntan, Alf replied that he'd been on the beach all morning. He always felt much better about himself when he had a good tan.

'At the forces club?' asked Peter. Alf nodded his assent.

'I was going to spend some time there myself, but a colleague took me swimming some distance from here to swim at Fig-Tree Bay. Never a more peaceful spot will I be able to find, with the trees as a backdrop across the potato fields, and the shallow bay with the small island. Superb.'

Despite the trouble brewing on the island, trips nearby were frequently made without mishap and the coastline between Dhekelia and Cape Greco beyond the part of Famagusta called Varosha, was beautiful and unspoilt. From the barracks to the coast was a journey best made by Land Rover through the orange and lemon groves. You could drive to Dhekelia and then double back, but it was longer. The beach was pristine and the water so clear you could watch small shoals of fish dart in and out of the submerged rocks in the bay.

As Peter continued to chat, Alf could distinctly hear a flutter in

Peter's voice. He noted a perceptible shiver run over the man's body, despite the warmth of the spring evening. Alf recognised this. He had experienced it regularly when aroused and was unable to be demonstrably sexual. Like during the interminable anticipation of a first kiss. Last time it was with a wife of a fellow squaddie, whose behaviour had been verging on tarty. Alf had become aroused, but realised that the consequences of following through were too risky; it would probably have led to a brawl, and on that occasion he knew he would not have come off well. So he had withdrawn from the social situation he was in, made his excuses, and nursed his frustrated soul in the best way he knew.

Peter enjoyed the anticipatory sensation before intimacy. The initial moments when one stepped into the unknown, making physical contact, not sure whether the act would be reciprocated, were exquisite. If the action was reciprocated the next feeling of relief mixed with excitement was equally wonderful. Man or woman—it was no different, but there was an added frisson with a man. The charge of energy Peter felt go through his body when he placed his right hand on Alf's thigh was, therefore, as good a feeling as he was able to imagine. Buoyed by the lack of response—this soldier didn't seem about to get violent or abusive—Peter slowly moved his hand around the inside of Alf's thigh and further up toward the crotch. Peter, hypersensitive to Alf's reactions, noted both a gentle relaxation in Alf's body, a heat from the skin, and a visible change of demeanour, the eyes belying the lack of reciprocation with a look of guarded pleasure. There was a slight smile on the lad's face, he thought.

Alf was now certain about Peter's intentions. It was not unheard of in the forces. Most squaddies knew which officers were playing that game and guarded their exits, as it were. But Peter was recently arrived and nobody had rumbled him. Alf's view was confirmed by Peter's obvious state of excitement and his eye movements darting rapidly over every part of Alf's body. Alf put his beer can down and swallowed, wondering how to extricate himself from the situation. His own body was continuing to channel adrenaline to its extremities, which was not unpleasant.

Alf's first thought was that Peter stroked Alf's thigh in a similar way one would lackadaisically put an arm behind a girl, across the back of their chair, as a signal of intent. Alf felt his frame tauten, but his body outwardly made no perceptible movement. He felt like a rabbit in the headlights. He was conscious, within himself, of a feeling akin to arousal, if not quite the same.

Peter, sensing no resistance from Alf, consolidated his position, gradually sliding his hand further up Alf's thigh.

Alf shifted now to bring his thighs together and once again look into the officer's face with the unspoken questions, 'What? Why?' Alf realised Peter was now breathing more heavily, spreading his body more across the sofa cushions towards Alf's rigidly upright torso. Peter's hand pulled apart Alf's closed thighs and cupped Alf's crotch, gently pummelling him. Alf's body relaxed in autonomic response to the latest physical contact. That was unexpected. He was confused now, not about what was happening, but about how he should respond. His internal dilemma was whether decisively to put a stop to Peter's advances, or not. His own heart was gathering pace, his breathing erratic, he was taking pleasure from the attention he was getting. He still didn't want this. Or did he? Then, like a bolt of energy, he thought how he might throw away the chance of a career if he did the wrong thing now. Should he could go with it; reciprocate; or try to escape?

Peter's other hand started probing between the buttons of Alf's shirt. Peter's lips sought his. Alf lifted himself off the sofa, and standing, turned to Peter who was left awkwardly prone—Alf's countermeasure had caught him unprepared.

'Listen, sir, I'm sorry, but this just isn't my cup of tea.'

Peter didn't think that the reaction quite matched the body

language. He thought he could bring the lad back into the frame to enjoy, to participate. He sat upright opposite the standing lad and began to unbutton Alf's fly and top button to release the pleasure that lay within, his hand traced the outline of Alf's erection through the underclothing.

Alf had made his decision. He brought his hand down to prevent further exploration. Peter then stood impossibly close, facing Alf and embraced him. Alf pulled his face away and wriggled out of the embrace to a position near the dining table, re-buttoning his open fly and tucking his shirt firmly into his slacks, at the same time propelling himself into a monologue.

'Listen, Peter, I may be about to say something that will end my career in the Army, being as you are a ranking officer and I am not. I know this sort of thing happens and people turn a blind eye, or keep it under cover. And I cannot ignore the fact that you have managed to arouse me, but I can't go through with this. I am not usually turned on by men and I wasn't expecting this evening to turn out like this.'

In fact, he had acknowledged to himself that there was a 50 per cent chance that it would.

'I'm not going to say anything about this to anyone. Put it down to a misunderstanding on my part if you wish. I hope you won't take any sort of revenge because I've stopped. I'm sorry. You don't have to try to get that electronics job for me. Please don't do anything that means my billet buddies get to know about this.'

Peter looked helplessly around as if wondering what he'd just done wrong.

'Sorry, Alf, I thought that wouldn't come as a surprise to you. As you know, it can get lonely when you're away from your other half; I just thought you were expecting something and going along with it.' He sorted out his own state of dress.

'It won't go any further. I don't begrudge you. Don't worry, and thank you for not breaking my jaw or punching me in the face. Sorry.'

Alf, calmer now, his barriers still up, said, 'OK, sir. I should go now.' He made to leave the room and approached the external door. He knew his exit would be awkward and he didn't know how to handle it. A handshake? Just turn and go? In the end he turned and smiled briefly after he was across the threshold, then kept walking. He walked the long way back to the camp main entrance, past the taxi rank where the drivers were smoking, sat the wrong way round on their chairs, and engaged in a frantic game of tavli while waiting for a fare. He had confused, jumbled thoughts. He wondered if things could be the same again, whether life choices would ever be straightforward, whether the same thing could happen again, whether he'd let it happen? Reason kicked in. The law was clear and so were the Forces. There wouldn't be any repeat.

Peter noticed Alf's smile on his way out the door, like a concluding punctuation mark. He closed the door as Alf walked away and returned to the sofa, wondering how he had misread the situation, then querying whether, in fact, he had. He was more or less sure that the lad did not fit the profile of the antagonists he was seeking, although if the lad cropped up again in his investigations, he'd need to take a hard look at the circumstances. He thought his earlier throwaway comment about electronics opportunities would not have been taken seriously, but he thought he'd try and follow it up, given that the lad had been so reasonable. If the lad tried to expose him, he'd need something to barter with. Overall, he reflected, a good evening, albeit no climax. He would see to that shortly.

Chapter Fourteen
Mehmet's Story

My Turkish Cypriot existence is a mass of irreconcilable conflict. My family is full of contrariness. My nation is contraposed. In the minds of my compatriots, the other is always the cause of their woes, blame being applied disproportionately. Even outsiders, people not from my village, or even from my country, say there are contradictions here and forever try to impose their explanations and solutions. Let it be so, I say. It is God's will.

When I was born that day in 1931, contradicting themes were already shaping the pattern my life would take. But I should not reveal too much of this story so soon. And I cannot ignore the tremendous pleasure and prestige my parents gained from my birth. My father married well, to the daughter of the wealthiest merchant in the area. Sepia photographs fix beams of pride on the ageing faces of the respective grandparents, telling everybody who knew how these things worked that they were the architects of this union. They were the transacting parties. Not that use of such a word in any way conveyed some grubby back-room deal to stitch together two random people. This was all above-board, pre-ordained and endorsed by the whole extended family of bride and groom, although, as is the tradition, neither the bride nor groom had any say in it. I was loved and cherished from the day I was conceived by two people with very modern ideas about such things. I am extremely grateful for that fact. Imagine how it might have been to be conceived by two complete strangers who could never be other than intolerant of the other. This, my friend, is the beauty of a well-arranged union.

There are few moments in the life of people in our village so important as the birth of a child. Birth is the creation of a new line of ancestry, an expansion of the family name, in time another pair of hands to work the fields and fill the grain stores, another fine body to continue the family name into the future.

In our country, in our culture, we have weaved together a beneficial partnership of old and new ideas to create the best possible opportunities for husband and wife, whilst not forgetting that the imam feels the need to retain a hand in steering the family's spiritual development, and the mukhtar feels the need to be a civic guide. It is like we are weaving the seat of a chair, but some improvements have been agreed to make it stronger, more resilient, and more attractive. So, unlike our kinsmen from the mainland, we do not try to empty the coffers of the bride's family to facilitate a marriage, but we do follow the tradition of our religion. We do not commit the bride to virtual slavery in the home of her husband's family; we ensure that they have a home of their own, but if the family can't afford one, the bride's family will host them first. So there is the first of the contradictions. We don't do things like our kinsmen. Yet what we do is shaped first by their tradition and secondly, inseparably, by their—and our—religion. And at the same time, what we do now is informed by the more liberal views of outsiders, those who will never be able to participate in our customs, who can be observers and guests but not, as it were, parties in these things. So we have the enlightened ideas of the British to thank for their liberal attitudes to the role of women in our society. We thank them also for the role that education will play in releasing our women from the yoke of oppression. And we have the Greeks, our neighbours, to thank for having a better arrangement for dowries than our forefathers and their forefathers. Is this not all the proof you need that we are not poor, illiterate, peasant farmers, but progressive, intellectually open . . . poor peasant farmers. And which one person do we have to thank for all this? Well, you can't even count individuals on one hand.

Perhaps we should be thanking His Excellency Lieutenant General Sir Garnet Joseph Wolseley, or Queen Victoria for appointing him, whose Diamond Jubilee proclamation of 22 July 1897 referred to us using such phrases as: 'Warm interest . . . in their prosperity,' 'Afford to the people blessings of freedom, justice and security,' and 'Respect to the maintenance of their ancient institutions, usages and customs,' but then with the colonial proviso, 'That they be consistent with just and good government.'

Or maybe we should thank beloved Mustafa Kemal Ataturk, who died when I was just eight years old, but left a legacy of pride and unity amongst my kinsmen wherever they lived, and a doctrine to challenge the stultifying influence of the Ottomans and religion on the development of a modern Turkish nation.

Maybe we should thank one particular governor for the gift of education which, for all children, became compulsory during his rule. Of course, it was always the claim of the Ottomans that their education system was the driver for the sustenance and confidence of the Turkish people. But the further you travelled from the centres of power, the less you felt the confidence that education gives you and the more you felt a hunger for something out of reach. For us, in our villages, there was no education until the British. My grandparents were illiterate; each of their parents before them also. They managed to get by in life, but the predominant guide for all of their actions was Islam and the customs it perpetuated.

Do not misunderstand me, the importance of Islam in our lives is unquestioned, but since Ataturk and the British, we have found a way of making our faith our private business. As I am speaking to you, dear reader, in English, might I assume you are a non-believer?

If I am correct, I believe you might underestimate the central role of Islam in our lives. The Declaration of Faith and daily prayer play just a small part. If you are a believer you will understand. Let us leave it at that. My faith is central. But it should not come between us. And we should not forget the role of our own parents in taking the information and intelligence they gained and implementing it in their daily lives, and forcing it upon us, their children. We should thank them for making use of it.

But I digress, you will want to know how my life was lived, and what made me a man. Every child in my culture has a prayer whispered into its ear as it is pointed in the direction of Mecca before it is a few days old, then later its name is given by the imam. If it is a boy, he must go through sunnet when he is older—his foreskin is taken away. Then he passes into manhood and everyone celebrates, except the sore host. But from birth a child is celebrated. As soon as the birth has happened, there are parties and festivities, and the proud families show off their new acquisition. In some cases, among those who follow the old customs, the mother stays indoors for forty days. To do so was an anachronistic luxury in our village, especially when there are crops to be tended and harvested. My mother told me that within days of my birth she was back doing the chores, and I went with her to the fields.

But how glorious was my childhood! From the first day I can remember, I was a happy smiling child nurtured in a poor village, but raised on a rich mixture of love and nature. In common with other families in rural communities throughout the world, children are the justification for being, the purpose. It is never different. I could remember being able to roam free, to play with other children, especially my cousins and school friends: Yusef, Irfan and Ismael; and Takis and Dimitri. We would, when we were old enough, run across the fields, play the battles of military history with wooden guns and scimitars, divert water from the stream to make mud for our forts, use our slings to kill birds, take our fill of oranges from the cool groves in the late summer heat and sleep innocently in the security of our homes. At school we learnt our lessons: we were taught about our country, about our people, and about our environment. But the teacher in our village was Greek, so we grew up with a view of the world that should not have been our own. Some of us that were not Greek would grow up to resent that teacher for feeding us the lies and corruption of others. It would shape my view of the world I lived in; it would help sharpen my senses to the xenophobia of others. It would be my justification when I became politicised, it would set contradictions like cement. However, it is probably unfair to pile all the blame on the teacher.

But, as I say, my childhood was glorious. Until I left school, I only have good memories, although my parents are quick to shatter the illusion by claiming that I was a troubled adolescent. I never knew what they meant and they didn't ever elaborate. They carried that with them to their respective graves, and I helped to seal the issue with the three handfuls of sand I let flow over each of their bodies as their taut souls searched for Mecca. That I have become a troubled adult is not to attribute blame to anyone. As I have said, my childhood was joyfully innocent. My memories are filled with smells and aromas: of the fields after the first rains; of wild thyme and oregano crushed underfoot as I walked in scrub land; of chamomile; of cardomom-imbued coffee; of cumin; and of the zest of orange. I remember the feeling of a slingshot in my hand, or a whittled stick, or of the birds we caught as children for the pot. You cannot describe what friendship in childhood feels like, other than a vestigial warmth beneath the breast and a longing for reunion with your pals. But you can always recall the sensation of love for your closest ones whether they are parents, siblings, best friend or betrothed.

The only harsh memory was of sunnet, but I was told I should be proud of that time, the time I was told I became a man. My cock was very sore after the practitioner did that thing. It was painful to pee. But the passing discomfort was soon forgotten.

We had five years of eduction in the rural village. Five years longer than our predecessors. Our school was in the nearby village close to the Greek church. After completing our schooling we were sent on our way, usually into the fields or, if our parents could afford, secondary schools in the towns. My family could afford to send me to Magosa—you may know it as Famagusta—for a secondary education because of the fortuitous pairing of my parents and the previously mentioned dowry. My younger sister was not so fortunate, but she self-educated herself in later life. I still returned whenever school was out to work with my father in the fields. Those days at the village were idyllic.

But all was, as you realise, not well with the world. We had lived as a self-contained rural community alongside our neighbours, and the events that impacted upon our nation were slow to reach us. As children and teenagers we were insulated from the worst news about what our compatriots were capable of doing to their neighbours and friends. However, we were never able to escape the terrible spectre of war with Germany. The British forces were quick to build up locally. Before the war, my father told me there was but a single company of British soldiers, but soon after Mr Hitler invaded Poland and the British and French declared war on Germany, the military capability on the island increased to several battalions. As the war continued and I grew from three feet high to four-feet-two, the numbers of soldiers continued to increase. If British troops came to the village, we boys would crowd forward to stare at them. Even though they were probably here for some insignificant purpose, they carried guns or pistols. That was as if the touchpaper had been lit on the fireworks of our imagination. We would go to the nearby fields and re-enact the latest battles we had heard about from the radio or newspapers that had found their way to the village.

At first the troops were all British, but soon there were also men in turbans and darker skin, more like ourselves than the white men from England. Father said the ones with Turbans were men from India who were British soldiers. The Indians were nice people. The white ones were from England. My father said they were white because there was never any sun in England and it rained a lot. He knew that because before I was born an English man called George, who worked for the governor in Lefkoşa, used to come to the village to watch birds. He was very popular and I believe he visited a few times and the villagers made him an honorary villager. He was present at my cousin Oran's naming ceremony and he was honoured as a friend of the family by giving Oran his middle name, Hasan. He suggested it because it meant 'beautiful,' but it was also similar to his father's name and his grandfather's name. Little did George know, but that is how our names are chosen anyway.

My father's brother Ozan lived in England in a big town called Bethnal Green. He worked in a factory making clothes. Father said he left Cyprus when the opportunity to either remain Turkish or become a British Cypriot was offered by the British Government. He was a nationalist and was very interested in Ataturk; isn't every proud Turk? He said he'd rather be a Turk than a Briton, but it was better to have a job in England than to have no job in Turkey. So he became a British Cypriot and went to England to behave like a true Turk.

By the time I was twelve, the British started to recruit local Turkish people for the Cyprus Regiment. I remember my father showing me a poster nailed to the mimosa tree in the village telling potential recruits how to join. It wasn't, he said, so much that local men wanted to fight against Hitler (this man with his funny moustache had never even been to Cyprus, let alone invaded), but the British Army was a good employer and they sometimes took men to Egypt to train them, they fed them and made sure they stayed healthy, and if they needed medical treatment it was free, and then it might also open up a world of opportunity. My mother added that good young men would be wasted on the battlefield and it was important not to forget that they could also end up dead and that it wasn't all glorious. Most of the village men who applied went on the trail to the rural health officer, then to the police station. These places were miles away from here and they needed transport. Then they would wait until a letter from the district commissioner called them to an interview. Having made that additional journey, they would wait again to find out if they were selected. I think about ten men from our village were called to an interview, but only two were recruited. My father said that the entry conditions were set high; if you were illiterate, sick, not very tall, were known to the police, had been to prison, or were a communist, then they wouldn't take you. I didn't know what the eight men from our village had done to be turned down.

The rest of the villagers were recruited and paid to do manual work in the area. It wasn't very good money, but it helped to buy seed, fertilisers, school fees, and building materials. The war made the villagers more prosperous than they were before.

As for me and my friends, in our pubescent enlightenment, we began to take an interest in the affairs of government, bureaucracy and conflict, and awoke to a litany of injustices and man's inhumanity to man. The fires of unrest slowly took hold within my soul. A Turkish proverb speaks to this experience 'young wood burns fiercer than old wood.' I was perhaps fifteen when the Second World War came to an end. The British forces were now present in huge numbers on our island and the port of Famagusta was bursting with grey naval warships and cargo ships plying in and out of the bay to some unfathomable schedule. As secondary school kids, we used to walk down to the walls of the Old City and look down onto the dock across the barbed wire perimeter fencing to watch the crew preparing for their arrivals, or departures. There would be cranes bowing to offload vehicles, sacks, boxes of provisions, crates of weapons, light artillery pieces. Everything the British needed would come to Magosa or Limassol by ship. We would be amazed at the efficiency and haste with which everything was completed, the regimentation, the organisation. Coming from a rural village, life was governed by nature and the pace of life was never faster than nature herself dictated.

There were a number of British military sites where the goods would be taken to. One was not so far from our school, a dusty geometric compound demarcated by metal poles and high wire fencing topped by barbed wire. The tarmacadam roads around the site were marked out with rocks and kerb stones meticulously painted in white, even the trunks of the eucalyptus trees under which the semicircular Nissen huts sat were painted white. Everything in its place. The stockpile of armaments and vehicles were lined up in a regimented fashion. We knew that the staff on the sites were both British and Cypriot. My uncle once worked for the British Army. His job was to help keep his base tidy. He said his job was to paint the rocks and stones white. As a teenager, I simply couldn't understand how anybody could earn money painting rocks, or how rocks painted white contributed to the winning of wars. My uncle joined the police in Limassol after the war.

So you see, before my voice had deepened, I was already building a list of contradictions within myself: I followed the customs of my kinfolk and I did not; I was Turkish *and* British; I was and was not a villager.

As my maturity progressed my shoulders broadened and my spindly arms and legs thickened as my muscles reacted to the toil of rural life. I also began a journey of self discovery. My father once took me to Lefkoşa. It was a big city, very busy, with traffic and shops and factories and houses. We saw the Ledra Palace, we drove down Ledra Street and looked at all the wealthy people shopping for luxuries. We went to the airport to see the aircraft that conveyed people to new lives in England, America and Australia, or brought visitors to our island. We went to the site of Government House to see where George Holdsworth used to work. We ate western food. We bought ice cream. It was a visit that confirmed to me that I could not remain a village peasant; I would have to be part of something more exciting.

It was 1949 before I burst from the cocoon of the village and I was eighteen years old, although, as you know, I attended school in the city. To my parents' disappointment, I decided to flee without having being paired up with a wife. It was to my eternal shame not to have acquiesced to the wishes of my parents. I believe they were seeking a suitable bride for up to a year before I announced my departure for Magosa. Whilst I have always said that my parents were progressive, the institution and process of marrying off their only son was too great a milestone for them to be anything other than devastated when I announced my departure. They said, 'What is to be gained by leaving your home now? What are the chances you will make your way in life without a sound basis of family and home? How will you compete for work with all the men who have became unemployed after demobilisation, even though they have learnt skills in the Cyprus Regiment? And you, Mehmet, *you* have none of these skills, nor any history of work. Where will you live? How will you pay your way? If you have no work you cannot eat or pay for your lodgings. There is no money to help you. Only family.'

And they were right. After several difficult weeks searching for any sort of work, I returned penniless to the village like a dog with its tail between its legs. My parents were as understanding as it was possible for them to be, but it was a skirmish with them and I had been roundly beaten. Now they had lost face in the village because they had to restart the protracted negotiations to secure a bride, and families in the village were reluctant to engage with them because of my unscheduled departure.

But during my time in Magosa I had become more aware of unfolding political developments. The British administration had, post-war, become the legitimate target for criticism from virtually every creed on the island, and from many foreign governments. It was failing to stimulate economic and social development for the Cypriot people. It had become clear that despite assurances to the contrary, the British were not putting the interests of our country's people first; they were participants in a game between the USA, Palestine and Russia, along with political leaders of Turkey and Greece. The British wanted to maintain a balance of power in the region that was beneficial to them and the Americans; economic or social development and enhancements to daily life in Cyprus were immaterial, and no amount of media manipulation claiming otherwise convinced anyone. In addition, the British were being coy about the increasing prominence of the enosis movement being advocated by prominent Greek Cypriots and other politicians outside the island. Like the turning of a screw, one turn after another, the pressure mounted on Turkish Cypriots like myself to protest, to reject, and to lobby to have this injustice strangled. Nobody listened to us. That is how I became involved in the long struggle.

Chapter Fifteen
The Briefing Room

Peter didn't make any further progress with his covert operation the day following his tryst with Alf, nor indeed the day after. The whole company was drawn into patrolling Famagusta because of a flare-up in inter-communal violence. This happened, he had been informed, from time to time and was usually precipitated by some event or other elsewhere on the island. Prior to the start of patrols, he and his fellow officers were being briefed about the situation by OIC defence operations at the camp. Peter thought Goff a competent, if somewhat officious, WO2. He told them that both Greek and Turk were agitating for greater say in the island's running. Paramilitary groups on both sides were, as they had been doing for several years, targeting each other, as well as British interests.

Peter knew that after 1955 there had been a lull, thereafter an escalation in tensions. EOKA's campaign against the British in particular had ebbed and flowed. Recently, due to several murders of servicemen and policemen elsewhere on the island, the death penalty had been reintroduced for carrying weapons. Then the penalty had been relaxed again, no doubt as a result of delicate negotiations and compromises between Greece and the UK around some highly polished table in a European city. Peter knew that EOKA were playing their cards very deftly, accusing the British of atrocities against the local population, hence his own role. Political machinations, notably in Westminster and Washington, were delaying the publication of the most recent plan for the island. The delays were rumoured to be so that Turkey's international position as the West's only ally in the Middle East could be materially recognised. Turkey was concerned that any move toward self-determination would at best marginalise and, at worst, lead to the extinction of a Turkish voice in the running of Cyprus. Everyone knew that the proposals would be biased towards Greek demands, toward EOKA demands.

WO2 Goff waved his pace stick between the blackboard and a map pinned to the wall of the cramped classroom in the administration block, and said, 'The February 1958 plan for Cyprus put forward by Selwyn-Lloyd has yet to be published. This has spawned conspiracy theories among Greek and, more particularly, Turkish Cypriots. They think the content is being compromised under diplomatic pressure. Both factions suspect each other and their respective funders and backers. Bear in mind that the document has not been seen in entirety, so their views are speculative, or only partly informed. The Turks believe it includes a plan for the creation of a Turkish security area—an enclave—under Turkish sovereignty on the island. This would go some way towards meeting the Turkish position's demands for partition of Turkish and Greek sectors. If this were true, the British would also retain sovereignty over the two large Sovereign Bases.'

He shifted position, leaned on the edge of the table, put his pace stick down, and launched into an off-the-record monologue about the balls-ups being committed in London. 'Between you and me,' he began, signalling to the audience that this was his own interpretation of events, 'it follows that someone is going to be seriously pissed off by this plan when it comes out. The Greek government changes its mind more often than a woman. One minute it says union with Greece is the only way forward, then it says it isn't feasible, then it gets uppity when Turkey proposes partition because it thinks the island is Greek territory. Then we have the Turks going along with the enclave idea, but really seeking partition, and the British caught in the middle.'

Peter thought Goff's views were ill-informed. His assessment of the British predicament suggested a somewhat benign role. Peter understood it to be anything but. The British were in effect boxing and coxing to get the best deal for themselves and the USA so that they could snuff out Russian interest in the region and neuter the activities of the Russian military through their Black Sea ports and those of their Soviet Union neighbours. There was no way Cyprus would be abandoned by the British—neither they nor the Americans would even countenance the thought, given the security situation. The major powers' hidden agenda had little to do with the well-being or self-determination of the Cypriots. Peter knew there was a further dimension, a war of words and policies between the Conservative government and the Labour opposition in London. One favoured the plan which had yet to be published, the other favoured self-determination with no possibility of partition.

WO2 Goff stood and paced across the front of the room and back, swinging his stick and then tucking it under his right arm as he stood to face the assembled officers. He was on message again. 'This flare up has been initiated by the Turks. It began on June the sixth with the distribution of a leaflet originating in Larnaca from a Turkish youth organisation calling the youth to rise up "Partition or Death!"' He took a sheet from the desk and asked for it to be circulated. 'This is a translation of the leaflet. There have been signs of agitation for some days. The focus of the action was in Nicosia where the Turkish Cypriots started fires. Last week a bomb exploded outside the Turkish press office, perpetrators unknown. The trouble has spread to other towns. A singular act of savagery occurred in a suburb of Nicosia. Almost a dozen Greeks were massacred, hence the current Greek response. The agitation doesn't seem very well organised, but news is travelling fast. The Turkish youth there seem to have much pent-up anger about the lack of political progress.'

Goff went on to describe the current situation as one of the most serious inter-racial conflicts for several years and there would be a knock-on consequence for all British forces.

'Our immediate priority, as always, is to uphold law and order locally, protect British interests, and prevent unnecessary loss of life. Moreover, we need to ensure all British subjects are safe and remain so.'

The thoughts of those in the room hovered heavily in the air, filling up the space between the assembled men. There would be disruptions of routine for the foreseeable future; the married men were thinking about how best to protect their families and that the latter could be repatriated to the UK, depending on the seriousness of the situation, whilst they themselves remained behind; the single men were realising that it would mean an indefinite confinement to barracks, other than for sorties.

These possibilities were corroborated in the following minutes when Major Ellis, sitting towards the front of the room, read from a document outlining the interim evacuation and security plan.

'In addition,' he said, 'it has been decided by London to increase the number of troops on the island by a further five thousand. The majority would be additional postings of National Servicemen, billeted in tented camps either within or adjacent to existing British camps. At this stage, I have no details about the impact on this camp.'

He went on to describe their immediate responses to the situation, which consisted of more sentry duties, tighter security, stop and search, weapons inspections, armoury inventories, cancellation of leave, etc. All, to the minds of the officers assembled, welcome distractions from the boredom of CB.

Major Ellis's intervention was met by uneasy murmurs around the room, the sound of less than palatable information being processed by men who were less than happy, and who would shortly have to disseminate the same message amongst the ranks and to their own families. Several questions were tabled by the audience, seeking confirmation, or requesting further detail.

The briefing was terminated and the men fell out. Peter observed the impact of the news on the men as they left the room. He was listening for inappropriate comments, watching for misplaced emotions, and looking at what groupings the men fell into after their dismissal. He was convinced senior officers were involved in Saddleback. The Forces were under strict instructions from the new governor to root out and deal decisively with those involved. He knew the current situation would place more pressure on him to report positive progress to his CO. He walked back into the classroom, made some notes, then marched alone to QMS, where he briefed the quartermaster and his staff. They received his brief with predictable coolness. They discussed logistics in the event of an influx of National Servicemen, then he retired to his office for the remainder of the day. His main thoughts were of Victoria and whether the change in situation would delay her arrival, or scupper their reunion altogether.

Chapter Sixteen
The Paramyrsina Incident

August was a hot, dusty month. Tempers were flaring across Cyprus. From briefings at the camp, Alf was aware that the country's problems were once again rearing their heads. Sporadic outbursts of violence between Greek and Turkish Cypriot communities were more frequent. The camp was locked down. The frustrations created by this alone were palpable. Minor scraps between squaddies were a weekly occurrence. To divert the energies of the men, the CO scheduled more square bashing and pointless drills, more kit inspections, and more time-wasting; although the red dust that got everywhere in some way justified the need for constant washing and tidying. Non-ranks engaged in erecting more tents and NAAFI tents, and laying pathways around the site in preparation for the influx of more troops. The incoming troops would be expected to dig their own latrines and build their own ablutions blocks.

British efforts aimed at bringing an end to the troubles in Cyprus were being resisted by the Turks who were now campaigning for partition, their word for it was 'Taksim'. The BBC World Service was the main source of any information about the trouble, as well as British newspapers which appeared in camp several days after publication. The officers told them very little about what the situation was like. Alf believed the truth was always twisted by the British press to create a better story. He also thought the British government might be promulgating misinformation.

Alf gathered that the new governor, who had visited the camp a couple of months previously, had given an upbeat assessment of a move towards self determination for the Cyprus people (he'd failed to mention that the British would remain top of the heap). It was true that several months ago it was a very pleasant place, but since then, things had changed again. Alf thought that just a few words on a communiqué or in Hansard, or spoken in a summit in a posh hotel somewhere in the world, whether true or not, had changed daily life on the ground. Cyprus and its inhabitants were once again being troubled by an unfathomable agenda. It was difficult to establish the facts: unrest, violence, murder, assassination, and maiming were the currency of the negotiations. Peace was elusive. Alf and his fellow soldiers were being ordered to act out their role in this tragedy. Confinement to barracks was only the start of the consequences for ordinary servicemen like him. Almost every day, sometimes night and day, they were being ferried to different parts of the locality to play a 'peacekeeping' role. By the time they were deployed, it was usually the case that several people on both sides had been killed or injured, so the routine was to arrive and establish a level of respect using the superior fire-power at their disposal. It meant a noisy game of pinning back poorly armed snipers on both sides until they were out of reach of each other.

Such was the case when they were deployed one night to the village of Paramyrsina to relieve another company. The company was briefed by the camp commander before leaving the safety of the camp. There had been a flare up of violence after Greek Cypriot villagers had formed a vigilante group to protect their interests against the incursions of a neighbouring Turkish Cypriot village. A surprising burst of Greek infighting had followed whereby the vigilante group, largely made up of left wing sympathisers, was attacked by right-wing EOKA. The result had been one death and an unknown number of injuries.

Alf's colleagues murmured that they wouldn't be able to tell who the enemy were. At least with Turk on Greek hostilities you could usually spot the difference; here there would be three hostile entities in the same theatre of engagement, each blaming the British for their plight. The trip to the village in the back of the three-ton trucks was a sombre one. The trucks proceeded in convoy through the dark, star-encrusted night along rural roads, passing successive roadblocks. Each man armed, battle-ready and on a hair-trigger, was a sitting target in the un-armoured lorries. Deep in thought whilst crouched on the bed of the lorry, Alf wondered what had become of the slightly ajar door to a job in electronics that could have kept him out of trouble and negated his physical presence in conflicts.

Somewhere around 0200 the convoy arrived at their destination to a fanfare of sporadic rifle fire, a show of strength from respective combatants. The streets of the village were otherwise eerily silent. Between the rifle fire, the sound of the cicada beetles could be heard, resuming their chatter after the rude interruptions. It was a hot, dusty night and the full combat uniform was making the men irritable. Having taken up positions, relieving their outgoing colleagues, they settled in for the night, taking turns at being on watch. Other than a few shots from the hidden snipers which went wide, there was little enemy activity. Once the morning chorus began and the cocks started crowing, the situation changed. Alf was in a small party separate from the main body of men. There was a sudden shift in the position of the troops placed towards the centre of the village. Alf was not party to this movement and, because they had been separated, received no instructions relating to it. Some sort of strategic offensive was under way. The sergeant in charge of Alf's party asked the men to cover the advance of the troops, but not to participate further.

Alf and his mates peered at the action which was backlit by a low sun, making it difficult to be sure about what was going on, although it seemed that his colleagues in the village centre were advancing on a sniper position. Alf and his party briefly fired covering shots, but the soldiers quickly reached their target.

Between short bursts of rifle fire, Alf could clearly hear the animated and unmistakable voice of Ewan, then some mumbled shouting as they entered a building. A couple of muffled pistol shots rang out, followed by a short moment of quiet before Ewan reappeared, dragging what appeared to be a bloodied and incapacitated Greek Cypriot youth into the yard in front of the building. Ewan and three other men then proceeded to give the boy a brutal kicking, blow after blow making contact with head, shoulders, ribcage, groin and legs. After thirty seconds, the youth lay motionless. The men withdrew to their original position and the village went quiet.

The chaos that followed acted as a counterpoint to this brief tranquillity. The Greek Cypriots suddenly retaliated with any available weapon: rocks, rifle- and pistol-fire rained down on the British positions. The Turkish Cypriots took the opportunity to fire on their adversaries. Alf and his colleagues were pinned down by fire from both sides for the following hour. Frantic messages and shouted commands oscillated between positions as agitated officers tried to bring the situation under control. It was not until several hours later, when reinforcements arrived, that the British were able to get control of the situation.

No injuries were sustained by Alf's colleagues, despite the ferocity of the villagers' attack after the beating of the youth, save for one NCO's impalement on a rusty nail during a hasty repositioning under enemy fire. The journey back to camp was less than enjoyable since news of the event had spread from village to village and the convoy attracted a noisy and deadly volley of shots as it passed each cluster of buildings, resulting in the British returning fire from machine gun turrets within the convoy.

Steve Lockett, another billet colleague of Alf's, received a bullet to the arm whilst lying on the sandbags in the back of Alf's truck; the bullet having ripped though the canvas cover beneath which they were all crouched.

On their return to camp, Ewan and his two accomplices were quickly placed on a charge. Some of the other men clearly knew something was going on; they smirked and swaggered as they carried out their duties, and were clearly pleased by what had happened. The anger within the officer ranks, however, demonstrated that what had happened had not been officially sanctioned and that they were shocked by the event and its consequences.

Tension persisted for the remainder of the summer and into autumn. In an attempt to understand the state of affairs, Alf tried to get information from whomever he could. He asked those of his colleagues he thought were approachable what they made of the events that morning at Paramyrsina. He kept a keen ear out for any gossip around the camp. Tempers, emotions and hormones were at boiling point. Alf guessed the prostitutes of Varosha would be facing lean times—the energies of the men were instead being channelled into preparations for an escalating conflict.

He visited the camp library in an attempt to read up on the political situation in the British newspapers and to try and piece together the jigsaw.

Miraculously, Ewan had escaped any subordination charges and was released from detention several days after the event. Among Alf's colleagues there was a perceptible confidence in the rightness of Ewan's actions. A recovering Steve Lockett was hostile to Ewan, who he saw as culpable in his injury. Alf found himself drawn to Lockett during this time, for despite this simmering resentment, he was good company, and someone who also sought to understand what was happening.

The answers, when they came, were from an unexpected and not entirely comfortable source. Alf was reading through a piece about the Macmillan government's handling of the Cyprus situation in the *Telegraph*, which was already two weeks old, when Captain Jarvis appeared at the door of the library. After a brief nod between the two men, and an uneasy silence for a few moments, Jarvis opened with an enquiry about what Alf was reading.

Alf had not given a great deal of thought about Jarvis and the events back in May in the married quarters, thinking it best to let sleeping dogs lie. Jarvis, perhaps more confident in his situation and bolstered by rank and marriage, was clearly not phased by this encounter. Alf had no interest in resurrecting either the memories or the actions of the past, and acted as normally as one could when being addressed by an officer.

'It's an article in the *Telegraph* about the decisions the Macmillan government have been making about Cyprus. I hadn't realised there were so many things happening and so many different governments exerting their muscle. The Yanks seem to be deep in on it, even though you don't see them on the ground.'

'That's right. I think they are pulling strings within the UN. The role of Mac and the Turks and Greeks, whilst completely relevant, is being framed by what the Americans are seeking to do. That has as much to do with Russia and Cyprus's strategic position at this end of the Med as it has to do with what is going on here right now. Are you seeking anything in particular?'

'Yes, I was trying to make sense of what happened at Paramyrsina and why Corporal Mathieson did what he did, and why he suffered no consequences.'

'Ah,' said Jarvis, who suddenly found himself engaged in a dialogue which he wished for no part of. His body language changed as Alf continued.

'A lot of the ranks and NCOs know what happened, but nobody's coming out and explaining it to us who aren't in the know.'

Jarvis wondered if Alf was an outsider, if so, he was less likely to be a suspect for his investigations. Or was this a clever ruse?

'I can't help you, I'm afraid. I would take it easy if I were you. Don't ask too many questions.'

Alf nodded his thanks to Jarvis, who smiled a curt, clipped smile and proceeded to another section of the library, noting Alf's comment that some colleagues knew something. Alf took his advice. He turned to the rear pages of the paper and escaped into the sport. He read about a local derby between Sheffield United and Rotherham. At least with soccer you couldn't fabricate the reporting.

As tensions persisted it became less clear who was fighting whom than it had been for some time. The political machinations in London, Athens, Ankara and Washington DC had, above all, proposed the retention of the Sovereign Bases and British military presence in an otherwise self-determining entity. But now there were real and bloody conflicts between Greek and Turkish Cypriot communities, and intra-communal violence between different factions among both communities.

Chapter Seventeen
The Taxi Journey

The military health clinic was an angular, official-looking building constructed of corrugated iron around a courtyard, within which grew a majestic jacaranda tree, its lilac floral display contrasting with the dull metallic cladding of the building, the dullness was flattened further by the hues of the shrouded sky. Like the NAAFI elsewhere on the base, the clinic was a focal point for squaddies and camp families. In a gloomy, echoing hall inside the clinic, empty save for a line of chairs, sat a male orderly behind a desk.

Today, the Blidworths' baby girl required her second set of childhood vaccinations, having received her first prior to departing her homeland. The appointment passed unremarkably, the child accepting the treatment with only a few tears and some little commotion.

The family took a taxi from the stand on the roadside, where a group of middle-aged Greek Cypriot taxi drivers were smoking, legs straddling the backs of their wicker chairs, talking, arguing light-heartedly, and playing tavli in pairs. They would wait in vain for more business now that the troops had been confined to barracks. Nobody had told them. But this was their livelihood, their families depended on the income, so they would wait and hope.

Having been breastfed before leaving the clinic, the child fell asleep before they had even taken the taxi back to their hotel in the town, their temporary residence for the last few days since their arrival from England.

The taxi headed across the windswept landscape, a mixture of dark-green orange groves and stubbly fields of closely-shaven pale straw that occupied the flat earth between the contoured rocky outcrops, little good as commercial land, but a haven for wild flowers, birds, wild thyme, cactus, snakes and lizards.

After a mile, the car passed the military post office, another corrugated building with a sloping roof, its design devoid of character but familiar to all who had served in the forces in India, Libya, Malta, and Aden. It was simply the portal for communication with friends and family elsewhere. Beyond the post office was a military vehicle compound, surrounded by a high wire fence topped by coils of barbed wire. It was several times larger than it had been a few months ago; the new space was occupied by orderly rows of Nissen huts and a concrete water tower. Amongst the huts were parked dozens of military vehicles, Land Rovers, armoured personnel carriers, gun carriers, and military ambulances in their sand and olive camouflage. This was the vehicle depot overflow area for all the extra vehicles that were required at times surging hostility. It was about half full; a barometer of tensions in this colonial outpost.

Further towards the city, the suburbs had begun to spread along the highway. Isolated stands of concrete and breeze block constructions stood with their rusting reinforcement ironwork poking from their corners like antennae. Their flat roofs had been utilised as living spaces. Some of the buildings were painted, usually in blues and brilliant whites, some were just plain concrete or grey blocks. The fields adjacent to houses were being invaded by newer ranks of the same one- and two-story concrete buildings at varying stages of construction.

Chapter Eighteen
Takis and Costas Charalambou

Days of anarchy in Famagusta forced Alf and his colleagues to discharge their peacekeeping role to the best of their abilities. There were frequent skirmishes, particularly near the boulevard linking the Old City to Varosha. It was to this location, one cloudy and windy day in autumn, that Alf and his colleagues were again posted. Their tasks were to man the barricades and search vehicles, go on anti-sniper duty, or man the sentry positions. Alf was posted to a sandbagged sentry position closer to the city walls than previously, just outside the range of the Turkish Cypriots' rifles, but nonetheless exposed.

Around the trio was a scattering of buildings, displaying bullet-marked walls and mortar damage on the walls facing the Old City. Bizarrely, the commercial proceedings that went on in them continued mostly unfazed by events, unless it was clear there was going to be trouble, because on most days there was no danger whatsoever in this area. Buses made their way along predestined routes, shoppers returned from the market carrying their loads in woven baskets, large candy-striped sacks, bicycles or on the backs of donkeys. The businesses plied their trades: shipping agents, insurance, domestic electrical, ships' chandlers and so on. The cafés served their customers. The hospital, always a busy hub, continued to function. Today the streets were, whilst not deserted, very quiet, devoid of pedestrians. If you needed to pass along the boulevard on days like this, you made sure you could make a quick exit when needed. The alternative routes were equally dependent on passage alongside or near to the city walls, and thus also risked drawing the fire of angry and vengeful snipers. A long detour was the only safer alternative, so most people got on with it and dodged the occasional bullet.

* * *

Takis and his younger brother Costas were pinned down by the wall of the hospital generator block, close to the perimeter of the civilian hospital. They had been separated from their four colleagues. Apart from the boatyard to their left, which was bounded by a high perimeter fence, there was little cover from the sniper fire coming from the Old City walls. Every attempt they made to move came with the percussive accompaniment of rifle fire; they needed to move as soon as they could, but there were half a dozen snipers on that wall who were firing simultaneously from several angles. It was a hopeless situation to be in. But if one of them was able to slope away, drawing fire from several snipers, the second man setting off might just succeed.

It had all started as a particularly hot-headed venture earlier in the day. Incensed by the massacre of so many innocent Greek Cypriots at a Turkish Cypriot village outside Famagusta the previous week, the group of eight men in the EOKA brigade had taken instructions to agitate and create mayhem in the inter-communal locality close to the Old City. It was familiar ground to them since there was an assumption that this was the ideal venue for theatrical displays of military strength.

Whilst the British forces were legitimate targets for EOKA, the British seemed happy to let Turkish Cypriot and Greek Cypriot take it out on each other without the British joining in. From time to time, the Greek Cypriots had targeted the British Army and they would respond, otherwise it was Greek and Turkish Cypriots against one another. Almost never was it Turkish Cypriot on British.

Takis had been trained in the hills of Troodos, an EOKA stronghold. He was well practised in the kind of guerilla tactics used by EOKA. It was only recently that he had been sent to the southeast of the island to support the current strategy of passive resistance rather than open hostility and combat. He was always wary of such shifts in tactics. He fully expected a return to the old, more familiar ways. But for now he was pinned down with his brother, diverted from passive resistance because of a daft order from their commander, who had been drunk and almost incoherent at the time, to avenge the murder of the men in the massacre. He and five others, including the younger brother he would die to protect (although he believed his father, Stavros, would kill him a second time if he even thought about dying), were to try and take a Turkish life. Or two. Or more.

Under a leaden sky which signalled the onset of cool, wet autumn days, Takis and Costas were trapped behind the generator block drawing fire from several positions. They were certain the snipers were using bolt action rifles and were re-loading between shots. The armaments available to the Turks were fairly rudimentary, some dating back to the First World War, but these guys seemed to be using more modern weapons with good accuracy and range.

Takis counted the intervals:

'Sixteen seconds from the left position before a second shot from the same. Eleven seconds between shots from the centre left, less from the positions on the centre right and far right. If we run towards the trees and the road, the building will shade us from the firing on the right and centre right.'

Costas responded with his assessment, 'So if we fan away in this direction,' he waved his hand toward the road, 'on the count of three after the centre left guy has fired his shot, we should manage to draw fire in two directions and increase our chances of escaping unhurt.'

They agreed this was the appropriate action to take, an act of self-preservation in the wake of executing an order from a drunken fool; but they had known better than to challenge the order; a bullet to the head, or perhaps a beating at night down a dark alley would have been the result of that. And their assailants would have been those they believed to be their comrades in arms. Loyalty was paramount. Replacements were cheap.

* * *

Mehmet took aim at the position where he believed two Greek Cypriot fighters were hiding. He pressed the trigger and the shot produced its acoustic signature. In the intervening second and a half before the target gave off a puff of white dust, he was able to pull back his gun from the edge of the turret so that his location couldn't be determined. He moved position several metres further to the left to get a better shot. He took aim at the same position and fired the .303 bolt action rifle again. Again, a puff of dust. Just as he was about to re-load, he noticed the men running off in different directions.

Chapter Nineteen
Sentry Duty

Alf had been on duty for several hours. At present he was the sole sentry—one of his mates had gone for a piss behind a nearby wall, the other had been called to support another position. Sniper fire had been sporadically going on all morning. As the low clouds scoured the sky, a group of two or maybe three Greek Cypriot men could be seen shifting from building to building in order to gain a better position beneath the snipers.

The hospital site was adjacent to the focus of activity. Patients were moved to positions of safety within the building on days like this. Occasionally, innocent patients would suffer bullet wounds or be cut by shards of shattering window glass in the crossfire. But today there had been adequate warning and all patients and staff had moved to safety.

* * *

At the appointed time, the two brothers embraced each other and made a run for it. Costas's gun kept banging against his thigh as he ran, crouched down, away from their last place of cover. Because he had been unable to gain a good spot from which to fire, his ammunition belt was nearly full, so this was a further burden to his progress. The brothers' strategy did not quite go the way they had anticipated. Spurred on by the sudden activity, the snipers started to fire with remarkable accuracy, many different bullets emanating from slightly different positions sought the brothers. By far the larger volume of fire was directed toward Costas, but his nimble crouched weaving helped him to avoid the fire he was drawing. He noticed some of the shots tracing a route to the right of a British sentry post manned by a single soldier. He surmised that his brother was drawing that fire and that Takis would need to take a risk and run directly toward the British sentry. Costas corrected his trajectory, continuing his random pattern of zigzags but making progress across the footpath, past the storm drain, and onto the road.

* * *

Alf watched as the solitary Greek gunman ran across the main road, crouching as he ran with what appeared to be a rifle carried low in both hands, the ammunition belt banging on his thighs as he ran. The man wasn't concerned by the closeness of an armed British position.

A second man appeared and took a different track. Alf's attention was drawn to the ammunition belt the man wore. His route was bringing him closer to Alf's sentry position and he was drawing fire from the Turkish Cypriot positions as he made progress. Alf thought this move wasn't quite natural, and began to believe this man's intention was to draw Turkish Cypriot fire towards the British—this had happened previously when British positions were inconveniently located. He was in the way of today's strategy, so the Greek Cypriots were drawing the Turk's fire towards his sentry post to make holding his position untenable. The stock response drummed into the sentry guards was to respond with non-targeted fire towards, but not at, fighters to deter them from pursuing this strategy. It was, in effect, a tripartite battle of wills.

Alf, reluctant in any circumstance to draw arms against another human being, began to fire across the path of the running man. He was flustered by the sudden escalation of events and shouted for his mate to join him quick, whether or not he pissed his trousers. There wasn't any response, so he just kept firing to deter further gunfire. A couple of sniper bullets found the sandbags of the sentry post, which rocked Alf since he understood the position to be out-of-range of Turkish guns. He continued to fire, alternating first across the now deserted road, then toward the position high on the city walls from where he understood the fire to be coming.

The elevation in conflict drew the attention of the other British position some hundred yards away, and frantic shouting could be heard from that position requesting backup from further along the line. Alf was pinned down and alone, shouting desperately for his colleague to return and support him. Then, as he continued firing, it occurred to him that his mate had been killed, injured or abducted, and wasn't going to return to support him. Alf's stress levels were now sky high, and as the adrenaline pushed fear through him and the firing/reloading cycle continued, it dawned on Alf that this might be a moment of real danger. Alf, now panicking and convinced his mate had been taken in some way, sought to defend himself. A warning shot immediately in front of the running man failed to stem his progress, a sniper shot rang out as it glanced off a wooden post only a few feet from Alf. The man running forward looking directly into Alf's eyes. Alf took aim at the legs of the man, whom he was now convinced was out to get him, and fired a shot intended to bring him down. The man stumbled in the middle of the road and fell forward, twisting his foot beneath himself and landing motionless in a heap. His shoe had come off and landed some feet away.

* * *

Takis was unaware of the expression of terror in the sentry's eyes, the sight of the rifle barrel-end pointing directly at him, the muffled

ROADS TO VAROSHA

shouts above the sniper fire to halt, the screamed orders coming from the shocked sentry. And then there were shots.

He felt the pain first. It only slowly took the breath from his lungs and interrupted his forward progress. His brain was still intent on reaching the safety of the park. His body capitulated. The second bullet had penetrated his thigh and brought him to a halt; in the process he twisted his foot under his body. Takis Xenis Charalambou wasn't aware of much else. Except the pain in his chest and thigh. And his need for his brother.

His last conscious thought was of pain.

Chapter Twenty
Blood. Orange.

The sniper fire abated. Alf, stunned and in shock, retreated behind the sandbags and slumped to the floor. The body on the road was lifeless. Alf's mate Bob, appearing from behind the post, returned to the position and shouted for back-up, pushing Alf to one side so that he was behind the wall of bags and explaining to him how sniper fire had pinned him down behind the wall where he had gone for entirely innocent purposes. Bob surveyed the area of the now subdued fighting in case of reprisals. He was more battle-hardened than Alf and he had an air of detachment from the events that had preceded his reappearance. He worked steadily to consolidate their position, keeping a careful watch for movement and shouting the odd command down the line to the next post. Alf, drained of energy and purpose, sat crumpled, silent on the dusty ground of the sentry-post.

* * *

Mehmet watched the scene below him while he was reloading. He had been astonished to see that man tumble forward into a heap on the road. He thought he had heard a couple of shots ring around the natural amphitheatre created between the city walls and the shabby buildings some hundred metres away, but the echo had made it difficult to work out from where the noise had originated. He took a quick look to his left and right. He was expecting to see a dance of celebration from one of the four other men placed on top of the walls with the same task. But there was no sign of triumph. None of the men thought they had fired the shot that brought him down.

Shouts seemed to be coming from the British positions, way over near the park. There was a flurry of action on the ground around a sentry post which, since he and his team had acquired a cache of British rifles, was now in range. He and his men were Turkish Cypriot; they had no reason in today's conflict to fire at the British. The British were legitimate targets, under different circumstances, yesterday or tomorrow, Tuesday or Sunday, but not today.

For many years the British had tacitly been benevolent supporters of Turkish Cypriots, especially in their fight against EOKA. He and his colleagues knew that their fellow Turks were loyal and hard-working men who did the work required of them. Most of the police force under the British officers were Turkish. Generations of Turkish Cypriot men had joined the police, fathers and sons following each other into the profession. They had been targeted by the Greeks. Now Turkish Cypriots were targeting each other for unpatriotic acts, acts against Taksim. How strange the world had become. Was it God's will that this should happen?

He shouted for his compatriots to pull back and disperse from their positions on the wall into the narrow streets of the Old City, thinking that there would be little to be gained by hanging around and being implicated in events. Better to melt into the business of the compact Turkish community on this side of the walls. He would send a scout out to see how events were unfolding later. The weapons would be returned to the makeshift armoury down one of the souk-like side streets close to the ruined Crusader-era church. In fact their arms cache was in one of the crypts.

* * *

Within minutes armoured back-up had made its way to the sentry post and Alf was transferred to a safe position. He and his mate Bob had been relieved by other sentries. The body in the road was guarded and covered by an olive-green blanket. Several troops were detailed to clear the area of other Greek fighters, including the dead man's compatriot, who they cornered and arrested. Neither side sustained further losses, but the dead man's comrade, who was called Costas, was treated roughly by the jittery troops. Several soldiers were dispatched to place some heavy fire-power toward the sniper positions high on the city walls; an army helicopter whined close by some minutes later to fire on the placements. The area fell silent. But throughout this incident the traffic continued to flow along the boulevard, through the barricades, and on past the blanket on the road.

* * *

'Sir, there's been a shooting in Famagusta, a soldier shot a Greek Cypriot.' Lieutenant Tony Surridge was duty military police officer on the afternoon his second lieutenant shouted across the barrack room from where he was holding the bakelite earpiece. 'They need you to go to investigate, sir.' Tony propelled himself back from the desk, his chair rolling back across the concrete floor on five dusty castors. The castors complained noisily like a knife scraped down a pane of glass, making all the staff within earshot cringe. It was the tenth instance today he had been reminded to oil the bloody things. Tony tasked the nearest private to do so and the lad scampered off to a storeroom in search of the oil can.

He drew himself out of the chair and launched his heavy frame towards the other side of the office to answer the phone. Incidents like this were an increasingly frequent occurrence in recent days, signalling the tensions the men were facing. He prepared to take initial details of who was reporting and the general turn of events. He asked the soldier's name, but it was not familiar to him.

'Where is the soldier at present?'

'Where's the body?'

'Right. Leave the body until I can inspect. Divert traffic until we can remove it. Keep the private at the sentry post. How many men were on duty at the post when the incident took place?'

'Yes. I'll be there in fifteen minutes if I can find transport'

Lieutenant Surridge placed the handset into its cradle and stared at the cluttered surface of the desk. What pressures might the soldier have been under, he wondered? Then, less charitably but nonetheless objectively, what if this is part of the pattern of reprisals on Greek Cypriots? This needed to be investigated with an open mind in case it was not self-defence. He wouldn't know until he'd gathered the facts. Surridge decided immediately to call the SIB officer to put him in the picture. He'd not met the man, but could tell he was efficient and incisive by the exchanges they'd already had.

Surridge managed to commandeer Redcap transport to ferry him to the site of the incident. Roadblocks had been set up, causing severe tailbacks and simmering resentment, not least among the Greek Cypriot lorry drivers trying to reach the port. He reckoned the drivers would already know what had happened. An atmosphere of frayed tempers, shouted insults and accusations, gestures and gesticulations, and general ill-feeling toward the British troops was developing. Militarily the lid was on this simmering pot, the fracas that precipitated events had been controlled. The situation was now largely one of civilian and military policing and traffic management.

On arrival, Surridge approached the body lying on the bloodstained road, raised the blanket and inspected the injuries. It appeared that there were only two entry wounds, one to the leg and the other to the lower trunk. It would have been the latter that killed the man and created the pool of blood, since the main artery appeared to have been penetrated. Dried, darkened blood traced a track over the road from the body.

There was little else to note. The man apparently had not been carrying a gun, but had a half depleted stock of 9mm ammunition around his waist. It suggested the man was previously carrying a gun, but had jettisoned it. He sent officers to try and recover the missing weapon. They spread out across the road in the direction of the hospital perimeter wall.

Surridge paced the few yards to the sentry post and inspected the two or three bullet holes and chunks taken out of the woodwork. He took out a penknife and dug a bullet from its point of penetration in a sandbag. It wasn't 9mm. It had been fired, he thought, from a .303 rifle. He guessed this was sniper fire from the Turkish position. It was strange that the Turkish were using 303s; perhaps they were spoils of a previous encounter. It did, however, explain how the firing had reached what was understood to be a safe position. He'd need to check the facts to determine whether his hypothesis was accurate. He spoke to the senior officer and advised him of his interim thoughts, suggesting that the sentry position be pulled further back in light of the weapons that the Turkish Cypriots appear to be using.

He returned to the jeep and drove to the fall-back sentry post where Private Holdsworth was sitting, alone and dejected. He had been given a canteen of water, ration biscuits and an orange, but was otherwise looking quite bleak. Focussed on his task, Surridge began to strike up a conversation with the soldier. It was almost definitely the case that because of the circumstances he would be interrogated at least two or three times to see if his story held consistently, so it was important to obtain as much detail as he could.

He approached Alf, who stood and saluted, telling him to be at ease and sit back down.

'Private, we need to investigate the circumstances leading up to this event. Are you aware of the protocol for opening fire?'

'Yes, sir,' said Alf in a voice quietened by shock.

'And you'll know then what sort of questions I'm going to ask you?'

'Sir.'

'Before we get to that, I want to inspect your gun.' The weapon had been taken from the private, but was now retrieved and given to Surridge who identified that there were twelve bullets remaining in the self-loading rifle's cartridge; eight presumably having been fired. The gun was otherwise in very good order, clean and well looked after. He briefly left the sentry post to clarify the log entry, which indicated that Private Holdsworth had been issued with the gun and a full magazine at the start of his duty that day. He returned without saying anything about this to Alf. Instead he asked him to describe in his own words the events leading up to the shooting, preparing to take notes as the soldier spoke.

Alf went through the events in detail, he was clearly shaken and on several occasions retraced his narrative to include something he'd missed. He'd clearly had time to think about what had happened. He was also very structured in his recollection, following without hesitation the steps all soldiers had drummed into them regarding what assessments and actions should be taken in such circumstances, the 'Instructions for Opening Fire'.

'Sir,' began Alf, 'from the start of this skirmish Turkish Cypriot sniper positions on the city walls had been taking sporadic shots, mainly at buildings, as well as at a few Greek gunmen, who had good cover and were moving easily from shelter to shelter beyond the hospital. We could see this as it happened. My colleague and myself believed we were not in any danger. We were under order not to fire unless there was danger to ourselves or colleagues. We weren't being attacked or fired upon at this point. My mate decided he needed to go for a piss, so darted behind the nearest building.

He was gone a very long time. I was getting pretty nervous about being on my own whilst these guys were running around firing at each other. Then there was an increase in the rate of firing from the Turkish side. They appeared to have routed the Greek Cypriots from a hiding position. One Greek man, then the other, began a run across the road, the second man running toward the sentry post. I shouted out for my mate to return, but heard nothing. In my mind I was worrying that he'd been taken out and I was being attacked, so I fired some warning shots. I shouted at the Greek fighter, but my shouts were drowned out by fire from the Turkish side, which was being drawn towards our position because the fighter was running towards us.'

Alf stopped and looked around him at nothing in particular, apparently helpless, drained of energy. He gathered himself for the next instalment.

'Then I shouted a warning because I reckoned the guy was going to fire at me. The Turkish bullets were now hitting our position.'

Sturridge had been keen to ask for clarification at different stages of this narrative, but held back, allowing Alf to order his thoughts and recount the episode in his own way. There was a long silence.

'By now I was convinced my mate had been shot and I was under attack myself. I took aim as the fighter ran towards me; I was under threat. At that time I fired whilst shouting out at the top of my voice. I didn't even know I was shouting, or what. I meant to fire one bullet to bring him down, but my finger remained on the trigger and squeezed a second bullet out. He fell. That's all.'

After perhaps a thirty-second silence, Surridge started to seek clarification.

'Your mate wasn't hurt, though you thought he was. When did he reappear and where had he been?'

'After the shooting. In the moments of quiet afterwards. He'd gone for a piss, but had been pinned behind the wall by sniper fire.'

'You seem to have assessed the situation. Did you think there were other options to opening fire?'

'Yes, if my mate had been there it would have turned out differently because we could have decided together whether we were in danger.'

'Did you consider firing back at the Turkish sniper position? Would that have led to a different outcome?'

'I didn't fire toward the top of the wall, but I did fire some warning shots. The snipers move position all the time. I didn't know where they were firing from. I was alarmed at drawing fire from them at all because we're usually out of their range here. You will, probably, have been on top of that wall. It's very easy to move along without any danger. The bloody thing's been there for hundreds of years. It's a sound defensive position.'

Surridge thought Alf had made a valid point.

'So you thought you were in danger and you fired an aimed shot?'

'Yes, sir, two shots.'

'Would you have fired any more than two?'

'No, sir, why would I do that?'

'Maybe you were so deep into things that you just kept squeezing the trigger?'

'No, sir. I didn't want to kill anyone. When I was called up I thought it would help me to get a trade. I wanted to be a radio operator. Killing people wasn't an ambition of mine. I know you end up doing that when it's necessary, but I'm not one of the numbheads that enjoys the feeling. If you forgive me for saying, sir.'

'I'm here to conduct an investigation. I need the facts, motives, circumstances.'

'Sir, I want to know why I'm being interrogated. I haven't done anything wrong. I reacted by the book.'

'I need to find out certain things. That's what I'm here to do.

When things are calmer we can work out if you've done anything wrong.'

'Sir,' said Alf resignedly.

'One last query: when you thought the Greek fighter was going to fire on you, could you see his weapon? What type was it? Rifle? Pistol? Was he aiming directly at you?'

Alf was silent as he thought specifically about each point. The traffic commotion outside the sentry post encroached on the solemness of the interrogation. He was briefly distracted by the noises before answering.

'I saw his ammo belt, he was moving swiftly towards the sentry post. I don't think I recall seeing the gun let alone identifying it.'

'Do you think it possible he may not have been carrying a gun when he ran towards you?'

'I don't know. I thought he was carrying one. I can't think clearly enough about that. Bullets were hitting the sentry post. I was in a panic. Are you suggesting he wasn't carrying one?'

Surridge left the question unanswered, thanked Holdsworth for his detailed recollection and left to go and interview Alf's mate. He would need to discuss everything with Captain Jarvis. Lieutenant Surridge instructed that Alf be taken back to the barrack room and be held until someone could interrogate him further. He privately thought that Alf may be masking some darker intention aligned with the paramilitary organisations.

Two military policemen escorted Holdsworth to the camp.

* * *

'Okay, Barbara, we're coming up to the tricky spot now. Is there anything we've got with us to distract Mikey?'

'I can give him an Opal Fruit and talk about oranges.'

Under the mottled grey sheet of fast-moving low cloud an easterly wind cut through the gap between the Old City wall and a raised embankment, behind which laid the municipal gardens. Only a few hundred yards away were the docks, from which direction the onshore wind was being channelled.

Barbara rearranged the sleeping baby girl resting on her lap so that she could reach the handbag in the foot well. She took out several items—handkerchief, lipstick, make-up compact, bottle of Milton (for there was an unspoken rule that at all times in a foreign country a bottle of Milton had to be to hand) before locating the cylinder of colourful confectionery. Tearing off the waxy wrapper she picked out the first sweet—strawberry—and was about to unwrap it when she spotted the second in the stack was orange. Saving the strawberry for herself, she unwrapped the orange sweet and gave it to the child. In a quiet aside to her husband she said triumphantly, 'I was hoping it was going to be an orange sweet. It will give me a lead into the distraction conversation.'

Her husband gave the shallow, silent, comprehending nod of a person preoccupied. Shortly before the roundabout were rows of shops, workshops and restaurants on the roadside. The road was frequently used by the camp residents and soldiers, so there were sign-written translations above those businesses that were restaurants: 'souvlaki', 'shish kebab', 'doner', 'Lamp chop [sic]', fish and chips, meze. The street divided into two distinct linear national and cultural entities. One side of the street had 'shish kebap [sic]' and 'doner kebap [sic]' and on the other were meze and souvlaki. As if to underline the cultural divide, Coca-Cola and Keo beer was marketed on the Greek side, Bel Kola on the Turkish. For decades, to a greater or lesser extent, the communities had coexisted in this way. Now Greek and Turkish Cypriots railed against each other and against the oppressive colonial administration. Each would boycott the other's products, hence the stark choices faced by customers on the left or the right of the street.

The silver Mercedes approached the first roundabout, it was

like the stage of a circus with its spectacular backdrop of the imposing honey-coloured, rough-hewn stone walls of the Old City. The taxi driver turned off the Greek music as if to presage the possible tensions they were about to meet. In broken and heavily accented English, he spoke to Barbara's husband, Tom, his anxiety clear on his moustachioed, walnut-tanned face, 'Many military, too much, this is dangerous area; today is not a good day for taking children here.'

Tom, in the passenger seat, his apprehension multiplying with every furlong, acknowledged the comment with another silent nod. It was the only route into that part of the town from the health clinic. He silently resented his wife's insistence on taking this journey because he knew about the increasing military tensions, and had heard about the fighting near the boulevard towards which they were inescapably headed. He also knew there was no reasonable defence against his wife's protectiveness towards her second-born. After all, it wasn't her who'd agreed to accept the foreign posting so few weeks after the child's birth. Now he would reap the consequences of taking her and her children from her familiar world into this alien land. He knew she would cope by adopting her obsessive-compulsive behaviours that emerged under stressful circumstances.

The taxi negotiated the roundabout, the driver's worry beads, which were hanging from the rear view mirror, described an arc in the cool air as they turned. The city walls loomed as the road passed close by. They passed a turn-off where a military road block—a chicane of barbed wire mounted on a cross frame of white-painted wood bookended by red-and-white horizontal striped, concrete-filled barrels, was manned by a pair of neatly presented riflemen in green mufti, weapons drawn. A white sentry box was the only respite from their lonely duty.

The car and its occupants approached the second roundabout,

the crossroads between the new part of town—a Greek metropolitan melding of historical stone structures and post-war modernist concrete with aspirations to be a popular holiday destination— and the Old City, inside the walls of which little had changed for centuries; the lives of its occupants, their buildings and trades, were all suggestive of times past. They seemed unable to adapt to the modernisation outside their walls. The stark contrast was a marker of the relative inequality and diverging economic status of Greek and Turkish Cypriot.

The car took the third exit. The boy stared out beyond the familiar family unit at every passing building, tree, wall, person, donkey, bicycle. He had a fascination for things. In the blink of an eye, as the vehicle passed by, each image would be swiftly replaced by another. His thought processes were seemingly shallow and transient, but they were creating fresh synaptic connections that would enable recall of images, sounds, noises, moods and flavours.

Barbara, seeking to engage the boy, said, 'Mikey, do you want an Opal Fruit? It's an orange one, and look, we're just passing the municipal garden where soon we will go to the Orange Festival. Did you see that postcard of the festival with all sorts of shapes and designs made with oranges: dolphins, carriages, birds, aeroplanes and ships. It will be so spectacular to see. And there is free orange juice for everybody. Thousands of people will be there, there will be dancing, music, food, and play. We'll go when the festival opens. There's nothing like it in England.'

Mikey ceased his regard of his passing world, transiently attracted by the prospect of the sweet, and now engaging in animated conversation with his mother about where oranges came from. He unwrapped the sweet; chewing on it, he released the sweet citric flavour, the sensation of bitter, sweet oranges exploding in his mouth, his tongue picking up the sourness, sweetness and pleasure while his mind continued to play with the new concept as the taxi slowed. Oblivious as the boy was to other events, he looked toward the gardens with the fully engaged imagination of his five years, seeking the mirage of bustling municipal gardens full of orange people, orange cars and orange fish, all drinking orange buckets of orange juice, orange sweets cascading from the orange waterfall.

The concentration of military uniforms and vehicles hit its peak along the straight boulevard immediately after the entrance to the gardens; Tom stiffened, the taxi driver shrank back into his leather seat, and Barbara kept up her engagement with the child. Suddenly, the vehicle was flagged to a halt by military police. The occupants were trapped in a queue of lorries, cars, buses and carts. There was no way the child could be distracted for the next few minutes as long as they remained in the queue.

Tom hoped that the car would be diverted to one side of the commotion while the boy continued to look out from the right-hand side of the car where he was sitting. Seconds passed, then minutes. Anxious young British national serviceman peered through the windows at the occupants, weapons primed, inspecting the underside of each vehicle and rifling through the boot. Everyone was shouting, pointing, groups of military men were engaged in conversation, then dispersing, then shouting instructions, the actions of subordinates adapting in response. The car was ushered forward at a snail's pace, the resentful taxi driver following the instructions of the military. There was a sudden diversion of traffic to the left. As the procession continued, Tom realised he could not shield his boy, could not protect him, from the image he was about to see.

Mikey, peering out once again, was excited no longer by oranges, but by the imaginary war he was fighting alongside the soldiers and military policeman. He caught a glimpse of an ambulance, and then of a man, perhaps his father's age, lying on his side in an unexpected pose in the road, a blanket pulled aside whilst a soldier searched the man's pockets. As if somehow contagious, the man lay there with a respectable radius of several feet between him and any of the surrounding commotion. He was wearing a brown jacket and dark trousers, torn at the knees. A hat had been cast free from his young, dark-haired head. A shoe, scuffed by contact with the tarmac, had been thrown clear to one side of him. His body was lifeless, his youthful brown eyes expressionless and staring forward. A gun had been recovered from beneath a tree perhaps fifty feet away and was placed adjacent to the body. A stream of red clotting blood emanated from a wound in his chest and streamed away in two rivulets which followed the camber of the road.

Mikey took it all in, a theatrical set framed by the chrome trim of the rear passenger window. He unconsciously sensed and stored the images, sampled the sounds, the smells. His eyes, wide open hazel orbs and sparkling whites in his young face, bearing none of the stresses shown by the other players whose emotional intelligence was being assaulted by the experience. The boy became silent and withdrawn, no longer chewing on a sweet.

The taxi pressed forward slowly as instructed, then picked up speed as it moved away from the site of the incident. The surrounding city swallowed up the car and its passengers into normal metropolitan life, which continued unabated despite the event. Their destination, the hotel that was temporarily their home, was reached minutes later. The adults were emotionally scarred by their experience.

The taxi driver hurriedly toked on a cigarette even before the fare was paid. He assimilated a different set of thoughts and resentments. This was his home. The troops and his passengers were colonisers. But the man on the ground was one of his kinsmen.

Inside the boy's head the images were being committed to memory like an action onto cellulose film. By now he was walking through the hotel entrance, his left hand held by his dad. Friendly staff tried to distract the boy, having found out what he had experienced. But they had no effect on him. His dad was grim with concern for what his family was experiencing, the effect on his young son.

There were only two words in the boy's mind: 'blood' and 'orange'.

* * *

Mehmet and his men met up in their coffee shop later. Their compatriots in the bar, mostly elderly men with no cause to sleep through the siesta, viewed Mehmet and the others suspiciously as itinerant youth, suspecting they were probably TMT footsoldiers, who were prone to abusing and attacking their own neighbours in support of Partition. As the thick, brown, syrupy coffee was prepared by their colleague, part-time soldier and shop owner Ismael, Mehmet watched the small white cups and the glasses of water being placed on the nickel-topped bar and the syrupy mix being poured into each cup. He was deep in thought. As their section commander, he asked each man for his version of events. He had assessed what had happened, quietly, purposefully adding each new perspective to the information he was assimilating.

'So we were all firing at different intervals, but on the same target. We managed to rout them and a couple made a run for cover. That took one of them across the road and toward the British sentry position. Then he fell to the ground and remained in that position, but none of us fired the shot that felled him. Is that what everyone thinks?'

'So was he shot, and if so, who shot him?' Said Gunar.

'I'd guess it must have been the British. Neither they nor the Greeks were to know that our range of fire off the top of the walls had been suddenly increased by our latest acquisition. Did anyone fire on the British?'

Osman said he'd traced the path of the Greek man and had fired a couple of bullets. He didn't know where they had ended up.

'Was that in the direction and proximity of the British sentry?'

'Yes, I suppose it was.'

Mehmet looked at the floor and returned to his thoughts, whilst the others took their drinks and engaged in several excited and simultaneous dialogues, each man with a view, a conviction deeply held, each trying to vie for the loudest and most extreme slur on the adversaries they had been firing upon.

'I would go down there and cut him open and trail his bowels along the street!'

'I would cut off his head and then kick it into the gutter!'

'I would relieve him of the burden of his festering balls!'

'I would spit on his mother!'

And so on. Each phrase was met by a roar of approval within the group.

By way of an uncanvassed reward, the winner of the competition— Oran, Mehmet's older cousin—was given the task of returning to the top of the wall unarmed and then reporting back to Mehmet on what was happening. He dismissed the other men ordering them back after their siesta had finished; unless there was cause for them to regroup.

He received a quicker than expected response to his enquiry. Oran returned breathless and agitated. He spoke in short bursts between gulps of air. He had not been able to get to the top of the wall. There was a British helicopter hovering around and firing randomly at their former positions. The turrets were, of course, now deserted. The wind from the helicopter rotors was stirring a cloud of dust from the fortified positions and redistributing it willy-nilly under the dark skies.

'The British are firing towards the top of the walls. They would kill me if I went up there. I didn't get closer than the cover provided by the cluster of houses across the road from the wall. I stayed in an alley and watched them.'

Mehmet thought through what might be happening. Did the British shoot a Greek Cypriot fighter? He may or may not have been a threat to them. The British may have thought the Greek Cypriots were firing on British positions because the knucklehead Osman had thought fit to fire so close to the sentry box. That would have heightened their fear and strengthened the conviction that they were being fired upon. They might have decided to attribute the death to Turkish Cypriot sniper fire. The British were now putting on a very public display of retribution, seeking to snuff out reprisals.

But, he thought, there is one less Greek Cypriot fighter than there was this morning.

'OK, Oran, go about your usual business. Melt into the background. Regroup at 16:00.'

Ismael saluted and went through the coffee shop door. Oran drank what remained of Ismael's glass of water. He thought about what his usual business might be. At one time it might have been chasing a mule around in a tight circle in their father's village to draw water from the well. He thought about how the mule would always be blindfolded to avoid it getting completely dizzy. They used his late grandmother's bra as the blindfold. It was a family tradition. They fitted the animal very well. Or he would be in the fields tilling the dry soil, keeping the crops watered, weeding around whatever it was that was being grown—green leaves, aubergines, herbs and spices, perhaps the large irregularly shaped carmine tomatoes their cuisine was reliant on. But what was normal business now? He thought back to his school days. He had only studied at school for a limited time. He started when he was six and had left school by the time he was twelve. They taught him to write and do arithmetic, taught him about the Turkish nation, about religion (but the Imam had taught them more), about right and wrong, and about the troubled country that surrounded him and his family. He had left school to help in the fields. His father was getting older, less able to do the work of a donkey each day; his two older brothers had been killed in the struggles during the 1950s. The only man left in the household was himself. So, at the tender age of twelve, he was the best educated shepherd and farm hand in the village. He had wanted to become an engineer. The proud standing walls of the Famagusta Old City were testament to the engineering skills of those who had lived centuries before, the ruins of Salamis stood as a monument to those engineers who had calculated and drawn two thousand years previously. But his own engineering aspirations were curtailed by the reality of an impoverished farming family.

Several years ago, Oran had become involved with a group of youths in his small village north east of Magosa. They were all at that age where passions ran high, dares got ever more challenging and the young men were naively searching for their personal mission in life. Turkish nationalism was running high; at school they had been taught about the mighty Ottoman empire and how Turkey would one day rediscover its Ottoman spirit and vanquish its enemies. He didn't subscribe to the view because he had always been brought up to think that Turkish Cypriots were not the same as Turkish mainlanders, that they were proudly peaceful and could live in harmony with other people. Indeed, in his village were several Greek boys. They played together, spoke each other's languages, laughed together at the same things, and had the same aspirations.

Then the youth group became more militant. The teenagers more angry, and just a little bit more violent. They were influenced by older men with their own agendas. The men wanted Partition of the island and were organising groups of patriots to achieve this aim. Oran was bewildered by the conflicting emotions of youth, by the desire for peaceful co-existence and simultaneous revenge. Perhaps his colleagues were similarly confused, but they were too proud to acknowledge it to each other. So they evolved into paramilitary thugs, held together by a loyalty to one another that emerges when children grow up together and develop as men together. The creation of TMT was just a convenient conduit, like the irrigation ditches on his father's fields, along which their teenage anger had been channelled.

They were asked to do things that in childhood would have seemed preposterous. If they saw a Turkish man smoking a Greek cigarette they would circle him and give him a kicking whilst shouting at him the error of his ways. If there was a Turkish woman buying Greek washing powder in the village shop they would abuse her and reduce her to tears, and abuse the shop owner for stocking the filthy product. They were not above acts of hooliganism and retribution. If someone stood up to them they would take revenge by following them to their home, then daub pro-partition slogans on the walls of their building. They were thugs, but thugs with purpose. It was lads like themselves who had attacked the Greek men that had been dumped outside the Turkish village, whipping up anti-Greek sentiment among villagers.

Now Oran and his closest friends from that time were part of Mehmet's paramilitary section. They still bullied and harassed innocent peace-loving Turks and their families, they attacked 'legitimate' targets, they beat up vocal non-partitionists. They were loathed and loathsome, but they had a true purpose. Mehmet wasn't an extremist in any way—he and his mates were perhaps more feared and extreme than Mehmet—but they had to admit that while he lacked thuggery, he possessed great leadership skills and was adept at strategic thinking. It wasn't in those terms they thought of him, their education wasn't sufficient to articulate those ideas, but they knew that he led and they followed, he instructed and they obeyed him.

Oran decided his usual business was more of this behaviour, so after siesta he met up with his two mates and they set about searching for more non-partitionists.

Mehmet took himself to his quarters: a bare, spartan room built into the Old City walls, the only furniture being a rustic wooden bed frame with a mattress stuffed with animal hair, a wooden chair with woven reed seat and his own crate of belongings. He had set up a makeshift fireplace in one corner where the smoke was vented out of the space and dissipated above an adjacent yard. The building was part of the old Lusignan fortress which made up the fortifications around the Old City. The walls were feet thick, impenetrable. The military quarters were labyrinthine, so it would be difficult to seek and find any individual. He reflected on his surroundings at length. There was some irony in the fact that Richard the Lionheart, whose emblem was everywhere in the fortifications, had built the fortress during the time of the Crusades, and now it was being used to defend against not only the Greeks but also the British.

He was not a natural military man, but he was fighting a cause, and found he could lead men. Whatever it took to vanquish the enemy was a valid strategy. The Turkish didn't have an army as such, but there was an informal military command over a disparate group of fledgling partition and resistance organisations. There was clearly some superior military organisation orchestrating the partition struggle, whom he believed to be mainland Turks with military backgrounds and strong links to the Turkish Nationalist cause. On the other hand, most of his subordinates and his immediate superiors were local men.

He found himself reflecting on his own family as he stoked the embers and brought the fire back to life with another log. The fire in his parents home was the focus of cooking and eating, the family centre. His brothers and sisters, their own village life, simple, peaceful. He lay on the bed. His specific memories were often prompted by food, none more so than today when he had the urge to eat one of his favourite dishes, fried aubergines, cumin and minced lamb. He had smelt the tell-tale aroma during his walk back to his room and his thoughts had turned to his mother cooking this savoury masterpiece, and his own role in the affair, helping his sisters cook the flat-breads on the inner surface of the clay oven. This led his thoughts beyond the beautiful taste sensations of the dish, of the sweet buttery texture of the bread and onto baklava, his favourite.

He awoke with a start from an impromptu siesta having realised he had dreamt his way through a three-course meal at the family table. It was the sound of a gunshot that had awoken him. He was off his bed and out the door in one motion. He thought to himself that he had now become ravenously hungry and would seek out food. In fact, the gunshot was only a man shooting at a migrating flock of birds, hopeful for a snack. So he tracked down the source of the smell of cooking in the hope that he may purchase or be given some.

At 16:00 the group of men reconvened at their usual meeting place and received their instructions for the evening. The routine of his team's activities had returned to normal following the events earlier in the day. Tomorrow may bring some new excitement, perhaps their target tomorrow would be the British?

Chapter Twenty-One
Interrogation

Alf was transferred the several miles back to camp in an armoured vehicle. Even before the vehicle drew to a halt outside the barrack guardroom, Alf had had to repeatedly describe the events of the shooting to his sergeant major, who had accompanied him. The tone of the interrogation—interrogation was the right word—seemed to be that he had somehow lost leave of his senses and fired at will on the man. Despite protesting that he was in fear of his life, and was defending his position, his story was drilled into with ever more detailed questions. The transfer to the barracks resulted in Alf being placed in a cell, just a precaution, he was told, whilst awaiting a medical officer and military police officer to take a statement. It seemed to Alf, who was still suffering from shock and not quite in the present moment, that he was virtually being accused of murder.

Back at the barrack block, Surridge heard Alf protesting about why he was being treated the way he was, saying he hadn't done anything wrong. He had heard from staff that Private Holdsworth, even under pressure, had not altered his story.

He discussed the case by phone with his SIB counterpart, Peter Jarvis. Jarvis suggested he keep Holdsworth for up to forty-eight hours. He said he'd get some material across to Surridge, lines of questioning. Then, before the forty-eight hours had expired, they'd talk again about the charge options. Jarvis mentioned to Surridge that the turn of events had precipitated the need to question several other men, not directly connected with the incident, later in the week. He'd keep him up to date on how that went.

Jarvis booked an urgent meeting with the CO.

Investigations continued into a second day. Throughout this time, Alf was held in the barrack room cells. He was subjected to several further interrogations, all requiring him to clarify aspects of his behaviour whilst on duty.

Jarvis felt his hand had been forced too early by events. He couldn't be certain that Holdsworth was guilty of any charge, but there was sufficient clarity that the man was unarmed when shot, although Holdsworth himself fired in the belief that the victim was armed, and circumstantial evidence suggested he *had* been armed until shortly beforehand. Nevertheless, Jarvis pulled all his mostly circumstantial evidence on Holdsworth, and went to the CO's office.

'What do we have, Captain?'

'Questioning of Private Holdsworth on a possible charge of insubordination, conduct prejudicial to good order, namely not following the Instructions to Open Fire drill, sir.'

'I see. Has this chap been in trouble before?'

'No, sir, but he has been in my sights for a while. I don't think he is implicated in the Saddleback thing, but he certainly mixes with a few who are. The incident at Paramyrsina involved serviceman Mathieson who is billeted with Holdsworth. I don't think they get on, but there seem to be too many coincidences. I was hoping to pursue the more senior controllers of Mathieson for a while longer. We released him after Paramyrsina to see if he would make contact with other Saddleback colleagues. He has certainly got some allies, senior officers included. I have been researching and building portfolios for each of his contacts. I am not completely finished with my investigations yet, but I'm sure we have five or six who are implicated.'

'Right. Very worrying to know some of my senior men are rotten. How long will you need?'

'Another five days should do it, sir. We can interrogate them after arrest before bringing charges.'

'This Holdsworth man. Is he still on your list? You said he'd been in your sights.'

'No, sir, I'm pretty sure he is not involved. But my hand has been forced, precipitated by his action, right or wrong. Now we have to pounce on the Saddleback men, citing this as a potential incident. Ideally we should charge all the Saddleback men at the same time.'

'Do you want to include Holdsworth? Should he be charged separately, if at all? You know he'll suffer at the hands of Saddleback sympathisers if there's suspicion that he has been implicated in events leading to their arrest.'

'I think we should include him. But if we charge him first the others will be more cautious and I won't have the edge in my investigation over the next five days. Anyway, his arrest links the incident to their other activities. It'll soon come out when I interrogate them whether the two strands are connected. I expect at that time that Holdsworth will be found innocent, that he made a mistake under duress and shot an unarmed Cypriot.'

'What do you want to do with him? Charge, extension of detention, or release?'

'I think we can charge him with insubordination and conduct prejudicial to begin with. If we omit any charge specifically related to Saddleback, then it won't spook the others.'

'What about the others? Do you think you'll have enough to charge them with in five days?'

'I do, but I could do with some more support in the meantime. I think we should charge all of the men—including adding more charges to Holdsworth's original charge—at the same time. If we prepare the charge sheets, you can sign them off, and then we can make our move on Thursday afternoon.'

'Fine. I'll have a word with Lieutenant Surridge. I think we can allocate a couple of men to Surridge. Keep your own cover though. He can do the interrogations under your instructions.'

'Right, sir, thank you. I'll get the police to collect statements from Holdsworth and keep him until Thursday. I have another man in his billet I can utilise to keep an eye out.'

'Good,' said the CO, satisfied with Jarvis's progress. 'I expect to see you on Thursday with the paperwork. I suppose we need to schedule summary hearings. I think if we could avoid the court martial procedure it would be better for the reputation of the camp. Try to couch the terms of any charges in something that doesn't precipitate automatic CM. Don't give anyone a reason to opt for CM.'

'Sir.'

Jarvis left the room and headed back to his office to continue his task. Several minutes after returning, he was informed by Lieutenant Surridge of the names of the officers allocated to him. Jarvis lost no time in setting Surridge and his men interrogation tasks. It was the opportune moment to find out as much as possible about Holdsworth's potential involvement in Saddleback using means he himself hadn't been able to employ.

* * *

Alf had been asked repeatedly about every detail of his actions. He knew the Instructions for Opening Fire drill inside out and was surprised his interrogators were fixated on whether he had followed it to the letter. He was now being asked about other things: his part in the incident at Paramyrsina, the time he and Gatbrook were in the town, about things he wasn't even a part of. They asked for his alibi on each occasion, a witness to his version of events, character witnesses, and who else he would expect to find on a charge.

Alf was no snitch and chose not to name anyone, not even

Mathieson, in response to the last question. He received no personal visitors, apart from Gatbrook, who informed him he had also been questioned about his and Alf's movements on the day they went into town, and that the police had searched Alf's locker. Alf was perplexed by the scope of the investigation against him.

Alf was charged and interred pending a hearing. He sought the friendship of Gatbrook during this trying time, but Gatbrook now chose not to visit him. Instead, Steve Lockett, another billet-mate, came to see him. Lockett was keen to proffer empathetic noises. Alf mentioned nothing beyond his own recollections. Lockett was also a Yorkshireman, so the rapport Alf felt they had previously built created an easy, comfortable atmosphere between them.

On the following Thursday, shortly after lunch, there was a flurry of Military Police activity in the camp and married quarters. A large number of policemen armed with charge sheets were dispatched to take seven people into custody. Ewan Mathieson, a lance corporal, then two corporals, a captain and a sergeant were all picked up. All were held separately so as to be unable to communicate.

Alf was mostly unaware of these goings-on, except for what had happened in his own billet. His extended charge sheet was presented to him by the MP officer who had interrogated him most frequently. It cited several charges, insubordination, conduct prejudicial to good order (which he'd already been charged with), disobedience, aiding and abetting, encouraging or assisting others, conspiring to possess inflammatory materials and the means of their production; it didn't elaborate whom his fellow conspirators were. He had to sign a form to say he'd received his new charge sheet, the summary of charges, the list of written evidence and a copy of his disciplinary record to date, which was blank, because he had no previous offences. The officer asked him to nominate a representative, an assisting officer, to which Alf had responded by nominating Captain Jarvis.

Alf, with only the charge sheet to refer to, was perplexed about the additional charges. He recognised the link between the content of the interrogation and the charges, but he couldn't protest his innocence enough. He was informed that the summary hearing was set for Saturday morning. In the meantime, he would just have to sit it out in his cell. He asked for a pen and paper so he could build a defence for when Jarvis came to see him.

Later on Thursday he was told that Captain Jarvis had declined his request to be his assisting officer. He felt he had been spurned by the one person in the camp who had the greatest insight into him. Then again, he thought Jarvis was probably avoiding being seen to have too much of a connection with him. He had to choose another nominee, selecting Sergeant Davis, his billet officer, thinking that he would believe in his innocence. Davis came almost immediately, he had been contacted and was only too happy to be Alf's representative. The two of them set about preparing themselves for Saturday's case. Davis was good at explaining the ins and outs of a hearing because he frequently acted as nominee when some of the younger lads were on charges of asleep on duty, drunkenness, wilful damage—the sorts of thing young men get up to when their self discipline or esteem slips. Davis knew the process. He also knew more about the other people arrested, which brought a new dimension to Alf's isolated perspective on his arrest.

On Saturday, Alf's case was heard in the CO's office. The CO and another senior officer were on the panel. Alf was marched into the office by the RSM, he saluted, gave his name, rank and number. His representative was beside him; opposite were those there to judge him. As statements were already made and witness statements had been collected, the whole business was to him one of unfathomable process, reference to documents, and with few direct questions. There was hardly any need for Alf to speak, other than to reply when asked whether he was guilty or not guilty. The judiciaries mumbled to each other, presumably reaching some conclusion about the preceding statement. Only on three occasions was Alf asked to clarify something. He was marched out to an anteroom whilst those assembled reached their conclusion. Then he was marched back into the hearing to be given their decision.

'On the charge of insubordination: charge not proved; conduct prejudicial to good order, namely not following the instructions to open fire drill: charge proved, although the mitigating circumstances of your having been deserted by your fellow soldier on his call of nature at a critical moment led us to be lenient. On the charge of disobedience: charge not proved; aiding and abetting: charge not proved; encouraging or assisting others: charge not proved; conspiring to possess inflammatory materials, etc.: charge not proved.'

The CO shuffled his papers into a less disordered pile whilst his fellow officer read out the punishment. 'You are required to carry out additional drill and extra work as specified by your mess sergeant for a period of fourteen days, and will forfeit fourteen days' pay.' An orderly informed Alf that he had the right of appeal and that it should be lodged within seven days. He also said that if he was charged with other offences in the following three months the original charges would also be re-heard. Alf was somewhat relieved to get away with light punishment, but was also resentful that there had been a charge in the first place. He had not really grasped the meaning of the last sentence. He was again marched out of the room, to be reunited with Sergeant Davis, who, full of sympathy for Alf's predicament, assured him his extra work would be nominal. His mate was reprimanded for leaving his post.

Alf was so relieved to put the whole thing behind him he was oblivious to the more severe punishments being meted out to his co-charged. Later that day, the charges and punishments should have been the talk of the camp, but a subdued and slightly menacing atmosphere had descended. People were keeping themselves to themselves. Alf's fellow billet colleagues were definitely giving him the cold shoulder. Not even Lockett was giving him the time of day, although Gatbrook did seem once again approachable. But Alf didn't have long before he was whisked off to complete his punishments. His time in his billet was largely spent asleep, sometimes interrupted by acts of vengeance from friends of Ewan Mathieson, whose sentence was severe—detention in the guardhouse for sixty days and loss of pay for the attack on the Cypriot youth in Paramyrsina; but he was also found guilty on two other serious charges. Apparently he narrowly escaped dishonourable discharge. Nobody could pin the counter-propaganda and leafleting campaign on those detained, but it wasn't long before they identified and charged the perpetrators.

Chapter Twenty-Two
Turfed Out

Due legal process did not, however, placate the Greek community; in fact they were largely unaware that there had been any repercussions for the soldier that had shot Takis because the whole process had been engineered to avoid a court martial. Civil unrest around Famagusta district had begun immediately after the shooting and had peaked several days later. A British Army nurse was wounded by a gunshot to the legs as she walked along a street close to the beach. She was hospitalised and recovered. The unrest abated after several weeks.

The remaining months of Alf's National Service were fraught with unpleasantness, malicious behaviour from Ewan and his mates, and violent outbursts from Ewan himself who, once he had been released from incarceration, targeted Alf as the person who had dropped him in it. Nursing occasional black eyes and bruised ribs, Alf persevered with his duty, but was seething internally, hating every minute, willing his return to the UK. Barely within the three months after his hearing, he was on a further charge for drunk and disorderly conduct, for which he lost entitlement to leave and had additional drill. That triggered the reinstitution of charges previously not proven, although they were once again rejected. Then he was falsely accused of theft by one of his billet colleagues, which also wasn't proven, but he was given the wrong hearing date, so failed to turn up and was again punished with extra work. Then he was caught brawling and was interred for fourteen days. Eventually he was discharged when there was no longer space to add any further items to his charge sheet, and the repetition of drunkenness charges wore down even his most loyal supporting officer.

PART FOUR

Chapter Twenty-Three
Costas, July 1974

Costas Charalambou pulled on his trousers and lifted himself from the single bed. He peered out through the shuttered windows of his rented room overlooking the crystal clear azure seascape, shallow waves appearing capped by crystal shards glinting in the sunlight. He admired the beauty and also the commotion of his adopted home town. The sun was making its way above from behind the port area. At times like this he thought about the family he had abandoned, his wife and child in the Peloponnese. Then he muttered to himself the same words he had often uttered in the past year, 'What went wrong? I had a beautiful wife, a good dowry, a beautiful son, my cousin Tassos, who was also my best friend, and I left them all to fight this battle I am still fighting.' He had never been very good at managing relationships. Some people could master them, seemed to get so much pleasure out of friendships and family. He struggled. Even here, he was the outsider. He spoke Greek with the accent of a mainlander, so that set him apart from the Cypriots; he had given up trying to bond with his work colleagues—for their part they studiously avoided him, other than in matters of importance.

Costas crossed himself as he passed the icon on a makeshift shrine dedicated to his late brother Takis and their extended family. It was the only chattel accompanying him everywhere he travelled. He left the room both satisfied and saddened. In some small way, every day, he painfully recollected his past life and his family. He descended the stairs on the outside of the building, taking in the noises and aromas of the busy town. He had been living there for the past year, having returned to the island from Athens.

In an attempt to organise his thoughts before his coffee, he muttered to himself as he walked down Afxentiou Street. He called in at the baker near the market for bread, then took his coffee at an outdoor table near the bus stop. He tore the bread, sipped the sweet drink and followed it up with a mouthful of ice cold water. In reality he was not a major player within his organisation, but he been around for a long time and had built the trust of his superiors. He had never, over the years, been far from Dighenis, Ioannides, or Afxentiou when he was alive, and was readily recognised by each. He paid his respects privately now Grivas had passed away. His job today encompassed the final preparations within his cell to ensure that the plan could be executed with the minimum of resistance.

After paying for his drink, Costas continued down the road until he reached the rented office where his colleagues would be working at desks and in an anteroom between the office and stairwell. The space had become known as the control room because decisions were invariably sealed there. Only days previously they had been in another building, but the government had latterly outlawed the organisation and so they had had to go underground whilst they continued to make preparations. Costas realised, as did all his colleagues, that the government was onto them. His main task for the day was to meet with a sympathetic National Guard chief, a Greek national, and his deputy, a Greek Cypriot. He and his colleagues were seeking assurances that there would be no sanctions against the organisation in the aftermath of the executed plan. He travelled by bus to the National Guard campus. The meeting was cordial, he felt comfortable discussing the issue with a Greek National because there were, he reasoned, shared values, a common agenda—despite the public perception of the purpose of the National Guard. It had all gone his way. Before leaving he was invited to talk to the recruits about the objectives of the National Guard in securing a stronger Greek identity, a topic he felt able to orate upon without preparation. On his return to the office he found out some of the executive were due to visit the town that afternoon, an unscheduled event (although for reasons of security virtually every meeting was 'unscheduled').

In fact, the executive branch of the organisation were advocating a further meeting with the National Guard officers to plan post-coup strategic moves that they were expecting the Guards to take. This meeting would go on into the night in a private location. It was 13 July; plans were being made for all activities to occur simultaneously with a Greek military advance on the fifteenth. Costas had been responsible for organising several attacks on police stations and had continued his role as agitator-in-chief in the Varosha area. After the coup was announced, he would be promoted.

Costas was aware that close attention was being paid to Cyprus by foreign powers whose shared intelligence networks suspected trouble. The United Nations, the Americans, the British, the Turks, the Russians and the Greeks—the latter being ironic as the Greeks were seeking to extract political advantage from the situation to support their crumbling military junta—were all capable of sharing intelligence, and each did a good job of appearing to share it without revealing anything. In this environment it was somewhat easier to plan their activities because no powers possessed all the intelligence. At the local level, however, all talk of international powers was irrelevant.

The radios in every café and store in the street were cranked up to the point of distortion, reporting news of trouble brewing because Turkish Cypriot nationalists had been proposing partition: Taksim. Counter-propaganda messages came from the far right Greek Cypriot minorities. In the past there had been strong popular support for enosis, but the political climate of the country had changed. He couldn't believe that under Makarios, after all the years of preparation, the Cypriot people had decisively chosen to follow a path away from enosis and towards a resurgence of Turkish nationalism. He had been fighting this battle for over twenty years; his group could already have reached their objective were it not for exterior political interference. At times it had been difficult to fathom the rules of the game being played by the major powers. Now he was convinced that the next few days would at last signal the most important and decisive shift towards union with Greece. It was such an audacious plan, and so few trusted people were involved in its execution that it would either succeed magnificently or fail spectacularly. It would have been easier if the Cypriot nation were as supportive of enosis as they had been in the past.

Overnight on 14 July all the preparations that had been made were put into action. A coup d'etat was announced as a solution to prevent internecine war in the Greek population. The unwitting leadership of the National Guard realised they had been infiltrated by pro-coup officers by stealth. The reservists were not a problem since they would be instructed by their senior officers to do the business of the coup leaders, and sufficient reservists would support the enosis cause wholeheartedly.

From the senior command point in Lefkosia, announcements and press releases were sent out at 8 am on the fifteenth. The whole of Cyprus simultaneously became aware of Athens's plan. The role of the National Guard was to maintain order throughout the difficult times ahead. It was made clear that the Turkish Cypriot minority had no reason to fear these actions, although the announcement ignited predictable terror amongst Turkish Cypriots. The most poignant announcement was that Archbishop Makarios had been deposed and killed and the National Guard had taken control of the government, installing a new president. There were predictable warnings that resistance would be swiftly and assertively managed.

Immediately afterwards, military music was played across all radio stations and all other programs were cancelled.

Costas now assumed his role in directing the National Guard in their work in Varosha; a militiaman in charge of the military. A number of sporadic demonstrations were taking place and some armed resistance had been experienced. The armed perpetrators had been pursued and demonstrators detained in hastily constructed detention camps—little more than barbed wire pens in the rural areas. From the office close to the beach he was able to direct operations, and also took the time on that first day to dine at the Neon Phaleron restaurant which was known to be excellent for fish. This was going to be a golden era, he decided as he ate.

* * *

All was not well. From Costas's perspective the most immediate problem was that Makarios was neither dead nor in captivity. He had managed to escape, having been assisted to flee the country with 'external support'. The consequence was that those opposed to the coup became more assertive while its advocates became less confident.

The coup fizzled out only two days later, by which time the whole débâcle had brought down the Greek military junta in Athens. Costas found himself without purpose. He and his fellow conspirators were ruthlessly pursued in the following days.

In those brief moments when he successfully sought refuge in the churches of sympathetic enosist priests, he was able to reflect on his life. He, in a mood of contrition, concluded that he had neither been a good father, a good husband, or a particularly effective militiaman. He wished he could have done better.

Chapter Twenty-Four
Michael, 19 July 1974

Dom's voice bellowed around the office, ricocheting off hard obstacles to be absorbed by the room's human occupants. Everybody was affected by Dom's penetrating deep base attention-grabbers. To most it elicited a frozen, guilt-ridden stance and a surreptitious sideways glance towards its origin, fearful of what might follow if you were the target. To some it was the early warning alarm for an opportunity to perform, to demonstrate skills, to go and get that real story. The demographic divided on seniority lines. The older crowd thought they might be in for some browbeating, pulled up on some detail of a piece they had submitted. Sub-editors thought they'd been caught making the wrong decisions, whether it was about an angle or who they'd sent to cover a story. They hadn't been roving hacks for years, they'd settled into their comfortable lifestyles; their free time dominated by the schedules of families and friends in Islington or Primrose Hill, their work time dominated by the pressure to perform for Dom and the shareholders. The eager young reporters, still cutting their teeth under the protective wing of their more experienced mentors, heard one of Dom's bellows as a rousing call to the converted. That call generated a spurt of adrenaline through their hearts, senses suddenly put on alert; fight, not flight.

Mike looked up from what he had determined was a dud parochial story about double white lines through Dorking; it was sucking the life out of him. It wasn't his brief—he was covering for Julia who usually did the domestic stuff—but he was trying to make a go of it. He'd only been out of college for six months and his first job on the nationals was the exhilarating experience he'd sought when he first made the decision to go into journalism. But sometimes you had to fall back on the academic discipline of your years at college and write something your heart wasn't in. His passion was international conflict; his background demanded it of him. Ever since he'd been a boy he'd wanted to convey the observed and the hidden into printed text that transported the reader to a location, a setting. He wanted to convey sensual experience. Feel the fear, the danger, the anguish, the love. Hear the conflict unfold. See the battlefield and smell the acrid fumes of war. Seeking to achieve this was his version of religion. But there wasn't much to feel, hear, see, or smell in Dorking. All he could imagine as he sat making copy were two parallel white lines trying to join before reaching infinity somewhere close to Box Hill.

Dom had wrestled the attention of all in the room onto him. He took a breath to infuse his oversized frame with oxygen. He focussed on a point somewhere in the middle of the room. The typewriters stopped chattering. The hubbub of the crowded room descended to a baseline rustle of clothing, breathing, the odd cough, distant ringing phones and the background clatter of the ticker-tape. Those who could, sat down. If there was a wall to lean against it was utilised by staff expecting a lengthy sermon. Eager freshmen and women clutched a notepad and pen ready for the instructions they hoped to receive. The hot July morning was in full swing beyond the office's dusty windows. Passers-by dressed for summer, tourists gawking at whatever was on their list for the day. Traffic continuously flowed past along the busy thoroughfare. The office was hermetically sealed to exclude distractions.

'I've talked to you before about the emerging situation in the Eastern Med—Cyprus, Greece, Turkey. To date we've had only news feed from AP and Reuters to draw from, as well as Alexis

sending copy from Athens. At first people thought it was a storm
in a teacup because they didn't see much strategic significance in
a military coup on so small an island, but I think we need to do
despatches. The ticker-tape is reeling off stories of ethnic conflict,
outrage and disconcerting murmurs from major powers. Those of
you who've been around a few years know Cyprus is like a sore that
opens up regularly. I reckon we're going to see it become inflamed
again. There are plenty of Brits out there: servicemen and families
on military bases; the resorts were full of tourists as well. It's a pot-
boiler and it might well spill over.'

He paused to recharge his lungs, pushed his thumbs beneath his
favourite purple braces and scanned the room like a chef searching
for ingredients in a kitchen. 'Bill, you cover this. Get on the ground
out there, do conflict and human interest, see if you can get the
political angle. April, you work at it from here and see if you can
pump some information out of the Americans, Russians, Israelis,
Foreign Office, embassies. I'll get Alexis on the case in Athens,
because the coup appeared to have been backed by their junta. We'll
get someone in Ankara too. This may be a big story and it may not,
but we need to keep ahead of that curve. The other broadsheets
haven't picked up on it yet, so there's the possibility of exclusives.
Get out there ASAP Bill and take young Mike with you. I've looked
at his CV and he knows the place inside out. OK, thanks everyone.
Back to business.'

'Yeesss!' An involuntary cry from Mike's lips, heard only by his
immediate neighbours on the pod of desks. His colleagues regarded
his muted celebration with a tinge of jealousy. His dream was coming
true. He looked up from his typewriter towards the international
desk at the front of the room. He'd not worked with Bill before,
but everyone knew of his reputation for ruthless directness in any
dealings with humankind, for always getting the story, and his huge
appetite for beer. International was what the paper was good at. Bill

was at the top of the heap. Mike thought about what his role might be, whether he'd get treated like some kind of lackey. He stiffened up in his seat at the thought, preparing to fight his corner for a decent professional opportunity.

The travel office was onto him in minutes. They called to say they'd booked him and Bill onto a flight from London to Nicosia via Rome that evening. If he could come up to the office and pick up the details he could get his ticket at the airport. Mike tried to envisage some kind of schedule to get to the airport by 5 pm. He'd have to grab his luggage from home before that, then make the journey out on the tube to Hounslow West and get the bus. He sought out Bill, who it seemed was writing another piece, determined to complete it before the dash to the next story. 'Bill, how's it going? Do we need to talk?'

Bill responded without looking up or stopping what he was doing. 'Not unless you've got material for me.' The sheet of paper in front of him was pushing itself up through the typewriter rollers, being pasted with words that would be read in homes and trains throughout the country the next morning. 'If you've got anything to give me leave it there, if not, go home, wash behind your ears and I'll see you in the departure lounge at five. Don't forget your passport and press pass.'

Sarcasm was the source of his infamy. Everyone knew it when Bill had given them a lashing. He was about fifty, slim, bony, but fit as a butcher's dog. People speculated about how he managed to stay so slim when he drank like a fish and was known to have a tremendous appetite. Most put it down to nervous energy, his body burning calories at several times the rate of a normal person. He didn't seem to play sport, but he had been known to play a round of golf when etiquette or office politics demanded it. He was single, a confirmed bachelor with a shaved head that would otherwise have been a receding strawberry blonde, his moustache was greying slightly, his eyes a piercing blue. He was not someone you thought of messing with. Few did.

'Oh, and do you have a flak jacket?'

'No.'

'Well you might need one; I'll see what I've got at home.'

'OK.' Mike was a little deflated by Bill's tone, especially the last lines because he couldn't tell whether his senior colleague was joking or not. This was his most significant assignment, but Bill wasn't going to let him celebrate. Mike wandered back to his desk and ensured that the adrenaline and caffeine-infused attention made the white lines in Dorking meet before the bottom of the page, passed the piece to the domestic sub-editor, caring little whether they published it or not, and went up to the travel office to pick up the documents. They had booked the two of them into a hotel in Nicosia for five nights. That was, Dom had obviously decided, how long the story would need.

Mike was out of the door by midday, he grabbed a sandwich from a little booth he often went to (pastrami, rye, mayonnaise, gherkins, a packet of crisps, and another coffee). As he sat on the stuffy Tube finishing his lunch he thought through the domestic arrangements he would need to change. His coffee was in a covered plastic cup between his feet, the heat scolding his ankles. His shoulder bag with the significant documents was on his lap. It was sweltering in the crowded carriage, full of holidaymakers following a weary route along the Central Line between one tourist ghetto and another. He was uncomfortable, perspiring, his bag making it worse. By the time the train reached Shepherd's Bush and he stepped onto the platform the crowds had thinned considerably. He reappeared at ground level, made his way across the scruffy green then down the Shepherd's Bush Road to Cromwell Grove.

The flat he shared was bijou and adequate for three; there was private space for Sally, Liz and him. They had met up in a previous larger flat share and when the tenancy ended they mutually decided they could share as a threesome and took this flat. A sometime visitor to the flat was Ali, his better half, a strong Lancashire girl who, although they lived apart, was his soul mate since before leaving college together. Sal was Australian and Liz was broad Selby. It was with Ali that he'd have to rearrange the schedules. He got in and plonked himself on the floor of the hall next to the phone. He picked up the green hand piece and called her at work.

'Hi lover, just a quickie to say that I've been given an assignment and will be away for a few days.'

'Where to, is it lucky or unlucky?'

'It's Cyprus, Nicosia.'

'Lucky then.' She knew his past and his passion for the place he'd been brought up in.

'Yeah, I reckon so. At least I won't feel out of place. Listen, I know it's a long shot, but do you have an hour or two this afternoon?'

'Sorry, I can't, unless you come over and we do it in the staff toilets.' She had cottoned on to him, but it wasn't going to be possible.

'Nah, what do you think I am—some grubby exhibitionist?'

A chuckle of delight on the other end of the line 'Exhibitionism, *you*? Would I suggest such a thing?' Mock affront, knowing full well that he could be outrageous at every opportunity.

'Well, I've been given five days away so if it all goes to plan I should be back by next week. But that means I'll have to def out of the weekend in the Lakes and that party on Thursday. Sorry, Al.'

'I'll just have to pin you down to another weekend in the lakes. I'm still waiting for you to take me there.'

A smile spread across his face at the outbreak of innuendo. 'Hmm.' He twiddled the coiled green phone cable as he chatted to her. 'All in good time. Anyway, I have to go because I've got a flight at seven, so there's not a lot of time to spare.'

'There was enough time a minute ago to meet me.'

'It would have been a quickie.'

'Just the sort I like.'

'Stop it!'

'Have you seen Sal and Liz?'

'No, they're not around.'

'Leave them a note and say hi from me then.'

'OK, I will. Love you!'

'Farewell, my love! See you when you get back.'

'It's a date!'

'Bye, Mwah!'

He put the phone back on the cradle, clambered up from the floor and completed his preparations: passport, insurance, press card, money, credit card, travellers' cheques, cheque book—just in case—Eurocheque card, several changes of clothes, shorts, swim gear, shoes, flip flops, toiletries, washing liquid, elastic washing line, notebooks, pens, pencils, camera, dictaphone, batteries.

It was a well rehearsed routine, changing only according to the purpose of the trip or climate. His assignments to date had been Monmouth, Elgin, Belfast, those sort of places. No need for trunks and flip flops.

By 3 pm he had walked down to Hammersmith to catch the Piccadilly line out to Hounslow. By 4.30 he'd picked up his tickets from the Cyprus Airways desk and by 5 o'clock he found himself sitting next to Bill in the departure lounge. Bill was no longer the terse, absorbed man he'd left behind in the office. Now he was openly welcoming, friendly, chatty. He explained that he was always glad to be out of the dog cage, as he referred to the office. Mike thought Dom must have been the dog and everyone else his bitches. Bill seemed now to take a lot of interest in Mike's background, about which he'd never before enquired. Bill asked all the usual questions and chatted about what he knew of the island, which turned out not to be much, for although he'd been on holiday there five years previously, to stay with forces friends in Dhekelia, he hadn't strayed far from Larnaca, other than the mandatory tours of nearby archaeological sites. He did like the place, but thought it had a bit of the fish and chips, Marks and Spencer, Double Diamond culture associated with the forces. Mike accepted that that was true, but only if you shopped where the other Brits shopped. Mike tried to persuade him that alongside those things there was a traditional culture, even within the same towns that catered for the forces families. Bill was reading a pile of newspapers he'd bought at WH Smith in the terminal building: *Herald Tribune*, *Washington Post*, *The Times*, *Telegraph*, a couple of French titles. He had meticulously sought out any story about Cyprus and jettisoned the rest of each paper. There was a pile of discarded newsprint next to the seats. The cleaners weren't quick to claim it, it was something to do with the look Bill gave them each time anyone looked like attempting a grab.

'I'm collating a time line of reported events. The military coup seems to have been orchestrated by Athens to force the Greek Cypriot government to take a more enosist stance than they have been happy to do so far. Here's the bare bones,' he showed Mike a quickly sketched summary, narrating his way through it, 'Brigadier Ioannides in Athens orchestrated the coup with the support of the Greek Army and perhaps tacit support of the generals. In Cyprus the old pro-enosis fighters had re-formed under a returning Grivas, who had subsequently passed away. The new EOKA-B organised themselves to support the 15 July coup d'etat. President Makarios was taken into custody. Nicos Sampson was installed as a puppet president. Makarios escapes custody and broadcasts to his people; Turkey advocates an end of the coup, citing the danger to the Turkish Cypriot population despite the Greek Cypriot contingent insisting this was an internecine Greek dispute not affecting Turks; there are news blackouts in southern Turkey; Turkish diplomatic efforts take place in UK; Turkey threatens invasion unless Makarios is reinstated within twenty-four hours.'

Bill hadn't omitted anything, but he carried on poring over his cuttings until he was satisfied.

'What do you know of enosis and EOKA-B?' he asked Mike.

Mike began his narrative in the 1920s and continued until the present day, explaining about the island's long history of violence and terrorism, the rapprochement of recent times as the republic sought to escape its past and re-establish itself as a united independent state under Makarios. He described how the right wing elements of Greek politics had always been pro-enosis and had been deeply involved in armed insurgency that sought those ends. Mike described what links existed between the Greek military junta and EOKA-B, painting a picture of the late Grivas and his band of resurgent activists.

Bill's knowledge of the Cypriot independence struggle and the EOKA era was sound if not detailed, although he'd never reported on it. His knowledge of more recent times needed Mike's support, and he asked Mike many questions before they were called to the departure gate for boarding.

They were surprised to find so few people preparing to board. Mike counted six passengers, and estimated as many cockpit and crew. Bill was surprised there weren't other hacks on board, chasing an unfolding story. He said to Mike that either they were ahead of them, in which case they would need Mike's knowledge to catch up, or they'd missed the story so far, which meant they would have a series of exclusives. Mike hoped for nothing more than to get a scoop and be able to put enough authoritative dissection of the background into the story to bring him to prominence under a byline, if Bill would sanction it.

Chapter Twenty-Five
Michael, Overnight 19th–20th July

The Trident was pushed back from the terminal and became airborne on schedule, soaring over the Home Counties. On the ground the summer evening was unfolding for the millions of inhabitants of Great Britain who were sipping beers in riverside pubs, walking the dog, or heading to the park to catch some evening sun. The rush hour was beginning to tail off, but still there was heavy traffic on the M4 west.

Bill and Mike settled down on the evening flight to Rome, appreciative of all the attention the cabin crew—whose staff-to-customer ratio was 1:2—could offer. After a pleasant meal over the Alps and a couple of drinks, the two men had bonded well. Mike was relieved that he wasn't being treated as a lapdog. They discussed their tactics: what Dom had briefed Bill to report on and how they would split their time. It was decided that Mike would write a human-interest story, seeking out examples of intimidation or mistreatment, and Bill would tramp around Lefkosia to get the political low down. They'd get to their hotel, try to catch a few hours' sleep before dawn and get out there as fast as they could. If Bill found other hacks in Lefkosia he'd be able to tell how much they'd need to do to catch up. Mike said he'd probably head for one or two Turkish Cypriot or mixed villages to find out how the coup was impacting on the community and its individuals, then seek out servicemen and their families for a good person-centred take that resonated with a British readership. He was already writing out ideas and drafting phrases.

Their stop in Rome was only for refuelling. The passengers disembarked and walked across the hot runway to the airport's lounge; the stale air of the plane replaced by a curious mix of jet fuel and fragrant flowers, hot tarmac and diesel fumes. Once on the plane again they expected a short journey and an estimated landing time of 3am. Bill and Mike dozed on and off in the subdued lighting, relatively undisturbed by the clutch of other passengers scattered sparsely across the cabin in the unfathomable way that loading factors dictated.

Mike was awoken by a change in the engine note, a sign—he thought—of descent prior to landing. But as he sat in the world between sleep and wakefulness he realised that the plane was repeatedly changing direction: it would fly for several minutes, then turn, then turn again as if criss-crossing the same area. He pulled up the shade on the window, but revealed little more detail in the pre-dawn dullness. He could vaguely make out lights below clustered into settlements; he could just make out a coastline and assumed, if the flight was on schedule, this was the northern Cyprus coast. He was expecting the plane to take a path over the Kyrenia mountain range and into Nicosia, but it changed route once again and seemed to fly north before finally turning 180 degrees and starting its approach. Mike could make out through the window a collection of vessels near to the port he assumed was Kyrenia. He guessed they were fishing vessels, but their number surprised him. They also looked quite large. Before he had a chance to look again the cabin crew began their preparations for landing. The plane was now flying over land, the pilots trying to minimise the effect of a side-wind as they flew over the hills and lined up for the airport.

The flight landed at 3.55 am. Bleary eyed passengers sauntered across the tarmac toward the small terminal building, as the pilots powered down the plane for its overnight stop. The airport was not quiet, especially for the middle of the night; there were people crammed into the departure lounge.

Mike thought of the times in his childhood when he and his sister had left Cyprus at a moment's notice, shepherded by their mother, urgently making towards a waiting plane, ushered forward by British consular staff. His father was never with them, always remaining behind to continue his 'vital' work. He thought of the times that followed every flight from trouble. The absence of his father created a feeling like acid burning a hole in his soul. He needed what only his father could provide at times like those. He was desperate for the hug, the protection, the love. For months at a time it would only be his mother that could provide those things. It seemed sufficient, but he needed his dad as well. Then, like nothing had happened, the three of them would be on a plane back to their house in Cyprus, the family complete again, his soul repairing itself.

As he stood waiting for his papers to be processed, Mike started mentally replaying what he thought he had just seen. It was odd and he wasn't sure he could rely on himself to interpret it properly. There were only six passengers. The cabin crew, smiling as always, had ushered them off the plane with remarkable speed. As the passengers were descending the steps, all the flight crew were descending immediately behind them. At the base of the steps were a welcoming committee of several military staff and police officers. They immediately took the pilot, co-pilot and navigator to a waiting Jeep and drove away at speed towards the control tower. The rest of the crew were whisked off by military personnel at such a pace that they reached the terminal building before the passengers. The plane had barely powered down, the jet rotors still turning slowly with kinetic energy. In the distance, several aircraft were taxiing toward the runway, the first taking off just as Mike and Bill reached the terminal. Within two or three minutes, all the other aircraft had ascended. In the departure lounge waiting passengers were listening to announcements which, though his Greek was rusty, seemed to be asking them to make their way to another lounge as a precaution.

Precaution? Against what? This was 4 am. There were no visible planes on the tarmac other than the one that had just arrived. Yet there was a terminal full of departing passengers. It didn't make sense. The immigration staff, considering there were only a few incoming passengers, were disproportionately agitated, their furrowed brows signalling some crisis, staff shouting to each other distractedly as they processed passengers. Mike tried to ask what was happening. The officer dealing with Mike told him that as a precaution the departing passengers were being moved to a place of safety and he and other arriving passengers should make their way as directed as soon as possible, once they had collected their luggage. Mike, using his best Greek, asked why the precautions. He was told that the military had identified some unexplained air and shipping movements, confirmed by their pilot who had seen the same during his descent, and there was an alert in place. He conveyed this information to Bill and explained what he had seen when he looked out of the cabin window. The pair wanted to ask further questions, but the immigration officers were packing up and running toward their offices immediately upon the last of the arrivals being processed. The terminal building was on the move. Departing passengers were snaking their noisy, disgruntled way toward the designated safe area. Children were crying, men were shouting, alarmed mothers were shepherding their children as instructed. Holidaymakers, mostly British, were looking bewildered and tired.

The first plane that flew over the airport at that moment neither sounded like it was one that had recently taken off, nor was flying a permitted route. It was a fighter. There was a short silence as it pulled away, only to return seconds later. An explosion outside, a secondary explosion, the sound of mayhem as the fixtures and windows shook. The glass skylights high above their heads shattered, sending deadly shards raining down. The two men darted for the cover of a corridor to one side of the baggage reclaim hall. Plumes of dust were billowing from sections of the roof, from windows, and engulfing the vast hall. Then a second explosion was heard further in the distance. Mike peered towards a window, but was unable to see anything. Then there was a third explosion, close to the terminal. Shards of metal from outside the building shattered the windows in the adjacent departure hall where minutes previously hundreds of innocent passengers had been penned.

Mike shuffled forward in his half-crouched stance, trying to get a view outside. What he saw shocked him. The plane from which he had, moments before, disembarked was a bombed-out ball of fire. The fuselage was in two pieces, the wings now broken and sagging towards the ground. The detached cylinder of the fuselage was burning fiercely. Acrid black smoke rose from the wreckage. Jet fuel, now ignited, was forming lakes and streams of fire across the tarmac. Seconds later a jet passed over and strafed the airport and the jet with machine gun fire.

The screams of women and children could be heard, then mens' voices shouting urgent commands. Fire alarms were activating, parts of the building were groaning in protest at their attack. Fixtures randomly hit by bullets or shrapnel were peeling or sagging. In one part of the building a sprinkler system had activated. More fighter attacks picked off targets on the airfield; in the distance another parked aircraft outside a hangar was targeted. Particular attention was given to the tiny three-storey control tower which was repeatedly strafed as one jet after another targeted its deadly armaments at the building. The deserted runway was a scene of complete destruction.

Barely ten minutes of Mike's visit to Cyprus had passed and he and Bill had enough copy to fill the pages of tomorrow's papers; they didn't need to type it or make notes. It was their living reality. But there was no way they could call the office to dictate the news. There were no working telephones, no opportunity to look after anything but their own safety.

As quickly as the attack had started, it finished. In the few moments after the sound of fighter jets had receded there was the kind of silence one rarely experiences in crowds. No human being volunteered to break it. The nerves of the young failed first, prompting spontaneous sobbing and screaming, then the crying of the women, and finally the regrouping calls of the alpha males.

Normal humans rush to patch up their psychological being after such an event, paying more introverted attention to their souls in those few minutes than during the rest of their lifetime. Journalists, on the other hand, seek answers, explanations, photographs and bylines. They switch from rational beings to predatory story-seekers. Mike and Bill didn't need to regroup; they knew they had a story here and it needed to be told. They roamed the corridors of the airport, now dressed in their press vests and flak jackets recovered from the hold luggage. They put their press cards around their necks, looking for the best source of explanation they could find. When they latched onto a Cypriot National Guard officer they weren't going to take no for an answer. He passed them to a senior officer, busy with the need to initiate retaliative action. The belated response from anti-aircraft batteries around the airport perimeter and the adjacent military airfield could already be heard sending messages to the departed aggressor. There was no longer an aerial attack over the airport; the jets had moved on to another target. Cyprus isn't such a big island that you can't get a sense of what is happening in another part of it. The fire power was over the northern mountains.

From this brief meeting, Bill and Mike drafted out their first news story. When content with it, they located a working telephone, courtesy of the officer, and urgently dictated their copy to the office. As it was only midnight in the UK there was a chance the story would appear in the later editions the next day. Then they sent a truncated version of the same story to a syndicate. It was Bill's idea, and he worked under a different name when he penned it.

They were instinctively working like a hunting pack. Mike sought out the departing passengers until he found a holidaying British couple who were being sent home early because of the coup. The pair were trembling with shock and barely intelligible. They were from Colchester and had only had the first week of a two-week holiday before their travel company had offered them the option to return, which had been recommended. Fearful of future trouble, they had opted to return and were due to fly out on one of the planes Mike had seen taking off.

Mike spent his time patiently drawing out their story, asking how their first week had been, and what they had seen of the island. He enquired about their feelings as they had watched their flight depart without them. He quickly put together the article and rushed it over to Bill. The edited version was phoned through courtesy of the goodwill of the Greek Cypriot senior officer. The latter's goodwill wasn't entirely altruistic; he wanted the world to know what Turkey had just done, how Cypriots should be portrayed as innocent bystanders. Perhaps the truth was something else, thought Mike.

They didn't have much more opportunity to put another story together. The Cypriot National Guard secured the airport quickly, for fear of further Turkish—or Greek—interference, and arranged for the locally based United Nations contingent to evacuate the terminal passengers and staff to a place of safety in Nicosia. It was a confusing time for all. No sooner had the passengers overcome the shock of the attack than they were told that the Turkish Air

Force had bombed the airport and had rendered it inoperable. They were informed that the Turkish Navy had carried out an invasion on the north coast. Then they were herded onto buses hastily marked with UN insignia and driven to the city. There were no onward arrangements, but all of those moved were taken to a reception centre—an empty sports hall attached to a technical gymnasium (a technical secondary school).

Mike and Bill worked quickly to gather as much information as they could from the passengers. Most of the staff had dispersed from the airport, they were happier to be with their families in these times of conflict. All the staff were Greek Cypriots. There hadn't been a single Turkish Cypriot on duty at the airport since the coup several days earlier.

Greek Cypriot residents were surprisingly willing to speak to them, claiming that this coup and the resulting invasion was nothing to do with Cypriots and that they longed for a return to normality. On that basis, Mike and Bill got a lot of help and telephone time enabling the pair to report to the outside world what was happening. Of course there were Cypriot newspapers reporting on the affair, but there hadn't been anyone else from the international press on the ground; so at least Bill and Mike's stories were exclusives.

Despite their having a hotel reservation, they continued to work the passengers until after midday, then took themselves to their hotel to freshen up. Upon their late arrival the hotel was reluctant to release the room, but with the offer of a small consideration the issue was resolved. Bill put down a holding payment covering the next ten days, conscious that if people were fleeing conflict then hotel rooms might be in demand.

It had been a tough few hours.

The Turkish invasion from Kyrenia had quickly expanded south and was encroaching onto the Messaoria plain by midday, only meeting resistance at several spots in the mountains. Their advance onto the plains had been remarkably unchallenged. The baking hot day was punctuated by sporadic machine gun fire, explosions, the squeals of tanks on the move and the sounds of fighter plane activity to the south. The Cypriot National Guard were putting up a spirited defence with inferior armoury, but they were significantly overpowered and out-gunned by the superior Turkish military. After all, it was no secret that the US and NATO had been arming Turkey for some time—though not, admittedly, to perpetrate the sort of invasion that now faced this tiny island.

The residents of Nicosia had matters of survival prominent in their minds and were stockpiling items, anticipating days of disruption. There was a brisk trade at local markets. Bakers and butcheries sold whatever was available until they ran out. The city was preparing for lock down. Whilst there were no battles yet on the streets of central Nicosia there was sporadic sniper fire around the densely packed shopping streets that straddled the Green Line (the United Nations Buffer Zone). The city's inhabitants were increasingly displaying signs of fear and stress. In their confusion they were simultaneously preparing to remain and to flee, confused about whether and where to go, and when. Their options were limited only to Limassol or Larnaca.

Chapter Twenty-Six
Secure Passage

Bill was doing all he could to secure UN attachment. He was a professional in these matters and knew how to foster good relations with peace-keepers and aggressors alike, he knew which buttons to press. His couple of hours on the phone achieved the outcome he had sought; they could travel as embedded reporters in UN vehicles for the next three days. He set off immediately to fetch the paperwork. Together with Mike, Bill had agreed to split up to cover the main stories. If the situation changed they'd have to rethink, but it would be more difficult to organise once they were apart. Bill would be based in Nicosia at the hotel for as long as was possible, taking the political stories, the Nicosia local interest angles, and using the UN patrols to get to hard-to-reach spots. Mike would use his knowledge of the island to find the kind of stories they needed. Mike reckoned that if he could get to a couple of villages on either side of the conflict he'd be able to report on how communities that were traditionally mixed were handling the events of the last few days. If he could also get to Famagusta he might find a good story or two because the Greek- and Turkish-speaking communities were—more-or-less—segregated by the Old City walls, and the Greek Cypriot area was of commercial importance to both, as was the port.

As he sat in his hotel room, Mike realised he hadn't eaten since the previous evening on the plane. A sudden hunger and thirst overwhelmed him; his relative inexperience as a reporter in the field meant that he hadn't planned for the basic human survival needs.

He realised Bill had negotiated for himself the easier task, taking advantage of his colleague's unworldliness. He sought bottled water in the room, then at reception. Eventually some was brought to him. He drank it and immediately requested another. He wasn't able to persuade the hotel to make him any food. Much of the stock had been plundered by employees, but he was able to obtain some crisps, bread and honey, which he devoured without ceremony. When Bill returned with the papers they needed, he told Mike that he was to meet up outside the hotel with a team travelling toward Kyrenia at 3.30 pm. That was in only half an hour's time, but Mike's mind was still firmly focussed on food. Despite this, the pair urgently drew up contingency arrangements to ensure they could remain in contact. Mike was to telephone three times a day to the hotel, at 6 am, 2 pm and 10 pm. The 10 pm was the most important, so if he couldn't make contact on the previous deadlines, he must try on the third. He could dictate his copy to Bill or direct to the news desk, but Bill preferred it to come through him so that overall themes could flow through both men's pieces. If injury or sickness prevented him working, or if he became trapped by military activity, Mike should at least contact the UN. If that wasn't possible, or if he'd gone missing for more than thirty-six hours without contact, Bill would assume Mike was in trouble and would alert the London office, the British Embassy, and the local UN command. His priority was to position himself to get the stories. From the news and from his own sightings whilst on the plane, he and Bill knew that Mike must travel to Kyrenia. It was going to be difficult, but it was the only way the story of the moment could be obtained.

When the UN transport failed to arrive at 3.30 Bill again contacted their press officer. He was given a polite explanation of why the trip to Kyrenia would not be possible. It wasn't quite what Bill was expecting given the prior assurances he had received. The press officer for UNFICYP explained that it was almost impossible to get non-peacekeeping personnel through the Turkish-declared enclave whose boundary followed the main road and stretched for five miles from Kyrenia to the base of the mountain outside Nicosia. He said that because there was no international support for the Turkish action, so the role of the UN had been be interpreted by the Turks as optional; they were using the peacekeeping contingent to their own advantage. The *laissez-passer* usually negotiated for the UN was, for the time being, inoperative.

The Turkish offensive on that first day was staggering in its scope, leading both Bill and Mike to conclude that the strategy and logistics for this invasion had been carefully planned and rehearsed. Wondering how Mike could now get to Kyrenia, they went back to their hotel and talked it through. It seemed that any unilateral attempt to cross into Turkish-held territory would result in detention or worse; it was too risky. The pair embarked on further lobbying calls, to UNFICYP HQ, the British High Commission, and to a British commander with the peacekeepers, hoping to pull strings. It was a hot evening, they consumed servings of Souvlaki from a street vendor and chased it down with beer from a nearby bar to an echoing soundtrack of distant rifle and machine gun fire: a hollow, muffled din echoing off the mountain range. Mike, content and replete, was privately relieved about his aborted departure. He reflected on the risk of a Turkish invasion of Nicosia. The locals were going about their business as if that prospect was not imminent. Experience had taught Cypriots that conflicts can be compartmentalised, so Nicosia's commerce was functioning relatively normally, believing the buffer zone wouldn't be breached, albeit there were runs on essential items. On the other hand, families were preparing in the event that circumstances changed. Mike recalled how in the Famagusta of his childhood the worst conflict could be similarly compartmentalised whilst communities went about their normal routines just a few hundred metres away.

Bill and Mike had still to secure Mike's passage to Kyrenia. Bill drafted out a couple of stories between their lobbying efforts. Late in the evening they returned to the UNFICYP press office, by which time the effects of their lobbying would have trickled down. They managed to secure passage for Mike the following morning. He was glad, at least, to have eaten before he was to be chauffeured by his white knights with their blue berets into the jaws of a military onslaught.

He was to join a vehicle that was travelling to reinforce a small group of UN troops guarding the Dome Hotel. The hotel had been hastily re-purposed as a refuge for displaced tourists and a small number of local Greek Cypriot dignitaries whose future, because of their status, would otherwise be precarious. Although Mike didn't wish to be confined to the company of the UN throughout his visit to Kyrenia, the press officer signalled that he would be constrained by events.

Chapter Twenty-Seven
Michael, 21–22 July

Mike returned to his hotel with Bill after midnight. Having been deprived of the luxury of sleep for thirty-six hours, he settled down for a few hours rest and slept well. His travel alarm clock awoke him early. He washed and shaved, packed his essentials into a small holdall and made his way immediately to the UN base. He was assigned to a vehicle travelling almost immediately, crewed by several northern-European soldiers. Their knowledge of the situation was as sketchy as his, but they did help to fill in some gaps. From what the troops told him, the invasion was precipitated by the Turks' demand to maintain the safety of their Turkish Cypriot counterparts although, as Mike was fully aware, Turkey had been interested in the partition of the country for years. The Greek-backed military coup had acted as the catalyst for the Turks' long-planned action. The arrival of substantial naval and air power overnight on 20 July had been met by a robust response from the Greek Cypriot National Guard. Naval gunboats sent from Greece to intercept the Turkish naval attack were immediately bombarded from sea and air, resulting in substantial loss of life. The Turks were continuing to flush out resistance from Greek Cypriot National Guard positions in the mountains. Many Greek Cypriot reservists had reportedly been killed in these attacks. Some bombing had missed military targets, resulting in the dry, resinous pine forest igniting and burning unchecked. In the still morning air, smoke rose like a wall from the smouldering mountainside before a high-level crosswind took the smoke away from the ridge, giving the appearance of an overhanging shoulder atop a massive perpendicular surfing wave.

As they travelled across the green line through snaking chicanes into the Turkish side of the city there was significant resistance to their progress. Numerous roadblocks had been put in place by the Turkish troops which slowed the vehicle significantly on its route towards the mountain pass. Prior to the invasion, the military bases north of Nicosia had been prominent elements of the island state's defence. A significant offensive was ongoing to wrestle control of the area, through which passed their white and blue vehicle with its flapping white flag. As they reached Five-finger Mountain, Pentadactylos, the occupants were astonished to see the deployment of a significant number of paratroopers from a low-flying Turkish aircraft, which had then landed on the plains north of Nicosia. There was gunfire from Cypriot positions, but their airborne targets were out of range. With monotonous regularity, the UN vehicle had to make way for oncoming military vehicles. Despite fierce resistance from Cypriots, the sheer volume and fire-power of the Turkish invasion was overwhelming their opposition. There were a number of places along the road where bodies of National Guard soldiers lay. Bombed, bullet-ridden and burnt-out buildings on the roadside were evidence of a brutal onslaught.

The sparsely populated area had been home to the residents of a small number of mixed Greek and Turkish Cypriot settlements. The UN vehicle passed through villages where it was apparent that the Turks were conducting a concerted and systematic separation of Greek and Turkish-speaking residents, and men from women and children. The Greek Cypriot men were being treated brutally. Turkish troops could be seen beating men with the butts of their rifles. Random kicks and punches rained on defenceless civilians. Greek Cypriot women and children were not spared rough treatment. This was not military action, it was a venting of xenophobia upon innocent villagers. Mike wanted to stop and document the troops' behaviour, to speak with villagers who were being detained so brutally. It epitomised a story he imagined would touch the world, an account of the brutality of the conflict. His hosts did not agree to his requests, nor to his suggestion that he might photograph events from the vehicle. He was restricted to observation and furious note-taking; no time to craft the story, just getting impressions down on paper.

It took one and a half hours to reach the northern coastal strip, very slow progress for a journey of only a few miles. They had been stopped at hastily constructed roadblocks no less than eight times. Each roadblock was guarded by young, nervous, very trigger-happy soldiers. Whenever there was an unexpected movement nearby they would open fire. Livestock and dogs were the main recipients of their jittery actions. Civilians fleeing villages to escape the Turkish troops were at risk of being fired upon, trapped by wildfire, or most likely of being rounded up and detained.

As they approached Bellapais, from which there was a view of the coast, the true scope of the military effort became apparent. Some twenty naval vessels were anchored off Kyrenia, offloading troops and heavy armoury. The constant noise of military aircraft flying to and fro along the north coast was a distraction from the human cost. Mike made a mental note to write more human interest pieces.

In the village, a convoy of buses was moving civilians under armed guard. Mike could only look on in horror as this military force was taking innocent people against their will from their own homes to an unknown destination. Greek Cypriot youths and men were being forcibly separated from women and children. The Turks were intent, it seemed, on cleansing the entire area of its Greek-speaking inhabitants.

As the UN vehicle eventually drove into Kyrenia, Mike remembered childhood holidays spent there. The Dome Hotel was on the waterfront close to the harbour. Dozens of people were queueing patiently and apprehensively to gain access to the hotel through the UNFICYP-guarded entrance. The numbers queueing were far in excess of capacity under normal circumstances. It wasn't until he entered the hotel that Mike realised that perhaps six hundred people were being herded into this eighty-bedroom hotel, western tourists (mostly British), Greek Cypriots, sailors whose yachts had been impounded, functionaries, professionals, men, women, and children, all in a state of bewilderment and fear.

Mike had been informed *en route* that the Dome would be his base for the foreseeable future and he wasn't likely to be treated any differently to the other 'guests.' His freedom of movement around Kyrenia would be zero. Dejected by this dawning reality, he recovered his camera and notepad, left his baggage at the reception desk, which resembled a luggage store, and began to obtain accounts from those present. He had no opportunity to feed news articles to Bill or London because there were no working telephones. He quickly drafted his articles from the available material.

From this material he could conclude that at first light on 20 July, everybody had been awoken by a Turkish aerial and naval bombardment, quickly followed by the arrival of significant numbers of troops on the ground whose aim was to secure the northern part of the island. They created a boundary behind which the Turks were systematically separating and removing the indigenous Greek population, leaving their Turkish Cypriot compatriots alone. In each village, among them Lapithos and Bellapais, the action was being repeated. The few villagers who had managed to travel unobserved to Kyrenia were witnesses to the brutality of the operation. None had the opportunity to collect possessions. Families were desperate with anxiety about the fate of missing relatives.

Mike, still drafting his work, crafted descriptions of the treatment that people were being subjected to. He listened to a Cypriot woman's account given through an interpreter: 'My elderly mother had been threatened with a gun when she refused to leave the home; she had lived there for eighty years. She was hauled from her kitchen with nothing but the clothes she was in, not even the medication she required. She, together with other residents, were taken to a school in a neighbouring village where she and her compatriots were locked in and guarded.'

Mike wondered how this first-hand experience could have been passed on to the daughter, he was suspicious of whether the daughter or the interpreter were fabricating the account, and why the daughter hadn't also been detained.

When he spoke to the British tourists, especially to those who had been elsewhere at the time and who had seen what was happening in the villages, the accounts of brutality toward Greek Cypriots were corroborated.

United Nations troops who were guarding the hotel residents were themselves being observed by a cordon of Turkish troops. Mike discreetly watched the Turkish troops, seeking to confirm his suspicion that Greek Cypriots coming to the Dome seeking refuge were being taken away before they reached the front door, but there were no Greek Cypriot arrivals in the half-hour or so he observed them.

His portfolio of stories both from British tourists and Greek Cypriots, together with some insights from United Nations troops he had interviewed, formed a powerful story. He could hardly believe what was happening in this civilised, westernised nation so close to Europe. After collating and editing stories for three or four hours he arrived at a sufficiently brief piece that he could telephone through as soon as he could find a working phone.

He was again thirsty and hungry; tired and sweaty; there was nothing to eat or drink, and nowhere to sleep other than the floor. Earlier arriving guests had organised themselves into groups of six or eight per bedroom. Late arrivals—like Mike—were less fortunate and could select a strip of ceramic floor from rapidly diminishing options.

The Greek Cypriot hotel staff had fled leaving the UN to organise things. Only the manager remained, like the ship's captain unwilling (and unable) to abandon his vessel. Mike suspected the manager was more focussed on preserving the integrity of the hotel during its unplanned appropriation than on customer care; he was jealously guarding chattels and erecting protective cordons around the more delicate fixtures.

Mike slept fitfully on the floor of the large dining room, its windows overlooking the concreted pool area and the deceptively calm, blue Mediterranean beyond. He was able to observe naval vessels offloading their contents and gunboats firing into the mountains to support ground forces. He witnessed one of the Turkish vessels being sunk by an Turkish air force plane. It was snippets of factual information like this that would make his articles publishable.

Some of his fellow guests had transistor radios. The news broadcasts were on twenty-four hours a day, they kept a worried audience informed and offered a wider view of the insurgency, allowing listeners in the Dome to place their experience into a broader context and be thankful for a veneer of security. Many of the Cypriot and British radio stations were based in Nicosia or Limassol, so were not presently being affected by the invasion. Mike's professional view was that the broadcasts were potentially one-sided unverified accounts from the underdog in this particular battle. They did, however, offer a truly gruesome picture of human rights abuses being perpetrated by the invading force. Just about every news item reported the tremendous political and human cost. It was too early to estimate numbers, the names of those who had lost their lives, or the fate of those that had been driven against their will from their homes. There were rumours of surrendering

Greek National Guardsmen being transported as prisoners of war to the Turkish mainland. If the rumours were correct, the detainees would be brought to Kyrenia and boarded onto ships taking them to the mainland port of Mersin. Mike wasn't able to spot any activity consistent with this.

In the early hours, the UN troops informed those hotel residents who were awake that a ceasefire was being negotiated, but there was no clarity about its implementation. Mike internalised his ongoing frustration at his inability to leave the hotel and again fell asleep on the segment of dining room floor he had commandeered for himself whilst others, prompted by the announcement, busied themselves with premature preparations for departure.

The ceasefire was called at midday on 22 July. Following the announcement, the UN began to transfer tourists in Kyrenia to the Greek Cypriot sector of the island to be repatriated to their respective homelands. Mike understood from conversations with the UN staff that the ceasefire agreement would limit the Turks to territory they had already secured. He was aware that the significant troop movements out of Kyrenia and over the hills suggested military preparations for a further push. It was no surprise to hear on radio reports from Nicosia that the Turks were consolidating their position and moving laterally away from their forward positions. The Turks had succeeded in securing a bridgehead to Nicosia. The conflict would be taken to the capital, traditionally a flashpoint of inter-communal violence and activity. The Green Line was the thinnest and most tenuous of boundaries.

Mike had been able to persuade the United Nations to telegraph his pieces to London. They also agreed to convey him back to Nicosia. He thought his five-day posting could become open-ended if the story kept unfolding and the world kept listening.

It was with relief that he travelled back to Nicosia in the same United Nations vehicle that had conveyed him several days previously. *En route* to Nicosia he and his fellow passengers observed huge numbers of exhausted and frightened women and children being transported over the mountains and down towards Lefkosia. They were being taken, he was told, under the terms of the ceasefire agreement to be handed over to the Greek Cypriots in an exchange of prisoners of war. He had probably seen more than a thousand women and children being moved in this way. He reflected on the population living within a radius of ten miles from Kyrenia and assessed that these beings were a tiny proportion of the total in the region. He wondered what was happening to the others. Clearly, the menfolk were being held or detained and, if rumours were correct, deported to Turkey. He wondered whether people were still hiding either in their homes, or in the mountains away from the attention of their aggressors.

Exchange. Prisoners of war? Mike thought there would be a similar movement of displaced Turkish Cypriot people, none of whom were by definition prisoners of war. He wondered if the same inhumanity and lack of dignity had befallen the Turkish Cypriots. He imagined that because the situation was so emotionally charged, the likelihood was that Greek and Turkish Cypriots alike might have descended into acts of retribution, casting aside their humanity towards one another, and forgetting their former—although sometimes strained—co-existence. It would be left to UN officials to be objective and officious in their management of what were now refugees, and for politicians to salvage whatever they could from the situation.

By the time Mike reached Nicosia and crossed the now heavily fortified Green Line, he was extremely weary and hadn't eaten properly for some days. He made his way as soon as he could to the point that he had been told was the handover point of those women and children who had been transported south. It turned out to be one of the large hotels close to the Green Line which had also been commandeered as a reception centre. As the harsh sunlight hit the front of the impressive building, the buses disgorged their human cargo. Crowds of highly charged, emotional, tearful, shouting onlookers, desperate for sight of their relatives, pushed forward against the cordons separating them from the official handover process. Women and children were crying and screaming, officials in highly excited states were trying to systematically record details of each woman and child and their experiences.

When Mike had witnessed this distressing procedure for an hour or so, he made his way by taxi to his hotel, grabbing something substantial to eat and drink on his way. He waited in the hotel gardens until Bill returned. Under the combined effects of the summer heat and a post-prandial blood glucose spike, he dropped off to sleep in the hotel, dreaming terrible nightmares of depravity.

It was dark before Bill returned. He spotted Mike in the hotel's lobby. Whilst he was glad to see him alive and well, he chastised his colleague for not staying in regular contact before being appraised of the impossibility of such a plan. Placated over a beer, Bill conveyed his grasp of the political situation. Mike, in turn, described events north of the mountains, ready to produce all the copy he had been drafting over the last few days. Bill had been regularly cabling his own and Mike's pieces back to the office; the sole news item that Mike had managed to get out of Kyrenia via the UN had been published under his own byline. Mike let out a whoop of celebration at news of his status as an international journalist. After he had completed Mike's debrief, Bill's conversation turned to Mike's dishevelled and malodorous state. Mike realised how unpleasant it must have been to be in his company for the last couple of days. He took himself off for a cool shower. Reunited with his luggage he was at last able to change into clean and fresh clothes.

Chapter Twenty-Eight
Costas, Famagusta, 12 August

The unfulfilled life of Costas Xenou Charalambou ended shortly before dawn on 12 August when he and a colleague were shot dead in a deserted Hippocrates Street by a team of Greek Cypriot National Guard troops loyal to the Cypriot government. The National Guardsmen had been under orders to relentlessly pursue and eliminate the cell that had supported the Greek coup. In the minutes before his death, Costas heard jets flying overhead and the distant sound of bombs. He assumed it was National Guard activity in response to the Kyrenia invasion—he was oblivious to the reality that a Turkish assault on Varosha had begun.

Foolishly, somewhat carelessly, he had surmised that the guardsmen who had approached him were benign and sympathetic towards his cause. They, like him, were unaware of the nascent Turkish attack on Varosha, although minutes after the assassination they would become aware. Charalambou and his compatriots had, inadvertently, secured the most significant change in the political landscape of Cyprus for a hundred years: partition.

Nobody mourned the passing of Costas and his colleague; nobody buried them. In a brutal, calculated move, the two men's identities were erased, mechanically disfigured using knives and the butt of a rifle. Their anonymous bodies were abandoned in the street; identifying and interring the bodies would only have risked creating martyrs of the men. Having neutralised their targets, the guards moved on to the next names on their list.

Chapter Twenty-Nine
Michael, Famagusta, 12 August

After his return from Cyprus, Mike had spent several weeks in London, pumped up with his newly earned fame amongst his peers. Events conspired, however, to prevent his return to normality. Turkish forces continued to press forward across Cyprus and by 12 August the port of Famagusta was in their sights, albeit they were temporarily held back by a spirited defence from the retreating Cypriot forces.

Mike, recently arrived via a Royal Air Force flight, secured UN passage to a barracks on the northwestern edge of Famagusta. Unencumbered, except with the relevant papers and a change of clothes, he arrived at the camp in the early evening of the twelfth with a brief that he estimated would take a day or so to fulfil.

The white UN vehicle transporting him pulled into the gated compound, negotiated the blue and white-painted oil drum chicane, and parked up in formation against other identical vehicles. Each peace-keeper he travelled with was relieved to have survived the trip from Nicosia. The camp was to be his base. It afforded him the opportunity overnight to be fed, watered, clean up and rest something he valued more highly since his previous trip to Cyprus. The troops he'd travelled with were a friendly bunch, the Indians were a bit wary of their guest, but a Danish soldier thought he was OK. 'I think you are a little bit crazy to want to get into the Greek part of Famagusta,' he had said matter-of-factly in his careful English diction after Mike had outlined his plan to him.

When he arrived in the compound, Mike used the UN phones to contact London. He chatted for a couple of minutes and dictated a small amount of copy to them, a reflection of his journey. Mike told his colleague he planned to set off in the morning to get into Varosha.

Mike left the camp on foot at 0630 on 13 August, having being asked to sign a disclaimer in the event of his death. He was loaned a bullet-proof jacket over which he wore a 'press' vest. It was a hot morning and the additional burden of the protective gear caused him to sweat profusely. Apart from the clothing, he carried his leather shoulder bag and, in one hand, a large bottle of water. He hoped to find food and water from time to time, anticipating that he would have gathered sufficient press copy during the day to be able to return to the camp that evening, so would not be deprived of food for long. On passing through the camp gates, his first instinct was to travel directly along the main road towards the conflict. He could skirt around the edge of the Old City walls. He had not progressed more than two or three blocks along the main road before dismissing this as an irrational plan. Turkish troop positions were attempting to push forward beyond the city walls towards the adjoining Greek Cypriot town. In the neighbourhood through which he walked he was a bold target on a main thoroughfare, there were few other remaining civilians; the small number who had not fled did not dare to go outdoors. But he rationalised the risk; it wasn't as if he was close to any conflict. The occupants of a procession of erratically driven vehicles fled away from his intended destination. The occupants' weathered features were imprinted with fear and regarded with incredulity the foreigner walking in the wrong direction. He was approached by a slowing vehicle crammed with more occupants than seats, plus all the luggage they could cram into the remaining space, the vehicle groaning under the burden. The occupants yelled at him in the Turkish Cypriot tongue he could not understand, then realising he was foreign, in broken English beckoning him to join them.

'Very dangerous. To be dead that way. Come, come, this way, friend. Safer.'

He thanked them for their concern, turning his back for them to read his 'press' vest. In English he thanked them for stopping and wished them well as they drove away in a cloud of dust and diesel smoke from their over-worked vehicle. He could imagine the conversation the occupants would be having about him as they drove on: some murmurs of comprehension at his purpose and the chatter of incomprehension from others. They would talk to distract themselves from the dangers they themselves might yet have to face. There were no guaranteed outcomes for fleeing citizens of either side. Their trajectory might take them into mixed communities of Greek and Turkish Cypriots, the common village ties hewn apart, the inhabitants treated differentially according to whether the occupying militia in each village were pro-Turkish or pro-Greek. As the events of July and August progressed, an informal partition had begun to play out, with many families moving to voluntarily divide themselves along ethnic lines.

In the background, Mike could hear the sound of Turkish Phantom jets flying backwards and forwards along the curving coastline of the Karpas peninsula, which pointed like a forefinger toward the nearby Syrian coastline. He could also hear mortar fire, explosions, machine gun and intense rifle fire; all other background noises were absent. The nervous sound of the cicada beetles had been silenced by the noise of war; the barking of dogs, confused by the abandonment of their owners and missing their familiar routine, was absent. Any remaining outdoor life was now battened down behind hastily constructed barricades. Car horns—each normally an instrument playing the abstract soundtrack of Cypriot daily life—were silent, their driver-percussionists presumably fighting or having fled. There were palls of thick black smoke rising from different parts of the Greek Cypriot town. He knew he needed to get nearer to the town centre and decided to travel in an arc through the southwestern flank of the Greek Cypriot area, then to proceed north toward the centre. At the first opportunity, he dodged down a deserted residential street. From behind the fences of barricaded properties, he could occasionally hear women exercising that part of their vocal range reserved for extreme circumstances, animated, high-pitched, urgent instructions to children, animals, parents, other neighbours. There were no men in the neighbourhood, patriotic duty had presumably driven them to take up arms. Occasionally he would hear sniper, gunshot and machine gun fire, their distinguishing aural signatures resonating as they ricocheted off masonry and steel. Despite this soundtrack, he sensed there was no conflict in these residential streets. Nonetheless, he felt increasingly exposed, and took to darting from building to building, conscious of a need for bolt-holes. He sensed many eyes upon him from behind makeshift barricades. He felt utterly alone and isolated. Beads of perspiration passed down his face and neck, drenching his eyelashes, soaking into his hat and the layers beneath his safety vest. He could not afford to use the precious water to cool his face, and took a breather in the shade of an abandoned shop, slumping to a crouch against a dusty whitewashed wall. For the first time on this sortie, he thought about his girlfriend, knowing she would not approve of his crazy mission. He tried to dismiss those thoughts, but he knew she was right. What was he going to achieve on his daytime mission? What was his objective? For whom was he doing this? The answers eluded him because he was too focussed on survival, but the questions floated prominently in his mind, sowing doubt, nurturing a feeling of futility.

Setting forth again, he rationalised a sense of professional purpose, getting the story. He knew he was out of his depth, more so than on his trip to Kyrenia, but he couldn't allow himself to doubt his purpose—his motivations could be analysed some other time.

Somewhere in the middle distance he could make out the unmistakable sound of heavy tanks moving, their over-revving engines and the signature dusty squeak of metal tracks on tarmac. He didn't know if they were Turkish, Greek Cypriot or British. They were not close enough for him to be immediately concerned. He proceeded along his route, but virtually all the buildings he passed in the Greek Cypriot neighbourhoods appeared to have been hurriedly abandoned. Windows and doors were ajar, washing was left on the line, dogs were unleashed but left to defend gated properties. All commercial activity had been abandoned, the shops shuttered. It was difficult for him to imagine that people had just left everything and run for their lives. He had no prior reference point for such an experience. The scale of the upheaval in the area wasn't really a scene of warfare, more a saddening depiction of mass abandonment. He found a solitary old grandmother, 'yia yia' in local vernacular, going about her daily chores, dressed in black, her tired frame enacting the domestic routines of a lifetime. He tried to hail her. Even though he spoke Greek Cypriot to her she regarded him suspiciously and scuttled inside her home, locking the door behind her. He persisted, calling in a friendly manner to enquire if she was alright. Moments later she appeared, a silhouette on a first floor verandah, the extending overhead awning fully engulfing her in shade.

'Ya ya, I want to know if you are well,' he explained, careful to remain cognisant of his surroundings, looking out for risks, at the same time respectful to her as an elder.

'I am well, son, and you?'

'I am well, under the circumstances. You might recognise from my accent I am Inglezo, a journalist, a reporter for a newspaper. I am making my way to report on the fighting.'

As if choreographed, a large explosion perhaps half a mile distant punctuated his sentence. Both individuals looked skywards for smoke, trying to locate the blast. He took a long overdue swig of water.

'You are crazy.' He made out the screwing gesticulation of her clenched right hand against her temple that went with the statement, a familiar taunt from his schoolboy days just a few miles west of where he stood. He smiled, his first that day.

'Ya ya, do you have anybody to look after you? Do you have everything you need?'

'I have what I need, some vegetables in my garden, some water from the well behind the house, lemons on the tree. I can make bread in my oven, and I have my memories. Thank you.'

Mike gathered from the way she was dressed that she was widowed, perhaps familiar with coping alone, perhaps left to her own devices by her extended family, except for celebrations, name days and moments of family solidarity. 'Where are your sons and daughters?'

'My sons have gone to fight. My daughter and children have travelled to Larnaca. There is only me. Nobody will bother about me. I will be safe. If the army does come and kill me then my tragedy will be over. Until then I will stay here. Where would an old woman go? Who would wish to be burdened by one like me, although I have my health?'

Mike guessed she, like her older peers, considered herself a draw on her successfully fledged family and didn't want to inconvenience them.

'Ya ya, you must not think like that. Every life is precious. What is your name?'

'My name is Androulla.'

'Well, Androulla, ya ya, I wish you luck and safe keeping. With good fortune this will be over quickly.'

'It has taken many years for the angry boil to grow and burst, son, but now the poison is released and might kill the patient. I am not optimistic.'

'Are your neighbours here?'

'My neighbours, all old like me, have been taken away by their families. I would not go.' She was lost in her thoughts for a few seconds, he made out her gaze as she scanned the local environment.

'You can take my neighbour's son's bicycle if you need to be quick.'

'Stay well, ya ya, and keep safe, and thank you, the bicycle will be useful.'

'Stay alive, Inglezi!'

Mike commandeered the bike from a cool veranda beneath a burgeoning grape vine, checked the tyres were inflated and pushed it into the road. He careered down the street, fathoming the bicycle's idiosyncrasies as he went, ready to jump and take cover at the slightest indication of risk—either from this bike that had no brakes or from the military onslaught.

At a junction with an arterial road from the town centre, Mike prepared to cross without attracting attention. He pedalled furiously to cross the broad carriageway at right angles to the vehicular flow. A saloon car—the occupants' possessions in plastic bags piled high on the roof, covered by sheeting and tied down with ropes—narrowly missed him, its cargo lolling from side to side as the vehicle swerved. Other vehicles passed, an open boot filled with children, terrified live chickens tied by their feet to door handles, deflated tyres rumbling past. Lorry loads of human cargo trundled past, aiming for the Greek Cypriot zone. Resourceful, frightened people were escaping by whatever means were possible.

Those residents who were too afraid or immobile to escape were remaining in their own houses or apartments, not knowing their eventual fate. Mike knew there was a substantial community of British Forces families living in the town; unless those families had been pre-emptively relocated to the camps, and Mike could think of no reason they would yet have done so, mothers and children would be stranded in their homes as the likelihood of conflict grew. He imagined the difficulties they faced, in desperate need of defence from the camps several miles away, reliant on a functioning town for food and water, power and services. There was no indication that the British military or United Nations troops were rescuing anyone.

Crossing another arterial road he saw a procession of Greek Cypriot military vehicles travelling toward the conflict, diesel fumes clogging the suburban streets, their din echoing between the buildings. Troop carriers passed by with their cargo of uniformed regular and reservist troops. The expressions on their faces reflected their terror, their fear of mortality, their anger and outrage. There were lightly armoured vehicles and articulated lorries carrying heavy military equipment. The vastly superior Turkish Air Force had all but extinguished aerial combat. Arterial routes were being bombarded to prevent National Guard forces entering the theatre of conflict. Collateral damage along each arterial road was evident. Mike decided it was safer to keep to back streets and disappeared on his borrowed transport back into the suburbs. He was acutely aware that anyone with a gun who had done Cypriot military service would be contributing to the defence of their kin, nation and property, if only from their apartment windows. Almost anyone was a legitimate target if they couldn't be identified as friendly. His press jacket and bicycle combination were probably of little assistance to him. He crossed into Iraklis Street before heading towards Democracy Avenue, past the theatre where, as a child, he had been to see the Russian Cossack dance troupe. Opposite the theatre was a shuttered record shop where as

a fourteen-year-old he had taken his pocket money and bought his
first Beatles single. His thoughts briefly strayed to recall happier
times.

He decided to abandon the bicycle because it prevented him from
taking refuge without injuring himself in the rapid dismount. Until
this point, Mike had not encountered any bodies, but it became
apparent that Turkish forward positions were focusing on several
Cypriot military targets. His own movement was now attracting
occasional sniper fire and he was having to dart from hiding place
to hiding place to keep safe. He had been on the move for a couple
of hours and was already at a disadvantage through the tiredness in
his legs, his thirst and the need for sustenance and salt to fend off
cramps. Having only just arrived in the conflict zone, he could not
yet distinguish where the battle lines were. He found a sheltered
alleyway and took stock, drinking water and eating a piece of fruit
he had found in an abandoned store. He saw plate glass windows
shattered by machine-gun fire, glass shards spread like confetti across
the pavements, window displays and shop floors. Everywhere was a
layer of dust from the rattling and shaking upheaval of previously
settled structures. Cars parked in the streets were shrouded in dust,
or mangled by mortars, or punctured by gunfire and small bore
projectiles.

Mike spotted, amongst the debris in the street the mangled
frame of a tricycle, its wooden frame and now shattered glass
windows still discernible as those of a mobile food hawker. His
thoughts once again drifted toward his childhood, remembering
when he was very young a sandwich seller on a three-wheeled
bicycle who could always be found plying his trade in this street.
The small glass larder atop his three wheeler was filled with
ingredients. The torpedo shaped baguettes would be made to
order, filled with sliced roast lamb, crisp, fresh cucumber and
flavoursome beef tomato. Mike recalled the unpleasantness of

being marched to the hairdressing salon in the same street and the subsequent reward of a baguette. The salon remained, but had been ransacked, its glass frontage shattered. Two civilian bodies lay further along the street, a rivulet of blood from one body had cascaded over the kerb into the gutter before the heat of the sun had congealed it. On closer inspection, he noted gruesome mutilations intended to anonymise the victims. He wondered who they might have been and why they were targeted. Moving again, he progressed towards the junction of Democratis Avenue and Evagorus Street, bizarrely, the traffic lights were still changing rhythmically, independent of the failed electricity supply around them. The restaurant on the street corner was now a burning monument to war. To the south he couldn't hear any sign of gunfire. He took that route, carefully trying to avoid any attention from troops or snipers, and darting from shop front to shop front, pausing in alleyways and doorways to avoid being fired at. This took him several hundred metres off his route, but he made his way down back streets and service roads to return to his trajectory. As he passed what used to be the municipal post office, he realised how much effort was being expended and the size of the armaments the Turks were utilising in this attack.

It reminded him of the photographs from the TV news of Beirut during the 1967–68 period in which the whole city appeared to have become a battleground. He had paid much attention to those pictures as a boy because he lived less than one hundred miles away from that reality. Here, as in Beirut, there were pockmarked ruins surrounded by mounds of rubble and glass, tidily maintained streets replaced with chaos. His childhood self had once wondered how long it took to demolish a building using only the weapons of war. He was again reminded of that question.

Fixtures and fittings were dangling, fabric awnings over shop fronts were tattered and bedraggled. Amongst the dust and rubble were twisted metal structures, window frames, shutters and street furniture that had been catapulted across the street. Shrapnel, spent bullets and cartridges were becoming increasingly prevalent on the streets. Mike was repeatedly pinned down by invisible, nervous combatants, who, latterly recognising his press affiliation, shouted at him, demanding that he leave the area.

He was now several punishing hours into his mission and his senses were being challenged, his orientation, sense of hearing, sight, and smell submitting to a weary numbness, his body demanding nourishment and rehydration. His only thought was of survival. He had never been in the Forces, but imagined that at some point in armed conflict sensory shut down or a developing immunity to horror might facilitate the perpetration of unimaginable actions. Perhaps, he thought, that is partly how inexplicable events occur in conflicts like Korea and Vietnam, a combination of mental overload, depravity and the lack of a moral compass culminating in an outburst of sub-human retaliation.

He attempted to focus his thoughts on his present predicament. If he could reach the beach front along Hippocrates Street he would be able to locate British families in the beach side apartments and find shelter. When he had recovered his sense of purpose, he could build a story from his own experience and from that of the people he would now seek out. As he passed different residential buildings he could again sense eyes upon him; the eyes of the incarcerated, bereaved and terrified.

Another mortar exploded, perhaps one block away. For several seconds afterwards the echoes resounded down the deserted canyons of the residential thoroughfares. A dust cloud belatedly puffed out from an adjoining street. He checked he was not exposed and saw several troops taking aim towards him from a junction several hundred metres away. He darted behind a low wall and sneaked out of sight. They were seeking uniformed opponents and strategic targets.

If any citizens became victims then he suspected the Turkish troops would consider that to be collateral damage, but it seemed they were avoiding civilian casualties. As he lay in the dust and rubble of the concrete forecourt behind the low wall, he became aware of a black clad arm and hand beckoning him towards a ground floor doorway, which had opened up slightly to allow him entry. Realising that he had placed himself in more danger than he would have wished, he decided it would be best to enter the relative safety of the building.

'I am Despina Vassilides,' said the woman once he was inside. She was perhaps sixty years old. 'Please, you are welcome to my home. You will be safe for a while.' Her warm smile softened her tired face. She closed the door and, with his help, barricaded it again with a wardrobe.

Mike noted her eyes had beautifully clear whites, like a child's.

'Thank you, mama. My name is Michael,' he said between panting breaths, still trying to compose himself after his brush with the Turks. 'You are very good to me.'

He still could not understand how, after all the indignities forced upon the Cypriots during their long colonial past, they could be so friendly, so hospitable to foreigners. Perhaps their memories were short. Since independence in 1960 there may have been a long enough interlude of peace to forget their pain. In his mind a simultaneous counter-argument was demanding his attention: he knew Cypriots forgot nothing but had an immeasurable capacity to forgive.

The apartment was in darkness, made darker by the amount of large wooden objects shifted to obscure windows and external doors and give the illusion of security.

'Do you live here alone?' He said, convinced that the heavy removals must have been the work of a man.

'I live here alone, my husband Nico is departed. My children live in Lefkosia and Limassol.'

'How have you been today?'

'I have been awake since before the cockrels' crow; three in the morning the bombs started on the plains. We are very frightened. How have you come here, what is happening?'

'I came on a bicycle, from the UN camp on the road to Salamis. Then as I came closer to the centre of town I abandoned the bicycle and proceeded on foot. There are many Turkish troops; they are trying to take Varosha. Many are very young and inexperienced, as frightened as you and I, that is why they are dangerous.'

'My friends and neighbours have left their apartments. We believed they were going to kill us.'

'You should remain indoors until you are told it is safe to leave. I do not think they want to kill civilians, especially women or children. They have another purpose. Do you have food, water, electricity, telephone?'

'Only some food from two days ago, water I saved before the water stopped. I have no telephone. The electricity is off, the refrigerator no longer cool. Food is wasting.'

'You need to conserve what food and drink you have. Are there other people in the apartments?'

'One or two. Many left as soon as there was news of a possible Turkish invasion of the town. They just drove away before dawn, left me the food in their kitchens, they wanted to take me with them, but I would not leave. I will be OK.'

The fear and apprehension showed in her features, belying her apparent stoicism. In the background he could hear a transistor radio broadcasting ongoing coverage from a safe studio, perhaps in Limassol. Her radio batteries were draining and the distortion made it difficult for him to understand the excitable, rapid dialogue. His Greek Cypriot was not good enough to follow it. He asked if he could tune into the BBC World Service, but he heard little of use. The world was not yet awake to the unfolding crisis in Famagusta. He commented that there was no news report yet.

'Even the Cyprus radio does not have enough detail, not enough to help us understand whether it is safe to leave. So we'—meaning her remaining neighbours and herself—'just stay where we are.'

'Mama, I am a reporter for a British newspaper. I am here to report on this crisis.' He deliberately utilised the word 'crisis' a Greek word transposed into English. 'Can you help me understand what has happened during the last day or two?'

She recounted for him every detail of how she had witnessed events. She spoke carefully, switching between relatively good English and Greek Cypriot. Mike assumed she had been well educated or had long term contact with English people. Nothing she recounted was previously known to him, and he scribbled notes to catch this very personal interpretation of events. Her careful, purposeful gauging of every word was evident to Mike, he believed she was holding back emotions that, once unleashed, would be difficult to regain control of.

'I know the military coup frightened many people, Greek and Turkish speakers alike. I do not understand the politics, I do not understand why Greek generals think they should have some control in Cyprus. We are independent of Greece. Enosis was in the past. Leave us to get on with our lives. I am not surprised at Turkey for taking action, because the Turkish Cypriots were intimidated by the coup. But,' she searched for the words to describe her perplexity, 'it is a catastrophe. In the days since the invasion of Kyrenia my neighbours and I have seen the mountains burn close to Kantara, seen planes flying, seen television pictures of paratroopers falling onto the plains outside Lefkosia.'

She paused, taking a tissue to mop tears from her eyes.

'We could hear the gunfire and explosions in the distance. None of us understood what was happening. We didn't know who was fighting who. We didn't know whether we should feel safe or not. Some of my friends fled after the first invasion, to be with their families in Larnaca, Lefkosia or Limassol. Their sons and daughters came to collect them, or they just went on a bus. I told my son not to come. Then the National Guard mobilised every man that had trained, every man eager to fight for his nation. Now my son has left his wife and children behind; I don't know what has happened to him, my only son.'

She sobbed, hiding her face from him whilst doing so, shuffling uncomfortably to avoid communicating further. Mike tried to reassure her, but he refocussed for a while on what the radio was reporting.

Some minutes later she had regained composure and asked if he was hungry.

'I am hungry and thirsty, mama, but I want you to conserve what stores you have for your own use.'

'There is no problem. I have bread and cheese, olives, some tyropita. I have some bottles of Coca Cola.' She shuffled into her kitchen to prepare food, then returned with small plates of food for him, and a room temperature soft drink.

'Thank you, mama,' he said, tucking into the offering, downing the drink.

After he had eaten, Despina returned to her narrative of the situation. She recounted reports from neighbours who had stealthily sought provisions before dawn.

'The post office and police station have been hit by rocket fire. Our church has been hit, why would they do that? The church is the centre of our peaceful lives.'

Mike held her hand as she sobbed, her lace handkerchief drenched with tears of despair. His feelings of sorrow triggered by Despina's desperate situation caused him to change tack, to prepare for departure.

'Mama, I am trying to reach the apartments along Hippocrates Street because there are probably British service families trapped there by the trouble. Which is the best way to get there?'

She described a route, advising him to wait until dusk—a recommendation he disregarded. He thanked her for her hospitality and left the building; darting through the scrub like a gazelle, he set off trying to avoid the attentions of any military presence in the vicinity. He knew he remained a target for trigger-happy young recruits when there were so few people on the streets. Of the Turkish troops he'd met, even at a distance, he could surmise that most were immature, mainly teenage recruits from the mainland, perhaps as frightened as everyone else. By darting from block to block, Mike was able to make his way slowly in the mid afternoon heat towards his planned destination. He had to zigzag a couple of blocks in order to reach the long street flanked on one side by the row of tower blocks that was his destination. He was hot, he was thirsty, he was frightened. Frightened not only for himself, but also for the fate of the country and its people. He hadn't seen any proof of atrocities in Varosha like he'd found near Kyrenia. It was likely that the bodies he'd seen would have been participants in some form of military resistance, although he hadn't seen any weapons near them. There was certainly no evidence yet that the Turks were forcibly removing Greek Cypriots from the town, although their presence in this part of the town was limited.

He was surprised to immediately become the target of an invisible sniper. He barely felt the passage of the bullet as it grazed his lower calf, but he did feel the trickle of blood down his ankle. He zigzagged his way past pungent palm trees, stands of flowering shrubs, bamboo and ripening figs, too preoccupied by the danger to feel pain. As he managed to skirt back round a concentration of National Guardsmen, he darted into a bolt hole and rolled up his trouser leg to assess the damage. It was only a graze; fortunately there was no serious damage, but it did look messy because blood was being absorbed into his trouser leg and was running down his calf to fill his sandals. He didn't have any bandages with him so the best he could do was to get to the block.

It was difficult to gain entry at first. All the windows and doorways had been barricaded from the inside. There were people on guard duty at ground floor level. He banged on the door, shouting that he was British.

'Alright, alright, there's no need to break the door down. We can hear you're British, so we'll let you in as soon as we can. There are a couple of bits of furniture to move first.'

The accent on the other side of the door was, thought Mike, Lancashire or Manchester. When the door opened, and was again sealed shut, the adult who addressed him said in English devoid of any accent, 'I'm Martin. I guess you're looking for some shelter?'

A lad of about fifteen was helping him with the barricade. It must have been his voice, thought Mike.

'This is my son, Darren.'

I'm Mike, I'm a journalist from London, working for one of the newspapers, covering the story of the Cyprus invasion,' He fumbled beneath his bullet proof jacket for his press pass. 'Here's my ID. I came to this block because I knew there would be British forces families living here.'

'How did you know?'

'I used to live in Famagusta. I went to school here, dad was with the Forces. There were always British forces families living in these apartments so I thought it was likely there still would be.'

'Well, you're right, and fortunately you haven't been shot getting here.'

Mike drew attention to the trickle of blood down his leg.

'Not strictly true,' he said, 'a sniper managed to get me just a few minutes ago, but it's just a graze, looks worse than it is.'

'Lets get you patched up. You'll have to walk up to the fifth floor. The lift isn't working. No power.'

His short-fire sentences were matter of fact, his manner crisp, perfunctory. Mike guessed he was an officer. Used to issuing instructions. Used to being obeyed.

'Yeah, no problem. So are you off-duty, is that why you're here?'

'Correct. Finished a shift yesterday. Due a couple of days leave. Thought I'd spend it with the kids. Get some skiing and snorkelling in. Unfortunately, other parties put the kibosh on the schedule.'

'So, you work at the local base?'

'That's right. WO2 Davis, Signals. Can't tell you any more, I'd have to kill you.'

Mike smiled. As they talked, Darren said he wanted to go and check on troop positions, he leapt up the stairs two steps at a time, the echo of his clumsy footwork receding. The lad clearly relished the opportunity to be a deputy soldier under his father's command. They followed.

'Before we go any further, I'm putting together stories of people caught up in the Famagusta invasion. Would people mind if I took notes so I can include them in an article?'

Silence for several steps, then at the next lobby Martin turned to Mike, who was still ascending slowly on account of his bloody leg.

'As long as the whole thing is anonymous—no real names, no addresses, nothing that would identify us—then I don't think we would object. You'll have to get consent from the others, of course, but I guess they'd be happy for their story to be told. Darren can give you lots of information; he's living and breathing the whole thing, but check with me first.'

Mike noted the loss of the clipped response, this was more prosaic. He wondered why there was a difference. Perhaps it was emotional.

'OK, thanks, I'll just get to know people first, make notes about how the thing has played out so far. If I use a human interest angle, I'll get consent.'

'Just one more flight of stairs. My family: me, the wife, three kids—Darren's the middle one, the older brother's at boarding school in the UK.'

Inside the apartment, the same careful barricading of doors and windows. One advantage of this block was the integrated metal shutters, rolled closed over each window. What would normally be an airy beach front luxury apartment was presently a dingy, claustrophobic series of chambers. He sensed the whole family had been allocated tasks and asked to keep a stiff upper lip, although that might have been a slightly unfair assessment.

'This is Maureen, my wife. Darren you've met, this is little Lisa, my daughter. Maureen looked as if she'd hurriedly put her face on in the bathroom at the prospect of a visitor. Perhaps Darren had alerted her.

'Hi, Maureen. Hello, Lisa, how old are you?'

'I'm nine, and daddy says I'm very grown up for my age.'

Martin smiled, 'That's because she's been bearing up very well these last few days.'

Maureen dealt with Mike's first aid needs, cleaning up the wound with TCP, wrapping a dressing across the graze. It was a deep graze, but hadn't penetrated to the underlying tissue. He would have to put up with the bloody clothing for the time being. Water was in short supply.

'Would you like a drink, Mike? I've only got squash. We're using water from the header tank on the roof. We're boiling it; not very palatable, but it tastes OK with orange in it.'

'That'll be fine, thanks.' He followed Maureen into the kitchen. On the worktop a Primus stove was heating water, beside it a row of filled recycled bottles kept closed with aluminium foil and rubber bands.

'You've certainly got yourselves organised here.'

'That's Martin's doing, I'm afraid. He's Mister Organised.'

'How are the kids coping?'

'Darren's in his element. If he wasn't doing this he'd be ambushing snakes, planning an assault on the Naafi shopping trolleys with his friends. I think he's going to be a soldier.'

'How do you feel about that?'

'Probably happier than were it ten years ago. I think the world is a less dangerous place these days.'

Mike thought briefly about a response then decided to keep quiet. He wasn't certain she was right. The Yom Kippur war had been the previous year, and several conflicts were slow-burning in Rhodesia, Malaysia, Cambodia . . . the list went on. And they were right in the middle of a global oil crisis.

'And how's Lisa doing?'

'She's fine. There are friends her own age in the block, so she just gets on with enjoying herself. She's always been a bit of a carefree girl. Maybe because she has two capable and protective older brothers.'

'And you, how are you coping?'

'I'm a Services wife,' she said, as if that was all the explanation that was required.

He drank his squash and rejoined Martin and Darren. Darren spent several minutes pointing out where fighting was taking place. The trio of men peered through a chink in the metal shuttering. There was a view from each side of the building. The overview was as good as any military commander could have required. His knowledge of the town and observation skills were superb. Mike made chronological notes to describe the developing conflict; he realised his story would be enriched by the lad's effort. He'd have to find a way to acknowledge his input.

Martin launched into a summary update.

'There's a company of Turks to the north east, several pockets of fighting in the town centre, near the market. South and southwest there is little going on. The Cypriot National Guard are coming in from Larnaca, trying to pin the Turks back towards the Old City. They're not succeeding. The Turkish jets are providing air cover. They bombed the main public buildings, the big hotels, the military positions. They frequently strafe this bit of beach.'

'How long do you think this can last, and at what point do you think Britain will retrieve you?

'Difficult to say. I've listened to BFBS for information. We're ordered to stay indoors. My understanding is a negotiated ceasefire on humanitarian grounds is being prepared. At that point we will be rescued and the rest of the town folk will flee. I'm not too worried that civilians or foreigners are in danger, it seems the Turks are careful to meet their Geneva Convention obligations after their post-Kyrenia mauling by the international community. My sense is that they are simply securing a partition line that happens to include Varosha. There will be more important things to see to before they think about the civilians.'

'But some of those troops out there are trigger happy teenagers, frightened and in a foreign country.'

'True. And that is a risk for everyone. Staying out of sight is the best option.'

'I was thinking of trying to get closer to the conflict zone near the George Hotel. Is that a possibility?'

'Do you have a death wish? Think about your family and friends first. I wouldn't advise it even if you were being paid a fortune to do it, and I guess you're not.'

'What about if I take off in the morning to join the exodus of people fleeing on foot towards Larnaca. I need human interest stories.'

'There's less risk to that, but it isn't without risk. Go before dawn. Tread carefully. Head for Paralimni, then Ayia Napa. It's safe over there for the time being. I doubt the Turks would push that far beyond the historical green line.'

Mike met other families in the apartment block that night. He worked hard to build up material for his articles and talked with each family about how best to hide their identities. He found a nickname for Darren only his extended family would recognise him by, so he would be able to acknowledge his contribution. He slept in a corridor on the cool ceramic floor. It was uncomfortable, he was awoken regularly by the sounds of the conflict, but he managed to get some rest.

The guard on lookout reported that many Greek Cypriots had taken the opportunity to escape their homes under the cover of darkness. They had fled southeast. From their vantage point on the fifth floor, the lookouts were able to see a significant amount of movement approximately two to three miles west along the beach and promontories towards Ayia Napa. From time to time the lookouts would see Red Cross ambulances, a white flag, white handkerchief, or dressing being waved through the vehicles' windows, appearing to rescue infirm, bedridden, mostly old people from apartments. They may have had knowledge of the whereabouts of the most vulnerable. That was a selfless and brave mission. It was only a matter of time before a negotiated relief mission would take place to rescue the remaining British families. Mike tried to convince himself everything would return to normal, but he got the feeling that this was not going to end well for Famagusta—for Varosha. Even if the Cypriots continued to hold back the Turkish invasion, even if the Turkish invasion was dispersed across such a broad front line, even if it could not sustain a forward push, the reality was that there were too many Turkish troops in the country and little credible opposition. There was nothing to stop the Turks from quickly taking the whole of Varosha if they had set that as their strategic objective.

Mike's thoughts took him along uncomfortable trails, his girlfriend, his longing for their comfortable urban life together, of his friends and parents, of shattered reflections of childhood, of mourning for a country he loved. An outpouring of emotion hit him unexpectedly. Peering out beyond the closed shutters, he sobbed quietly to himself as he watched the town that he had grown up in being fought over, destroyed, its inhabitants' fate unknown. In that moment he realised that he was so engrossed in what was happening around him, he'd completely forgotten about everything else in the world.

His cousin Eric was meant to be island hopping in Greece and had intended to visit Samos, which is perhaps the closest Greek island to the Turkish mainland. Mike imagined that any holiday plans in this area would have been quickly scuppered by the current conflict in Cyprus and wondered what had become of Eric's. He speculated that tourists would be quickly and hastily repatriated to Athens. For all he knew, those islands might also have been attacked and invaded by the Turkish like in Cyprus, in which case Eric's fate was less easy to guess. As for Mike, his colleagues, Bill, and the management, they were probably imagining the worst.

Before the dawn of 14 August, he ate a ration of biscuits and jam with a cup of Naafi-branded tea. It was heated on a Primus stove using water from a header tank on the roof with Carnation condensed milk to taste. He was grateful to be offered anything.

He continued to discuss with Martin and the other occupants how they saw the current situation and whether they had any intelligence. He quickly realised that they had little more to add to what he already knew.

After thanking his hosts, he left the apartment block at about 0500 (Darren had taught him to speak of time like that) under the moon shadow from the apartment blocks and progressed south, firstly down Hippocrates Street itself then along Livadia Street and Miaolis Street. He passed the house where his family had once occupied the first floor apartment. It was saddening to be reminded of his past under such circumstances. On impulse, he called at the flat of the woman who had lived on the ground floor. There was no response.

He continued further south, joining an exodus following minor roads. Groups, families, singletons; on crutches, on foot, by vehicle, by bus, if they were fortunate—everyone was on the move. It was a depressing end to what might be his last visit to his home town. As he walked at the same pace as other evacuees, he chatted in his, by now confident, Greek tongue to get a picture of their respective last few days. All were clearly traumatised by events and had had little warning of the advance on Famagusta.

He spoke to Chloe, a conservatively dressed woman of about forty whose husband was away on business in Limassol and whose children were at the gymnasium in Lefkosia. Her partner on the journey was her ageing mother dressed in traditional black, hobbling along the route fearful of any obstacles or challenges. They had left behind their one-storey home which they had owned and occupied for three generations. Every item in the house had been left behind with the exception of a couple of changes of clothing, medications, water, and a small amount of jewellery. They had barely enough money between them to afford food. The pair were devastated and very tearful. The grandmother could not walk fast so she and Chloe were falling behind the other people. When asked where they were going they said they didn't know, they were just walking away from trouble.

Would they try to reach Limassol and her husband, asked Mike.

She said she didn't know; why would they go to Limassol, her family were all from Varosha. When asked what was the most traumatising thing for them in all of this, it was that her husband and children were not with her and it was difficult for her to imagine how they might ultimately be joined together again. She had no money and nowhere to live, she didn't even know where she was going to be at the end of the day, or where she was going to be tomorrow. But she was glad that she had managed to escape.

Mike spoke to Vassili, a small businessman in his fifties walking alone. He carried a backpack containing his 'whole life', or as much of it as he could carry on a journey without a destination. His trade had been in consumer electricals. Vassili described business as good until the invasion ended his livelihood. He had had to leave everything behind, knowing that he would lose his stock to looters and encroaching forces. He described his state as a living death. He couldn't find it in his heart to forgive anybody. He had been a single man. All of his emotional strength had been invested in his business, only for it to be left abandoned in a lock-up in the town centre.

Mike asked him who was to blame. His answer, after a brief reflection, surprised Mike 'the Greek generals.'

Mike asked him whether he thought the Turks were over-reacting. 'In this part of the world everybody over-reacts. I wouldn't have expected less of them, and nor should the Greek generals.'

Mike caught up with Daphne and her three children, one young enough to need carrying. They had come from the outskirts of Varosha. Her husband was a reservist who had gone to fight two days earlier. She had already received the news that he had not survived the first day of the invasion. Her determined face hid the tremendous sorrow and hopelessness that the tragic loss of a partner can bring. She was trying to be strong for the children, but they were traumatised by their father's loss. The three kids were, he was told, fourteen years, eleven years and eight months. The older pair were clutching a small plastic bag of belongings, mostly clothes. Apart from the eight-month-old in her arms, Daphne was also carrying a large woven plastic bag containing the things she believed would be necessary for the journey. She had started out with two bags, but it had not been possible to carry everything, so they had jettisoned one bag having recovered from it whatever necessities she thought it possible for the children to carry. Each unscheduled stop slowed their progress and used up precious water, she told him. She had a lot to say, and Mike assumed she talked incessantly because if she stopped her grief would engulf her. He knew people develop routines and behaviours to distract them from their immediate reality. Few people he met were trudging along the road with a clear mind. They neither knew what they would achieve, nor where they would end up. They were just going forwards. As if to reinforce the magnitude of this human tragedy the route—along which hundreds if not thousands had already escaped—was marked by discarded luggage, items of clothing, packaging, paper, and plastic bags; a garbage trail, like cairns marking an exodus.

The further they went the clearer it became that the numbers fleeing the town were significant. Drawn from a population of perhaps twenty-thousand Greek Cypriots, even on this second day of hostilities, he counted several hundred people along the road in the two hours since he'd set out. He knew there would be more. He knew that at some point Varosha would be a ghost town. How long would that situation remain?

At the first opportunity he attempted to telephone the office. There was no working telephone line in Derynia village, which he passed through. Like everybody else, he ambled on, his leg sore, his feet aching, the sun and heat of midsummer taking its toll. There was no breeze. He had barely enough water to sustain him for the morning. He was thirsty, but hadn't dared to drain the bottle. Liquid issued forth from his pores, streams of perspiration made their way under force of gravity down his calves, thighs, torso, arms. Drops irrigated any ground he lingered over or it simply evaporated on his skin, its salty residue matting his body hair. Everybody had to migrate forward, in search of the caravanserai of their imagination as if their lives depended upon reaching it. Whenever Mike and his fellow émigrés passed through a village it was a relief for them to be able to walk into the shade and refill their water bottles.

At midday the sun robbed everyone of shaded respite, their
rate of progress checked by the searing heat. Between villages
were orchards of unripe oranges and grapefruit. People were
picking them to obtain a package of acidic liquid refreshment. The
Mediterranean temperament was at its least attractive under the
extreme circumstances. Many raised voices and altercations took
place, despite the fact that everyone was in the same predicament. It
became difficult to catch one's breath as one penetrated the veils of
hot, still air; each step was a challenge. The temptation to sit down
and give up was never far away. Mike felt the cast of dry blood on
his calf, the underside of his heel cloyingly sticky inside his blood-
filled sandal. Then, about mid-afternoon his body just gave up.
Every muscle fibre simultaneously revolted, deprived of the oxygen-
rich blood they required, his body suffering muscle cramps and
weakness. He was forced to rest on the roadside, an overwhelming
tiredness descending upon him. He watched as better-prepared,
more resilient souls continued past him during their expatriation.
After stopping an hour he had recovered enough to proceed, by
which time a rearguard platoon of refugees was flowing along the
road towards and past him.

For a short time he fell in with Antonis, a young man of about
sixteen, with a fiery hot teenage temperament, resentful and
angry. Some days earlier the invasion had separated the boy from
his family and he wasn't sure when he'd see them again. He was
walking with a purpose, in the process consuming energy a mature
person would see sense in conserving. His pace and his anger
burnt calories he was unable to replace. He wasn't prepared for the
journey. Apart from a bottle of water, long ago emptied, and the
clothes he stood up in, he had nothing. He told Mike he wanted
to go and fight for his country. He had turned up to volunteer as
a reservist but they'd turned him away because of his age. That
made him sore because he felt impotent. Mike was unable to keep

the pace that Antonis had set himself. He disappeared further into the distance, until he was a diminutive character on a broad horizon as they crossed stubble-filled wheat fields, Mike thought about the folly and impetuousness of youth, drawing again on his own past. Antonis was in a hurry, to go where?

Mike, suddenly finding himself alone in this weary nomadic cortège, reflected on the senselessness of combat, the inhumanity of military action that draws innocent civilians into its arena, its mendacious propaganda, its bloody skirmishes, the random slaughter; embodiments of hatred and evil. Territory? Resources? Religion? Are these justifiable reasons? When warmongers take stock and review their gains and losses they fail to realise that they are so imbued with hatred, so coiled like combative springs of action–reaction that retreat seems virtually unimaginable, unattainable, undesirable. At what point does the mass suffering of the innocent force intercession and mediation to save humanity from itself? At what point does the collective conscience of humanity shout loud and long enough to pacify the unpacifiable, silence the wails of war-makers, bring sense to a lost cause? Why, across the millennia, had nobody crystallised the point before the carnage; created a sensor which could warn humanity when it crossed the line that would, if left unchecked, lead to mass suffering, annihilation, the retrograde moment when the fulcrum teeters and the balance of peace is destroyed? Why hadn't the human race found a way to throw a switch to prevent the warmongers? A solution involving a deciding game of football, maybe, or cricket? His mind drifted, his sentences ceased to form, key phrases coalesced and repeated themselves in his mind. He realised he was too tired to think straight.

As night fell, many of the walkers settled by the roadside close to villages where it might be possible to get provisions. The chaotic events had disrupted supply chains to the villages. There was water, but not for drinking. There was food, but it sold out as soon as it appeared. There was nowhere to wash with dignity. Everybody rested—hungry, thirsty, desperate—under the stars, listening to the sounds of distant gunfire and cicada beetles, in the company of mosquitoes, howling dogs, crying children, and the wailing of the bereaved. Bereaved by the death of their kin and their town. Because of the perceived danger of aerial attacks on the refugees, perhaps more rumour-driven paranoia than fact, many people headed towards the British camp at Dhekelia, thinking this would be the best place to find safety.

So, as everybody awoke at daybreak without the routines of ablutions and breaking their fasts, they just got up, relieved themselves, gathered their belongings and walked. Later that day, when all the refugees were tired beyond imagination, they reached the boundary fence of the Sovereign Base Area. The British military had set up facilities to process them and allow them inside the perimeter fence. Mike made himself known to one of the senior officers and explained his situation. He was escorted to the administrative offices of the camp and introduced to the press officer, who had been alerted to his unscheduled absence. Mike's dishevelled status was much the same as it had been after his trip to Kyrenia, so as soon as he was able, he excused himself to freshen up. He requested access to a telephone to post his press copy, which was provided after negotiation. He explained the need to contact his girlfriend, the UN in Famagusta, and his office in London to let them know he was safe and well.

Later that day, as soon as his priority tasks had been completed, Mike was provided board and lodging in the Sergeant's Mess. It was the first time in three days that he had been in a place of safety without the need to depend on his survival instincts. He explained to his hosts that he had started from the apartment block in Hippocrates Street and queried whether there had been attempts to rescue the forces families from Famagusta. He was informed that a recovery exercise had taken place the previous evening. Mike, in the comfort of the mess quarters, was more fortunate than his refugee counterparts who, having reached the Sovereign Base, were herded into temporary tented compounds with basic facilities.

At the press office the following day, he was told that a United Nations vehicle would collect him and return to Nicosia that day. For now his ordeal was over, but there were many more stories yet to be posted. Mike was repatriated to the UK by the RAF with other British citizens three days after his exodus from Varosha.

Over the following weeks a number of initiatives were agreed, including the exchange of prisoners of war and repatriation of Greek Cypriots from detention camps in Northern Cyprus. Greek Cypriot combatants had been shipped to Turkey and put into camps against their will. Those men who had survived the experience were returned and handed over to Greek Cypriots or United Nations representatives in Nicosia.

Michael Blidworth had, through his reporting of events in Famagusta and Kyrenia, launched his international career.

PART FIVE

Chapter Thirty
Simon Holdsworth, Malawi, 1999

The heat punched his chest as he descended the stairway, struggling to breathe the freshest air he had been offered since Sheffield, the moisture-soaked air of an African night. Familiar aromas assailed him: wood smoke, jet fuel, the wet tarmac surface of the runway, the unmistakable smell of moisture-laden vegetation, the sweet fragrance of a jasmine bush nearby. The heavy cloud cover that had buffeted the airliner like a fairground dodgem on approach to Lilongwe was hanging threateningly above them. He knew that it would not rain; it would fall on schedule at 7 am, when the ground would be provided with its quotidian opportunity to absorb the gift. After two hours the storm would pass and oppressive humidity would conspire with fatiguing heat to limit productivity. He was glad once more to be in this paradise.

He had been home to bury his father. It was no big deal. He hadn't got on with him for years and the man treated his wife of forty years—Simon's mother, Doreen—like a maidservant. In some ways it was a relief, a release for Simon and his mother to have put the man to rest. His mother had always been loving and loyal to her husband. She was rewarded with spiteful indifference, tinged with menace in recent years as his condition had gradually invaded his personality and replaced it with that of a stranger. He was never, as far as Simon could remember, other than a spiteful old man with a chip on his shoulder. Simon had never understood where the smouldering resentment emanated from. His father did not have much ambition, didn't expect a great deal from life, and seemed to begrudge what it offered him. Doreen often told Simon about the happy times she and Alf had shared during courtship, of the joy of his birth, and of the comfortable but meagre living they had carved out for themselves in his family's home city. Now Alf was buried. Doreen could do what she needed to do with her life. Simon had made all the necessary arrangements after the funeral to ensure his mother would neither be bothered by bureaucracy nor by the financial challenges of old age. Her pension was adequate and the household bills would be paid through Simon's account. He kept an open return ticket in case of a crisis.

As Simon reached the terminal building he felt the spirit of the continent embrace him. It felt like home. England, in contrast, felt like a foreign place populated by people whose motives and lives he couldn't really fathom. Here everything seemed simpler, people were content; desperately poor and without prospects, but seemingly content with their burden. He was sure that if he scratched the surface, the naïvety and offensiveness of his sentiments would be quickly exposed.

His spirits were temporarily checked by the realities of African bureaucracy. Officials meticulously carry out their duties with curt, almost sneering dedication. All paperwork has to be in order; all stamps must be applied; every bag must be searched. A superior official has to be consulted; the paperwork and bags again surveyed. Then passengers spew out into a huge, virtually empty, public area, its only inhabitants family members or besuited drivers with placards waiting for expatriates or government officials. But for Simon there was nobody.

As soon as the last passenger had been processed, the officials disappeared home, air crew, drivers and family members headed to the sleeping city, cleaners dozed on wooden benches next to their buckets and mops. The arriving aircraft lapsed into silence. A gentle background chorus played, provided by cicada beetles and croaking frogs overlaid with the distant glissando banter of a couple of guards talking to keep themselves awake outside their sentry box, their voices spanning base scales. Otherwise the airport was silent.

After waiting for half an hour, Simon heard the roar of his colleague Richard's car. Richard rolled into the car park at the wheel of his battered old Morris Marina, drawing to a noisy halt outside the main doors. Simon was informed that the car had shed a temporary repair to the exhaust somewhere between Capital City and the airport. Simon bunged his luggage on the back seat and clambered into the passenger seat. He did the local handshake, glad to see the familiar face. In the twenty or so minutes it took to reach their shared apartment they discussed the flight, the weather in England, the funeral (briefly), and what had been happening since Simon's departure. They stopped only to pick up the sliver of hammered out oil can that was the lost exhaust repair. Through the dark, silent African night, the only other movements were of occasional human silhouettes along the roadside or the lope of a hyena, eyes reflected in the headlights as they darted back into coppicing plantations lining the roadside.

Simon clambered from the car when it reached their gated compound, as he did so greeting the informally-dressed security guard who had come running from his hut to open the gates, his panga knife in hand in case of trouble. First stop was a beer from the fridge, a chance to settle back into the familiarity of his surroundings. Richard explained the mess by saying there had been a few friends around earlier that evening. The polished concrete floor was littered with discarded groundnut shells and pumpkin seed husks. Available surfaces were filled with empty beer bottles. A few forlorn over-ripe bananas in a dish sweetened the air with their pungent aroma. Nothing had changed.

A few short hours later, Simon awoke to a familiar wood smoke aroma wafting through his shuttered windows. An early wood fire meant there would be hot water. It was still dark, but there was a buzz of activity in evidence. Cockerels announced the forthcoming dawn, birds initiated their chorus of tropical calls. Mothers gently encouraged their children to face another day. Simon clambered clumsily out of his mosquito net, tramped to the bathroom and emptied his bladder. He looked at his face in the mirror. It was pale and drawn, the consequence of dehydrating aircraft air and dismal British weather. He checked there was hot water before he stood beneath the spout of water emanating from a broken shower rose, soaping and shaving himself. Mosquitoes hovered just beyond the splash zone hoping for the opportunity of a blood meal. Then, with his towel around his waist, his flip-flops clacking over the hard floor, he went to the kitchen, filled a kettle and made tea. There wasn't any fresh milk, there had been none in the supermarkets before his return to the UK. He used the powdered milk on the worktop, picking out a couple of ants as he heaped a spoonful into his cup. Then, as he was in the habit of doing, he went out onto the *khondi* (veranda) and sat watching the day start anew. A procession of soldier ants caught his attention as they crossed the lawn. A retinue of sleepy men and women passed on the other side of their fenced compound on their way to work. He listened to the banter of the people, their tongue mostly undecipherable, save for a few words. He heard children from within the compound's staff quarters and knew he would soon smell the familiar maize porridge cooking on a wood fire in the yard. Later, from their quarters, carefully dressed and groomed schoolchildren would make their way to school.

Simon pulled on his work clothes and crash helmet and left

the bungalow with his satchel of papers over his shoulder. His trail bike was in the yard, close to guard's hut. After a couple of failed kick starts he ran it across the gravel courtyard and jump started it. He didn't use waterproof gear because, by judicious scheduling, it was usually possible to avoid the heaviest downpours. After light showers it was usually better to be able to air-dry. In Africa, in the rainy season, every garment rotted and emitted a rank mouldy stench. No clothing dried completely, week after week, unless you were wealthy enough to own a tumble drier. Not until the winds lost their humidity would Simon get stuff dry and smelling fresh. He could clear a room in minutes just by walking into it.

His work was as a volunteer trainer in a college. His office was shared with another tutor, his colleague Watson Mphiri. Between them they taught healthcare studies. Simon gained a lot of satisfaction from doing the job. By and large the students were willing and capable, glad of an opportunity to get on a career rung, even if at the outset they had little idea what the Ministry recruiters had allocated them to. His role was as lecturer, tutor to a small number of students and deviser of practical exercises, experiments and demonstrations. This was his first role abroad and he fully expected that his whole life would be spent in similar roles, facilitating those who had no resources save for their intellect to make their own way in life.

Mindful of the weeks of teaching he had missed, he needed to do to catch up and so chatted briefly with Mr Mphiri over a cup of tea to find out how his students were progressing, what teaching cover had succeeded or failed in his absence. Simon was perpetually in awe of Mphiri who made his tea so weak but then piled seven spoons of sugar in each cup. The prospect of diabetes was never far from Mphiri's mind, but in his defence he would proclaim this was his way of stoking up the fire every morning, that the country was awash with sugar cane syrup, and that he couldn't understand foreigners' 'need for strange foodstuffs at their breakfast ceremonies: cereals, bacon, eggs and whatever.' Simon would sip his no-sugar tea, glad not to share his colleague's addiction. It was no surprise to Simon that the teaching cover had completely failed to materialise and his students had found themselves with free time without any academic demands being placed on them. His immediate task would be to recover the lost teaching time so that the curriculum would be covered by the end of the year. His first lesson was a doddle since his input was a repeat of the identical session he'd prepared the previous year. Afterwards he'd been quizzed by some of his students about his trip home.

In the hour or so prep time before his next lecture he popped out to a lane behind the college that was turned each day into a food market to cater for the teaching staff and nearby hospital workers. There was the usual range of prepared foods: fruits, bread, mandasi (maize flour doughnuts), bottles of soft drinks, prepared sandwiches and chips fried in makeshift cauldrons made of oil cans shaped into metal hollows filled with cooking oil over a wood fire. He reflected on how nobody ever enquired about the provenance of these foods. He imagined that somewhere in the slum townships a night-long shift of food preparation took place in oil lamp-illuminated poverty and grime with sleeping children nearby. All this to make enough on each transaction to pay for the following night's family meal of *nsima* (maize meal) and leaves. It was the epitome of a hand-to-mouth existence.

He made, as he often did, a decision to buy chips on the basis they were cooked *in situ* so were relatively safe to eat. He also bought *mandasi* and a bunch of bananas. His mandasi were sold by a lad of perhaps fifteen with youthful unblemished skin, his beautifully innocent personality shining through his eyes. This lad was not the usual mandasi seller.

Simon asked him in Chewa, 'Where is the other seller?'

The lad shuffled uncomfortably.

'My sister is sick and my mother told me to come in her place.'

Sickness had a number of interpretations, given the poor level of health, but the dominant cause was malaria, thereafter the curse of HIV or TB. The lad spoke English well.

'What would you be doing if you were not selling mandasi today?' asked Simon.

'I would be at school, secondary grade four, with my brother.'

'Then you must be studying for your secondary certificate soon?'

'Exactly, master.'

'But what lessons would you miss today?'

'Science and religious studies.'

'And will you be here tomorrow?'

'Maybe, if my sister remains ill.'

'What is your name?'

'My name is Duncan.'

'That is not a Chewa name.'

'No, it was the name of the doctor who brought me into the world. I am sorry, master, there are some people who want to buy mandasi.'

Simon apologised and stepped aside to allow commerce to proceed, eating his chips out of the newspaper they were served in. He wandered off down the vehicle tracks of damp red earth, back to his office where he cleaned his shoes off with a tissue. He thought of the precariousness of Duncan's life and wondered how he and the rest of his family, parents, brothers and sisters would fare in this world. But when he thought things through logically he realised that as the lad was in secondary school—which would be fee-paying—his parents could not be the poorest, if they had been, they would not have been able to afford the school fees.

The next day he was again buying his mandasi from the stall in his lunch break. The rains had persisted uncharacteristically long and hard that morning, disproving his schedule of predictable weather events. Simon's clothes were damp. He was, as a consequence, not in the best of spirits. Today it was the boy's sister selling their produce. He tried to engage her in conversation, but he had always found her to be shy and unfamiliar with discourse with Azungu (white people). He didn't get any further with his enquiries. But the mandasi were, as usual, good.

PART SIX

Chapter Thirty-One
Ioannis Georghios Panayiotis, born 1985.
His Life in Greece Before Adulthood

My mother talked with different voices. Some were soothing, as required when I had fallen and grazed my knee. Some were cautionary, as in 'Yianni,'—that was my nickname—'you'd better clear up that mess before I come into the room,' conveyed with firmness, but steady in tone and force. Others were, how should I say, 'war-cries.' These you ignored at your peril. Depending on the reason, the tone, pitch and force of the war cry would change. If you were late in doing something and you were barely in earshot the war cry would be a two-parter: starting low and finishing in a falsetto cry, as in 'Yia-*nniii*! Come and get washed and changed for church.' Another more serious voice was the nakedly aggressive call to account—a strident, barbed call to account. 'Ioannis Georghios Panayiotis, come here immediately and herd all the goats back into the pen and don't leave the gate open again!' She didn't call me by my full name unless I was in *big* trouble. My father said my mother was a temptress and could use her voice to good effect in getting what she wanted. I didn't understand what he meant, in the same way as I didn't understand my father's comments about her bedtime voice at the time. For me she used the two-parter at bedtime.

On this occasion it was the two-parter; I was under the fig tree with Dimitri and Photine, my best friends. We were stuffing ripe figs into our mouths, splitting them with our thumbs and peeling the flesh away from the skin with our teeth, enjoying the fresh, sweet fruit and building up a pile of discarded skins in the process.

We would have to hide the evidence if we were to avoid the call
to account voice which my mother would apply if she thought her
supply of figs for preserving was being scrumped. Late September
had its advantages. The figs were ripe, the harvest was in, the
unrelenting summer heat was on the wane, my father would be at
home more. The downsides, if you were of the view that these were
'downs' and not 'ups', was that junior school started—everybody
called it *dimotiko*, but I don't know why—and the storms would
soon start lashing rain onto our little peninsula and the sea would
turn grey. So here we were, in September, eating figs, after school,
and at least it was still summer.

'Yia-*nniii*! Yi-a-*nniii*!'

The three of us looked at each other and briskly gathered the
skins. Dimitri said he'd take them and throw them into the roadside
undergrowth on the way home. I stood up and knocked the sandy
dust off my shorts with both hands and ran towards the house,
shouting a departing 'see you' over my shoulder.

'Mama?' I then shouted, to acknowledge the two-parter.

She saw me approaching the house. She probably knew where
I had been and what we had been doing. I expected a telling off,
but she was different. My father was at home as well, which was
uncharacteristic. He worked the morning in our field and during
the afternoon and evening for an agricultural machinery company
on the outskirts of our village.

'Come in, Yanni, your father and I have something to tell you.'

My older sister was already pensively sitting on one of the dining
chairs. Mysterious? I couldn't imagine what would need to be said
in such a formal manner. Was it a telling-off? Had my schoolteacher
told them about the fight I had with Albert that morning? It was
nothing really, but he stole my ball off me. Papa cleared his throat.
Even though he wasn't old, he had to do that because he smoked
cigarettes. Mama kept telling him not to, and my teacher said that

people who smoked might die. I was sad for my father and I often told him to stop, but each time he just said something like, 'Won't anyone lay off applying guilt? Go to your room Yanni.' Why did I get the punishment for his smoking?

Mama started, even though Papa had cleared his throat.

'You know we have lived here for many years, and our families have farmed this land for many generations. Your great-grandfather Panos Ioannis farmed this very plot and lived in this house. Your great-great-grandfather also farmed this land. But each generation that passes has less land to farm. Now all we have is the yard and the field. We can't make money from what we grow. That is why your father works at AgriMex as well.'

Then Papa continued, 'Times are difficult since the fall of the generals. In all the years that have passed since they fell, Greece has been in turmoil. There are not enough jobs in the countryside. You will not remember the generals, but they ruled Greece with a steady hand. If you behaved like the generals required, people could live a pleasant life, go to church, walk freely in the community. If not, they would imprison you. Now we have a democracy. Democracy started in Greece. If you have not learnt this at school, you will do soon. But with democracy comes the responsibility to make choices to look after your family and children.'

Then Mama took over, like the whole conversation was rehearsed, 'So Papa is trying to make our life and your future better. We have made a decision that we think will make your future better.'

I was still mystified. My emotions erred toward fear and trepidation. My sister fidgeted in her seat. I wondered why they didn't mention grandfather Costas Ioannis, since they seemed so eager to cover the family history. They rarely mentioned him.

'Your Mama and I have decided that we are going to sell our plot and move to Athina. I have secured a new job with the company I work for. We will live in an apartment. You will go to junior school and Mama will find some work as well,' then, his gaze settling on Elie, he continued, 'and you will go to gymnasium in Athina.'

Elie and I sat silently, taking in this bombshell. I stared across the darkening room toward the early evening brightness on the other side of the threshold, the sun falling gently towards the west, casting a rosy hue through the doorway and across the wall where the icons were looking back at us.

'How will I get to dimotiko?' I asked.

'You will be able to go to a new school with other children. You will make new friends. There are many children moving with their families to Athina. You will meet children from all over our country, Greece.' Papa's voice quivered a little when he said 'our country.' Mama always said Papa was a staunch nationalist. I didn't know what that meant, but it made him cry sometimes. Mama told me that the priest once had to comfort Papa when news of his father's passing away reached him, but that was before I was born. I wonder if that was because he was a nationalist.

'I don't want to go to Athina,' I finally blurted out, tears welling in the corner of my eyes. 'I want to stay here with my friends and uncles and aunts and cousins.'

It was fair to say that most of the village was related in some way or other to us. Even Dimitri and Photine were related in some way. About ten families were called Panayiotis. And then there was my mother's family, whose name was Papadopoulos, were a very big family right across the Peleponnesos.

Elie looked shell-shocked as well. She was holding her hands together interlocking the fingers and trying to turn them inside out. I knew she was thinking, silently and hard. But she didn't cry. She was twelve and she was a bit more grown up than me. I ran out of the house and into the yard toward the grazing donkey, from whom I could obtain solace.

It was in that yard, next to the donkey that my mother joined me and said in her soothing voice, 'Yanni, don't be upset; it's a good thing that Papa is doing; it will be exciting for you and Elie and you will be able to get a good job in Athina when you grow up. We don't want to leave you and Elie with so little land that you can't make a living in this part of the country.'

She ruffled my hair as she spoke and I felt the warmth and certainty of her caressing hands on my cheek. I leaned in towards her and nuzzled her hip. I could smell the traces of mint and cinnamon from her preparing the evening meal. She dried my tears with her handkerchief and stooped down to look me in the eye, her voice careful, measured and loving.

'Now I don't think we need any more upset from you before *vrathino* (the evening meal). It's not good to go into a meal at five years old crying. I have cooked your favourite.'

It was odd to eat a proper meal in the evening. That usually only happened on festivals and adults' name days. But I was sufficiently distracted from my thoughts by the encouraging prospect of Pasticio. My mother had convinced me. For now.

Of course, even a child knows how good his mother's cooking is. Mama masterfully commanded all the local ingredients to produce the mouthwatering pasta dish. Relatives always found reasons to drop by when news of Mama's culinary activity was abroad. Which was no bad thing because Elia and I were usually brought some small present by whoever came to eat with us. Mama always cooked much more than we could eat because of the arriving hordes. But today there was only enough for the four of us. As if Mama knew nobody would come. We ate purposefully, each lost in their own thoughts of a future without description. I kept asking questions when they formed in my mind. There was no flow, they just came out abstractly and were answered by one or other parent as best they could whilst distracted by the task of eating. For once the television was not playing to itself in the background.

'Who will live here when we leave?'

'Why are we going to Athina? Why not Kalamata?'

'Why will I have to change schools?'

'Will we come back to stay in the summer?'

'Can I come and see my friends and cousins?'

'Will there be a field with the apartment in Athina?'

'Will we have a fig tree?'

After the last question Mama looked up at me and knowingly glanced at my shirt, stained by the red of the figs Dimitri, Photine and I had been scoffing. She made no comment. But she knew.

My final question was the one whose answer I remember to this day. It was the promptness of the response and the pressing timescale that etched itself on my mind, as if this had all been worked out well in advance of that day and Elie and I were just being informed prior to the event.

'When are we leaving?'

'November,' said Papa.

That night it was a long time before I drifted into sleep. Even then I kept waking up imagining men moving about the house, directed by Papa to pack things into crates. Even my bed with me still in it.

Next day I was tired and couldn't concentrate at school. I kept my news to myself. Dimitri noticed my distraction, but didn't enquire. He just kept looking across at me in class. I wondered if everyone in the village, including Dimitri, knew my news. Later, after school, Dimitri, Photine and I met up. I said our family was going to Athina to live in an apartment. They were surprised, so I don't think they had known. We talked for a long time that evening about what it might be like and whether we could write to each other. I said we would stay in contact forever. Dimitri, for whom this was a replay of events since his other best friend, Savvas, had also moved to Athina some months prior, simply said he'd try, but he didn't see much purpose if we weren't going to see each other again. Savvas had promised to write to Dimitri, but he had not done so. Dimitri felt abandoned and hurt by this. I thought he was probably reacting to my news by insulating himself against future disappointment. Our evening drew to a close with a lot of unresolved issues, and at least one saddened participant.

When I had, several days later, become used to the imminent prospect of a life in Athina, I began to reflect on how the family had been changing in recent weeks. It had only been this news that had sensitised me to the realities, but I remembered several events, several conversations between Mama and Papa ending suddenly on my entry to a room, more telephone calls into and out of the house, the occasional businessman visiting the house and looking around the yard and the field. The dialogue was tense, tempers were raised. I sensed this was not going as smoothly as was anticipated. Papa disappeared to Athina for two days one week. We saw him off at the bus stop. He first had to go to Kalamata, then change to another bus. Mama was sad when Papa wasn't there. She tried to hide it, but I could see the sadness in her eyes. When Papa returned he announced that he had rented a fifth-floor apartment with modern facilities in a suburb of Athina called Nea Ionia. He told me there was no field, but a park opposite where children played. The local dimotiko for me and a local gymnasium were very well equipped. He said one of the reasons he was moving so quickly was because myself and Elie were now only a few weeks into the school year and he wanted to make sure we were able to settle into our new school. It was especially important for Elie because she had just graduated from year six in my school to the first year of gymnasium. I was in year one of dimotiko and Papa said my main job was to make friends with other children this year because I wouldn't have any gradings yet.

During the wait to move to Athina, Mama packed everything

carefully that could be taken to the new apartment. As time
progressed it became more difficult to find anything. Items that had
remained in the same place all my life would disappear overnight.
Another box would appear, sealed with tape.

Another thing happened during this time. A procession of foreign
people came to the house, often clutching papers and pictures of
our house. Many of these people looked different to us and came
in cars. Almost nobody in the village had a car, but all the visitors
had cars. Elie and I quickly separated the visitors into two groups.
The first we called 'D-car people' because they all had a sticker
with a *D* on the back of their cars. The others we called 'NL-car'
or 'S-car-people', their cars had *NL* or *S* on them. We liked them
better than the D-car people because they were more friendly and
smiled. Mama and Papa had angry faces when the D-car people
came. I don't know why.

Some visitors even tried to speak to Elie and I, saying 'Kalimera',
'Posoeestay', or at least that was what it sounded like they were
trying to say. I just looked at them and responded meekly,
abashed. We couldn't understand how they spoke. Papa struggled
in conversation, Mama deferred to Papa with a shrug and a turn
down of the edges of her mouth. 'Don't ask me' was the message in
this gesture. Nobody brought children with them. Papa said these
people were looking at our house because they wanted to buy it.
I asked whether we could visit them and stay and he said not. I
was saddened by this because I wondered who would look after the
donkey, chickens and goats. But when I asked Papa, he said our
uncles and aunts would take the animals away and look after them.

'So what will these people do? Do they have their own animals
to bring?'

Papa smiled and said, 'I think not. I think they just want to sit
in the sun and look out over the sea.'

I didn't think that was a very good idea because Mama was

always telling us to stay out of the sun. 'As long as they promise to keep looking after the fig tree.' I said.

To which Papa replied, 'I hope so too.'

Between the time Papa and Mama told Elie and I we were moving and the actual time we moved there were a number of holidays, festivals and name days. As is tradition, we all celebrated each and exchanged many gifts and ate a lot of food prepared by the host families for each occasion. Even I was allowed to have a name day celebration when it wasn't my name day. After we had been to church and paid our respects to the saint and to the priest we returned home. All the relatives came to the house and gave me presents. Even the priest came. Mama cooked loads of food: mezes, salads, pasticio, moussaka, souvlaki, barbecued fish, sweet pastries. Everyone talked, laughed, sang and danced. But everybody who came knew we were moving. They all knew what it meant. Sad goodbyes were being hidden behind all the talking, laughing, singing and dancing. Elie said to me that she was very sad to leave. I was also sad, but I thought I could keep up contact with my friends and cousins by letter. So I convinced myself I was not really leaving, simply going away for a time.

On the day of our move Mama was very flustered and Papa had the job of greeting and despatching any visitors and well-wishers. A big lorry came to the house and three men began loading the boxes and furniture onto the lorry. One of the men kept stopping for a drink of water. But I could smell his breath and I recognised it as the breath of a man who drinks Ouzo. He became more careless as time went on, dropping boxes and banging against doorways. I didn't like him. It was windy and it rained two or three times. Everyone would dart inside and wait until it stopped to recommence whatever they were doing. The aunts and uncles came with trailers and borrowed cars or vans to move the animals. The donkey was walked to a neighbouring field. In the end, Elie and I just stood in the middle of the empty yard free of all livestock looking out across the grey autumn sea. Papa had once said to me that the fingers of the Peleponnesos were like the fingers of a hand, and where we lived was like clinging to the fingernails, careful not to slide down the slopes into the sea. I said I hoped there would be a view like this from our fifth-floor apartment, but Elie said I was stupid if I thought Athina's suburbs were scenic. I think she was upset, she didn't usually call me stupid.

At about 4 pm the lorry had been loaded and drove off down the narrow lanes leading to Kalamata. I could imagine our material lives being catapulted down the country roads towards Athina. We would be following by bus to Kalamata, then train to Athina. When we left our house everybody lined the street to wave goodbye, their handkerchiefs in their hands. We all cried. My uncle had a car and drove us to the bus stop on the main road. Whilst we were waiting for the bus, people kept coming to us and hugging us, kissing and wiping tears from their eyes. I wondered why we were making this move if we were crying and everyone else was crying because we were all sad about our leaving.

Papa had arranged for us to stay overnight with relatives before catching a train. When we arrived they greeted us and gave us food. We were all very hungry and tired. I can't remember much about that stay.

It was the first time I'd been on the train to Athina. I spent almost the whole journey looking out of the window, as if I was recording the journey on a video in my head so I could replay it backwards. I thought it would be possible for me to imagine going home any time by doing that. I would probably get lost though, because I had to pee sometimes and I fell asleep for about an hour, so bits of the journey were missing. I went to the toilet on the train. It was scary. There was a hole in the floor. You could see the moving ground through the hole, the sleepers passing beneath you as you tried to do your business. The hole made a noise at you, a roar that put you off what you were doing. The train rocked and rattled and I found it difficult to pee. Then you pulled a chain and water washed down the hole but some went on my shoes. I don't like train toilets.

It was late afternoon when we arrived in Athina. The station was Larissa and it was very busy. As the train had made its way from Kalamata it had picked up more and more people. When it arrived we all poured onto the long platform under a cover like a veranda. I remember the long platform because it had arches all the way along the walled side. Some had windows, but it was so long you could not see the end of the row of arches. There were announcements through the loudspeaker, hard, rough-edged accents unfamiliar to me, announcing trains so quickly it was as if the announcers were needing to catch the train and were afraid of missing them if they didn't hurry up and finish what they were saying. We had a small amount of luggage and Papa had arranged for us to stay in a hotel. I had not been to Athina before; it was very big—it took thirty-four minutes between the last fields and the station. There were buildings everywhere, all of them taller than any in our village or town. Everybody seemed to be rushing. People were not very friendly, and we didn't know anybody. Even people on the train who talked to us were now pushing past us to get to the exit or catch a bus. Some were even walking across the tracks, but we had been told at school not to do that if we were near a railway. Papa knew where he was and it was not very long before we had made our way to the nearby hotel. I had not stayed in a hotel before, but this one was like luxury. There was even a bathroom in our hotel room. It had soap and towels, a shower and a bath. We were four people in one room so my sister and I had to sleep in the same bed. Elie objected a bit but Papa arranged the bed so we were top and tailed—that was how Papa described it. There was no food in the hotel, but Papa took us to a souvlaki stand and we sat at plastic tables in the busy street eating our food and drinking Fanta, with Papa drinking beer.

We ate early because all of us were tired. The next day I woke up at 6:40 when Elie kicked my face by accident. We all showered and dressed. Papa said that hotels serve breakfast in the mornings to cater for Western tourists and we should eat because he didn't know when we could next sit down to a meal next. We sat down in a big room and then a man came and told us we could go to the food table and eat whatever we wanted. I ate something from almost every part of the table, even some food for tourists called cereal, which they eat with milk. There weren't many tourists in the hotel, but Papa said that was because it was November and they don't come in November.

Later in the morning we set out to reach the new apartment. Papa took us on the Metro, which is like a noisy train that goes under the ground. It wasn't always under the ground on our journey— perhaps they had to give the passengers some air. Papa got a map for me so I could see how we got to our new home. The stations were close to each other. I remember Agios Nikolaos, Kato Patissia, Agios Eleftherios, Ano Patissia, Perissos, Pefkakia, and Nea Ionia—this was our stop. Our new home. When we arrived at the apartment the lorry with our belongings was already waiting. As soon as the door was open our furniture and boxes found a space. There wasn't much organisation and tempers flared. Elie and I took the stairs to the roof of the block to escape the chaos. The roof was where other residents hung their washing. We looked out over the new view. All I could see were buildings: on hills like the hill our apartment was on, in valleys; in rows, in streets; right next to each other, and some on their own. And big flat buildings that Elie said were factories. There were many factories. But no fields, no livestock. The only trees were along the roadsides, on the path. You could walk into them if you weren't looking where you walked. We looked over the edge of the roof. The park was a tiny space surrounded by buildings. That was going to be our play area. Mama came up and gave us a spoon each and pots of chilled rizogalo with honey, and a bottle of water. That was my first food in my new home. Looking over the city I remembered that Elie said I was stupid if I thought Athina was beautiful. Now, in that moment, I understood.

* * *

Now I, Ioannis, live in Nea Ionia, I am thirteen years old and I have settled into First Senior High School, having graduated from the local dimotiko. The intervening years were a period of adjustment and learning about our new neighbourhood. We lived a modest life in the apartment. My parents became active in the local church and participated in each of the religious festivals. Neither Elie nor myself were as religious as our parents, but in Greece it is difficult to eschew religion completely, so firmly entrenched is it in society and nation, so we would go to the festivals, weddings, baptisms and funerals. Of course, everybody celebrates Easter too. Through the combined efforts of both Mama and Papa they made good networks with people. It was nothing like the community of the Peleponnesos village we had known, but good people helped each other willingly, although many other Athenians kept themselves to themselves. As for Elie and myself we had the dubious benefit of a socialisation of sorts in school. All the pupils lived locally in Nea Ionia, so our peers were known to us, as would be the case in any city suburb. We each had our scrapes with the underbelly of school life, made bad choices, learnt tough lessons by associating with kids who turned out to be the 'wrong kind'. Elie had now begun university, she had chosen to move away to Thessaloniki to study. I was still in the family home.

I woke up one morning and realised I was becoming a man. There were new dark hairs on my legs and under my arms. There was a growth of hair above my cock (that's bigger too and has a mind of its own) and I needed to shave my face. It seemed like it was not there the night before, and then it was! Although I guessed that would be impossible. My voice had been lowering in fits and starts for weeks, although it went higher and lower of its own free will. That was embarrassing for me to hear, and I was embarrassed because of other people hearing it. I was one of the first in my class this happened to, apart from those few boys who appear to have Neanderthal ancestry, who became men-children at the age of eleven. There were other changes too. My body was growing steadily, but then it put on height and weight so quickly. I was thirty kilograms for ages and suddenly I was almost forty. I was 1.2 metres tall only four months ago, now I'm nearly 1.4 metres. Ma and Pa looked at me and you saw their pride. I just think I was growing to be a man. It was a bit soft to see them cooing over their son. That's what's going to happen. We had a more adult relationship now as well. When Elie went to university they changed how they talked to me. They asked my opinion and everything. Pa tried to involve me in what he was doing when he was at home, which wasn't that much. I didn't like many of his friends. Ma tried to treat me a bit like a grown up, but she couldn't change the habit of a lifetime by stopping her war cries and her firm voice. Especially 'You treat the apartment like a hotel—there's no room service you know.'

I used to go to the kafenion with Pa. He'd walk past three to go to his favourite. I thought it was a dingy hole compared to some, but he met his friends there and it seemed like they ignored their surroundings. They all talked about soccer and politics. I had done a few years of Greek history at school so I thought I knew some of it, but these guys were all stuck in a time warp. They talked about the generals and mentioned events and individuals, they revered some of the junta like they were gods. They talked about Turkey, about Macedonia and about Cyprus—always that things were better before some figure or other did a stupid thing. I think Pa and they all belonged to one political party which I heard them talk about in code. Like they didn't want to let anyone know. Anyway, it was obvious they were nationalists because they were always going on about that and what should happen. Pa had always been a nationalist—I remember him talking about it on the farm. He said his family had a proud history of nationalism and activism. I thought that meant they were physically active, but now I think he meant they didn't just say they supported the party they did something for it. 'Loads of people on the Peleponnesos were nationalists,' Pa said, 'it went with the agricultural life.'

I remember in the kafenion once he shouted over the chatter to Tassos, to whom were are related, and ranted, 'But when you move to Athina there's all manner of crazy views. The Communists . . . *ftou, ftou*'—as if spitting—'they have a lot of supporters and we know what they stand for. Yet all the time we end up with parties in power trying to be so close to the middle they collide in the centre. Nobody knows what they stand for, other than other countries meddling with our affairs. At least with things like National Alignment, the Progressive Party, the National Political Union, and even those crazy 17N guys. Some are like reptiles.' I thought about Ninja Turtles as he continued, 'And now this other bunch,' not referring to them by name in case he was overheard.

This was the stock conversation for Pa in the kafenion. It all happened ages ago. Half the parties didn't really exist, they had no MPs. But at the bottom of an ouzo glass they lived vividly each day for these people.

One evening I asked Pa about our ancestors and whether there were any famous people in our family. He went all dreamy and mentioned my grandfather and great-grandfather, as well as my mother's great-grandfather. 'They were all nationalist fighters, farmers second and fighting men foremost,' he shifted position on his seat as he became animated. 'Our family are proud of your grandfather Constantinos. He fought in Cyprus. He was born in Greece but our family are originally Cypriot. The British exiled your grandfather's sister's son Costas for his involvement in an armed confrontation that killed his brother Takis.'

He described the situation Costas was involved in. It was amidst an armed struggle between the British and the liberators in Cyprus. He mentioned names I was familiar with from history. He referred to the centuries-long animosity between Greece and Turkey, the role of foreign powers interfering in regional politics, creating the circumstances that ignited armed opposition. He smiled as he reflected that grandfather may have been expelled, but they didn't keep him away from Cyprus for long.

We talked, or rather Pa talked and I listened, for perhaps an hour. I wanted to go to bed. He wanted to continue. In the end Ma rescued me by insisting I went to bed.

As the months progressed, as festivals were celebrated, as name days came and went, semesters passed, exams were taken, I became more of my own person. I thought I knew my mind and could hold my own in an argument. There were a lot of arguments. It seemed I couldn't keep out of them. My relationship with Ma and Pa had deteriorated. My school mates all agreed it was happening to us all. But Ma and Pa certainly despaired of, as they put it, 'the cuckoo, the nasty man in the household, the nice boy who had started to go bad.' I wasn't doing well at school either. My interests were not being catered for in class. I was rebelling and nobody knew what to do about it.

The first time I saw Ma drunk on brandy I was a little frightened. It was after a blazing row between us about something trivial. I boomed my deep voice, issuing forth foul language and half formed logic before storming out of the apartment. These days her voices had no effect on me. She could shout and wail all she wanted, but I could give as good as I got. Pa was not around very much because his job took him all over the mainland. Ma and I were the sparring duo. We weren't very charitable towards each other any more. Anyway, two or three hours after I stormed out I went to sneak back into my room. But Ma was sitting on my bed crying, and drinking directly from a bottle of Metaxa. Her movement was uncoordinated, her gaze imprecise, her speech slurred. She had been crying for a long time because her make up had run. She looked towards me as I entered my room. *My* room, and I shot her one of my evil glances. She ran out of the room but caught herself on the door handle. She screamed in pain and stumbled to the floor, then picked herself up and locked herself in her and Pa's bedroom. I looked about my room, emotionally bruised by the sight of my mother. I sat where she had sat. I lost myself in thought. Was I a bad person? Had I caught *matisma* (an evil spell passed by looking at someone) from somebody? Was I ill?

Before I went to school the following day, Ma and I faced each other and I was unable to hold my upset back. I cried and apologised if I had caused her to drink. She apologised for frightening me. I asked about her bruised arm from her collision with the door. She brushed her arm as if to say, 'I'm fine,' but I could see she was not. I went to school, but my mind was not on my study. I picked an argument with someone larger than me at break time and came off worse. I was called to detention. A black eye and a cut on the nose had developed during detention. When I returned home I looked ugly. My mood was correspondingly ugly too.

Another row materialised from nowhere between Ma and I. We polarised to separate ends of the apartment. I escaped as soon as I could, skipped a meal and sat in the park smoking and seething with resentment at the world. Oh yeah, I had found the pleasures and kudos of smoking.

This pattern of altercations at school, at home, and with virtually anyone, continued for weeks. I was not being bad, but nobody I was engaging with could understand how I felt. It's like I can't even explain it to myself, I just knew I was at odds with the world and I couldn't see any end to it. Ma continued to drink when Pa wasn't around. But sometimes she wasn't even at home when I returned. One night she didn't return at all. She wouldn't tell me where she'd been. Cue another row. I said some more bad things. She cried and then drank again. And so it went on. My life was becoming shit.

Chapter Thirty-Two
Volos

Then, on 14 June 2001, our world got hugely worse.

Ma was calmly cleaning the flat. I was excluded from school, even though it was almost the end of the semester, for threatening a teacher: *Malak*a (masturbator, as in a dope)!

The apartment stairwell suddenly filled with people. You could hear many steps coming all the way up from the ground floor. Other neighbours in the block were calling to each other to see who had arrived and where they were going.

A knock at the door. Ma opened it to find herself confronted by two policemen, one of whom was Tassos, my father's cousin. Both officers had removed their hats. Behind them two female officers hovered. They asked if they could come in. The four entered the main room and beckoned Ma and I to sit. They in turn sat. Tassos opened his mouth but no words came out. His colleague realised there was a problem and took over.

'There has been an accident,' he began, 'on the northern road near Volos.'

Ma took hold of my arm and with the other hand reached for the handkerchief tucked into her sleeve. She looked beaten, even before she heard the news.

'Your husband, your father, was in collision with a truck. He didn't survive.'

At that moment, before any further dialogue, mother visibly shrank. I swear, she lost five centimetres seated. She started shaking, like she was holding one of those road flattening plate machines and the reverberations were passing though her body and up to her head. At first there were no tears, then her handkerchief was mopping up buckets of tears, she was blowing her nose, attempting to hide her emotion-contorted face from everyone's gaze. She stayed like that for several minutes. Tassos also mopped tears from his eyes. Only the officer who we didn't know had managed to stay free of the hold that a relative's death has on people. I wondered how many times a week he had to do this.

Taking a dispassionate observation, that is me not thinking I was participating in the tragedy, I suddenly became aware of all the thoughts in my brain bursting forward simultaneously to the front of my head. Half-sentences issuing from my mouth, overtaken in my thoughts by hundreds more vying in the queue to be blurted out next, my face felt like it was working through every expression it had ever rehearsed. My eyes darted from face to face, wall to wall, to the door, to the window with the daylight outside it, to the picture on the wall—an image of the yard and field on the Peleponnesos. I recalled memories of Papa and me doing things together. My moist face belied the rush of emotional turmoil beneath its skin. My mouth was contorted by a jumble of juxtaposed words never before structured into a monologue.

Nobody was answering my questions, but maybe they weren't coming out as questions. Nobody was saying anything. In fact the only thing they were doing was pulling out paper tissues from the little packets you get in shops and pharmacies. Tassos, still in tears was handing tissue after tissue to Mama and me, then one for himself. A female police officer came into the room from the hallway. She took her place opposite Mama, I think so that mama was not in the sole company of men. Still nothing was being said. I could hear noises and voices in the rest of the apartment block, as neighbours relayed the unfolding crisis to others. At that time of the day the men were working and children were at school, so all you heard was the highly pitched tones of the womens' agitated calls to each other, like the calls of a flock of gulls.

It felt like my body wouldn't work properly. I tried to get up from my seat, but my legs didn't work. I tried to reach over to Mama, but my arms didn't respond properly and just flailed helplessly. It was Mama who was the first one to come out of the paralysis. The shaking had stopped and the tissues were drenched. She pulled me towards her side and enveloped me in her arms, pulling me closer until there was no air between us. It was uncomfortable and bits of me hurt while this was happening, but I thought that this was as good a place to be as any at this time. A well of tears unleashed themselves from my eyes as Mama's grasp continued. I was as sad as I had ever been in my life. My eyes and face ached with the pain of crying; my chest and throat ached from the emotion that seemed to be inside but was unable to fight its way to the surface. I just wanted it all to stop, but it didn't.

The officer who gave us the news went to the kitchen to get us water, coming back with a bottle from the fridge and two glasses. The female officer continued to ply us with dry tissues.

After several more immeasurable seconds, minutes, quarter hours, Mama, Tassos and I had calmed down. She and I were beginning to look at the officers and ask questions. Mama took the lead and I kept my questions to myself. My eyes and expressions were asking questions, but my mouth wasn't ready yet. Mama asked many of those that I was thinking.

'When?'

'Whose fault?'

'Where is he now?'

'How?'

'Where exactly?'

'Was anyone else injured or lose their life?'

'Has a priest been to see him?'

'Did he suffer?'

'Which direction was he going in?'

'Is the car badly damaged?'

'Was he taken to hospital?'

The officers answered each of these in a calm and sympathetic manner. It happened at about 6.30 am. The car was travelling north past Volos on the main highway when a lorry that was travelling south overtaking another on a hill experienced a sudden mechanical failure and was unable to move across to the right hand lane. Papa's car collided head on with the stationary truck immediately after he had come over the brow of the hill. It appeared that Papa was travelling quite fast and didn't have time to react before the impact. There was no chance for any of the occupants. The hill was close to a church so the priest was able to be on site quite quickly, but the occupants of the car died instantly. They would not have suffered. The description continued, the lorry driver was so badly injured he would lose one leg at least.

Occupants. Mama's lips sculptured themselves around the word but no sound came out. From inside my maternal cocoon, her arms still engulfing me for her comfort and mine, I felt her grip perceptibly tighten when the word was uttered.

The officer looked uneasily at Tassos, then quickly toward both of us and shuffled on his chair, as if he had mishandled the situation and now needed to go into further detail than he would have preferred. He stuttered at the beginning, then took control.

'There were three occupants. There was a woman and a child of about three years old. None survived.'

'But was he giving these people a lift, was this someone he worked with?'

Mama's confusion was evident on her puffed up face, her reddened eyes searching every feature of the officer's face for explanation.

'We found the documents of each person.' He stopped, looking as if he had already crossed to an uncomfortable place and wasn't willing to go further, he himself now displaying signs of emotional stress.

It was Tassos who took over. 'Despoina, what we know at the moment is that Georghios was driving these two north past Volos. Their papers suggest that they live in an apartment block close to where he has his up-country office base. He was carrying the keys to the apartment.'

'So you know that he knew the woman and child?'

'Yes.'

Mama had taken in this information, but was fearful of probing any further. She released the grip on my body and stood shakily to get the phone.

'I have to let Elie know what has happened. I wonder if she will be in classes yet. I'd better call her on her mobile.'

Tassos stood to catch Mama as she lurched towards the phone, put his arms protectively around her and whispered that he had already contacted the university and that she was aware of the situation; officers in Salonka had spoken to her. Elie was coming home on an afternoon flight. Mama slumped back into her seat again and searched the room for answers that made sense, certainties, logic. But there were none.

Tassos and the other officers had a quiet conference together and, Tassos excepted, took their leave, offering their condolences. The hours that followed merged into one another. During that time I was challenged by the situation in so many ways, the questions still inside me, but unable to be uttered. I can't remember what was said or how I felt during those hours, only that it felt as if an acoustic barrier of thick cotton wool had been placed in my head, blocking my ability to analyse the situation.

After Elie returned home there was another period of

unmitigated grief, raw emotional outpourings. We hadn't eaten. We weren't hungry. We weren't thirsty despite crying an ocean. Neighbours came to offer their condolences, having made what they could of the bits of information they had heard. Some bought simple, hastily baked foods, like *paximadia,* on such occasions and made drinks to sustain us through everything. I don't remember whether I ate and drank or not. But after dark fell I went to bed and slept fitfully.

At one point I dreamt vividly of a time when I was about four years old and Papa was teaching me how to round up the goats. I remembered his attention and care to ensure that I understood what he was telling me. I felt in my dream as if he was my protector, dependable and constant. I felt the warmth within me from that. I was the observer. I watched him looking out from our field towards the sea, when in the evening it was difficult to separate the sea from the sky just after the sun had set. He looked at peace with the world, comfortable with his surroundings and probably content with what he had achieved. A ship sailed across his field of vision from left to right, cutting a line in the apricot coloured void, only for the cut to repair, smooth over, like a crease in a piece of fine silk which in its own time flattens again. His mouth formed the description of our location 'Clinging to the finger nails of the Peleponnesos'. I was happy.

Chapter Thirty-Three
Ioannis Loses Sight of His Lode Star

The days that followed were a minefield of confused emotions, exploring mental territory that was foreign to the three of us in that apartment. Now my mood swung between extremes, my need for certainty never far from my thoughts, anger welling inside me, searching for an outlet. Whilst I was conscious that this was a difficult time for each of us and feelings of love, care, and protectiveness toward Mama were prominent, my teenage angst, for it had now begun to take on definition thanks to Elie's instructive chats, lashed out in unpredictable ways, after which I felt transitory remorse and disgust at how I could be so callous towards other people struggling to manage their own emotional nightmares. Mama and Elie were now dressed in the traditional black of mourning. I wore a black armband.

On one occasion, after I tongue-lashed Mama because of some minor issue and stormed out of the apartment shouting foul language over my shoulder, I paced the streets, seething. I had nowhere in particular in mind to go, nobody I wanted to talk to, and no desire to return home. I was of an age now that meant I had outgrown the play area opposite the apartment. The streets were my new territory, although I wasn't usually alone, and the boundaries were stretched further as weeks passed. I had enough money in my pocket for the fare and decided to take a bus toward the city centre. After about forty sweltering minutes I found myself in the Nea Iraklion area. I was so angry I did not think about how exposed I had become, so far from home, so far from anyone I could turn to; or what I was going to do next. This area was so much more scruffy than where we lived. It was like those images of Africa you see on the television. In the lobbies of old, dilapidated apartment blocks were groups of foreigners, standing or crouched against the wall in conversation, looking with fear through grubby windows upon each passing pedestrian, suspicion on their faces, and on those passing by.

I suddenly felt very alone and lost.

In an attempt to connect with some familiar Greek-ness I made for a kafenion, which Greek men inhabit as a proxy for social clubs. I realised I had insufficient money, and when I reached it found only foreigners sitting in the white-ceramic and Formica brightness. I turned away, seeking something, anything, I could identify with. The shops I passed were selling foods I never ate, displaying vegetables from another world. Anatolians in our neighbourhood had their own foods and spices, but these were quite different. I quickened my pace, looking for normality. I walked blocks along linear boulevards before I could feel that I had re-entered a Greek neighbourhood. How could a neighbourhood be so totally different from anything I had known and grown up accepting? Where had these people come from, what were they doing here? I felt as if I had travelled continents on that bus. And now, as I realised too late in my confusion, I was unable to take the bus home since I had no more money left, so I had to walk continents. I wasn't certain which direction to walk in at first and took a circuitous route through unfamiliar neighbourhoods. Then I found an arterial road I recognised and trudged with tired repetitiveness towards home.

Home. Despite my masculine adolescent urge to tear myself from it, the home in which Mama, Papa and I had lived in was the only place of safety and security I knew. That realisation was enough to summon up a pile of guilt at how Mama and I had clashed before my earlier departure. Tears welled, my throat ached holding them back.

I felt my face and lips struggle to hold in any noise. Then I crouched between two stinking wheely bins in an alleyway crying like a baby.

I resolved, having recovered my composition, to be more mature in my dealings with Mama, to act like the man I was becoming, and to behave in a manner that befitted a man of the house. I returned several hours after the fiery departure, exhausted and a little battered by my experience, full of intent to be a good son and feeling love and protectiveness toward Mama and Elie. That wasn't enough to avoid a thorough shouting match regarding where I had been.

The funeral was delayed whilst Papa's body was returned from Volos. Mama went to church at least every day. The priest visited almost every day to make sure we were all OK. Tassos helped with the arrangements. The telephone was constantly ringing as relatives and friends made contact and made preparations to attend. I don't know about other countries, but funerals, weddings, and baptisms are all big family events in Greece. Everyone who had been part of your life and is well enough to travel will turn up. They all need accommodating, feeding, talking to. Preparations are huge.

Throughout this time there was one topic of conversation that Mama said we couldn't talk about: who had also died in the car with Papa. Elie and I had discussed it without her knowledge and Elie said that the police had concluded, rightly or wrongly, that the car's occupants were a family unit, that the paternity of the child was not in doubt. They implied that Papa had a second family, that all his time away from home on business was also his alter-life. When Elie told me this I felt huge anger towards Papa for betraying me. Elie said we all felt betrayed and the priest was not very pleased to be having to bury someone who was so dishonest and uncommitted to his true family, but he had said that the funeral was best thought of as honouring the bereaved as well as the deceased. This was something of a departure in Orthodox custom, but Elie said that the priest was, thankfully, progressive in this manner and felt that if Papa was fit to be closer to God then Papa could discuss it with God directly, and in that knowledge he would conduct the ceremony.

My feelings of betrayal wouldn't go away after the funeral. I had millions of memories of Papa, more in the past than since we had moved to Athina, but all of them were so vivid to me, and in each of them Papa made me feel that I was the only person in the world he loved. Of course I knew he loved Mama and Elie too, but when he was with me it was as if his love was for me only. Now we knew that Papa's love, latterly, had been spread liberally and we had no sole right to it.

The funeral passed by without too much problem. Mama said she had poured out all her grief and anger beforehand and had no more to express by the time of the funeral. But she was still visibly upset right through the ceremony. His body, what remained of it, was laid to rest in the municipal cemetery; his grave on a shelf in a modern part, his photograph (taken the previous year) peering out at us from the head of the coffin. I always wondered, from previous funerals, why people choose the most sombre photographs to put in cemeteries. The style has changed little for decades. Nobody puts a photo of a smiling adult, a party-goer, a happy face, unless it was a son or daughter who died before their life had really got going. Cemeteries are depressing places. Mama didn't dwell long in that place. It turned out that the family of his mistress and their child didn't approve of the relationship, so there were no representatives of her family at Papa's funeral. That, at least, was a relief for us.

Chapter Thirty-Four
Guardian Angel

It was after the funeral that Tassos began to take more interest in our wellbeing. Elie had been so close to the end of her university year when the event happened that she was given a special dispensation and didn't have to return until next semester. So we were all living together, and Tassos and the priest would make frequent visits. Tassos took a particular interest in me. He knew I had been having a few problems at school and with Mama. He said to me that if I needed someone to help guide me through the future he would be happy to be there for me. I was touched by his offer, but I thought I could do without his keeping an eye on me. He did, I think, imagine that I was up to no good, other than during the bereavement and mourning period, when I had largely settled into compliant behaviour for the sake of Mama, especially after my journey to 'Africa'. I think he was right. Being the dutiful son does not feel natural most of the time. I would rather be out with school friends, immersing myself in what we felt we had in common—music, the culture of the street, girls. That didn't fit with being a dutiful son.

Tassos also offered to help me uncover some of my ancestral roots to, in his words, 'understand what had made me the person I am.' Years later, I can see that he had an ulterior motive for his interest in me, that he was grooming me in some way for a future I had not, at that time, imagined for myself. But at this time I was interested to learn what others had taken for granted I had known.

He said that we could talk this stuff over if I came to the apartment he and Auntie Adonia lived in every Tuesday.

I still didn't really know my own mind, but I thought it would be respectful to take Tassos up on his offer. At least he would think I had an interest, whether or not I had. I would have to practice the art of appearing engaged in what he would tell me. I'd not been good at doing this because my face gave away what I was thinking or how I was feeling. Mama used to say she could read me like a book, but she didn't say that any more. Now she said she thought there was a cuckoo in the home. The other thing I had to work on to please Tassos was my attitude. Like I really couldn't be bothered with boring shit. If I was in a group of kids outside of school and something in the street was going off and a passer-by stopped to give us a piece of their mind (it was usually a black-clad granny) I'd think 'whatever' and walk off whilst they were still talking, which made them madder. 'Come back when I'm talking to you . . .' they'd say, and we'd just ignore them. Then they'd shout along the street after us about 'young people being respectful of their elders' and stuff. It's easier when you're with mates because we could all walk off. Power in numbers. But with me and Tassos it would be one-to-one and he's a cop, and he probably thought I'm his cousin's skinny kid. That's what I mean. We see each other differently and I've got to put on a mask.

On the first Tuesday I went round, Auntie Adonia plied me with home-made food and clucked like a chicken as we waited for Tassos to return home. When he came in I was busy eating baklava and finishing my second bottle of Coke. A sweet and tacky layer of cola and syrup coated my teeth. As I ran my tongue over them, it felt like licking the surface of fly paper. Bits of pastry found their way into the pockets of space between my cheek and my gum. No amount of Coke would dislodge them. I stood up when he came in the room and choked on another bit of the sweet pastry as it caught in my throat.

'Looks as if you have been treated like a guest,' he said as he put his uniform jacket to one side. 'So how was it today?'

'Not so bad. I was hanging with some mates in the park.'

'Didn't get into trouble then,' he said, smiling.

I smiled in response, shaking my head.

After the introductory chatter he took me onto the veranda and we sat talking about more stuff, but I could tell he was moving towards a line of interrogation. Once a cop, always a cop, I thought. His theme was what other kids I knew thought of Greece, of Athina, and what thoughts I had of my own.

'Dunno, really. I haven't thought about it.'

'But you study Greek history at high school?'

'Yeah, but that's all in the past. How civilisation developed, what people lived like, what bits of today's society we owe to that time.'

'Exactly, so what does the past tell you about how we live now?'

'Well, there's government, and people, democracy, representation of the people.'

'And law and order?'

'Yeah, of course.'

'So what is all this for?'

'I don't understand.'

'So we have all these institutions and structures, what are they all for?'

'So people can live their lives?' I suggested uncertainly.

'Right, but do they have to fight, or can they just get on with it without fighting?'

'I dunno, Some people get on with it, others fight. Others take the piss.' I wondered whether this slip into how my mates and me talked would draw censure.

'What do you mean?'

'Well, some people couldn't care about stuff, they just go out and take what they want of the world. They pay if they've money, they thieve if they don't have, they fight for their corner. They don't care.'

'Care about what?'

'Other people. Rights. Feelings. Hurting people. Those kind of things.'

'Is that right? To not care?'

'Sometimes.'

'Really?'

'Yeah, sometimes there's no reason to care about what other people think or do. You just have to get what you want.'

'And other times?'

'There's stuff stopping you. Laws, other people, someone stronger than you.'

'So, the ones you don't care about, give me an example.'

The abstract suddenly needed real life experience, but my mind was blank. 'Like when,' I struggled to think, 'some guy wants to build a development and there's already people living there and they get thrown out so this powerful guy can build his development. Like in China.' I said thinking of a telly programme.

'Does that happen in Greece?'

'Yeah, of course.'

'But aren't there rules to stop it?'

'Yeah, but money talks. In Greece, money talks.'

'Are you suggesting Greece is a rotten, corrupt and lawless country?'

'Depends.'

'On what? Either it is or it isn't?'

'Yeah, it is. Papa was always saying he had to pay his taxes, but loads of people were milking the system, avoiding paying, doing cash deals, claiming for things they shouldn't.'

'You don't have a good view of the world.'

'It's what I see. It's what Papa saw.'

Tassos paused, looking from the veranda toward where the sun had set.

'OK, maybe there are some problems, but does everyone get on with their lives happily without fear?'

'Not everyone, only those that can afford to.'

'So it's still about money?'

I thought about this for a while. I never had any money, other than what Mama and Papa had provided, pocket money or 'allowance'. I was speaking from a position of having no money and no power. I lived in fear of having no money. A moth repeatedly head-butted the light bulb above our heads.

'Yeah.'

'How do you change that?'

'Why would I need to, as long as I had money?' I suppressed the urge to complain about never having enough money and not being taken seriously, which were the main gripes of kids my age. I guessed he didn't want to hear my moans.

'How do you get money?'

'Earn it. Speculate.'

'Speculate? How?'

'Get loads of money then put it towards something you bet will make a profit.'

'Like what?'

'I dunno.' I was bereft of ideas. I wasn't sure what I meant by speculating.

'OK, back to Greece. Who lives in fear in this country?'

'Old people who can't look after themselves. Victims of thieves and violent people. Sick people.'

'That shows a good awareness.'

'We're taught about citizenship, so that's where I learn about it. But what you see on the streets tells you about other people living in fear.'

'Like who?'

'Immigrants.'

'So what have they to fear?'

'Everything. They aren't Greek. They don't speak Greek. They have come here, but they bring nothing, so they must only take. The newspapers and television report about them and wind the Greek people up against them. The police harass them. The politicians beat them with their words. Hooligans kick them with their boots. I think I'd be in fear if so many people in a country were against me.'

'Do you think immigrants are treated properly?'

'Dunno.' I really hadn't thought about it, but it occurred to me that I didn't see people in Nea Iraklion looking very happy. They all looked as fearful of everyone else as I was of them.

Uncle Tassos went and got a beer from the fridge and commented about his working day. I think he'd reached a point he wanted to get to with me. The visit ended and I sauntered home along the darkened canyons between tall apartment blocks, listening to Greek city domestic life, televisions, arguments, dogs, cicadas, and police sirens puncturing the background din of a city in motion.

Alongside my trips to see Tassos that summer, and perhaps prompted by what I was taking away from these chats, I was exploring what my mates and I understood about politics. I had always understood—without thinking about it much—that Greece had a long tradition of what Tassos called polarised political opinion. The story of Greek history is punctuated by rebellions, coups, riots and wars. We were a warring nation. We fought the Turks, mostly the Turks really, but other countries as well. Whilst I have been on the planet there have been no wars, but the one people talk most about is the war with Turkey in 1974 after they invaded Cyprus. And the coup of 1967. And the problems with Macedonia. I didn't know much about any of these. But what I did know was that every Greek adult had a view about everything and nobody agreed on anything.

So you had loads of political parties and protest groups. Hardly a year went by without a riot in Athens; war on the streets. Papa used to stay clear of activism, never thought to go to demonstrations. He said there was nothing to be gained from hooligan behaviour except a split skull and a bloody nose. I think that's why I didn't know much about things myself.

By now I was sixteen. My mates had a much better understanding of politics than I did (although I don't know where they got it from). Manos, a classmate, said his older brother explained to him about communists, anarchists and fascists. I think he said his brother was an anarchist. Papa and Tassos said our family were nationalists and I didn't understand where that fitted in with all the other parties. Could you be proud of your country, a nationalist, and at the same time be a communist? I didn't know.

So my summer of enlightenment helped position my views on a scale of what I understood to be: right, left, fascist or communist. I still struggled with the idea of Greek nationalism, to me, nationalism was the identity which truly Greek people shared. It was the glue which held us together, our history and pride in the significant contributions Greece had made to western culture were part of our national consciousness. But as far as I was concerned, I could only see Greece as it actually was, speaking the language it had always spoken, practising the religion it had always practised. Even the priests, their tongues loosened in discussions outside the kafenion, staff in hand, legs apart, sat bolt upright, could only advance a nationalist opinion. They were virtually the standard bearers of nationalism; as long as the Orthodox church had a tight grip on Greek social and political existence then nationalism would prevail. Yet still I struggled to comprehend the spawning of so many different colours of the Greek political spectrum. How could people even begin to think they could change society with some alternative view that failed to embrace nationalism and the religious dominance of the Orthodox Church? I couldn't see how, for instance, communism could survive in Greece, despite its many attractions. So I decided that I was Greek, and that as long as I was Greek I would be a nationalist. Not left or right.

Tassos talked to me one evening about our family's nationalist past. He explained how our family had straddled the countries of Greece and Cyprus, how our ancestors had fought for the principles of nationalism. How some of our ancestors had died for the cause of nationalism in Cyprus and some had also fought for terrorist organisations in Greece, supporting the nationalist cause. Tassos was proud of our family's past.

I queried how someone born in Cyprus and, after all, had a different passport, could be a Greek nationalist. He said it was complicated and even he had hated history at school (so why did he know so much about politics) so his understanding wasn't good, but it was something to do with the fact that many Greek-speaking Cypriots considered themselves an extension of the Hellenic nation; that there were always going to be other opinions, cultures and political opponents, so under the leadership of the Orthodox Church, and with the blessing of the British who had colonised Cyprus, the idea of Greek nationalism had flourished. There was and still is, he told me, a strong movement for union with Greece—enosis—among a large proportion of Greek Cypriots. I had heard about this, but hadn't really paid attention.

Chapter Thirty-Five
In a Dark Place

By the end of summer that Papa had died and abandoned me and Mama, I became a youth with a political viewpoint. I hated Papa sometimes because whilst he was developing another life and another family somewhere else, I was sitting in Athina crying out for some guidance. If he was here today, I still don't think we'd have had the discussions I have had with Tassos, and I think I would still have been in the dark.

'In a dark place' was where I think Mama was for the remainder of the year Papa died. Despite the support she was getting from Tassos and Auntie Adonia, and from the priest, Mama couldn't cope with the sense of abandonment that had exposed itself at the moment of Papa's death. I tried to follow through on the promise I had made to myself months before, to be dutiful son and the head of the household. I took this latter role very seriously, seeking to protect Mama, doing all the things men did in the household. She appreciated it, I think, but I did realise that whilst she held up her head when we were together there was evidence of the sense of deflation she felt when I was not around. Although she tried to hide the evidence I think she secretly tried to re-inflate herself by drinking. There were never any bottles around the house, but she behaved differently when I returned home in the evenings. Sometimes she had gone to bed very early and locked her door. She wouldn't talk to me through the closed door. She wouldn't even acknowledge my presence. At times like that I felt helpless and angry, frustrated and yet filled with tenderness, all at once. It screws you up when that happens. I sometimes punched a wall or a door to release the tension. I don't know why—it never helped.

I was beginning to find her behaviour odd. As Tassos put it 'when the hormones of youth clash with the vulnerabilities of adults there are likely to be some heated reactions.' Indeed there were. On occasions my rows with Mama became so vocal that the neighbours would knock on the door or shout from the floors below to tell us to keep the noise down. Greeks love a heated discussion, but my exchanges with Mama were in a different league. What then developed to avoid these problems was that I would increasingly not stay in the apartment and Mama would see less and less of me. I would hang with my friends, try to sneak a meeting with a girl I fancied without her parents knowing, play soccer, swim, or do other stuff on the streets my mates and I had claimed for ourselves. Things came to a head between Mama and I when I came in after midnight one school day and she accused me of having smoked. I thought Nico, Manos and I had managed to avoid getting our clothes smelling of the stuff because we'd stripped to shorts only; don't ask, it was a crazy evening. Mama could smell something, but she wasn't to know it was weed. It wasn't the first time.

She began to go out in the evenings, 'to Auntie's' she would say. I would go out with my mates and come home late. Mama and I would have shallow, neutered conversations. The apartment became a no man's land that neither of us wanted to occupy or fight over, and the outdoors were what I thought of as the place where I could stretch my mind. Nothing to do with weed, of course.

One wet November evening she came home drenched, her hair matted to her face, her clothes dripping, her mascara in rivulets down her face. She had been drinking. I had only just returned home and was in my room. I think she thought I was still out, but I sneaked a look at her from my room as she searched around the house before going out onto the veranda and gesturing to someone below. Seconds later the front door opened and closed, a man's whispering voice, a girly giggle, then Mama's door closed and the lock turned. I realised there was a man in the house. I quickly began to get a feeling in my chest, a tight, wringing sensation, my heart beating and my skin starting to sweat. My muscles seemed to tense up and I couldn't get them to relax. It affected my legs, arms, neck. By now my whole body was contorted with the rigidity. A pain in my chest. I thought I was having a heart attack. I was afraid to go out of my room. I lay on the bed, got up, paced the room, lay down again and tried to distract myself by playing a computer game. It didn't work—I couldn't concentrate. Then I heard noises from the bedroom which I thought must have been the pair having sex. I couldn't believe my ears. My body was in outright revolt. I grabbed my Walkman and ran from the apartment slamming the front door on my way out. I didn't know what I was going to do, but my whole body was still tensed right up. The rain was the fine, thick, drizzle that drenches you without your knowing. I was soaked in minutes and had come out without a coat. It was a cool evening as well, so minutes later I was shivering and seeking shelter. For about three hours I paced the streets, wherever possible taking shelter when the rain got too much. I cared neither for myself nor my mother. How could she betray me like that?

I thought about going to see Tassos, but it was too late. I thought about going to the home of one of my friends, but thought the idea stupid. I walked aimlessly, my thoughts like a smokescreen. I was unaware of where I was, passing dog walkers, party people, and avoiding the packs of dogs which roamed the neighbourhoods barking and in turn catalysing an endless chorus of responses. Cars passed by occasionally, their red lights disappearing into infinity along the gridded streets. Trains rhythmically clattered over their points toward their distant destinations. The nightscape of our city.

I didn't go home. I couldn't. I didn't even know if I could ever go. In the end, exhausted, I found shelter under a bridge, pulled some discarded cardboard boxes around me and tried to sleep. It was impossible. All I could think of were the images in my mind of my mother with someone else, the remembered noises, the mascara stained face. Each time I thought my pain was easing the thought of what was going on tensed me up again. Sometime in the night I was disturbed inside my boxes by someone close by. I guessed it was someone trying to steal something, but I couldn't get a view of them. Maybe it was some pervert preying on whoever they could find out at night, alone and vulnerable. I had images of an old man ready to molest me, or perhaps wanting me for some weird sex thing. I thought I was ready to jump up and retaliate if anything happened, but I was unprepared for what happened.

The first blow was across the cardboard covering my legs. Under the cardboard I instinctively curled into a defensive posture, knees against chest. My legs were smarting form the blow. Before I could respond a second blow connected with my back. I caught sight of a booted foot retracting before receiving a second blow to my shoulder. The pain was unbearable. I was frightened and gasping for breath and fighting off tears. Blood began to trickle down my collar bone and onto my breast. More blows from above onto my torso; it felt like a piece of pipe, only slightly cushioned by the cardboard.

Then an agitated shout, 'You fucking immigrant. We'll take your head off. We will cut your cock off, you fucking foreigner. We're going to kill you, you shit fuck.'

I was writhing in pain, packaged in cardboard, under a bridge and I was going to die. All I could think of doing was to shout out. 'I'm Greek, my name is Ioannis, don't hit me,' before curling tighter, tearful, into a huddled ball, like a hedgehog.

The blows ceased. The attack suspended. Then, as two hooded men with black scarves across their faces pulled away the cardboard, they bleated apologetically, 'Sorry mate, really sorry,' and ran off into the night.

I pulled myself into a position so that I could look at the injuries. I couldn't think straight. After a couple of minutes I tried to stand and fell back onto the cardboard. I stayed still several more minutes before again trying to stand. I was trying to catch my breath between holding it each time I moved an injured limb or bruised part of my body. I was a mess. Blood started to seep down my back from the shoulder wound. My t-shirt was turning from yellow to red.

Then, as if planned, not five minutes after the event, a police car screeched to a halt under a bridge and a couple of officers rushed toward me. They settled me into a position and called for an ambulance. There was no hint of malice, only concern for me. They kept asking whether I was alright, what my name was and how many fingers were they holding up. They searched me for identity papers but I had none. It didn't seem to bother them. They were only full of concern for me. When the ambulance came I was taken to Evangelos Hospital, way down in the centre of the city. My mother was summoned and because she'd told the police about Tassos he was coming too. Despite being so late at night the hospital accident unit was awash with the sick and injured of Athens. Queues of resigned, triaged patients with blank expressions waited in the corridors for the doctors to work through their lists until every patient was attended to. The atmosphere was desperate, a cohort of patients demanding quicker attention outside the doors to the treatment rooms—the last doors of the lengthy triage. I was wheeled into the department, then parked in an anteroom whilst my details were processed, then through the crowds immediately into the chaotic treatment room. It looked like a traffic jam of beds and trolleys loaded with gossamer-white old people breathing what could be their last air; blood-covered accident cases; and the walking wounded; whilst doctors and nurses darted erratically around and dealt with the night's unfortunates. My bruises and contusions were developing into a range of puffy purple-black-yellow hills all over my body. Some were being dressed with gauze and lint. I was so stiff I could hardly move. I didn't know whether I was hungry or thirsty. I was shaking. The doctor gave me some medication and I felt calmer. The pain eased. I was taken for an x-ray, then returned, each time through the throng of the triage.

Tassos was the first to arrive. It was about 6:30, the rain had cleared, the sun outside the window had poked its head above the hills. The cityscape to the east was silhouetted against the red-grey backdrop. I was relieved that my mother was not first. Tassos was beside himself with concern for me. Our voices collided as I tried to communicate the thoughts uppermost in my mind. He wanted to know who had done this, what had happened. I wanted him to make sure my mother did not come in. We talked over each other. We tried to get words in edgeways. In the end he let me talk, but either I couldn't explain, or he couldn't comprehend the reason why I didn't want to see my mother. I said she had upset me. He said she must be allowed to see me because she was my mother. I said she wasn't my mother. He looked perplexed.

When we could hear the animated voice of my mother approaching the ward, Tassos took on a role as welcoming committee member to prevent her immediate access to me, but it was no use. Her maternal instincts prevailed, her clucking attention was unchecked. I, for my part, was determined to have nothing to do with her so I tried to maintain a defiant silence. But I soon burst into tears, ashamed of my obstinacy; needing unconditional love, my mother cradling my head, kissing my forehead repeatedly. Tassos looked on from beyond the end of the bed, conscious that this was a private family moment. He remained perplexed at my earlier admonishments to keep my mother away.

With no serious injuries I was discharged later the same day. Tassos and my mother remained with me until I was allowed to go. Tassos drove us home. I returned to my room. Any evidence of the precipitating circumstances of the night before had been removed, obliterated from the apartment, but not from my mind.

Chapter Thirty-Six
Political Awakening

As soon as I was well enough to attend high school, I returned and was treated with careful respect by fellow pupils and teachers alike. They had heard about the attack because the local newspapers and TV channel had reported the story. The story carried the theme of mistaken identity by far-right sympathisers. It implicated people close to the police as the perpetrators, claiming only someone well-connected could have been so quickly in contact with the police. The editor of the newspaper was renowned as a socialist thorn in the side of the right who took every opportunity to snipe at what he perceived to be the out-of-control elements of the far right and their infiltration of the police. The sub-theme was one of solidarity with the immigrants who sustained unreported attacks such as these on a regular basis. They weren't able to interview me because of my age, but they managed to get hold of a photo from somewhere. I was disappointed that the photo was of me about two years previously. I looked like a boy. Any kudos I could get with the girls from the event would be wiped out by that photograph.

Mama never again returned to the apartment with a man, but she did regularly stay away nights. If I was able to predict when these would be ,I'd make sure I'd invited a few mates round, and hopefully some girls, although it was near impossible to achieve the latter. We'd smoke some weed, maybe drink some beers or vodka if we could buy some. The biggest draw for these evenings was Internet porn. Mama was quite oblivious to the uses kids were putting their parents' computers to. There were no blocks or password controls. The Internet was quite a recent addition to the household and Mama didn't understand it. Several of us lads would click page after page of free access porn, getting more excited as the evening went on. We'd fool around a lot, and on one occasion we all had a group jack off. None of us had done that before and it started off being kind of weird. The more daring or uninhibited lads stroked themselves before others had the nerve to join in. I was neither the first nor the last to join in. One mate just couldn't face it and went home. We haven't done it again because afterwards everyone felt self-conscious about it, even though it felt fine when we were all doing it. I don't even remember what we were watching. We had loads of porno evenings like this in the end, but none got out of control like that again. Some of us were, by then, flirting by mobile phone with particular girls that we fancied at school, but there was nothing most of us could do to take it further because parents wouldn't allow the opportunity to meet.

After I became eighteen, Mama announced that we couldn't afford to stay in the apartment any more. We'd have to move to another part of town, to a less expensive flat she'd agreed to rent. It was a bit of a shock. The apartment was not too far away, but was definitely in a cruddy area. She took me to see the place. It looked a bit shit, but she said times were hard.

Athina was in the throes of a huge construction boom ahead of the Olympics. The traffic problems were terrific and the promised new metro lines had not yet been completed, so everyone was moaning about everything. The government was on some big ego trip about the Olympics and state TV was playing along with them. Everyone could see all the work going on and wondered where the money was coming from. In the end, the whole city accepted that the Greek people were ultimately going to pay for the developments: first through their taxes, second through their inconvenience; and third for seats at the events.

Seats were already being marketed, but the prices were astronomical. Me and my mates weren't as interested as we would have been if Greece was hosting the FIFA World Cup.

We moved to the flat. I had become involved in a political group, and several evenings a week I would go to their offices and help making banners, seal envelopes, make badges, and that sort of thing. Tassos had introduced me to someone who had invited me down. They were all very friendly and looked after me, drawing me into their banter as we worked, caring for my needs, getting me drinks from the kafenion downstairs. They were all nationalists, well, ultra-nationalists to be more accurate. Their flag flew off the balcony. Their aim was to smash the left-centre government and reassert pride in 'Greece for Greeks'. They wanted all the government ministries to promote nationalist ideals. They wanted to stop the watering down of our country with foreign workers and immigrants coming from or going to the rest of the EU. I didn't know how they were going to achieve this, but that was what they stood for. They didn't have any MPs, but their supporters shouted and demonstrated in Syntagma Square. I reflected that these were the same sort of people Pa used to engage with when he was in his favourite kafenion.

My time was split between studying for my exams and my political work. I managed to fit in the odd date with girls as well. Mama was still staying away at least once a week, but she kept from me the identity of the man was dating because she had understood what impact her behaviour was having. I still got upset that she was with someone else, but I now had my own life, my own girlfriend action. Knowing about her became less and less stressful, eventually having almost no effect on me. Then, after all my exams had finished, as me and my mates were preparing for a long summer of parties, not to mention demonstrations, Mama dropped a bombshell. She announced that she would be moving in to stay with her boyfriend. She said we would still retain the apartment for which she would continue to pay rent and bills, but she wouldn't be living there. I'm not sure how I felt when she announced this, because I was thinking more about the opportunities it offered, less about the down sides. All I could think of was that I had loads more freedom, a bachelor pad for parties and sex. And so it turned out to be; well, maybe not much of the latter. I don't think I regretted the departure of Mama after the initial surprise of her announcement. Perhaps I had decided when lying in that bed at Evangelos Hospital that the apron strings should finally be severed. Ever since that day she and I had been tolerating each other. She, no matter what else was influencing her decision, was obviously confident that the time when I no longer needed her had arrived. I was now officially free.

The nationalists were taking more of my time now. They would take me out on demonstrations where I would distribute flyers. They told me they weren't allowed to let me demonstrate because I was a minor and they would get into trouble. They were nice enough to me, but there were some real boneheads. Perhaps those people just needed some social focus. They would be at the office every evening. Although I was meant to be there only one evening a week I sometimes called in at other times to finish off tasks. I reckoned I knew more than some attendees—it was almost all men—about what the aims and objectives of the party were, but I also knew I didn't know everything.

In my own world, living independently from my family, despite getting involved in political activity and continuing my education, I began to feel I was hitting a wall. It felt like I was in paralysis. The biggest problem was education. Since the age of fifteen when I had left the gymnasium with a school leaving certificate, I had been enrolled in the next tier college, the Lykeio. It was in the neighbourhood and some of my school mates from gymnasium had started with me. Mama had always gone on about how it was better to get as much education as possible, but I wasn't interested;

I just wanted to work and earn money so I could pay for the things I wanted. I'd stuck it out at the Lykeio. I knew I wasn't getting anywhere, my coursework was being marked low, my attendance was crap. Whilst some of my mates were doing really great, I was left choking in their dust. In the end, the principal arranged a meeting with myself, Mama, my teacher, and someone from the municipal HQ. I was a bit pissed off about everyone talking about me not making progress, struggling, being absent from classes. I was in the room; nobody asked me—they chatted as if I wasn't there. It sounded like I was some sort of failure. I knew I wasn't, but it wasn't the right place for me to say anything. In the end they terminated my enrolment. They talked about me registering for a vocational course instead, to prepare me for work in a trade, but I was so stressed towards the end of the meeting I just said 'shove that.' I think they belatedly realised it wasn't constructive to discuss someone's shortcomings when the person was sitting at the table.

I ended up in a construction job. There were lots of jobs around because of the Olympic Games preparations. I was working on infrastructure, which meant I was digging roads, ditches, drainage. The pay was OK, but it wasn't going to secure my future. Some of the guys I had to work with were real thugs, they worked to earn money to drink, smoke and gamble. They drank, they fought, they worked, they drank again. I thought I couldn't get into that, but they were a good bunch to work with and I did occasionally drink with them. They were all unmarried, mostly from out of the city, dossing in high density squats or cheap housing. Some lived almost all the time in shipping containers on different sites, even in the heat of summer. Because the construction was falling behind schedule it meant that higher paid work was available all times of the week, day and night. I volunteered for the unsocial shifts. We worked nights, weekends, festivals, even Easter.

But when the construction projects were coming to an end there was a problem getting other work. Before the start of the games I had pocketed thousands of Euros. Most of it I was now spending on food, drink, weed, and wooing girls; all offered diminishing returns. The only positive use of the money I saved was to get a passport. Tassos and Adonia pestered me to get one, even though I could have applied after I was twelve. They said I should broaden my horizons and consider travelling. Greece had been in the European Union since 1981, but I had never travelled beyond the borders of my own country. Adonia said my passport would allow me to travel wherever I wished. She said it hadn't been the same for them. I gave in to their pressure and was taken to the police station in Nea Ionia to submit the application which I paid for. My photo had been taken when I was seventeen. When I received the passport I couldn't believe how young I looked in the photograph.

My colleagues and I were laid off in August 2004 and had to look for other work. I got a job in a restaurant washing dishes; I couldn't give a shit any more. I only lasted a few months. One day, having received my pay packet the night before, I just didn't turn up for work. Then I got work in a supermarket—that was crap too, but I didn't have any other options, so I just persevered. I had to learn to stop spending money on stuff; it was just a matter of trying to survive. Mama paid the rent and everything, but I agreed to contribute twenty Euros a week.

Chapter Thirty-Seven
Mama's Departure

The second worst time for me was in 2009, was when I was really having a crappy time all round. I was in with a group of lads and we were all looking for trouble or thrills. Our lives were chaotic, our allegiances were to no-one but each other. We smoked weed and drank when we could afford it and just turned our lives into a game of risk. My supermarket job was a drag. The apartment was falling apart— the fans weren't working, the fridge broke down, I couldn't organise myself to keep the place clean so I wouldn't bring anyone home, let alone a woman. My contact with Mama was almost non-existent. My visits to Tassos were getting less and less frequent although Auntie Adonia would wash my clothes if I dropped them off for her.

Mama called me one day to say we needed to meet. She suggested a restaurant, nothing special, just normal stuff—moussaka, souvlaki, fried fish, pizza. So I went to see her at the appointed time—actually I was late because I'd been on a hot date with a customer who'd chatted with me at the supermarket and whose husband was away on business. I still had that sensation in your groin like your balls and cock have been pummelled to infinity when you've just had sex. I greeted my mother, sat down, ordered food and drink and tried to concentrate on what my mother had to say. I picked at bread and scooped up taramasalata between mouthfuls of beer. I was starving and it was the first proper meal I'd sat down to in days. I wasn't really listening properly until she said, 'So I've given notice on the apartment for the end of December.'

'What?'

'I knew you weren't paying attention. Your problem is that you don't pay enough attention to anything, Yan. I wish you'd sort yourself out. You'll be going nowhere if you're not careful. I said that I have split up with Mikis and he's thrown me out.'

'No, that's not what I was asking about.'

'So you didn't really hear anything I'd just said? You don't care about anyone but yourself. My life is in a bad way and I can't get any attention from my son let alone sympathy.' She was getting flustered, on the verge of a crying bout.

'I *said*,' she dragged out that last word whilst she composed herself, 'that my move out of Mikis's apartment has come just at the wrong time and my work contract is up for renewal. In a flash of clarity I've realised that I don't need to be here at all, that I can move back to the village and stay with my sister. I've got a pension pot and things look OK for the future. I can get work locally. You're in a job, getting paid. So I'm not going to renew my contract at work and I'm giving notice on the apartment for the end of December.'

The consequences hit me.

'So what am I to do about somewhere to live after December?'

'You can rent a room you are able to afford. You wouldn't be giving me money any more, not that you regularly do that at the moment, but you'll have enough to live on until you've got some direction in your life.'

'But, but . . .'

I was lost for words to express my exploding crisis.

'Listen, Yan, you're twenty-two now; you can sort your own life out. You don't need me, I know, because you hardly ever contact me. You're an adult and you should take the responsibilities that come with being an adult.'

'You're throwing me out of the apartment? Just like that?'

'I'm not throwing you out. I'm ceasing to be the tenant. If you want to be the tenant and want to stay there talk to the landlord. Otherwise, look at other options.'

The food arrived, but our dialogue was distracting me. The plate of kalamari failed to get my attention. I was shouting, pointing at my mother with a crust of bread in my hand as I issued forth, my voice taking on a menacing tone, my face sculpted into a scowl.

My mother had rehearsed this conversation and she was delivering it like a business boss would deliver a redundancy notice to an employee. There wasn't any emotion in her voice now, there wasn't any sign of the caring mother that I remembered from childhood, nor from the hospital. I was a stranger to her.

'I can't believe you can do this to your own son,' I said. I knew that any reasonable family would cover their only son with cloying claustrophobia, and like a parasite he would be a sitting tenant in the family home long past his moment of independence. I had kind of banked on that scenario for myself, hence the jolting shock to my system, the untouched plate of kalamari.

'My son? My . . . *son?*' she exclaimed, prodded by my one-liner into an emotional delivery 'What sort of son have you been for the last few years? You don't phone me, you've never come to see me. You take and take from people and give nothing back. What right have you to think I must any longer consider your well-being above my own? You've got a nerve. I have stayed in Athina for years on account of you. I have compromised and made sacrifices since the moment your father passed away to make sure you could carve out a future for yourself. If I had taken you back to the Peleponnesos all those years ago you would have found yourself without a decent education, no chance of work, no future.'

'And you think you've provided for my future here?' I shouted.

A table of customers shuffled around on their chairs, glancing in the direction of this altercation, unwilling witnesses to an unravelling family.

'Well you had the opportunities, you just couldn't be bothered to take them. You're lazy and can't apply yourself to anything. I've had enough of this.' She got up from the table, chucked a twenty Euro note onto the table to cover the bill, and stormed out of the restaurant without a further word.

I sat motionless, sensing the air refilling a vacuum created in the wake of her rapid exit. One of the fluorescent lights in the restaurant was flickering. Flies and moths were being annihilated randomly on the zapper hanging from the ceiling. The television behind the counter was playing yet another crappy game show. Then I distractedly forked lukewarm seafood and fries into my mouth. Customers sneaked glances at me. I glowered in their direction. The waiter, perhaps worried that the character reference he'd just heard might mean I would make off without paying, scooped up the note as he passed the table.

'That didn't go well,' he postulated.

'Ante gamisou,' I shouted, dropping my fork noisily onto the plate. Without finishing my food, I followed my mother into the night. She was long gone—I was glad.

The letter turned up from the landlord a couple of weeks later. My departure date was two weeks after the end of December. If I wanted to take over the tenancy he'd need a deposit and a month's rent in advance. He would inspect the property and decide if any of my mother's deposit could be payable to her after reparations. My mother had written to say she'd ordered a van to collect the major items of furniture on the last day and would pay a cleaner to tidy the house ready for the landlord. She had softened her stance and agreed to leave me the basic living requirements, bed, chairs, table, fridge. She suggested I go to the municipal office to see what help I could get regarding housing and financial support. That was the last I heard from her. When the van came to get the furniture, I made sure I was out.

Chapter Thirty-Eight
Squatter

Some days you wake up and see life for what it really is. When I woke up on 7 January 2010, my mind was clear. For once I would be decisive about my future.

Several days earlier I had been to the public housing office and had not been offered any local accommodation in the municipality. The best they could do for me was to offer a one-bedroom apartment in Korydallos, a northwestern ghetto suburb with a poor reputation, mainly because the prison was there. They could help me with initial costs and reckoned I could afford it on my supermarket salary, but I said it was too far from work and most of my salary and spare time would be wasted commuting. I went to see it on my afternoon off, but I wasn't impressed, so I let the offer lapse without replying. I had drifted into torpidity.

The clarity with which I had been blessed with today, focussed on two or three crunch-point decisions to bolster my increasingly marginal existence. First, I would not look any further for accommodation. Second, I would squat as long as I could in the apartment. Third, I would look at another nationalist group to see if they were more dynamic than the one I been festering unnoticed in for ages. I had done a bit of research on the landlord and the property and found that the building was an illegal construction that had escaped the attention of the municipality, presumably because the landlord was wheeling and dealing with the bureaucrats. I also found that the landlord was a non-resident Albanian whose wife was

Greek. All the letters I'd seen from him were posted in Athina, but it seemed he had businesses all over the region and didn't stay long in any place. I thought to myself that if I could resist the demand to vacate for as long as possible, I could live rent-free and that would give me an opportunity to get my life sorted. If I had any hassle from him, or anybody, I'd get some help from my nationalist mates before I jumped their particular ship. It felt like the best way forward at that moment.

On 14 January, the day I was meant to quit the property, nothing happened. Nor the next day, nor the next. In fact, it was the end of the month before anybody came. Because there was a vacant industrial unit beneath the apartment and it was tucked away under the lea of a hill, there were few passers by. One afternoon when I returned from work I found two guys trying to knock down the front door. I had made sure it would be difficult, barricading it from inside and using an alternative entrance on a first floor balcony. Because they hadn't got any equipment with them there was no chance they'd break in. I waited till they'd gone then entered my own way. I checked the door was holding, then got on with things as usual. Or rather tried to: I found the electricity and water had been turned off. I knew the stop tap and supply box was in the industrial unit below, but I didn't have a key. My mother had all that stuff and must have passed it back to the landlord or his henchmen. A temporary setback, I thought. I packed a bag and went out to see a mate who had a fitness club membership. I thought I could borrow his card, work out a bit, get a shower and go out to eat whilst I planned my next move. Nico said he wasn't a member of the gym anymore, but I could shower at his place and we'd get something to eat together. Nico was really helpful because he knew someone who could tap into the electricity supply and bypass the meters. He gave him a call and we agreed to meet up the next day.

Over a kebab, Nico and I were talking like you do when you're together with mates. He was saying he'd heard that there was a big crisis unfolding in the financial markets in Europe and that the stock markets had slumped alarmingly following the collapse of some bank in America. I didn't know much about that stuff and said that the rich bastards were probably just tricking everyone into thinking there was a crisis so they could make more money. Nico thought it wasn't the same scale as previously. I tried to steer the conversation to something else.

'You know how shallow I am Nic, I haven't got any interest in shit like that, and I don't have a telly so I don't even get any information anymore. I only know about the stuff me and the nationalists go on about, and they don't say much about anywhere beyond Athina.

'Anyway, how's it going with the soccer?' In fact, I didn't want to know about the soccer, but I also didn't want to talk about financial markets. It was never going to affect Greece, it wasn't like we were somewhere important like Germany or Britain.

Nico took the hint and we rambled on about other stuff, but you could see he was still worried by the news he'd picked up. There were other people around us talking about it as well. Anyway, our evening chat only moved forward when I told him I was thinking of chucking the nationalists.

'I've hung out with them for years, but each time they thought there was a reason to defy the government I haven't been more than a dutiful placard carrier in Syntagma Square,' I said, thinking that was most weeks. 'It isn't like I was expecting promotion, like in the army, but I'm still doing kid's stuff.'

'Yeah, but you haven't done your National Service. They probably don't like the idea that you're trying to dodge it. When you were in the lykeio that was fine, but since you've left you're not on the radar of the military because they probably think you're still studying. They're going to catch up with you eventually and you're just going to have to do it. I don't know why you don't want to do it, it's not like any Greek man has a choice. Most of them think like me, that it is my duty to Greece.'

I looked at Nico kind of strangely. I thought that he'd changed his tune since we were at lykeio together. Then we were all of the same mindset; to avoid conscription as long as we could. We knew you could dodge it for a very long time; we thought if we held out long enough it would probably be made optional. But here was Nico almost sounding like he wanted to do it.

'What? Six months ago you were all for dodging it, and look at you, there's a perfectly good excuse for you now you've gone from lykeio to university. You won't be doing it for years.'

Since the time I turned eighteen, I'd convinced myself that the draft was nothing to do with me, that if I studiously ignored it, then maybe I'd never get my call-up papers. And they hadn't arrived in the post yet. It wasn't like I was the only guy in Athens dodging it—thousands my age were doing as much as they could to avoid the twelve-month interruption to their lives. It also wasn't like I was against the idea of fighting and being trained to be a fighter, after all, I'd labelled myself a nationalist, and what could be a better demonstration of your credentials? I thought people who were conscientious objectors and got allocated non-combat roles were faggots. It was just that the discipline and servitude of national service wasn't for me.

Nico pushed the remains of his meal around his plate, deep in thought.

'You know, Yan, you can be a real dick at times,' pushing himself away from the table as he spoke, going outside to smoke.

I remained seated and tried to comprehend this sudden chasm that had opened up between us. I looked across to him outside the window. He wouldn't let me catch his attention. I thought that it would all blow over before we next met. I took my bag and left the building, walking past him, saying I had got to go. He didn't answer, just lifted his head in acknowledgement.

In the dark of night, I clambered my way into the flat. I'd have some power soon, I thought, I just had to get through the next day or so without it. But it wasn't a day or so. Nico's mate never came round; I'd burnt that bridge.

So from a day when everything was clear and real, I stumbled into a hinterland where things didn't connect with each other. The job was pissing me off, my flat was pissing me off. I had no power or water. The landlord had by now barricaded the main door from the outside, but it made no difference to me. I didn't use it any more. The nationalists were beginning to piss me off.

The news carried ever more frantic news of a financial crisis. I listened on my phone one day to a serious political station:

'Now with economic decline engulfing Greece, the population has begun to adopt new political identities. Some are aligning themselves with communist principles, some are hardening their nationalist credentials, some—many—lean toward the extremes, right, left or the technocratic middle. Others, especially the elderly, just want their own communities to be peaceful, populated by people who care about each other. If somebody doesn't fit into any of the above they're labelled as junkies, wierdos, anarchists, deniers; a surprisingly large and diverse demographic. Whatever the colour of your politics, whatever your age and background, if you are Greek then you fall into one of these categories.

'Yet, at the same time, people mourn the passing of the old ways of doing things, the old civic and political systems. "I'll rub your back if you rub mine." It was the sort of dis-organic, parasitic, leeching, black economy that landed Greece where it is. People blame everybody but themselves.'

Then they went to an outside broadcast to seek a more upbeat story, then the summary:

'Whatever the issues, Athenians now volunteer in soup kitchens, run free health centres, work with refugees. Some people are so ashamed of their circumstances they are unable to meet the eyes of another person in the street. Society is broken, but it is repairing . . .'

I unplugged my earphones. I just wanted it all to go away.

Next day I was sitting on a bench in a park. There were kids playing some game I had forgotten about and I was engrossed, trying to remember the rules. Two guys came up to me like they were canvassing or something. They were wearing black t-shirts and dark trousers, looking like those creepy American missionaries. They asked me how I was, whether I needed anything. I thought it was an odd question. I said, 'A home, a decent job and a point to my life.'

That had them smiling, saying, 'We'd probably all want to have those luxuries, but was it all that bad?'

I explained to them what was going on in my life and how I was squatting and the job was crap. They gave me a flyer for a food bank to get some food. They asked me if I was ill or anything because they could get me a doctor. I said I was fine. When we talked a little more they described the organisation whose name was on their t-shirts and said they were recruiting people to join them. I asked what it was they stood for. They told me and I thought this is maybe what I was looking for instead of the nationalists. I said I already did some volunteering with the nationalists. They were interested, but referred to the nationalists as a bunch of well-meaning middle income boys with no teeth. It was affirming to hear a couple of lads my age saying what I had been thinking. They gave me a card with a logo and a web address. Soon afterwards I'd lost their card and thought nothing more about them.

Over the following months I began to feel better about my station in life. OK, work stacking shelves in the supermarket was still shit, my mates and I were still getting into trouble and I never knew when I'd get kicked out of the apartment. But life would pick up.

I knew my uncle was keeping a close eye on me. Tassos had always thought of himself as a surrogate father to me, 'his cousin's son' as

Tassos was used to calling me. He said it was what he needed to do in memory of Georghios, my late father. Auntie Adonia would also do whatever she thought necessary. I thought their duty towards me was nothing to do with me, but it was useful to have someone to haul you out of the shit when needed.

One spring evening I was, not unusually, in a bit of trouble. I was having a perfectly legitimate evening out with friends when we spotted a girl one of my friends was attracted to, along with a second girl. The two girls were displaying interest in our small group of lads and more than a little eye contact was being exchanged. Vassili, my colleague whose particular interest had been hooked, approached the girls in a respectful enough way and engaged in conversation. The rest us lads held back in mock embarrassment. None of us was aware of the presence of a chaperone, normal in traditional circumstances. The subsequent argument, on that spring evening in the middle of a street filled with promenading Greek families, was probably a turning point for me. I was drawn into the altercation when the chaperone started pushing and being physically aggressive toward Vass. With my hot head, I was the first to plough further into the melee. Suddenly, the innocent evening turned more ugly, starting with shouting and waving of hands, claim and counter-claim, pushing, prodding of fingers into chests. The two girls melted into the gathering bystanders for protection. I threw the first punch. My mates knew I'd be the first because I was the one with the shortest fuse and was the least able to talk my way out of trouble. My clenched fist connected with the cheekbone of the taller of the two men. The resulting street brawl was, depending on one's age and gender perspective, either an ugly scrap between testosterone-filled young men; a diversion from the tedium of a normal day; a blood-spattered disgrace; or a display of virility for the girls.

I emerged from the altercation not as well as I'd hoped. By the time the police intervened I had sustained a black eye, was bleeding from my nose and ear, and had been kicked in the ribs. My evening ended there, bundled once again into a police van and being taken, again, to the custody suite with my friends. Onlookers did, however implicate me as the initial perpetrator. My mates had been drawn in because they felt they had no choice but to stand united. The upshot of the arrest was that I was booked for a minor offence and then I released from custody. How I again escaped detention had only been revealed later. It revolved around the influence of Tassos within the station. That same evening, after his spell of duty, Tassos had made a call on me in my impoverished squat. I think he was shocked at the state of the building and the poverty of my existence. He wasn't surprised that I seemed to be unable to plan a way out of any predicament. He had known me for so long. But to see me attempting and failing to live a respectable life, failing to cope with day-to-day circumstances, these things came as a wake-up call for Tassos. I remember the conversation.

'You are happy with your life?'

'It's what I have.'

'Have you a plan to make a better life for yourself?'

'No. How can I do that? There's nothing for me or anyone my age in this country.'

'But many of your friends are making something of their lives. Your cousin is training to be an accountant. He is courting a lovely girl. Do you have a girl?'

'No. My cousin is different to me.'

'In what way?'

'He had opportunities. He's sensible. He's boring.'

'But is your life boring?'

'No, it's not. I have a good time with my friends. The boring bit is work.'

'What do you want out of work?'

'Money at the end of the week.'

'Is that all?'

'What else is there?'

'Are you happy in this apartment?'

'I live here.'

'But could you live more comfortably?'

'Why would I need to?'

Tassos paused at length to think through this bleak dialogue before continuing.

'I think you may be well-qualified to be a model Greek patriot. I think you can improve yourself and be helped to put a little more structure around your young life. If I could do something for you to help you, to keep you out of the custody suite, to give you something to live for, would that be attractive to you?'

'Depends what it was. Would I have to move from here?'

Would you want to remain? If you work hard in this role, work day and night to make it happen, you may find yourself among others who bring out the best in you. They would be your brothers whom you'd trust with your life, and they would entrust theirs to you.'

'It's not the army is it? I don't want to join the army.' I knew I was not being offered a police position. My charge sheet was too long.

'No, not the army.' Tassos knew I was dodging the draft. He was irked by my attitude, but in this conversation he seemed to have put that thought aside.

'But in this role you must also learn to be disciplined, to control your anger, your impulses, and channel your energies. You must follow instructions. But in return, you will gain self respect, the respect of others, and you will be contributing to your country. I have a friend; my friend is very interested in giving young men like yourself this opportunity. In the beginning you will not be paid and will need to work during the day. But this role will increase to take over the rest of your time, it will build you into something others will admire. Women will admire you.'

Tassos knew what men my age wanted to hear.

I liked the sound of getting respect from colleagues and from girls. My success in this arena had been limited. I was still, despite everything that had happened, technically inexperienced in matters of sex.

'It sounds like fun. What do I have to do?'

'You'll be part of a very important and influential group. You will be applauded for your dedication. You will give yourself to the Cause'—I knew he meant cause with a capital *C* by the way he said it—'and make Greece once more the proud country it once was. Most importantly, by being part of this you will be able to take what you do best and apply it, make something of yourself.'

Tassos paused again, leaving a pregnant silence in the room with the grubby mattress and bare white walls.

'How do I know this is a good idea?'

'You think that I, your father's brother, would think of proposing something that might be worse for you than you have at the moment? Look around you, Ioannis. There's not much here for you really. A prison cell is more comfortable. The Cause will feed you, accommodate you. Here you have to scavenge like a dog to keep yourself alive. You have to work for the money you spend each week. You currently have no ties and too few interests. What I am proposing will make you a man to be reckoned with.'

I thought Uncle Tassos was selling this proposition very convincingly. It was a mystery why he should approach me like this, and there were too few facts. But I nevertheless nodded assent.

Tassos put in place one of his smiles that brightened rooms, lifted the souls of those around him and brought warmth.

'You will not regret this commitment,' he said. He was probably privately thinking that this might just be the best way to keep his nephew out of a vortex of trouble, out of custody, and himself from Adonia's endless nagging admonishments to do something about the kid.

I lost my job at the supermarket; natural wastage, last in, first out, blah, blah. I'd persevered for over five years. Losing my regular pay was the final straw in my descent into poverty. I was beginning to think national service might be a reasonable option for a year or so when I suddenly heard about a job in the neighbourhood at a plastics extruding factory and got a job offer for a probationary period. I really thought the work was beneath me, but I must have put on a good show at the interview or the supermarket gave me a shining reference to get rid of me, but I got an offer anyway.

For a few weeks more at least the work was keeping me in money and food. I'd hooked up a makeshift shower in the flat by running a hosepipe from a nearby neighbour's tap up to the balcony. I'd fill a container and put it on a shelf in the cubicle and turn the tap on. It was cold water, basic, but it kept me from smelling like a down and out.

But my employer thought differently. One day he laid into me.

'You look like a tramp, your clothes stink and you can't even turn up to work on time most days,' he said, effectively firing a warning shot, threatening my probation period.

He had a point in that I hadn't attracted any girls since the shit hit the fan. Anyway, I guess he was just mouthing off and I was a convenient target. He didn't do anything. The other lads said he was always bullying someone or other, so it was just my turn.

But he carried on picking on me, for weeks it would be my dress or timekeeping or my bad breath or my attitude. So one fine spring afternoon, when families were preparing for Easter, the congregations in each church were practising their processions, and mothers were cooking special pastries, I'd decided I'd had enough of him.

I became *persona non grata*. I had alienated just about everyone I had known. It was my fault that I couldn't keep friends and relatives on my side. I didn't know what the origins of that failure were, but these days I didn't usually hang around to see if I could make things right—as you will have gathered. My philosophy had always been move forward; never look back.

Tassos introduced me to Mavro, but before I took up the offer he had presented to me, there was the little matter of work to sort out.

Chapter Thirty-Nine
Transition, 2011

The job pissed me off. I didn't need it. I would be one of the Brothers advancing the Cause; they would look after me. When the time came there would be jobs aplenty for me and my fellows. I left the factory building in a furious mood, on my way hurling abuse at innocent bystanders, firing a torrent of insults, vile language, and volumes of spit in the direction of the boss. I cast aside the plastic mouldings and extrusions that had been the subject of my attention for these last few weeks, trampling on finished items, hurling mouldings across the room, angry at everyone.

As I made my way towards my neighbourhood I mouthed and replayed to myself all the foul language I had employed, smiling at the effect I believed it had achieved, shouting at the top of my voice, abuse ricocheting off the buildings. That had fucking told them!

Small children and women, conscious of the approach of a madman, scurried out of sight.

I turned up a side street on the way to the home me and mother used to inhabit before she took fright at the situation and went to live with her sister in the rural south. At that moment, thinking of Mama brought back memories.

I lived here, I asserted in my thoughts. The Peleponnesos wasn't home.

Mama had been unable to control what she called her 'wayward and bitterly angry son' so she had unwillingly and distressingly abandoned me to my own destiny. I think she was fully aware of the path I would be taken down. She despaired, but she would have lost her sanity if she hadn't done it. She had seen me drift from job to job, never keeping one for long, never seeming to secure any prospect of a future. I had held no job more than a few months: barman, security guard, shoe shine boy (that was a bizarre set-up), food store shelf filler, plastics extruder. Mama's repetitive chants included that I was an angry man, got in with a foul-mouthed crowd she described as being made up of 'druggies and mental retards', carving myself a niche amongst misfits and hooligans. I had never been far from trouble, but mysteriously seemed to avoid ever being held to account. Mama used to say to the police, on the occasions they brought me home from the arrest suite, that I seemed to like it more in the cells than with my family. My mother's boyfriend disowned me—and I him—we wouldn't even engage. The policeman who most often accompanied me home had known me since birth. He was part of my family, had known me since childhood and was there throughout my troubled teens. He regarded me as a symptom of a failing society. Nice! Not even a disease, a plague, just a symptom. Then again, Tassos, a police officer in the Zefyri division, proud officer and nationalist sympathiser, was the protector of his cousin's son.

The Cause to which I had become attached after that dire interview with Mavro was, as yet, an unknown quantity. I was told it would consume my time, my thoughts, my dreams and aspirations. I would be amongst friends, with men whose world view I would share, men who nurtured within me a passion, men who would make me feel part of their family. I had made the transition. By walking out of that extruding job I committed to the Cause, and my Brothers would look after me. I sealed the pipeline from my past by also walking away from my squat that same day. With the few possessions I owned I took off to meet up with my mentor, Steven.

In an apartment block in the Zeyfiri district I was introduced to Steven. He was of a similar age to me, but muscular, more alert.

He had an air of confidence and a friendly face, which frequently seemed prone to break out into a broad grin. His eyes seemed to hold a hint of mischievousness.

'I am your mentor. You are my pupil. How do you like being a pupil?' he asked

'I don't. I wasn't a good school boy.'

'This is different. You'll have to be open to new ideas, follow my lead, take instructions only from me, shadow me. Do as I demand. Whatever that means. If you had a life before coming to me—forget it. Your new life starts here. I will own you throughout your journey, and I will own your failures. Make no mistake, screw me over, give me grief, lose the plot, and I will personally see to your punishment. You will eat, train, sleep, and learn alongside me. You will live alongside me, and that means I require you to be compliant, clean, quiet, and eager. In the end you will think the same as me. The longer it takes you to learn, the longer you will be here with me. If you think you can shit on me, you will learn a very hard lesson. What do you say?'

'I didn't realise I had to be here. It's not a problem. I have everything I need with me.' But I was apprehensive about what he'd said. Behind his happy face there might be a sadist, or a sex abuser, maybe. Surely Tassos wouldn't do that to me?

'I didn't mean that. What do you say about doing as I demand, being owned by me?'

'As long as that doesn't mean I've got to be your whore.'

I hoped not. I thought Tassos would disapprove. So would I. I was petrified at the prospect of handing over my body and soul. I wanted to run. Fast. But I wasn't in a position to do that because Tassos had issued an ultimatum to me; it was this or prison. Prisons were about the same, right? Steven wasn't impressed by the response. The friendly face and mischievous eyes had darkened. I sensed menace.

'You will be the latest of five to join, so you will be at the bottom of the ladder. Get used to the idea. We'll go to the gym and work out. You can get to know us. Over the weekend we'll all work together and bring you to a point on Sunday night where you will pledge yourself to the Cause. We have done this many times before. All our men go through the same process. Now go.'

At the gym I was welcomed with noisy ceremony, more a statement of group invincibility than a greeting. I was introduced to each of my future colleagues. They all had pseudonyms. Even Steven wasn't, it turned out, his real name, but he didn't elaborate. I'd have to think up a name for myself.

Other gym users looked on bemused, fully aware of the nature of the gathering. We were there until dusk, engaging in displays of power, virility, bonding. Young men, part of the Cause, strutting the room, challenging each other to greater and more implausible physical tasks, shouting across the echoing space, oblivious to other users' unease.

'Who has pushed the most today?' I shouted.

'Alexi, he's done one-fifty.'

'That's nothing,' I said, perhaps over-confidently.

'You try. Get on there and do one-sixty.'

After a few minutes of grunting and puffing, I dropped the weight-laden bar hovering over my chest, but was saved by the two lads who relieved me of the burden before it crushed my ribcage.

'He's a novice says one, he'll need to build up to that.'

I was humiliated, so went off to another machine to do a few lat pulldowns. I worked alone until the shame softened. From time to time my colleagues pulled out their vibrating phones, peered at their screens and engaged with one another:

'It's kicking off in Agios Pantaleimon,' said one.

'How many?'

'They say twenty with about forty police.'

'Who are they going for?'

'Pakistanis.'

Then another text pings.

'There's a rally tomorrow when the leader will speak.'

'Where?'

'Volos.'

'It's too far to go.'

'Should be a riot!'

Laughter at the irony.

I was shattered by the time we returned to my new accommodation. We cooked a good meal, enjoyed each others comradeship, exchanged banter. It struck me there was little discussion of why we were all together, what the purpose of the Cause was. Steven was overbearing in his demands, nitpicking in his attention to how I did things, like someone always on your case. Like I imagined doing national service would be. I was 'billeted', as it was termed, with Steven. The bedrooms were minimalist, like barracks, but more comfortable than my own. The beds and bedding were army surplus stuff. I had to keep reminding myself that Tassos had assured me I wasn't joining the military.

After a good night's sleep, I was awoken at six. Steven issued me with a set of clothes to wear and requested that I shower, sort my bed and clothes and return to the dining table at 06:15. I was late and they were waiting for me. Another bollocking. We breakfasted on meats, cheese, bread and yoghurt. Then we all went to another room and received a briefing on what was to happen during the day. We would take a minibus to the suburbs and walk fifteen kilometres with heavy packs before returning to the apartment in the evening. During the walk we'd get the opportunity to do some rope-work and some circuit training. In the evening there'd be an 'enlightenment' session. On Sunday there would be further training in the morning, a support task in the afternoon, and the gym and dinner in the evening. It sounded like the army.

It had been some time since my life had been regimented and my time filled so comprehensively. The rest of my new colleagues were supportive and friendly, although I was obviously a drag on them at the moment, not up to the task really. I fitted in and tried to keep up. Steven was the sort of person you could follow anywhere, so skilled was he at bringing people on board and seeing them through tasks. He was a tough taskmaster, not one to let a problem go unpunished.

The only obstacle I found was the session in the evening, where the 'enlightenment' was communicated. Of all the events, sitting in a classroom and learning stuff on a Saturday night would not have been my preference. We were shown a DVD of the rise of ultra-right ideology, shown news clips of the shortages, factories closing, poor older people scavenging for food, of the bloated ruling class of politicians, told of the banking crisis and asked to debate whose fault it was. There seemed to be no particular political bias or idealogical emphasis to any of the information, but one or two colleagues were certainly eager to voice their forthright views. I lost track during a debate on what the reasons were for the problems in Greece. Then we were asked to decide on scenarios where we might support the Greek nation. Whilst I didn't altogether share the zeal of my colleagues, I went along with it. I had the feeling I was being judged on performance, engagement, and what I said.

On Sunday, another early start, then to the local park for a session of circuit training. The discipline was more harsh than the previous day, which had felt like a jaunt in the country with close friends. Today it seemed more competitive, more was demanded. On one occasion I was unable to achieve my target for push-ups. I was shouted at and had to do a different exercise as punishment, then restart and complete my push-ups again. Steven was more assertive than before, less friendly. My colleagues were accusing me of slacking, and Steven was quick to punish. Our task was to work at the office above the convenience store packing and distributing

food parcels for the elderly. I was told that food producers and
wholesalers had been encouraged to donate. I was impressed by
the largesse implied. Our weekend ended with another gym session
and an excellent meal. These guys certainly knew how to look after
themselves. I was required to wash up afterwards, which took a
while, with Steven rejecting many of the washed items.

Over subsequent weeks and months my colleagues and I were
inducted, indoctrinated, and coerced into submission to the Cause.
By August I could no longer imagine myself to have been the punk I
now realised that I had been. Now I had purpose, friends, and self-
respect. It was certainly the case that I felt better, that Tassos would
be content to know his advice was sound, and that Steven would be
rewarded for a good job well done. The Cause had gained another
footsoldier. I was ready.

The five of us were now attached to a larger contingent based
in another part of the city. We found our new colleagues, whose
company we joined, more aggressive, harder. Then, one or two days
afterwards, we lost Steven, as it seemed he was called away by the
senior team. Someone in our new company said we'd been dropped
off by the wet-nurse as if it was always the case that Steven settled
recruits in then dropped out. Now we would be truly fighting for
the Cause. It was tough, because unlike previously we were having
to assert ourselves amongst our new colleagues, and that led to some
tense face-offs. Ultimately, of course, we formed a tight-knit group
with a common bond. We were Brothers now.

I could see what the Cause was and how it asserted its will. I
could see my role in that. I was still oblivious to the broader political
landscape in Greece and Europe. Everything we were taught was
tailored to avoid unfortunate moral and ethical dilemmas. Tailored
to ignore inconvenient truths. I had become just what the Cause
required me to be.

Chapter Forty
Defending Greece

I had matured since induction into a more rounded, but also more dangerous, individual. I could now cook, clean, iron, polish, wash clothes, mend clothes, and budget an income. I was able to disable someone with a baton, fire small bore weapons, use a variety of knives, make Molotov cocktails, release a hand grenade, and beat someone to maximum effect. My other skills included bare knuckle fighting, high velocity verbal abuse and extreme coercion. I was more disciplined, but antipathetic toward those I saw as enemies of the Greek nation: Africans, Gypsies, Arabs, Pakistanis, Germans, student anarchists, communists, socialists, bankers, old guard politicians, and gays. I was trained to not think of this as racist, xenophobic, or homophobic; I was defending Greece. I was defending Greece for some time—nearly two years—before something changed.

In November 2013 I was assigned to a series of support operations in central Athens. The riot police would be called to deal with a situation and my company would be tolerated by the police command as we informally backed up the police line. Our assignment was to carry out 'routine stop and search' and 'crowd calming'. Each of these was not what it sounded like. Stop and search usually involved forcibly stopping those fleeing a demonstration and extracting a donation before sanctioning their release. Crowd calming could be, on occasions, an activity akin to a seal cull, although our demeanour, together with the threat implied by the sticks and bats we carried, was usually sufficient to pacify our targets.

I had become so well indoctrinated I thought nothing of rough handling people. But at the same time, those Greek people who were already, or could potentially be, supporters were treated with gentle respect and encouraged to sympathise by the offer of charity. It was the Cause. I was defending my country.

PART SEVEN

Chapter Forty-One
Simon Holdsworth in Sheffield and Athens

Packing cases once again filled the hall of the family home in Sheffield when Simon left for Athens in the spring of 2009. His mother was looking on as she had always done when her son was on his way to another job, another country. It meant she wouldn't see him for another couple of years. At least this time it was in Europe, so it was possible he would be back to see her from time to time. She'd watched as he re-packed the tools of his vocation into cases, organised his belongings, checked and rechecked his documents, his ticket, his passport and made sure his tin box of emergency things was in his luggage.

Simon was always conscious of his mother's disappointment at losing him once more, which was remarkable considering he was oblivious to the emotional cues of the majority of people he was in contact with. He knew that behind the oversized glasses the moistness was not, as she suggested, the beginnings of a cold. He had studied her covertly whilst she was busying herself with drying the pots or dusting the miniature pottery houses on the hall shelf. She was becoming old, her face a roadmap marking a tough life. It was rare to see her without some make-up, a mask over her furrowed features and sagging eyelids. She always tried to present herself well. She always spoke politely to strangers and on the telephone. She was a proud woman, brought up to be courteous, respectful and determined. Simon wondered whether she would survive for much longer. She was now almost sixty and her ailments were keeping the pharmacy busy and ensuring she was on first name terms with the GP receptionist. She wasn't ill, not chronically ill with a lifestyle illness, but she was high maintenance. Mercifully, she did not seem to be prone to losses of memory or the other signs of dementia. For many older people, their health became an obsession, a focus of their daily life, an albatross. His mum was the same, as her world had shrunk, so the importance of her ailments grew.

Simon spent so little time in the UK that, after his father's death, he had encouraged his mother to retain their old house, which was slightly larger than was absolutely necessary, on condition that Simon paid the outstanding mortgage, and the taxes, services and insurances necessary to keep it in good shape. In return, he used his old bedroom as a home office, bedsit and storeroom when he was in the UK, although he rarely spent much time living there.

It was the proximity and easy transport links to his ageing mother that attracted Simon to the Athens job. He'd been working in South Sudan when he saw the job advertised on the Internet, in the twilight zone toward the end of a fixed contract where one's attention was on the next job rather than the one you were doing. He'd reasoned that if his mum fell ill he could get back easier. Other benefits of Athens included the availability of daily low cost flights to and from home, the benefits of being within the EU zone, mobile networks, broadband quality, and the familiarity of a European lifestyle—he was not going to need to apply his amateur social anthropology skills as much in Greece as he'd had to in Africa.

So in April he'd set off for Athens for his new role in the refugee centre. He was thirty-six, well-qualified and relished the opportunity to work with so many different nationalities and with an NGO in a European country. His background research told him about the emerging economic crisis in Greece, which had impacted on the urban poor whose neighbourhoods were also the first to feel the consequences of the influx of migrants and refugees. Two years into his contract he renewed it for a further three. The economic and social situation had worsened and now resembled some of the parts of Africa he'd previously worked in. The daily problems of ordinary people were similar to those in Zimbabwe, the violence against ordinary citizens approaching that experienced in Harare, Eritrea, and countless others.

Six months into his second contract, in October 2013, Simon's phone vibrated in his pocket and his mum's neighbour had delivered a stark message that changed his diary. His mum was in hospital after a stroke. She had fallen down the stairs and had lain there for some time, nobody knew how long, but when they found her she had soiled herself, was dehydrated and suffering hypothermia. It was only the neighbours' familiarity with her routine that alerted them: she wasn't filling the kettle by the kitchen window to make cups of tea at the times they'd come to expect her to. Simon rushed back on the first available flight, had travelled from London to Sheffield and gone straight to the hospital. After some troublesome negotiation, because he was outside visiting hours, he had finally managed to see her at 7 pm. She was only semi-conscious, but was aware of his presence. It was as if she had held out awaiting his arrival, knowing he would come. In the remaining two hours of her life, he held her swollen hand tight, never letting it go until her breathing had ceased and the vital signs monitor had ceased to plot a regular pulse, instead charting a straight line across the centre of the screen. He cried the uncontrollable tears of the bereaved at her bedside, then again in the staff canteen when he was taken there for a cup of tea by the male duty nurse. That night had been the worst of his life. Having no reason to go to the house he'd checked into a budget hotel in the city centre. He was dog-tired after the travelling and the emotionally draining evening, but he found sleep elusive. In the early hours he somehow drifted into a proxy for sleep. Next day he tried to gather his thoughts. He had to contact relatives and make the necessary arrangements. He wanted to talk to his mum's neighbours and go to the house to cast an eye over the scene of his mother's last moments in this world. He felt different, but put it down to bereavement. He had a vague awareness of a buzzing in his head, it could have been the flight. It was like a hum, as if he was standing outside a nightclub and all he could hear was the base beat through the walls.

Almost a week later at the funeral, he was one of a surprisingly large number of people who had come to pay their respects, neighbours mostly, but with an expectedly large number of relatives coming from the four points of the country. His mum was never the most outgoing and confident woman, but those who knew her could feel her emotional warmth; her friends were loyal.

For an occasion as sombre and final as his mum's funeral, he'd hoped to avoid any conversation about his dad, but it was inevitable that someone attending would refer to the couple as being together, whereas those more familiar with the family would be careful not to mention them in the same sentence. Every time someone mentioned his dad, Alf, it was like somebody had attached a live wire to Simon's head. His body tensed, and an overwhelming feeling of revulsion and pain, like a migraine, washed over him. At times like this he had to resort to his tin of emergency tablets to keep up the happy mask that everyone else thought was the real Simon. He kept his memories securely packaged so that these thoughts rarely emerged. He was careful not to be reminded of the past. Today it was unavoidable. Now he would not even have his mother to look upon as a kindred spirit.

During the wake he fell into conversation with a couple of people who had been his mum's friends decades earlier, and who had remained in regular contact. Eileen and Ted were what could be called a salt of the earth, middle-of-the-road couple in their late seventies. They had met Simon's mum and dad before Simon had been born, when young couples had the freedom of a life in post-war, post-ration book Britain. They appeared to have had a whale of a time, and regularly went as a foursome to Butlins at Skegness for weeks away. This must have been the heyday of holiday camps and it was clear they had happy memories.

During the conversation, Eileen talked about Alf. 'Because your grandad George had been a soldier, Alf was happy to do his stint. Funny that he ended up being posted to the same place. When he demobbed to Civvy Street, he had just wanted to catch up with all the partying he could manage. He wasn't really the same person after the army, so your mum said.'

'Yes,' said Simon, 'there must have been some trigger for the bitterness he felt after leaving the army. Mum said he began to drink too much, which he passed off by shaping himself as a *bon viveur*, always out, always the centre of attention; but he was never out with my mum. He never had any money either.

'Mum told me there were some days when he didn't even come home; and these were the times when they were recently married. He'd miss days from work for no apparent reason, then somebody would find him in the boozer and bring him home. He would turn up at the house, often drunk, and start shouting, angrily throwing things around the house, on occasions breaking the furniture. Around the time my mum was expecting me, he started mistreating her, sometimes he was remorseful straight afterwards, but increasingly he was not. Money would start to disappear from the savings tin. We always lived close to the breadline in those days and the budget was carefully apportioned for different things. But food wasn't on the table some days.'

'He did over-do the drinking. Did he ever hit you?' asked Eileen.

Simon desperately wanted to tear himself away from this couple and their conversation. He tried to bring it back to a good memory of his mum, which after all was why he thought people were here. He was pensive for a longer pause than Ted and Eileen were comfortable with. They began to realise the conversation was straying into harrowing detail, their discomfort was evident. They all wanted the discussion to end.

'I think my mum got worse treatment than I did,' he said, leaving the indescribable images in his mind. 'She was a wonderful mother, very caring, very tender. She didn't deserve the ill-treatment that was meted out. We didn't deserve the life we lived.'

Again, an awkward pause. 'If you would excuse me, I have to mingle with some of the other guests.'

'Of course, lovely to meet you again.'

Then he fell into conversation with Matt, 'a drinking pal of your dad's,' was how he introduced himself. Simon didn't have a lot of time for the very people who accompanied his dad whist he'd fuelled himself up before coming home. Drink was at the root of the problem, Simon believed. Nevertheless, Matt seemed a lot more amenable and intelligent than most of Alf's known drinking buddies.

'My condolences,' said Matt, his only words of formality.

'Thanks, it's over now.'

'I knew a good deal about your dad.'

'I didn't, so you've got one on me there.'

'No, I can understand that. Listen, this may not be the place or the time, but Alf spent a long time putting something together to explain himself to you.'

'Can't say I've come across it.'

'From memory, I think he put it in a sealed envelope.'

'I haven't gone through all mum's paperwork yet, so it may be there.'

'I'd recommend you have a read of it. It explains a lot.'

'I doubt I'll be a willing reader. If I find something that fits that description I'll know what it is. Anyway, must move on, thanks for that information.'

Simon desperately wanted to move away from this man. It was

his mother's funeral, he thought; not a time for remembering a vile father and husband.

And he was gone, moving on to a clique of elderly relatives whose demeanour was universally as dark as sin. Hoping, despite his own grief, to inject a modicum of joy into the proceedings, Simon said, 'How are you all, everyone got their drinks topped up?'

'Oh yes, thank you,' said a maiden aunt in black, 'but we're only drinking tea; too early in the day for anything else.'

Simon saw he'd a mountain to climb with this group. He thought the likelihood of any of them getting more than a bit dizzy on a port and lemon was remote.

'Thanks for the lovely spread of food; very thoughtful. Your mum would have enjoyed herself here,' said Uncle Bert, oblivious to any irony in the comment. It really didn't matter which funeral you went to, there was always someone that said something like that.

'Thank you, Bert,' he said with a wry smile acknowledging Bert's unintended uplifting moment.

Bert got a stern look from Auntie Joan, who thought her husband required reining in a bit.

'Anyway, let your hair down a bit now, there's nothing else we can do except celebrate her life,' said Simon. To which all nodded solemnly. Simon took his cue to move on again to a younger crowd of neighbours who seemed the last bastion of hope in the otherwise morose or depressing crowd.

Following the end of the wake, Simon returned to the family home and gradually began to undertake the mandatory chores, such as reading all of his mum's papers and documents, and preparing for an appointment with the solicitor. He'd found the sealed envelope addressed to him, with the ominous words 'To be opened after the death of both parents.' He was too engrossed in process to deal with individual details, especially knowing what topic it contained, so he placed it in his bag where it would probably stay until he was back in

Greece. Much of the preparation was done on his mum's affairs; he'd seen to it after his last visit. The solicitor's appointment was just a formality. Further input from him could wait until he returned from Athens three months hence. The neighbours had agreed to look after the house, there was little need to undergo a house clearance yet as he wasn't intending to sell it. He just needed to work through changing all the accounts and bills to his own name. He kept himself busy until about 11 pm, working his way through a bottle of wine as the evening progressed. At twelve he went to bed and slept almost immediately.

The cupboard door pressed inwards into the space; then was almost ripped off its hinges as the booted foot attempted to gain entry. Simon was hiding inside, cowering in the dark space beneath the stairs hoping he would not be found. 'Fucking shitting door,' he heard his father shouting as boot mark after boot mark imprinted on the painted surface. 'Open this door, you little bastard. I'll beat you stupid.' His mother was in the background, a feint sobbing behind her pleading to leave him alone, attempting to deflect some of the anger toward herself so he could be spared. 'Shutupyoufuckin'cow,' he slurred, 'get back in the kitchen. I'm gonna get this fucking kid out of here and show him who's boss. Jesus Christ, how much longer will he do it?' The boy inside pushed himself further back under the lowest possible stair tread, willing himself to blend into the structure. In his damp blue flanelette pyjamas and cream dressing gown, this was going to be difficult. He could sense the overwhelming odour of warm urine on his pyjama bottoms. The hinge rocked again, the wood splintering around the hinge, pieces spraying across the chinks of light coming through the edges of the door. Then, with one last kick, the door caved in, flying into the void, narrowly missing the lad. He shielded his eyes with his arm, not from the door, but from what was likely to happen to him.

The man wrenched the boy from his hiding space, carelessly dragging his damp cargo from the doorway. He was small enough to fit under one arm and that is how he was carried into the kitchen. That was where the terrified boy watched the thick leather belt being pulled from the trouser hoops. His pyjama top was roughly pulled over his head and thrown across the room. The belt was raised above the man's head and brought down across his shoulder blades.

He felt the stinging pain a delayed second after the impact, the burning sensation sending a bolt of pain to his extremities. Again the belt came down, this time making contact with his shoulder. Again a bolt of pain. He cowered with his back to the perpetrator, waiting for the agony to stop. He knew it would stop. It always did. And, after six or seven strokes, the man stopped mid-lunge, suddenly coming to his senses, falling to the ground sobbing like a small baby. The boy's mother crying uncontrollably in the corner, the boy weeping. The scene in the kitchen replayed a dozen times over . . .

Simon awoke suddenly, a florid fever causing rivulets of water to run from his chest onto the bedding. His breathing was rapid and deep. His heart beating so hard his whole torso was pulsating with the rhythm. His eyes were slow to adjust to the sudden wakefulness. Nightmare. He reached for the bedside light and checked his watch, it was a quarter past three. He lay there for a minute before walking to the bathroom and getting a towel to dry off the sweat, then he returned to the bed. The noise in his ear was becoming persistent, such that in silent surroundings it sounded like a muffled conversation.

His dad was the only person he truly despised. He hadn't been afraid of him so much as afraid of what he'd do. He resented the man for destroying his mother's confidence, for turning her into a meek shadow of the person he had loved above everything else. When he was a child, he had wanted more than anything for his dad to leave them, never to return. But, of course, that wasn't to be. He had to wait fifteen years for the opportunity to bury the vile bully, to make sure that he never bothered either of them again.

He made a cup of tea and willed dawn to arrive, waiting for the milkman to make his way along the street, the refuse lorry to draw up outside, its noisy operators exchanging their inane banter. He waited for the nightmare to evaporate, to be overwritten by the mundane incidents of daytime. He took the last of the medication he carried with him, making a mental note to re-stock before returning to Greece.

On his return to Athens, Simon settled back into his job, accepting the condolences offered by many concerned friends. His flatmates were very supportive, making the effort to lighten the atmosphere. He thought a lot about his mother during the following weeks, and cried himself to sleep on occasion. He sought out the intimacy he craved, along with sating his lust, taking solace in the arms of others. Sometimes it was a stranger, sometimes someone closer. One friend in particular always seemed to be willing to accommodate his needs. Zoe, a flatmate, a Greek national working with the same charity, seemed to have a borderline obsession with him. At times her attentions were cloying. He tried to disengage himself from the emotional hooks she attempted to snare him with. The accessible intimacy and unquestioning fulfilment of his needs had to be offset against the very real danger that she would stalk him if he stopped seeing her. Zoe wanted from Simon more than he was prepared to yield. Her omnipresence tired him, and he was never certain whether or not she was spying on him. He feared her; he had reason to protect his inner thoughts and feelings.

He no longer thought of his father. To Simon Holdsworth, the man they referred to as his father was a nasty, sad, old loser who took his failures out on others. He didn't deserve a second thought.

Chapter Forty-Two
Mphatso, November 2013

Mphatso pulled himself from the loving embrace of his emotionally charged partner, breathless, satiated. His track record of encounters these days was poor, but not unreasonable for times of extreme hardship. As he pulled on his jogging bottoms, he thought about what this sexual encounter represented.

He reflected on what his parents had said to him as a boy. He had always been raised to appreciate that everything in life had a purpose and that when man and woman joined together there was a purpose in that event. It had taken him his entire childhood to fathom what his parents and grandparents were talking about. When he was young, running around the compound naked, when his mother was always there to look after him, when his father was always working in the mine, the words had no meaning. But, like other phrases he frequently recalled when circumstances triggered his memory, they were a moral code:

'Do not challenge your elders.'

'Follow the preachings of Jesus.'

'Education is the key to the future.'

'Health is wealth.'

And so on.

He admired the wisdom of his parents and grandparents because he knew they had no formal education. The structure of their society, the dominance of the Anglican Church, the poverty of their upbringing, all placed strict boundaries around everyone's interpretation of life, key events and aspirations. The witch doctor had his own code of social conduct, which spread sufficient fear amongst the villagers. No matter what the teachings of the Church, another, more familiar, layer of beliefs ultimately controlled the actions of each individual.

And so it was that Mphatso's mother and father worked their fields and the mine face respectively until their fingers bled, until their joints felt like they were being pulled apart. They worked long, long days to increase their income, to grow a bit more produce to sell, to gather enough money to send as many of their children to school as was possible. Indeed, they had been blessed with five children, not a large family—the only rebellion his parents fought and won was their resistance to producing a large family.

This had several consequences and one important outcome. First, because health was out of their hands, children died young, and mothers died in childbirth. His parents opted for a smaller number, and two were lost in infancy, so in his family there was Grace, his older sister; himself, Mphatso; and his younger brother, Duncan.

Secondly, because of the small family unit, the family were looked upon by the rest of the villagers as being unfortunate, different, even sick because they could not produce enough children for them to provide for their parents, work in their gardens and produce more children. They were outsiders, irrespective of the generations that preceded them in the same village, irrespective of the tribal ties they had with their neighbours. As such, the family adopted a increasingly radical approach to life, tried new ideas, did things differently.

The third consequence was that the family were able to provide for their children, give them a start in life, educate them. They would, in turn, have enough to provide their parents with a comfortable old age. Because his father worked in the mines he earned some money, so was not restricted to a subsistence lifestyle; he could afford to educate his children. And so it was that the family moved from the village to the township, took a rented plot with a small garden, and placed the children in elementary school when they reached the right age. Mphatso and Duncan were enrolled in the Kaziwiri Diocese Elementary School, and later managed to continue their education as boarders in the Mapulanga Secondary School, fifteen miles south of the township. Grace did not receive a secondary eduction; her skills would be in child rearing.

Throughout their education, the two boys, two years apart, devoured whatever learning opportunities they were given and participated fully to extract as much utility as possible from the chances their father and mother had carved out for them. It was tough at the start, the daily rituals were exhausting, even before school. They would arise at the first crowing of the cock, help their sister stoke the fire so she could make maize porridge and tea, fetch water from the stand tap down the road, wash themselves using a bowl in the corner of the compound, dress themselves in their uniform of khaki shorts, white short-sleeved shirt and blue necktie, then walk two miles to school. They would fall asleep in class in the summer because of the hot weather and the drone of the teacher's voice, especially after their lunchtime meal of *nsima* and vegetables. This was the case for all the children, but there was a trick that the teacher taught them to reawaken themselves—stand up at their desk and remain standing until the sleepiness had been overcome. So it was, then, throughout Mphatso's school days, that classes were characterised by a random pattern of children standing up, sitting, standing, sitting, whilst the learning continued. It was a habit Mphatso continued to carry with him. In Africa this was widely acceptable, but in other countries it was seen as a bit odd.

The outcome, for Mphatso, was that he found his way, like a lizard through the rainforest, along a convoluted path, to a formal apprenticeship and training course which, ultimately, provided him with the opportunity to leave his township and family and travel to other countries. His first apprenticeship was in mining engineering. He took the opportunity to focus on the electrical aspects, and in due course this led him into information technology. With this skill he was then able to travel. He was grateful—but nothing more—to the mine company for his apprenticeship. He took himself to Johannesburg, then Dubai, Switzerland, Sweden and Italy.

Now he was in Athens. He had been away from his family for so long that he did not feel any sense of anxiety about roaming the world alone. But there were people who, because of his colour, did not like him. Others resented his presence. He was marginalised in the way every immigrant is marginalised, by the narrowness of the indigenous population's experience of 'the other'. Xenophobia was escalating in Greece.

How his life had now changed! Through a strategy of calculated risk-taking, some privations, hustling, a good knowledge of the rights and wrongs of civilised society, he had achieved his aim of becoming a bona fide European Union passport holder. He chose Greece to settle in because it was the country with the kind of climate he'd sought.

He had moved from his original vocation, through a universally tradable skill in IT, and was now owner and manager of a kiosk in a fashionable shopping district of Athens. His business of three years had attracted many loyal and regular customers, intelligent enough to recognise him as a friend or colleague. His skin colour attracted some less welcome attention from xenophobic thugs and their followers. It could be worse, he thought, he could be in a poor neighbourhood where all of the population was squeezed dry by austerity.

His thoughts had taken him so far away from the physical world that it was a surprise when the woman next to him drew him back towards her, deftly pulling his recently put-on joggers down over his buttocks and legs, ready for another round of energetic sex. Her name was Mfunda, she was a fellow African, but from Cameroon, and was similarly at sea in this new culture. They sought solace in each other on the basis of their skin colour—well, there weren't any Greek women who paid any attention to him in that way. Their relationship was, in Western terms, a regular casual one. They had met when he was working at a refugee centre in Piraeus as a charity worker. She was one of the few women who had made the risky trip from North Africa to Greece; who had paid the masters of her destiny sufficient money, and too many additional favours, to get her as far as Athens. She was a good Christian girl, with a strong moral compass, who had been drawn into less savoury activities in order simply to survive. He had seen a spark of interest whilst assisting her at the refugee centre offices and had followed up with a date. That was several months ago. Now they were regular lovers, and she was again rediscovering her moral compass. She was no longer having to sell her body. She was no longer running the gauntlet of smugglers who wanted her money and cared for little else.

They engaged in a bout of tender massage, a prelude to another vigorous hour or two—she was insatiable on occasions. They were interrupted by his vibrating mobile. He reluctantly pulled away again, her hot, moist skin peeling itself away from his smooth torso, her fingers trailing down his hairless arms as they disengaged. He leaned across the bed to the shelf where the phone was dancing like a honey bee and reached for the device. He sat on the side of the bed.

'Neh, Alexis, Kala Soicitay,' he exchanged greetings with the caller.

Mphatso acknowledged what was being said by repeating 'ah-ha' which meant that he was listening and understanding. He had a brief conversation in Greek that Mfunda didn't understand, then ended the call and stood up.

He explained in French to Mfunda that he'd have to go, he was needed at the refugee centre. This was a common occurrence on Sundays, the only day he didn't work sixteen hours in the kiosk.

His role was as an interpreter, helping complete documents for asylum seekers or preparing court defence papers in immigration cases. His skills lay in speaking his own tribal language, Chewa, plus English, and a smattering of Greek, French and Italian. His incidental expertise in computers, the Internet and the Greek legal system were also often called upon. He had always found it easy to learn and use key phrases in languages, perhaps it was his drive to learn something from everyone.

From Mfunda his learning wasn't language, it was sheer pleasure. He had never in his life been as sexually aroused, fulfilled, or emotionally connected as he was able to be with her. Sex had turned from something he was taught to think of as a function, a duty of procreation, into a form of absolute joy, a release from the duties of daily life. So it was with some reluctance that he took his leave, knowing that by the time he returned she'd be gone, leaving only the smell of her beautiful body, stained and crumpled sheets, and a sink full of unwashed pots.

Chapter Forty-Three
Simon and Mphatso Work with Refugees

The rain fell in sheets on the cluttered streets around Victoria Square. After years of constant social unrest in this part of town, the cash-starved municipal council had all but given up on beautifying or cleaning the concrete landscape. The smashed up paving slabs and broken concrete that replaced them had been used and re-used as ammunition, defence, call it what you will. Rubble was now heaped up against dark, shuttered shop fronts, burnt out apartment blocks and building frontages demolished for their bricks, to throw or to build with. The crumbling rendering on each building was held together with layers of fly-posters, some charred and defaced, over-pasted with more recent slogans; poster hangers and taggers respecting no prior slogan. Mounds of congealed poster glue pointed upwards like stalagmites from the uneven pavement. There were slogans on every surface: glass, render, shutters, the ground, abandoned vehicles, street furniture. It resembled Beirut in the late 1960s, Mogadishu in the 1990s; but this was Athens.

Simon was picking his way through the rubble of the side street aiming for a squatted apartment block at number twenty-three. This was the residence of a community of Iraqis, stranded in Athens for months with no prospect of being accepted as refugees elsewhere, and no probability of obtaining travel documents. There were regular demonstrations here, not only against the refugees; everyone had a reason to demonstrate. But it was these streets that regularly attracted those who wished to keep Greece for Greeks;

as if the refugees would choose to remain, were they ever offered a choice.

The latest demonstrations were carefully monitored by the riot police, in their dark jump suits, gas masks, helmets and behind their perspex riot shields. Everyone knew that when the riot police were involved, behind them would be another, more sinister, force that would use whatever weapons were to hand. In these demonstrations the target was the refugees. Not anarchists, students, corrupt government (everyone took their grievances with the government to Syntagma Square), unions, nor the left or the right; but the refugees.

Simon located the block he was searching for and found his way in through their own tight, self-imposed security. The stench of human detritus was in evidence, it was said the sewers were blocked and overflowing. The heavy rain served to distribute the mess around the grid patterned streets. Simon scaled the ladder to the third floor—the stairwell had been barricaded to prevent incursions by the fascists. He located the woman he had been seeking, sitting on the floor in the spartan apartment, the window open to the falling rain, an occasional clap of thunder punctuating what would have been a tranquil sound in any other urban European setting. The Iraqis had attempted to make the room habitable. There were cushions around the walls and a threadbare carpet in the middle. All the room's occupants were seated against the walls. In the centre of the carpet was the tea-making paraphernalia. He took off his shoes by the doorway and was ushered to a cushion where he offered tea, which he accepted. They spoke in hushed tones, despite the bustling background noise of voices echoing around the corridors of the block, car horns, motor engines, mopeds, police sirens and the sounds of water falling from broken gutters, cascading to the solid concrete yard from five storeys high.

He told them of his reason for visiting. The woman and her young child had been ordered to be deported to Iraq. The refugee centre had objected to the deportation on behalf of the woman on the grounds that violence would be used on her if she returned to a non-Kurdish area. Deportation was to Baghdad or Basra; she would be placed in danger. He needed to know if she accepted the deportation. He came to her as he knew it would have been too dangerous for her to come to the centre.

There was a common nod of agreement from all those in the room. None, except the woman and child, were related to each other, but they felt a bond of filial protectiveness toward each other and the few women in their group. The woman spoke through an interpreter who addressed Simon. Through him she asked if there had been any development in her case or an alternative offer.

'Not as yet,' he said, 'but the centre is working to secure a good outcome. Are you sure that returning to Kurdistan is the best solution for you and your child?'

'We have been here for five months. We arrived with nothing, we landed on an island and were brought to this city, this prison of a city, by the police. We have been stranded here for all this time. We fear for our lives. We fear for our children. We want to leave. If we cannot leave for the Netherlands, or Germany, or London, then it will be better for us to return to our country.'

Simon recognised that the interpreter had put his own story across along with that of the woman he was trying to get answers from. She, not knowing what was being said, remained quiet. Simon probed further to determine that a return to Kurdish Iraq was what she wanted. He received the briefest answer in English from her, in response to the translated question.

'Yes.'

He sipped the hot, sweet tea, trying to finish as quickly as possible so that he could leave the building. He would ensure the centre did what they could to facilitate her wishes. He would come back in a few days to update her. He knew he had to be quick today, he wanted to make plans for the evening. He said his goodbyes and exited, careful to assess whether there were any thugs around to ambush him, perhaps to accuse him of collaborating with 'migrant dogs.' It was normal for him to have his wits about him. This neighbourhood was no place to be alone in at nightfall.

* * *

Mphatso left his apartment block and walked along the street to the Metro station. He waited twenty minutes for a train, despite the timetable advertising a service every five-minutes. The timetable had been daubed with slogans, as had the station walls, train carriages and windows. All shades of political opinion were represented. Most prominent were slogans of the far right. Mphatso knew he was in the minority as a black man in Greece; he received daily reminders. This was a country approaching meltdown. He realised it had been an unfortunate choice to settle here instead of the UK, but when he arrived in 2004 it was a country in the ascendant. It had hosted the Olympic Games; it was still a fledgling member of the European Union; it had embraced the Euro, and with the Euro the requirement to pump money into the European Federal dream. In return, Europe now seemed to be demanding more than it offered. His Greek friends told him the place was struggling before joining the EU, having lost its shipbuilding industry. The majority of the rural population were engaged in agriculture, many on the breadline. Those that moved, like moths to a flame, to large cities saw their living standards originally rise, but then fall. His friends described what they regarded as a corrupt political system, corrupt police, a creaking local government system, a tax regime that was easily avoided, and a pandemic of mortgage borrowing and lending from newly created banks and institutions. Even back then they had all thought the boom was unsustainable. Now, as the rest of Europe struggled, Greece had already been brought to its economic knees, burnt out after its burst of prosperity.

The Metro train rocked its way to his Attikis Square destination; a dingy, down-at-heel neighbourhood of older housing, squats, and abandoned premises towards the northern edge of the city centre. Light industrial units peppered the area close to the main railway, but many were vacant. Some had been built and never occupied. Among the buildings was a warehouse sheathed in a grey moulded metal sheet and a corrugated roof. A large glass atrium on the front of the building and a bank of air conditioning units humming away on the long side wall distinguished it from a sealed bunker. There was a three-metre-high fence topped with barbed wire protecting the building. The Refugee Centre, funded by the EU and a number of collaborating NGOs, addressed the demand for services from an increasing number of impoverished and vulnerable refugees, mainly arriving *sans papiers*. The influx of refugees and migrants threatened to capsize Greece in the same way as it threatened Italy. Refugees were a convenient target for xenophobes and racists. Resentful, hard-working and poor Greeks, themselves impoverished by the dramatic fall in their standard of living, believed they were competing for resources and harboured resentment towards the centre's clientèle.

Mphatso always experienced the same emotion when he approached the building: his heart sank. If he was dependent—as his clients were—upon it, its workforce and its purpose (which, mercifully, he was not) he thought he would have lost hope at first sight. It looked like one of those bland warehouses on business parks where a lorry occasionally drops off or collects cargo, but no other activity seems to take place.

There was nothing complicated in the case he was interpreting for, a twenty-three-year-old Mozambican woman who spoke only Portuguese and Chichewa. Mphatso imagined how this young woman's life had been moulded by conflict, how the terror of

Mozambique in the 1980s accompanied her entry into this world, how for years it was dangerous for Mozambicans to tread the ground for fear of APDs: land mines which maimed thousands of victims during the harsh civil war. Now, in search of a new beginning, she had pitched up in, of all places, Greece. Whilst not exactly the front line in a war, Athens did resemble at times, and in some neighbourhoods, an anarchic dystopia.

He listened to the female case worker, a middle-aged Greek social worker who worked for no payment at the charity, whose own income stream had been truncated a year earlier as a result of some savage public sector cuts, and whom he respected immensely for her dedication.

'It will first be necessary for me to decide whether she wishes to bring charges against the perpetrators of her beating or against the police who subsequently mistreated her.'

She looked through the papers in front of her. She read the invoice from a private medical clinic who had treated her after her attack, although everyone knew she could have been treated free at a public hospital, and addressed Mphatso in Greek, spoken at an alarmingly rapid pace.

'I assume she has no money for the medical bill, but we need to confirm this is the case. When I have dealt with that, I need to understand her domestic arrangements. She is very nervous to go out, and we may have no option but to place her into a formal detention centre. If we allow her to go back onto the streets, she will be exposed to further abuse and danger.'

Mphatso could just about understand all of what the woman had said, but clarified in English one or two points. The woman's heavily accented English was as much a problem to understand sometimes as her rapid-fire Greek.

'Of course, we cannot make her do anything, but if she returns to the streets, the same thing may happen again.'

He gave a nod of understanding to the case worker and introduced himself to the young woman.

'Muli bwanji achimwemwe,' he said, asking her how she was in their tongue.

'Ndili bwino zikomo, kaya inu?' She was fine, and how was he?

'Ndili bwino.' Fine.

Whilst speaking, they exchanged the formal handshakes of their shared cultural heritage. Despite her injuries, she raised herself out of the chair and bent her knees and her back slightly forward so as to be positioned lower than him, her left hand resting on her right forearm in the deferential manner of someone meeting another in a superior social position. She eased herself back down into the chair.

He apologised she had to wait for an hour-and-a-half for him to make his way there, then explained what he was there to do. They began a dialogue, Mphatso making occasional notes.

'Where are you from?'

'I am from Lichinga in the north, close to the lake.'

'It is a good place, near the lake,' said Mphatso, remembering his childhood spent on the opposite shore, close to the Livingstonia settlement.

'What has brought you to Greece?'

'My husband passed away and his brothers are all passing from AIDS. My children need feeding. My parents need looking after. I have had a spell placed on me so nobody will help me and my family. I need to keep sending money to my parents so my family can survive. I have travelled here so that I can do this.'

He thought that this story omitted huge chunks of significant information, which was unlikely to be volunteered. He filled the gaps in his own mind but did not reveal this to the social worker.

'How did you get here?'

'I travelled with truck drivers as they moved north, then I

prepared food on a boat from Kenya to Egypt, then moved to Turkey with groups of other migrants and refugees.'

'It is a long journey, sister. How many months has it taken?'

'It is fifteen months.'

'Ahh, that is a long time. How have you survived?'

'I eat when I am able, I drink when I can get water, then store it until the next opportunity. My small luggage pack contains what I need to make a fire, and some blankets to sleep under. I have no money, no papers, no way of going back.'

Mphatso stared into her emotionally drained face, a visage years beyond her true age, wondering what trauma she must have endured to reach this point alive, what abuse, what loss of dignity. He had heard similar stories from many other cases—clients, as the refugee centre would prefer they were called.

'How are you surviving here?'

'I am living in the parks, at the moment I stay in Pedion Areos,' her pronunciation of the place was wrong, but he knew where she meant.

'And it is safe where you are?'

'No, I have been beaten four or five times as I sleep. Sometimes it is Greek men in black who shout words, but I don't know what they say, sometimes it is the police with their shields, sometimes it is other refugees who are robbing me. But I have nothing to take.'

'When did you last eat?'

'Yesterday in the morning, when the soup kitchen was serving in Amerikas Square.'

'And how is your health? Do you get water easily?'

'My health is a bit fair. I have a cough, I have lost weight. I am sometimes coughing blood. I am sometimes sick.'

She looked in despair at the floor as she said this, for the first time averting her eyes from his, as if she knew what he was thinking.

'I see. When you came here did you have papers?'

'No. I have not had papers at any time, except my Mozambique permit.'

'How have you crossed so many borders without papers?'

'The truck drivers have hidden me in their lorries. The boat captain kept me locked up at ports, and I escaped only when the boat ran aground away from the ports. I am a very experienced refugee. I am lucky I am a lake shore girl and can swim. Many migrants cannot swim and are lost.'

'Where are you going?'

'To Germany.'

'How long have you been in Greece?'

'I cannot remember. Maybe three weeks.'

'Where were you before you crossed into Greece?'

'In Turkey. At a detention centre before I escaped.'

'And you were in hospital, when was that?'

'Four days ago, for three nights.'

'What were your injuries?'

'I have bruising on my side, I was kicked between the legs and it was very painful. The men in black hit me with iron bars on my back. My eye was also blackened when they kicked my face.'

He could see the obvious purple wheals on her brow, but she carried her other injuries without showing discomfort, although he knew she would clearly be in pain. He knew to display the grimace of pain was culturally unacceptable. He again regarded her and noted how horribly thin she was. Her destiny was unlikely to be in Germany. He was not a doctor, but he knew what her symptoms foretold.

'Sister, we are now in Athens. We need to make sure you have somewhere to go. I will need to talk with this lady. I then need to ask you some more questions and she will decide what we can do for you.'

She nodded silently, once again averting her gaze, her hands held in a tight grasp on her lap. Mphatso turned to the social worker and explained the woman's plight. He described the medical circumstances without making a specific reference to Tuberculosis or HIV. They discussed, in English, what options there were.

The social worker said, 'The medical bill will be met by the charity, she will just have to complete a form.'

Mphatso asked whether the woman could read and write; the response was negative.

Then the worker outlined what she wanted to tell the client. Mphatso relayed the options.

'The options for you, given the danger of living on the streets or in parks, are to be taken to a detention centre and await deportation, or to join a repatriation scheme. If you decide not to do either, your only option is to make your way towards Germany. You will not be able to claim asylum here, or in any other country, because your home country is stable and peaceful, and you would not be in danger if you were returned home. You will at least be safe, fed, and treated for any illnesses in the detention centre. You may eventually be deported, but only to the country you were in before arrival in Greece, which you said was Turkey. The repatriation option is better. In the meantime, we can give you a survival kit of food and essentials.'

She thanked the two of them and said she would need to make a decision after thinking. They gave her a leaflet in English and French which explained how to access the two main options, a voucher for a survival kit, and a flyer for a refugee mental health charity.

Mphatso and the social worker knew from experience 'having time to think' invariably meant that the centre would never see that individual again. They would melt into the fabric of the country, or die, or both. Mphatso knew that neither detention centres, nor repatriation, would help her get money to send back to her family. On her return she would probably have to face the loan sharks and thugs who encouraged and facilitated her departure in the first place.

The woman left the room and made her way down the stairs to the main entrance leaving Mpahatso and the social worker in the office. They looked at each other and they both knew the outcome of the session.

Mpahatso later found himself assisting another charity worker. Simon was a British man of about thirty years old who had come here to work in the centre, for which he was in some way paid. They had formed a friendship earlier in the year. He always appeared, despite choosing to work in environments characterised uniformly by despair, the most happy and spirit-lifting person Mphatso had ever met. He always had a friendly smile and jaunty conversation. He could joke and laugh despite everything around him being bleak. He was like a breath of fresh air.

Simon knew Mphatso was from a country he had worked in, so could identify with his culture and language. Mphatso was, as a result of his haphazard travel history, a UK passport holder. Between them was therefore a bond that others in the refugee centre did not have.

'Hey, Lucky Jon, muli bwanji!' said Simon as soon as his colleague approached him. 'Lucky Jon' was the nickname Simon had given Mphatso because of his charmed passage to becoming a British passport holder. To some this name and the reasons behind it would have seemed tantamount to a racist or xenophobic insult, but the recipient dismissed any such notion.

'Hi, Simon, I'm fine, and you?'

'Yeah, good. You've come to help me, I guess?'

'I just did a translation and now I've got some time.'

'OK, we need to make up more survival packs. On top of the people we've already got on the streets, there are about another two hundred a day coming from Turkey, heading towards Athens.'

Why they would ever consider decamping to a city and a society that was effectively disembowelling itself was beyond Simon. Athens should be the last place anyone would want to come to.

Mphatso and Simon settled into a routine of pack stuffing: one insulated emergency blanket; one waterproof plastic mac; one quick drying micro-towel; three bottles of water; toothpaste; soap; toilet roll; a pre-packed emergency food box, similar to the ones given to troops; a map of the principal sites where unfortunate recipients could get healthcare and mental health support.

They continued to pack, shouting across to each other from time to time, enquiring about their respective love lives, their past week, how it was in their neighbourhood and so on. Then it began to rain and the noise of the heavy shower on the corrugated roof extinguished any conversation. Simon wanted to get to a pharmacy. He'd tried several times, but the crisis was affecting medical supplies. The rain put him off the idea of going out unnecessarily, so he continued with his task. Afterwards, when Mphatso was preparing to leave, Simon asked him if he wanted to come to his apartment for food that evening.

'We can have some fish and vegetables. I think I have some polenta for you if you don't want rice, maybe a beer.'

Mphatso gratefully accepted. He had been to Simon's shared apartment before. The apartment was always a lively place, lots of people, lots of music when the electricity was working, and a good communal atmosphere. It was in Exarchia, one of the less well maintained neighbourhoods close to the archaeological museum; but he didn't expect trouble there.

They agreed a time and Mphatso left the building to return to Nea Ionia. He was grateful for the neighbours he had, and for their acceptance of him. Decades ago it was a settlement area for thousands of displaced Greeks when the Turkish expelled them from Ionia. It had a deep tradition of socialism, communism, and unionism. It was a solid little community and everyone pulled together. Elsewhere in Athens every other shop was shuttered and the streets were filled with litter, but Nea Ionia felt more prosperous and few shops were vacant. He was a British citizen, which tended to make him 'alright' according to the neighbours, and he had not experienced racism and xenophobia to the same extent as was meted out elsewhere. These were good people.

On returning to his flat he found Mfunda had, as predicted, left, so he busied himself with washing the dishes and tidying up.

Chapter Forty-Four
A Party in Exarchia

That evening Mphatso made his way to Simon's place. Evening was always a tricky time in Athens these days. The wealthy and those who still had jobs had returned to their homes in the prosperous suburbs. Tourists remained largely in the Monastirakis and Syntagma area, close to the historical monuments. Elsewhere, especially the area north of Omonia, there was an uneasy stand-off between political factions. Whether it was students fighting police, fascists fighting anyone, or anarchists fighting everyone, there were two or more sides to be taken and tensions centred on one of several streets or squares. Then there were the drug addicts, the refugees, migrants, and the homeless, all ending up in the same neighbourhoods as well. So here they all were, in Victoria Square, Agios Pantaleimo, Palaio Faliro, Omonia Square, or in the maze of side streets, parks and open spaces close to them. And in nearby Exarchia, packed with left-leaning and anarchist populations, Simon lived.

The rain had dampened peoples' enthusiasm for confrontation tonight. There were few people of any hue in evidence as he walked from Victoria Metro station to Simon's apartment on the busy street. Keeping his wits about him in the dusk light and avoiding the prospect of trouble, he reached the block unscathed and ascended to the fifth floor. As anticipated, it was buzzing with activity and the smell of food cooking hit him as he crossed the threshold.

The block was a seventies concrete structure, short on character, planning sense and soundproofing. Like thousands of apartment blocks across the Mediterranean, it was the sort of place where everyone knew your business. The apartment was typically white-painted and ceramic floored; sound reverberated around its reflecting surfaces. It was a noisy place.

Simon was in the tiny kitchen preparing part of a communal dinner of fish, rice, vegetables and Greek salad. There were perhaps ten or fifteen people in the flat. The talk was of inconsequential things, entertainment, football, gossip and humour, ribbing one another. It was the name day of one of the Greek women, so the evening was by way of a celebration. There had become over the last few weeks, by way of light entertainment, a kind of joke factory atmosphere within the apartment where the group tried to evolve new jokes about the desperate plight of Athenians of all creeds. It was disingenuous, but fun, and there were no shortages of targets. Just about every individual and organisation could be held up for examination and be found wanting in tackling the austerity, economic crisis, and social and humanitarian disaster that was Athens, Salonica, Sparta—Greece.

Someone started off a rant, and others added a line. It was democratic free verse. One rule: neither prose, nor haiku, rhyming nor metered. Anybody could contribute:

'Papandreou is a bloated old post-dictatorship has been,'
'With a mine of gold stashed away in Switzerland—allegedly!'
'A bland line in suits and ticket out of here,'
'Capital flight—political flight!'
'Who wears a suit in this city these days?'
'You wouldn't want to be mistaken for a banker.'
'That would have you chased up a street, perhaps more,'
'By students and anarchists.'
'And all the city's poor.'
'Of course, the police would stand by,'
'Everywhere the police go the fascists are two steps behind,'

'With their sticks ready to find,'

'Another nonconformist to beat.'

And so on, until either a punchline emerged or, more likely, a perfect example of innuendo.

As the warm up for the evening continued, everyone was caught up in infectious laughter, the jokes a counterpoint to the brutal reality beyond the apartment block.

Everyone knew Mphatso, but he was surprised to find himself inducted into such a vibrant and good-natured gathering. Past visits to see Simon had been coloured by politics and resentment, earnest debate and raised tempers. Many had honed their invective through their militant unionism, student politics and anarchist sympathies. The conversation was more likely to centre on Occupy, or Anonymous, their exploits and exposés. Tonight it seemed to be party night; but he wasn't sure if he was in the frame of mind for it. The journey had been a little difficult as he had had to continuously revise his route to avoid any possibility of confrontation. But after perhaps half an hour he had been fully integrated into the mindset and was enjoying the light relief. Fish, rice, bread, and salad, plenty of beers: a recipe for a good evening.

Towards the latter part of the evening, as those who had homes to go to drifted off, Simon and Mphatso sat on the battered sofa with cups of chamomile tea, and Simon felt the high spirited evening wash away, being replaced by feelings of fear, loss of hope. He thought it was to do with his mother. The night was cool. It was decided that Mphatso would stay over tonight because it was rumoured that there would be a campaign against immigrants each evening this week; they were frequently attacked by guys on motorcycles. The journey home wasn't likely to be safe. Despite Mphatso's air of self-confidence as he moved around daytime Athens, the thug on the street would not distinguish a black Briton from a black African. Chains, knives, batons and knuckledusters would work on either.

About midnight, when the evening had reached its natural end, the two of them moved to Simon's bedroom and prepared for sleep. There was an inflatable mattress for Mphatso; Simon busied himself with his routines. Mphatso slid into a spare sleeping sheet fully clothed. Mphatso could never fathom the degree of clutter and disorganisation Simon created around his room. It was as if Simon didn't even know how unsavoury his surroundings were. Mphatso always tried to put a layer of clothing between himself and the rest of the room.

When Simon came back from the bathroom he had obviously been thinking. His first comment was, 'I've never asked you before, but why if your name is Mphatso, is your brother is called Duncan. It seems a little strange.'

Mphatso remembered he had described his family set-up to the group during the evening.

'Mphatso is Chichewa for gift. It is a custom that when a child is born it can take the name of the first thing the parents or mother, or community birth attendant, or doctor think of. You get called gift, surprise, lively, lucky, all sorts of things.'

'So why is your brother named Duncan?'

'It is an honour in our village to be delivered by a doctor because there are not many, and the baby is usually born in the village by a community birth attendant. But my brother was delivered in the hospital by an English doctor whose name was——'

'Duncan.'

'Exactly!'

'I see.'

Simon had a feeling he'd heard this story before, but he was certain he and Mphatso had never spoken about it.

'And where is your brother now?'

'He is working in South Africa for an airline.'

'Do you get to see him?'

'Ah, not so much, he is my best friend and brother, but I only see him occasionally and speak to him on the phone a couple of times a year. How about you, do you have brothers and sisters?'

'No, I'm an only child. I haven't really ever understood what it is to have someone so close.'

'Oh, sorry for that. But you have a lady who is special?'

'I know an interesting and fun woman, but she is not the special one. I don't really do relationships.' He thought of the last few weeks since his mum's death, the frantic craving for physical closeness, the number of people who had fallen for his charms and who had been taken advantage of. 'I'm a bit of a loner when it comes to that.'

'Oh-ho,' said Mphatso contemplatively. 'I have Mfunda as a friend. We make good times together.'

He was unsure of the etiquette of pre-slumber conversation, but decided he was uncomfortable with the way this was going, whether or not intended. He faked a yawn and wished Simon a good night's sleep, rolled onto his side and fairly quickly his regular, deep rhythmic breathing echoed across the room.

Simon lay on his side regarding Mphatso, unable to sleep so quickly, watching him in the light cast under the door from the hallway. He was thinking about how his own life had turned out, his nomadic existence, his lack of family ties, his emerging sense of . . . he wasn't sure what. Whilst he watched the gentle rise and fall of the form beneath the sleeping sheet, he began to regard Mphatso with a sense of resentment. Resentment for having a family, a home life, a plan, a girlfriend, being successful in what he sought to achieve. Darker thoughts from his past crowded into his mind and took him into a troubled and restless night.

Later that night, unable to sleep, Simon's thoughts ran fast, swirling around his mind. Somehow, somewhere along the time continuum since he buried his mother, Simon had changed. He couldn't pinpoint how he knew, or what the result was, but he realised there was a deepening mood within him, a lesser regard for the feelings of others. His tablets had run out, so he couldn't easily lift his spirits. He lived instead under the grey cloud that followed him around, while maintaining his mask of congeniality. He had recognised within his thoughts, in sleep especially, a compulsion to thrill-seeking, gratification, the need to mistreat people in a way that did not form part of his earlier self.

The opportunities were all here: many people were living desperate and impoverished lives, and when that happened people were willing to take risks, sail close to the wind, knowing that there was dysfunctional law and order apparatus and that you could get away with many things under cover of societal breakdown.

Yet he was able to project himself to his friends and colleagues as the happy-go-lucky, cheerful Simon. More recently he was afraid of his own thoughts, and strangely excited by them. He heard someone telling him to start a fire one night in a deserted side street. He lit some rubbish and watched from a distance as an entire UPVC shop-frame collapsed, melted and scorched, windows shattering and shuttering sagging from the heat. He had not spared a thought about safety, for the possible residents, or criminal damage. Nobody knew why the fire had started. Nobody knew who was responsible. The fire service didn't turn up, presumably because of the danger of working in the neighbourhood at night, so the fire just raged on until there was no more fuel to sustain it. It would be written off as one of those sporadic acts of vandalism that had become commonplace. Simon, in the immediate afterglow of excitement, had internalised learning points from this: there was so much lawlessness here, you could get away with anything. He would look for more opportunities to feed his other self the oxygen it craved, the thrill it needed. He was beginning to lock his private thoughts further inside himself. So far inside that he had no idea about them until they reared up in his dreams and nightmares, or occasionally his actions. The thoughts took on a life of their own. They became his reality, no matter how bizarre or distorted they would seem to others. His mind assimilated the thoughts until they fitted his own logic. Wrong could be interpreted by him as right. His days seemed to involve an internal mental battle; conversations between the previous Simon and the new one. But he was sharp enough to keep in place the veneer of respectability and normality the other Simon had earned amongst his peers. He should refer to the other person as *not*-Simon. What name should he have? The previous night he had sought an easy lay with the first woman he had received a proposition from. He called himself another name, Harry. They did the deed in a park, not even bothering whether anyone was watching. He had treated her roughly. She had not been unwilling or resistant, but he had drawn from it a huge level of sexual gratification, an exhilaration greater than any he had previously got from 'loving relationships'. He had paid her. They'd parted company. It was sordid, dirty, violent, and gratuitous.

The two men awoke at dawn. It had been a quiet night in the neighbourhood. They prepared themselves for the coming day, Mphatso decided he would have to go to work in his current clothes, there wasn't time to go home first. He showered and checked his face in the mirror. His beard was slow-growing. He would get by today without a shave. His clothes were not so unkempt they would be out of place in his workplace. He left without having anything to eat or drink and returned amongst the morning hubbub, safe in the company of other employed persons on the streets, buses and Metro of early morning Athens. It seemed at times like two cities, one of commuters and payslips, the other of sheer anarchy; not parallel but existing in an alternating temporal series. Unless there was a general strike, the streets were occupied by workers by day, anarchy by night. The only interface that created a hint of menace was the switch-over in the early evening, after the workplaces had cleared out, before the darkness shrouded the malicious behaviours of the dispossessed. The morning was never a problem. Those active at night never emerged before midday from their lairs. They would lounge in menacing-looking groups, they would crowd around their dealers, they would attend their paramilitary meetings, whatever it was that turned them on, each to plan another night, another day. In fact they were recently becoming less ashamed of their actions, attacking people and property in broad daylight. Taking Athens on a perverted odyssey.

Simon showered after Mphatso, prepared himself for the week ahead, sure to check his mask was in place, grabbed yoghurt, fruit and coffee in the kitchen, quickly consumed them and sprinted off to his workplace. Another week!

Chapter Forty-Five
The Die is Cast

Zoe rented her own room in the shared apartment. She preferred the company of one roommate in particular. Today, she was alone in the apartment. She wandered into the kitchen and grabbed a Coke. Then she returned to her room and shut the door. She felt the need, as she did frequently, to connect with the object of her desire. She knew she shouldn't do it, but there was comfort in being in his room, touching his clothing, smelling his odour. She held back a moment, lying on her own bed, thinking. It was sufficient to convince herself to yield to her urges, to light the touch paper. She sensed the beginning of the arousal that his touch also prompted. She let it flow, her sexuality taking over her mind, her body. She began to writhe with pleasure. With her fingers she probed beneath her clothes, seeking her erogenous press-points, tracing her features, removing her clothing, electrifying her sensations. Her thoughts excluded everything except her immediate fantasy. When the fantasy finally displaced her grasp on reality, she decided to go, naked, to his room. She stepped in, observing details that would help her to withdraw undetected. She carefully noted the position of, then handled, items of clothing, paperwork, toiletries and cosmetics, she smelt his bedding, lay her face on his pillow, panting his name, all the time building herself to a sexually charged climax.

Then, when her heart rate had stabilised, her breathing normalised, she lay on his bed in an instant of serenity, her partly clothed body moist, her senses heightened. She looked around the room. Her attention was captured by a small tin pencil box she hadn't seen before. She opened it. There were identity papers from the charity he worked for, a passport photograph of a woman with large spectacles, a gold wedding ring, his passport, and two sealed envelopes. She studied each in turn, seeking a connection with him from handling his personal items. The seal of one had been compromised by frequent opening and resealing. She ventured deeper into the secret, opening it, pulling out a formal-looking typed letter in English. It was defaced in places with the header, address and name ripped off. It appeared to be old, dog-eared. She tried to read it, but the language was too technical. Did it pertain to him? She took fright at the sound of footsteps in the apartment stairwell. She immediately retraced her steps so nobody could suspect she had been prying. She folded the document exactly as it had been, resealed the envelope precisely and replaced it in the base of the tin, just the way she had first seen it. Then, restoring the other items in sequence, she closed the lid and repositioned the tin as she had first found it. She returned each other item she had handled to their exact position, made sure the toiletries and clothing were all the same way she had found them. She then attempted to re-sculpt the bedding, making the creases and corrugations in the base sheet resemble the way they were when he would have lifted himself from his bed that morning. She paced backwards through the doorway, checking whether there was any detail she had missed, anything that might reveal her interim presence.

The footsteps were a false alarm, but she was once again in her own room, she finished off her bottled drink, deep in thought. Who was the woman, and the ring—was he married? And what about the letter? The only section she had the opportunity to scan mentioned a sixteen-year-old. She didn't think he had a brother. Her thoughts circled around these new observations, distracted and pushed into uncomfortable territory. Was there another woman? Was that a threat to her emotional attachment to him?

* * *

Later the same evening, Simon's phone vibrated its way across the ceramic tiled floor of his bedroom, restrained only by the charging lead. He was out of the room. After several pulses it fell motionless again, only to emit a muted chirp a few seconds later: a voicemail. He was planning his meal in the kitchen, but he had little enthusiasm for cooking; indeed for anything. There was nobody else home. He decided to skip on cooking and produced a snack from the fridge. Cheese, hommous, pitta bread, dolmades, olives, beer. If he needed something else, he could grab a rice pudding from a shop.

The rain continued to fall in Athens, dampening the enthusiasm of the majority for societal change. Simon had not been warned of any demonstrations, any strikes. People just seemed to want to get home tonight; or stay in a bar to drink themselves into denial about their beloved country. He was, he realised, descending into one of his depressive states again.

It was about twenty minutes before he picked up the phone and listened to the two voicemails from Mphatso.

'Hi, Simon, it's me, Mphatso. Can you give me a call as soon as you can? Some Iraqis have just texted to say there's something happening near Agios Pantaleimon this evening. It looks like the neo-fascists are working with the police. They say there are about fifty police and a dozen or so of the others. Give me a call. We need to get down there to help.'

'Simon? Mphatso again. Please call me the minute you get this.'

He returned the calls and got through to an agitated Mphatso.

'Where are you?'

'At the centre, I didn't go home after my shift.'

'What is happening?'

'A group of riot police are sweeping through the side streets around Agios Pantaleimon; they seem to be looking for Iraqis, but it was an

Iraqi who told me this so . . . but I'm not sure there's any reason to think the police are targeting them.'

He was being distracted by someone talking to him in the office.

'Yes . . . Simon, you still there?'

'Yeah.'

'There are about a dozen neo-fascists with the police; they're armed with bats, knives and knuckledusters. We need to get down to the area to make sure we can hide or move as many clients as possible. I don't think they have stormed any apartment blocks yet, but the streets are chaos.'

'OK, I'll come over and meet you at Victoria. Give me ten minutes.'

'OK.'

In fact it was about twenty minutes. Simon dressed for a wet evening outdoors and placed his phone in his jeans pocket. On the way through the kitchen he ate what was left of his snack. As he chewed he began to hear the noise in his ears again. Then, as if directed, he returned to his room and took out a flick knife from a case at the top of the wardrobe. He slipped it into the right pocket of his coat and zipped it up. He descended onto a deserted street. Running towards Omonia Metro station he passed block after block of apartments, televisions broadcasting their eclectic mix of news, game shows and soaps through open windows and across the public space of the street. Athens was staying in tonight, he thought. Nobody would be witnessing events.

* * *

Simon met up with Mphatso and they immediately left for the troubled neighbourhood on foot. They made their way along quieter side streets away from signs of trouble. Mphatso was getting texts from the Iraqis, giving minute by minute updates. From time to time he stopped and checked to see if there had been relevant tweets from either side in this conflict.

Sure enough, he'd now seen a tweet from the police asking people to avoid Agios Pantaleimon whilst they conducted 'routine operations against a criminal element.' Then, from a political splinter group, a less sophisticated tweet.

'The Cause has identified a target this evening. The integrity of our nation will be defended once again tonight.'

Then another from the same source, giving latitude and longitude, then another warning 'non-patriots' to stay away or their intrusion would be met with force. Mphatso used the map reference and pasted it into his street map app to get the location and they set off again towards the Square.

There was no conversation. Mphatso thought Simon was uncharacteristically withdrawn, subdued.

When they got closer to the focus of the conflict it was clear that a lot of people had been drawn to the area by the tweets; the streets were teeming, as if a bunch of animated teenagers were walking to a music gig. They assessed the crowd to be heterogeneous, most of them were sixteen to twenty-five. That was the Twitter demographic. Within that there were factions: students, socialists, and some people wearing the paraphernalia of the far right. The tweets had not discouraged opponents, they had acted as a general call to arms. The streets had an atmosphere of a tense local football derby, or of a Roman Colosseum, the crowd watching anxiously to see which way the emperor would turn his thumb.

Mphatso remained alert to any possible trouble, waiting for the inevitable taunts, there were, in fact, none. He stopped again to check the information sources, then he tried to phone the Iraqis again, but he couldn't get a signal. Maybe they've disabled the mast, he thought.

When they reached the streets where the police and backup

neo-fascists were active it was a scene of chaos and anarchy. The police were focused on their task, proceeding in strict regimented ranks, their green jump-suits, grey helmets, gas masks and shields like a cloak of anonymity. The only distinction to be made between individuals was one of stature. At one end of the street there was a cloud of tear gas, and from several apartment blocks a shower of rocks was falling, landing with a dull thud upon an already concrete-littered street. The police were moving forward toward the gas cloud, batons drawn. A phalanx of police armed with modern sub machine guns was guarding the ranks. Some fifty metres behind was a noisy and darkly dressed group, well-disciplined and, again, focussed on their task. The police broke down barricades around an apartment block where a group of refugees were illegally squatting. They smashed the plywood and corrugated iron sheet blocking lobbies and ground floor windows. They moved systematically from one floor to another, but the occupants had fled. They were directed to break into another particular block.

Simon realised that this was a dangerous environment for an African, even if he was British. He tried to work up a strategy for his plan.

Mphatso led Simon in an attempt to get closer to the block where he knew the Iraqis were hiding. They needed to do so without drawing attention to themselves. Simon needed to keep Mphatso away from the neo-fascists. He checked his knife through the fabric of his coat. He checked his mobile, with its new SIM card, was still in his pocket. He had removed his wallet before leaving so it was less easy for him to be identified. Simon attempted to make Mphatso as inconspicuous as possible, hiding his colour and pulling his reflective over-jacket further over him to cover his skin. The jacket was marked with the charity name and the symbols of the EU, Greek government and Athenian municipal authority, which might offer further protection. Mphatso's face, except for his eyes, was covered with a tubular neck warmer and a woollen hat, and his hands by gloves.

Within the street were a combination of paramilitary figures, police and black-shirts, and various onlookers all shouting at one another, either warning or encouraging, cooling or inflaming tempers. There were gesticulations, shouts, chants, firing of tear gas canisters, and occasionally rubber bullets. The street was full of the noises of breaking glass as shop fronts, lights, and car windscreens succumbed to the onslaught of hammer and baseball bat blows, of steel shuttering being wrenched from guide rails, of splintering wood and plywood as barricades were demolished, of car alarms going off as the innocent victims watched from above as their vehicles were systematically trashed, of sirens, of helicopter rotors slashing the air above. At this stage there had been, it seemed, no human casualties, since the sophisticated network of escape routes, passageways, barriers and ropes enabled people to move from block to block when stormed.

Simon looked overhead, drawn by the noise of rotating blades to see the police helicopter hovering over the ravine which was the street, its walls the close packed apartment block façades. He spotted the tell-tale pod underneath the helicopter that held the high definition cameras. They were filming events and gathering intelligence. It would be risky, but not impossible. He would have to be careful when seeking his thrills tonight.

Simon and Mphatso skirted around the block to come up in front of the police. They made cautious progress, constantly on the lookout for violent outbursts targeted at them by anyone around. Some of the onlookers were antipathetic of the night's events, but nonetheless Mphatso remained on his guard. They moved steadily and without drawing attention towards the apartment block. They pinned themselves against the shuttered shop-fronts when trouble came close, Mphatso shielding his face from view. When they reached the building their next task was to enter the labyrinthine defence system without raising suspicion from either the aggressors or the inhabitants, since both circumstances could jeopardise the safety of the very people they were aiming to help.

They procrastinated whilst deciding how to reach their charges. Mphatso considered entering a neighbouring building occupied by Afghans then swinging into the Iraqi block, or scaling the outer plywood barricade. Simon was holding back, looking for other opportunities. Maybe they were too late. Maybe the chance had passed.

* * *

Ioannis had been allocated to support operations with his colleagues. He was happily—and with the required zeal—going about his stop and search duties. Summary beatings meted out to those few unfortunate members of the Iraqi community who were on the street were either met with roars of approval or disapproval from bi-partisan bystanders. Ioannis enjoyed his audience's reaction. His excitement was increasing, his over-zealous application to his task was being noticed by some of his colleagues. They knew how hot-headed and undisciplined he could be at times. They tried to rein him in. The crowds opposed to the activities in the street that night were receiving the appropriate crowd calming attention. Ioannis's focus on his task was absolute. He spotted two people he thought were going to be trouble. It was apparent neither was an Iraqi refugee, but both were foreign, one was white and one—whose features were carefully hidden—seemed to be black. The black guy was wearing some sort of hi-visibility vest with a logo on it. Perhaps a do-gooder socialist, he thought. The African made Ioannis think. He marked him as a target, his label immigrant, communist, socialist, student, queer—it didn't matter. He had made his decision.

* * *

Simon was thinking that his chance had not passed. He was scheming. He had spotted that it would be possible. He was now almost single-minded in his pursuit of his own objective. He motioned to Mphatso to move further along the street to where there was a small courtyard between two blocks. There was an overhang of a balcony, under which two shop fronts faced the street. There was a raised flower planter on the pavement, perhaps one and a half metres tall. The structure had been shattered, but the earth within retained its bulk and gave reasonable cover if they squatted behind it. The helicopter couldn't see them because of the overhang.

* * *

Mphatso was focused on getting to the Iraqi block and couldn't understand why Simon needed them to be there, but Simon was where he needed to be. He scanned the possible exit routes, checking there was nobody in the immediate locality. He once again checked his knife, then slowly unzipped his pocket. Even from this simple action he was able to extract a zap of excitement in the way he had got excited by lighting the fire, or unzipping a dress, or unhooking a bra on a successful date. He felt the sense of anticipation in this unlikely setting. He waited just a few seconds, before plotting his orchestrated steps towards Mphatso, drawing the knife, reaching his target, placing the knife, drawing it up, withdrawing it, standing back to watch as his control over the target became absolute, just as the noise in his head had dictated. He was aroused by the thought.

As Simon made the first steps toward Mphatso, out of the corner of his eye he noticed a black-shirted male approaching the two of them. He was armed with a baseball bat, drawn above his shoulder.

The man regarded them both; then he brought the baseball bat down vertically from a fully stretched position so that it connected with the shoulder of one of the cowering men. A crack of wood against bone echoed around the tiny courtyard in which they had been cornered. He kicked the ribs, and aimed for the groin, but the guy was well protected in his position. The force of the blow pushed the white guy up against a wall like a discarded rubbish bag. A knife flew from the man's hand, bouncing off the wall. The attacker drew up his left fist and cracked it across the cheekbone and jaw. The break of bone was marked by a wail of pain. He turned to the horrified second man who was pinned in a crouch against the planter. His first blow was to the man's stomach, then followed up with a powerful kick to the chest as the man crumpled to the floor on his knees. As a parting shot the attacker decided to deliver a carefully aimed baseball bat to the groin of the white man. All the time this was happening the police were no more than fifteen metres away, the rear of the procession of perhaps fifty men looking over their shoulders, regarding the event passively. Mphatso pleaded through his agony for the police to help them, but there was no reaction. The procession moved on, and with it, the passage of the black-clad men.

In the silence that followed, the badly beaten Simon lay motionless against the orange shuttering. Mphatso, incapacitated by pain, crawled across to Simon and checked he was conscious. He wasn't able to get a response, but his breathing seemed regular if shallow. Simon had received a blow to the face and it appeared there was some bone damage, and a lot of blood. He tried to raise his arm to push Simon into a sitting position, but a searing pain prevented any exertion, so he left him lying. He fumbled for his phone and dialled the emergency number asking in Greek for an ambulance. The operator took the details and commented that the street was one they would have difficulty reaching at the moment. They gave an estimated arrival time of ten to fifteen minutes, but could not guarantee it. They asked, 'Was there any other way of getting to the hospital?'

Mphatso looked around helplessly and concluded there was nobody there in a position to help. He took Simon in his arms and cradled him to provide at least the illusion of safety. He was himself unsure whether they were now safe, and thought that at any time someone could come and finish them off. In fact, a group of teenagers appeared and circled around the prostrate victims lying on the broken pavement. They were not, mercifully, supporters of the violence, but were here to oppose the actions of the paramilitaries, so offered themselves as a phalanx of defence against further attack. Mphatso felt as safe as he was able, awaiting the ambulance.

Chapter Forty-Six
Aftermath

Ioannis moved away and dropped the bat. He realised immediately what he'd done. He looked first at who he'd just floored. It shouldn't have gone that far; then he looked at the people around him. Some were looking at him, some were not. He looked at the sky, then at the ground, he was searching—he didn't know what for. As soon as his phalanx of colleagues reached a street junction, he ran, nobody stopped him, nobody came with him; nobody followed him.

When he was two blocks away the excitement that was present in the street had drained away like water down a sink. He just stopped and slumped to the ground. Rubble under his knees cut into his skin. He had no energy, it had suddenly drained from him. He tried to focus on something to bring him to his senses, but he couldn't without seeing blood, blood on the face of the lad. Had he done that? Was it him?

Time passed, Ioannis wasn't sure how much. It was raining; he was getting wet. He sobbed. Why did he sob? What was he sobbing for? Was the white man dead? *Did he do that?*

He needed somebody. He needed to touch reality. But he was living a fantasy. Did he get off on what he'd done? He didn't think so. Was he proud? He thought so, at least he'd set out thinking he would be. It was what they did. Every night. But it felt like this had affected him differently. This time his emotions had switched off, he didn't think he was capable of feeling love, hatred, compassion, revenge, anything. That single act was its own anaesthetic. The body's way of preventing self-destruction. Perhaps that's what happened when people who killed then went on to commit suicide. They broke through the anaesthetic. And the pain was unbearable.

There was no one on the streets here. Just him. He really needed somebody. Not to talk, just to be there. He had nothing to say; the anaesthetic stopped him. Nobody told him how to cope after doing something like that. It was like there should be a lesson in it. If it was likely to happen, like if you're a soldier, you could at least be taught what to expect, how it felt, how you could recover.

Ages passed; sand through one's fingers. He couldn't stop it. Now tears, real sorrow, aching sorrow. *Did he do that?*

Now he ran again, even though he had no energy; he stumbled a bit. He didn't know where he was going, or what he was going to do. When he couldn't run any more he just walked, he just carried on walking. All night. When he got tired he lay down and slept. He walked again; all the way to Piraeus, until it was impossible to walk anymore. Then he got a ferry, but he didn't know where to. He had enough money in his pocket to pay the passenger fare. People looked at him on the boat, probably because he looked a mess. There was blood on his clothes, his black clothes, so everyone could label him. Yesterday he'd been proud of his allegiance. Now it was a liability. He was alone in the world and he had just done something awful. *Did he do that?*

When people's suspicions were raised by his appearance, when he could no longer hide in the toilets from their accusing glances, and he could no longer look at himself in the mirror, he went on deck and waited for the inevitable time when a police officer would come to talk to him, would want to know why he was in the state he was in. He or she would recognise his clothing, the look in his eyes that said he wasn't really there, they'd think he was probably deranged. He would probably agree. They would arrest him, or arrange for his detention in a mental health unit until they could work out who he was and what he'd done.

Nobody came.

Nobody.

So Ioannis went back to Athens as stealthily as he could. He returned to where he lived to collect only what he could carry: passport, identity card, cash, clothes, toothbrush. He went in when he was sure the apartment was empty. Then he left; he was never going to go back.

* * *

Michael Blidworth tracked the attack victim to Evangelos Hospital. When he was told the second victim was by the bedside of the more seriously injured one, he blagged his way to the ward to catch a moment with them. It was already early morning. The ward staff wouldn't let Mike near the patient, but called his friend out to speak to him. The African guy was badly bruised, but suffering neither from concussion nor broken bones. He was reticent, suspicious, unwilling to divulge details. Perhaps it was a cultural thing, thought Mike. He attempted to approach the interrogation differently.

'Have the police been to see you?'

'Not yet.'

'Don't you think that's a bit strange?'

'Sure, but everyone knows the people who did this are close to the police. I doubt if they would follow it up.'

'Would you want the police to be involved?' Mike was checking that the guy he was talking to wasn't an illegal immigrant.

'Yes, sure. But how can we get any sort of justice?'

'Maybe if I used the British press to draw attention to you and your friend's plight. That would create a diplomatic incident the Greek government would need to manage. The police would be forced to give account of themselves and distance themselves from their uglier associates. What is his name by the way?'

'He is Simon, Simon Holdsworth.'

'And you are?'

'I am Mphatso. I am also a British citizen.'

Mike was unaware until this moment. 'I had no idea either of you were British. That makes the idea of press coverage more justifiable. I don't want to push you, but how do you feel about the world getting to know about this?'

'*Justifiable*?' He questioned Mike's use of the word. 'I can't speak for Simon. Nor can he. There's little likelihood of him regaining consciousness. But I want somebody to be held to account. You'd need to speak to his employers.'

Mike took down the charity's address and Mphatso's mobile number. He spoke to Mphatso for a few minutes more about why they were in the street the previous evening. He knew now that Simon's prognosis was poor. He needed to tie this story together quickly, to maximum effect. He sent a text to the London office telling them that the two victims of an attack in Athens were British charity workers. That the prognosis was poor for one and that he would be in contact in one hour.

Then he raced across the city in the morning rush to the refugee centre where he asked to speak to the contact Mphatso had given him. After a short discussion with the management, he left the building with a partial explanation of the work of the charity, their relationship with Simon, and his address. He thought he'd been remarkably lucky; in the UK he'd have been chasing around in circles for a home address.

Mike sent another text explaining that the charity supported migrants and refugees and that the two victims were trying to protect clients from demonstrators.

At the apartment block address he found a couple of house mates. They had only a vague idea of what had happened, Mphatso had contacted the charity and news had trickled down. He spoke to a

Greek girl called Zoe. She was devastated, as if an emotional grenade had exploded, though she labelled herself as a friend, a house mate.

'Simon is everybody's friend,' she said, between tearful moments, 'the sort of person who makes the room lighter when he walks in.'

'What about Mphatso?'

'He is a good man, helping the refugee centre by offering his services as translator. With some of the Africans they wouldn't be able to communicate well without him. These days more migrants are entering Greece without having English or French as a second language.'

'What events have Simon and Mphatso been at recently?'

'We had an impromptu party two nights ago. They were both here. It was a good evening.'

She thought for a minute, then continued, 'Simon's mother passed away recently. He has not been back in Greece for very long.'

'Do you know where his family lived?'

'No.'

'Do you have anything else to tell me?'

'No.'

* * *

Zoe was about as evasive and non-committal as it was possible to be with this British journalist, Michael. She was an anarchist speaking to a journalist, how could it be any different? But her evasiveness had more to do with the fact that she didn't want to blow her cover as Simon's stalker than because she despised the media. Then, of course, she felt that if any part of the media should convey this story, it should be a Greek station. She contacted a colleague, Maria, who was also something of an anarchist and had worked for the public television broadcaster before the government shut it down. Maria was now working for a radical private broadcaster. Maria agreed the issue must be covered and would send a news cameraman to see her. Zoe and Maria both wanted the story to come out, to seek revenge, retribution. Thinking she needed exclusive material for Maria, she returned to Simon's room, making a move directly to the tin with the unopened envelopes. She opened the first.

Our reference: DFX 4933673

Dear Dr Shah,

Re: your reference 3342865/ABS, male, date of birth [defaced].

Thank you for referring this sixteen-year-old male for psychiatric assessment. Your letter of referral kindly included helpful information on childhood development, known family and social issues and school record.

Simon attended with his mother. I found her to be polite and concerned for her son, although shy and lacking in articulation.

I found the patient to be somewhat withdrawn and suspicious of the purpose of the visit. I note that school reports have repeatedly cited fecklessness and inability to focus on school issues. His failure to interact socially or read emotions appropriately have also been noted.

I have utilised three methods of investigation. Separate from his mother, I utilised a non-structured self-reporting methodology, allowing the patient to speak about issues that he thinks have been significant in his life. He revealed, with little resistance, a history of physical abuse and psychological bullying at ages five to eleven, citing his father as the perpetrator. This appears to have tailed off as the boy grew in size and strength; now able to resist. Alcohol addiction appears to have been a trigger for episodes of abuse. The child did not volunteer a history of sexual abuse.

The patient reported several intermittent symptoms

including auditory hallucinations and low grade delusional ideation. His grasp of reality is variable, but not so impaired as to have impacted upon his education to date. It seems that these symptoms are prompted intermittently by external factors: danger, stress, physical violence.

In subsequent interviews with the patient, I applied standard validated diagnostic tests and carried out blood tests to exclude differential diagnosis. Serological tests for marijuana, cocaine, heroin and alcohol were negative. Blood tests were in normal range. Tests identified the presence of borderline Schneiderian first rank symptoms, rank 1–3.

I am unconvinced that the borderline level of symptoms implies a schizophrenia diagnosis, although his history carries risk association for psychosis. At this stage I do not consider him to be a risk to himself or others, but I think his social and emotional development will be aided by intervention sooner rather than later. In my opinion, the patient will require cognitive behavioural correction and a course of medication. I have received consent from his mother and will book him into a clinic over the summer. Thereafter, I believe his condition can be managed in primary care.

Yours sincerely,

Tapiwanashe Moyo (Mrs) MD, Fellow ABPD, Clinic Director.

The insight provided by the medical letter was already too much to bear. Zoe couldn't burden herself with more of his secrets. Simon was becoming her burden; her illicit relationship with his aura, his possessions, but not his body or soul, was her secret alone, even though the television station was to broadcast to the nation that she was his girlfriend. Her knowledge of his medical history would be known to, at most, one or two others. Zoe decided not to reveal this to Maria, nor open the second envelope. Whatever secrets were contained in the letter marked with 'To be opened after the death of both parents', she would ensure they were safely shredded.

* * *

Mike went back to his hotel and penned a follow-up article to his first rushed exclusive. He was going to describe the slaughter of innocents by an out-of-control fascist paramilitary group, raise the roof, bring the Greek government to account. If the Greek, European and English language media picked up on the story, the Greeks would feel the chill of disapprobation, feel their tourist income slip. He wondered if he should also address the migrant issues and the austerity he'd already written about.

The story was emailed for publication that evening. The press agencies would pick it up too, he was certain.

* * *

Mphatso waited two days in the room in the hospital at Simon's bedside for signs of consciousness. He didn't leave the building. There had been a steady stream of well-wishers to Simon's bedside, but Mphatso remained on constant bedside duty. After three days, the spirit and fight drained away from Simon and he succumbed to the effects of bleeding on the brain. The haemorrhage had paralysed him. He never regained consciousness.

* * *

Ioannis would never be aware of the fact that on that night he had saved the life of an African.

Chapter Forty-Seven
Road to Varosha

Now I, Ioannis, am in Cyprus, I've worked for my passage to Limassol. I'm working in a bar. But I'm not the person I once was. A metaphorical cloud hangs menacingly above my head, its micro-climate of despondency permanently engulfing me, draining me of energy, permitting me no interest in anything. I eat to survive. I sleep to recover. When I wake up, the cloud has been waiting for me. It seeks to suffocate me.

I've come to find the final resting place of Costas, my relative. I know he is here. I must find his grave. I know he was in Varosha because that is where Tassos told me he was killed in 1974. I will make my way there when I have enough money. Then I can atone at his graveside. Atone for my wayward life, atone for the miserable way I have treated my mother; atone for the death of a stranger by my hand.

Over the past weeks, I have considered, many times, handing myself in to the authorities for the attack I committed. I have even considered handing myself over to the family of the dead man. Yes, he died. I am full of remorse, I don't care what happens to me anymore.

He was British. A charity worker helping people through their austerity and pain. His girlfriend I saw on television pleading for justice, closure. His name was Simon. Nobody I had trained with would speak of it or reveal my identity. That is why I am still free. As soon as I can shed tears by my grandfather's grave, I will hand myself in because my life now feels worthless.

Now I have money to reach Varosha. I understand, from those I have asked, that the town is a shadow of its former self. Like myself.

I'm on the bus that will take me to Larnaca, then I'll have to make my way from there. I will need to locate Costas' grave, so I'm stopping in Larnaca to see if the authorities can help trace him. When they find him, I can visit his burial place. I can talk to him about what I have done and I will feel better; my pain will be over.

I have learnt that they can't locate him; they tell me that the Commission for the Missing may be able to help. I contact them, but there are no persons reported missing with that name, and none who have been identified fit the profile. They ask me if I wish to report him as missing. I stay silent, ending the call, knowing my options are diminishing.

Dejected, I decide to walk to Varosha, but a British Sovereign base lies in my path to Ayia Napa, to get there I must take a bus. It is winter now, the weather is depressing. In Aiya Napa, tourists huddle together in half-empty bars, or cluster in their hotel restaurants waiting and hoping for the next day to bring improved conditions. There is no work here for me to do, my passage is transitory. I walk, not quite sure what I am expecting to find. All the time I have been here I feel like I have needed somebody to talk to, but I keep to myself now. I have secrets to be shared with no-one. And now I am walking past the last inhabited area of Protaras. Before me, in the distance, is Varosha. Not shimmering like a mirage, but grey, sad, dilapidated; the only residents now are its many ghosts and the feral cats and dogs, rats, snakes and lizards. A tall barbed-wire fence blocks my passage, the guards look on suspiciously as I pace several hundred metres back and forth along its perimeter like a caged animal. I walk, following the fence, but it merges with the more significant fence of a British base. I can get no further. I sit down, dejected; the dark, low winter clouds blow quickly across citrus orchards and potato fields, squally showers dampen my clothes. The roads to Varosha are blocked.

I become lost in my own thoughts. I realise my desire to link with Costas, to make real my connection with my wider family, is doomed to failure. The burden of that thought pushes my weakened frame against the damp earth. The red ochre hue of the soil seeps into the fabric of the seat of my trousers as my thoughts crystallise; I cannot return to Greece, I cannot reconnect with my previous existence, I will be pursued by the police, by the Cause, perhaps by my mother, but most importantly by Tassos. He is the person who has guided me to this spot, to be virtually face-to-face with our shared heritage. Tassos would have anticipated more auspicious circumstances. He would be unhappy that only now, as an outlaw, have I become—by the act of acknowledging my family's past—a family member at last; yet I am simultaneously a criminal, and as such, in the same fleeting instant, am unceremoniously ejected from the family; that isolated moment of kinship slipping away unnoticed by anyone but myself.

My passport is only valid for a short time before it expires. It is fortunate that the teenage visage staring from its pages no longer resembles me. It has, I believe, saved me from detection so far. If I try to renew it, I will be snared by a spy in the microchip, the one who knows this killer's every biometric detail. I am trapped. I cannot be Ioannis. If I am not he, then I am not related to Costas, nor Tassos, who is the link between us. I am his cousin's son, and Costas was also his cousin. My destiny has been crafted by Tassos, not me. My role in it was unfortunate, yet I must still make amends, in particular to my victim. The attack in Athens was not the fault of Tassos.

Problems lie ahead of me. If I return to Greece my life will entail state-directed penitence, a spell in Korydallos prison, the destiny of the guilty. Beyond the moment a cell door closes behind me, it is difficult to envisage any future. My alternative future must be in Cyprus. I need to reinvent myself.

Costas. I could become Costas Charalambou, confident that his death has never been registered, confident that time has erased any memory of him. People might recognise the name as it stands, questions might be asked of me; I believe the names are common and popular. I would need to invent a past, invent the family described within the names I have taken. I have no idea whether or not this will work. I am going to have to learn. I am going to have to remain in Cyprus until Costas can become real. Nobody else will realise that I am paying my respects to the deceased, that I may be able to atone for Simon's death, that I will immortalise my association with my past family's hero.

Dark, low winter clouds blow quickly across citrus orchards and potato fields. Squally showers slowly soak my clothing.

The casing of an ugly chrysalis breaks open, its complex metamorphosis completed. The delicate wings remain folded until new blood fills their capillaries. After a pause, a light breeze between showers lifts the unique butterfly and carries it away to repeat the life cycle.

I am Costas Charalambou.

Epilogue
Alf in The Volunteer, Sheffield, 1992

Alf brought his pint glass to his lips and took a long draft of his usual ale. He was a Wards man; couldn't entertain the possibility of any of that Whitbread stuff. Stones was OK, but he preferred the taste of Wards. Even after all the changes in ownership, at least he knew the beer didn't have to travel far to The Volunteer, his regular pub, not his local, but he always drank there. It was Tuesday lunchtime. He was there every lunchtime. There wasn't anything else to do. Except pick up his dole money.

Drinking. That was Alf's occupation. As his world shrank around him, his outlook became narrower and his Yorkshire dialect became stronger, as if he wanted to belong in his world, talk and act like those he shared his world with. He was a chameleon.

That afternoon, as he set with his fourth pint, he surveyed his surroundings, trying to check his eyes could still focus. It became a problem after four pints. He regarded the panelled walls, the stone fireplace, the tar-stained ceiling, the sticky carpet with its wispy patterns that buggered your sight if you looked at them too long.

He didn't usually have drinking partners at lunchtime. Most of his drinking buddies worked. He could usually be found at the corner table just inside the doorway. Today was different. Matt had been to the doctor's and taken the rest of the day off sick. Matt was one of his intelligent mates, he held down a good job, earned a good wage, a sound local lad, quite a bit younger. They were chattering their way through the lunchtime, lubricating their tongues as they went.

There was some reminiscing about the past, something he didn't much talk about, but nonetheless it felt OK talking to Matt. Matt knew some of Alf's secrets. Not all.

'You never told me about when you got married, Alf. When was it?'

'The first or the second?'

'Now you're confusing me. I didn't even know there were two. To Doreen of course.'

'Doreen, 1971. It were a good do. Her family put a lot into the wedding, loads of money.'

'We don't see her very often these days.'

'She don't approve of me drinking. Never has really.'

'What about the first? Who was she? How did you meet?'

'Her name was Ella. She were an 'ungarian emigrant,' he dropped the *h*, 'came to England in 1958 after the uprising and after the second Russian invasion. She were beautiful, but a bit damaged by the troubles she'd been through.'

He reached for his pint again, watched a cheese bap on a plate hover past in the hands of the barmaid, destined for another table. He fancied one.

'Molly, get us one of those baps, will you?' He shouted as she returned to the bar.

'Cheese or ham?'

'Cheese.'

'Onion?'

'Yeah. Ta, duck.' Then he returned to his dialogue with Matt.

'I met her as an apprentice at Balfours. She were an apprentice too. Steel worker. The only woman on the shop floor. It were unknown then. Seems she were already an apprentice in Hungary, so when they resettled the unaccompanied teenagers—she were one—they brought her here and Balfours took her on as a sort of publicity thing. It were a bit out of character for the gov'nors. Nevertheless she did OK. I were apprenticed to the offices, not the works. She had a glint in her eyes, peeking out from underneath all that steelworker kit. And her name; it struck me because in Greek it's "come here".'

'How did she end up in Sheffield?'

'She told me the full history once. I were amazed. I were only sixteen when the invasion happened, so I wasn't really aware of it. But she was in with a political movement against the Hungarian government, lots of the apprentices were. They started at fifteen, the workers. She got into trouble in Budapest for demonstrating, was beaten by the police, then when the Russians invaded the second time, in—oh, I can't remember—she and some other apprentices escaped across the border to Austria. She said it had been hell in Hungary after the Russians had arrived.'

Alf's bap appeared on the bar, Molly gestured, a summons to Alf to collect it.

'D'you want another pint, Matt?'

'Alright, thanks, Alf.'

'And another two here, Molly, if you're not too busy.'

'Less of yer bloody cheek, Alfred! And where's your "please"?'

'Well, what's up wi'ya that *they* get their bap served,' nodding towards the other table, 'and I have to run about for mine?'

'Do you want it or not?

He collected the food and drinks, returning to his recollections between mouthfuls of bread.

'Anyway, she said it were better in Austria to begin with. All the villagers helped them out with food and warm clothing, shelter for the night, things like that. There were thousands of 'em apparently, flowing across the border like a wave. There was no-one to stop them to begin with because the Austrian military had been caught off guard. Anyway, once the numbers coming across got too great, the army started to collect the people together and put them in displaced peoples camps. She said that were the worst time of her life. These were camps left behind after the war, like concentration camps, with all the connotations of the war still hanging around them. There were lots of unaccompanied children, and they were really frightened to start with, but then the Austrians started moving people on to other Western countries, France, the USA, Canada, the UK, Sweden. Every country opened its doors to the emigrants. Loads came to England, thousands.'

Somebody put a record on the jukebox in the other bar. The music wafted trough the bar.

'She were allocated to a family in Sheffield, Hungarians who came during the war.' We started dating after she started at the works. She were difficult to get to know because of the language thing, also because she didn't want to talk about her past. I think if it were today, she'd've had a diagnosis of depression or summat.'

Alf was half way down his fifth pint. The patterns on the carpet were getting woozy. He needed a piss. He went off to the loo.

On his return Matt asked, 'Alf, I know you were in Cyprus on national service, and I know about your dad, he often talked about it when you used to bring him down the pub. But you don't talk much about the rest of your time. About all I've got out of you before is births, marriages and deaths. Even then you didn't mention your first wife. So this is new to me. Intriguing.'

Matt moved his beer mat about the table, what remained of his pint in his other hand, ready to order another before closing time. Minutes later, Matt placed full glasses next to the remaining drinks, together with a packet of crisps and sat down again. He was thinking about a proposal he'd wanted to put to Alf, but maybe not today. The round table was filling with glassware, plates, packets. There was little room left. Molly didn't look about to clear up. They finished their predominantly liquid lunch before being kicked out onto the busy streets of Sheffield. It was a long way home for Alf.

Several days later he met Matt again, the same place, same table.

Matt asked Alf the question he had been mulling over since their last pint.

'Alf, you've got a story to tell. Don't you think people like Doreen and your son would like to hear it?'

'It's nothing really. Not any sort of success story. They aren't interested.'

'It's more fascinating than you think, and if you've never talked to them about everything, how would they be expected to know?'

'I'd struggle to remember. Half my brain cells have been destroyed by alcohol. The rest seem to have emptied themselves and I've pissed their contents out. D'you know, I can't remember the day before yesterday. I'm always forgetting peoples' names. The other day I was just staring at someone's face, a good mate, known him for years. I couldn't think what his name was. It's like words. You speak a sentence and half way through there's a space where a word should be and your brain trips over and falls into the gap. You don't remember what should have been in the space till days later.'

'It's your hippocampus shrinking,' said Matt. 'Happens to everyone eventually. Maybe the time has come to preserve what you remember, what you want others to know?'

Alf didn't know what Matt was talking about, bloody hippos, but there was something in what he'd said that appealed to him.

'I thought a long time ago that I could do that, but they both loathe me. A harsh judgement, I think, but then things have happened. I thought I could write a letter.'

Matt nodded silently, understanding something, knowing part of the story, because he had been in a similar situation.

'Lets try it out. You dictate to me, I'll write, then we'll make it into a letter. You have control over the content. Not now, maybe in a few days.'

'And if I don't want you to say something?'

'It won't get said.'

'Sounds good. As long as I have something to leave my son. Atonement, like.'

At the appointed time the pair met at Matt's home, poured a beer and got chatting. At first Matt wrote nothing, just listened. Then, gradually he took more notes.

Alf talked about the time he went to Cyprus to do national service. He tried to explain why he was discharged, but Matt saw gaps in the account, so he probed a little.

'But what started you drinking too much when you were there? How did you end up on a charge? Who was this Captain Jarvis?'

'He was some good-looking, high-flying Sandhurst officer who just breezed into our camp one day. Me and my mates thought he was stand-offish, we were envious, he had it all. He had some role in Quartermaster's Stores, can't remember what. But here's the thing; every time you got into a bit of trouble he'd appear on the scene. Our paths crossed as officer and subordinate a few times. There was summat going on at the time with squaddies taking the law into their own hands, giving the locals a beating, that sort of thing, not me, but people I had to billet with. Jarvis seemed to know a lot about that stuff. Anyway, I lost it once and shot an unarmed local dead whilst on duty. He were unarmed when I shot him, but he wasn't just beforehand—he still had his bullet belt on him. I got charged, but they wanted to hush that and a few other things up, so I didn't get a court martial. Jarvis wouldn't help me, wouldn't speak in my defence. Before this, he'd made a pass at me. That's why I thought he'd help. I can't work out to this day whether he completely fucked up my life, or whether things would have turned out the same without him.'

Alf was comfortable talking to Matt about his peccadilloes because Matt understood what it was to doubt your place in society, overcoming society's obstacles to seek a vent for your emotions, seek a channel down which to guide your bruised spirit. He first met

Matt precisely in that environment, though both were 'in the closet' at the time.

'In the past you've told me nothing happened once you'd put a stop to it.'

'True, but it awakened in me those thoughts and needs. I'd denied them before, and tried to deny them afterwards for a while. Certainly until after I came back to Civvy Street.'

'You weren't discharged after the shooting?'

'No, my whole world just disintegrated after that. I were bullied, beaten, ostracised. It's no fun when the lads you bonded with doing national service turn against you. Miserable, it were. So I drank. That's why I got discharged.'

'Then you came back to the UK. Demobbed, so to speak. What happened?'

'You set yourself an objective. I wanted to start again. To find someone I cared about, someone who could keep my other side under control.'

'Was it long after you came back that you got the apprenticeship at Balfours?'

'Less than three months. People were crying out for workers. You were snapped up. Even though my military record was tarnished, they took me. I really tried hard to get that job.'

'Then what were your main thoughts about the several years after that.'

'It were about learning a trade, getting a qualification. I was only four years in before they made me a journeyman.'

'What's a journeyman?'

'Someone who's newly qualified, like after apprenticeship, who works for someone like a craftsman.'

'And you were courting by then too.'

'Yep. Lovely it were, the world was looking good.'

'Then you got married?'

'Yeah. The wedding wasn't much, just a registry office. There wasn't anyone on Ella's side to attend, just her adoptive family. We weren't the same religion or anything, but neither of us cared much for God. The marriage went well for a while, but there was, as I said the other day, some damage. She was emotionally damaged, like something held her back. Whilst we were courting there wasn't much obvious to spot, but after the wedding, it was clear that, you know, in bed, we weren't very handy.'

'Like something in her past had affected her?'

'Yeah. Something big. Then I began to think she had married me more for security than for love. I felt a right fool, like she'd cheated me. Well, what with not getting what a man needed from a wife, and the little issue of my other needs, the relationship soon turned sour. We'd argue, shout at each other in our own native language. The neighbours would complain. I'd be off out in the evenings, coming home late, really late. I'd be down the public toilets, you know the ones. Getting what I needed. Of course it was only a matter of time. In those days, before you were old enough to know, it was illegal. People would get drawn into a sting by good-looking policemen, posing as, you know.'

'So you were stung?'

'I should say so. There's no hiding arousal. What I never understood was how a policeman who was obviously enjoying himself could then turn all professional and slap you into cuffs. That bastard certainly did it for me. I was marched off and charged. In court I had to face him, all smart in his uniform, hair brushed and neat, and listen to him giving evidence. He fucking enjoyed every minute of our encounter.'

'It still happens, you know it does.'

'I know, but in those days the consequences were dire for anyone caught. I think in the months leading up to 1967, when they changed the law, the police really increased their surveillance of the cottages.

They arrested loads of us. The only crumb of consolation was after the law was changed the sentences were relaxed. So I only had to do six months inside. A nonce, that's what I was, am.'

Matt felt the chill in Alf's narrative. He stopped taking notes and poured another beer, opened a pack of salted peanuts. This was clearly something Alf rarely allowed himself to remember. The lesion had still not healed. Alf wasn't going to yield recollections of his incarceration.

'Tell me about when you met Doreen. Wasn't that a happier moment?'

'Again, I'd decided to put my record behind me, put the divorce into a bag marked "do not open". I wanted to get on with my life, find some happiness. And I was happy, for a while. Simon was born, and things were fine. I was getting all the attention I needed from Doreen. The boy was a little miracle. I was going to be such a good dad. I loved that boy, Matt, so much.'

He stopped, silent tears racing a pathway down the features of his face. Several minutes passed whilst Alf was lost in his own thoughts, seeking comprehension, mouthing unuttered words, wiping away his tears.

'I'll tell you what, Alf, why don't we call it a day and we can pick it up again another day? I don't want to cause you any pain. Things are obviously a bit raw.'

Then Alf composed himself, sat himself up and sipped his drink.

'I can't stop now, Matt, this is the only time I am going to talk to anyone about everything. Carry on.'

'OK, but you start from where you feel you want.'

'You see, the boy was beautiful, he was ours, I loved his smile. Everything went fine for several years, but then I started drinking again. I got laid off from Balfours when the steel industry began to collapse, when Sheffield started to go under. Just after we were married we did what young lovers do, going out dancing, going on day trips. That all stopped when Simon was born. Then the dole. And that boy, that gloriously beautiful boy, he wouldn't stop bed wetting. It drove me mad. I'd go out of a night and too often when I came home, I admit the worse for wear, all I could smell was stale piss. I was getting more and more trapped. I couldn't find a way out. I looked again in all the old places for the fun I sought, the intimacy, no strings. I still do. Sometimes I see you there. Ironic really, stale piss.'

Matt shuffled self-consciously as if he was being exposed to some hidden truth about himself, although he was much more comfortable with his life than Alf.

'Doreen was always the best mum she could be,' continued Alf, 'trying to manage the situation, but absolutely it all got under my skin. I just wanted him to stop doing it. I know he couldn't help it, but when I'd had a drink I just took it out on him and on Doreen. The woman's an angel really, Matt, but I can understand that underneath everything she has a real contempt for me. The happy marriage was, is still, a veneer—wafer thin. The marriage is a hook. The relationship was dead. Is dead. And that boy: how badly did I treat him. It was bad. I know how he feels about me now. There's no going back.'

'What's Simon doing now?'

'He's at university. Sussex. He worked hard at school and got good grades. He wants to work abroad, so Doreen tells me—he doesn't talk to me. Funny that, he'll be the third generation to travel.'

'Did you and he try to make up?'

'You know, I really don't know if we ever have. I think his barriers went up and emotionally he's unfathomable. He has a few problems, you know, like he doesn't really look after himself very well, doesn't click with people—seems friendly, but misses all the cues of friendship, and we had a scare a few years back when he needed medicines.'

'But he's OK now?'

'As far as I know.'

'Do you want to make up with him?'

'It's too late. I know I'm losing it, what with my memory and everything. Sometimes I'm walking home, just the same routes I've always known. Then I'm lost, don't recognise anywhere. And I panic. Then it passes again, and suddenly I realise I'm not two streets away from home.'

'Lots of people are like that. It doesn't mean anything.'

'It does when the doctor tells you.'

Matt held back after this latest revelation.

'So you telling me all this, it really is atonement.'

Alf made a shallow, thoughtful nod.

'And then I lost my dear mum. I'm having to put in a bit more time with dad, now there's nobody to look after him, but for his age he's doing well.'

'How was it when your mum went?'

'It's like an equation missing a constant. You'll never get answers. I wasn't there, and I'll regret till the day I die what I was doing instead. If you can't witness your own mum leaving the world, can't hear what she wants to say, can't see the message in her eyes . . .'

'Shall we leave it there, Alf?'

'I guess so.'

'Listen, leave things with me and I'll see what I can do with it. When I have worked on it I'll get back to you with a draft. A letter to Simon.

Alf had an immense sensation of tiredness, his huge emotional burden shared at last. He felt the need to lie down, to sleep. He slept for a while in Matt's spare room. Then he returned to an indifferent Doreen for an indifferent meal.

Matt took weeks to produce something for Alf. In the end, they edited it down concisely. Alf put it in an envelope, intended for Simon. He knew he didn't need to explain himself to Doreen. She was smart enough to know everything about him. He marked the envelope 'To be opened after the death of both parents'.

Acknowledgements

Thanks to those friends who encouraged me to put words onto paper, constructively commented on my output, and kept me writing to completion. Special thanks to Claire; Karen; Carol and Tim; and, of course, Rob.

Many thanks also to Dan and the small army of people who helped this book reach publication and the market.

ear reader,

I hope you have enjoyed reading *Roads to Varosha*. As a self-published author, I rely on reviews and recommendations to reach new readers. It would be appreciated if you could submit review on GoodReads (there is a link via the icon on www.krystofcarel.com), on Amazon, or your preferred platform or readers' book reviews.

Thanks in anticipation,

Krystof Carel.